THE
DATE

THE DATE

T. H. MURDOCK

Published by Thomas & Mercer, Seattle

www.apub.com

Amazon, the Amazon logo, and Thomas & Mercer are trademarks of Amazon.com, Inc., or its affiliates.

EU Product Safety Contact:
Amazon Media EU S.à r.l.
38, avenue John F. Kennedy, L-1855 Luxembourg
amazonpublishing-gpsr@amazon.com

ISBN-13: 9781662529337
eISBN: 9781662529320

Cover design by Dan Mogford
Cover Image: © Steve Collender © Weerawan Konkham / Shutterstock

Printed in the United States of America

THE
DATE

PROLOGUE

Caira waits, by the window. She sips her second small glass of Sauv, and watches for movement outside. The view from the living room of her basement flat is dominated by the stone stairway that leads up to the street. But when she stands next to the window, she can see a slice of the outside world above – enough to make out the tops of vehicles and the lower legs of passing pedestrians. If a passer-by's chosen path takes them close enough to the iron railings, she can see their shoes. It's possible to infer a great deal about someone from their choice of footwear. Sometimes, when Caira stands here and looks out, she can decipher a whole life story from a pair of battered old boots or shiny Mary Janes.

The next pair of shoes she sees might belong to her date. He will be here any second, assuming he's not another flake. He's a few minutes late, but that's okay; anyone flawlessly punctual would only grow frustrated with a person as chaotic as her.

Caira wouldn't normally let someone pick her up from her flat for a first date. But they've been chatting for a while. She's stalked the hell out of him on social media, and this guy seems as harmless as they come. That said, he's not what you'd call a first-tier dating candidate. He's too young for her, really. But this is the stage she's at with internet dating. To begin with, it seemed like an endless digital parade of bachelors. But that all changed once she filtered out the obvious red flags. First she got rid of the carp-holders, the shirtless narcissists, the straight-to-Snapchat adulterers. The gym-in-lieu-of-a-personality bros. The smileless men hiding their features under a cap and shades. The ones who list traits they don't want to see in a 'female'. When she ruled out the 'apolitical' (extremely right-wing), the 'purebloods' (anti-vaxxers) and the ones demanding 'no drama' (gaslighting bastards); and she weeded out the car selfies, the gym selfies, the bathroom mirror pouters . . . it became quite a small talent pool. More of a puddle, if anything. It only takes a couple of ghostings, a handful of disastrous dates and a few false starts before it all begins to look quite bleak.

Caira's nearly had it with dating apps, anyway. Using them feels soulless and transactional. She'd much rather meet some-one organically. But that isn't happening either. And so, with her options dwindling, she lied about her age – only by a year, and she'll be upfront about being forty on the date – and wid-ened the age criteria to fifteen years either side: twenty-four to fifty-four years old. That's a lot of life, right there. And that's how she ended up matched with Miles, who seems perfect if she discounts the fact he is – gulp – the tender age of twenty-nine.

Some movement. Okay, this might be him. A man has stopped directly outside her place. A smart pair of Oxfords – promising. The ample broguing on the wingtip speaks of a man at the bolder end of traditional. The newness of these shoes tells her he's got dis-posable income and takes pride in his appearance. Caira likes these shoes. And now they're making their way down the steps to her flat.

She suffers a micro panic about her own choice of clothes. Are they too old? Too mumsy? She's wearing a simple black outfit, albeit paired with a leopard-print scarf to prove she's not a complete bore. It's fine, she tells herself. It's fine.

Caira's heart flutters as she goes to the door. But the nerves ballooning inside her burst and disappear at the sight of him. He's holding a rose – that's a first. It makes her laugh. She suddenly feels far too old to be dating this sweet summer child. But also, really, who cares? They're both adults and they can do what they bloody well like. She's allowed to have fun. God knows she needs it after the week she's had.

Caira grabs her warmest coat and walks with him to the Olive Tree, a restaurant just around the corner. She's had dates here before. The waiting staff have probably noticed, she suspects. They sit Caira and Miles at a table by the window. It's busy in here – noisy and warm – and a sheen of condensation has gathered where the glass meets the freezing December air outside.

Caira asks Miles what he does for a living and pretends to look surprised when he tells her he's an actor. Of course, she knows this already. Of course, she googled him as soon as he WhatsApp-ed her and she found out his full name. According to his IMDb profile – which Caira has pored over several times – his credits are mostly for minor roles in TV dramas. She wonders if he'll oversell himself in an attempt to impress her, but he's modest if anything, explaining that he's just starting out, and taking on any job he can to gain experience. According to his profile on Starlight Casting, he has also modelled. But he doesn't mention that. It's easy to believe, though – he is too pretty in the candlelight. His skin is boyishly unblemished and smooth, and his brown eyes are sparkly and brand new. Being with him would be like making the first cut into a perfectly iced and beautiful cake – and that always feels wrong, however satisfying it's meant to be.

Curiously, though, Caira doesn't want the night to end. It's her who suggests going across the road for another drink. And closing time sneaks up on her like a fun-spoiling teacher clanging a bell to mark the end of break.

She lets him walk her home. There's no harm in that; he already knows where she lives. And he's done nothing tonight to change her initial assessment of him as completely harmless. This one was fun. *Really* fun. In many ways, it's been the perfect first date. But it's difficult to imagine it leading anywhere. Even in a late-night haze, it's impossible to escape the fact that he is practically – and *noticeably* – too young for her.

They stop on the street outside Caira's flat. Miles wraps his arms around himself. The soft curls that hang over his forehead tremble in the cold wind.

'Will you be all right getting home?' Caira winces inwardly as soon as the words leave her mouth. God, she sounds like his *mother*.

'I'll get an Uber.' His teeth chatter on the words.

She feels a need to wrap her arms around him. It's not a sexual urge, it's more nurturing than that – a simple desire to warm him up. 'Why don't you come inside?' Her words are out before she's had a chance to consider if that's a good idea. 'Just while you wait for your Uber.'

He flashes a smile. 'Okay, thanks.'

Caira descends the stone stairway, with him following close behind. Normally, she wouldn't dream of inviting someone in on a first date. But it's freezing, and it's only for a few minutes. And, honestly, what's the worst that could happen?

PART ONE

CHAPTER 1

ELEVEN MONTHS LATER

MILES

He sits at a table in a plain white room. The AirPods in his ears play an audiobook, but the words stopped registering at least an hour ago. That's because his head is already full of noise. There comes a point when the brain has been put under so much stress that it pulls up the drawbridge and refuses to allow in any non-essential information. His toes fidget inside his shoes, and what's left of his fingernails drum the table. Opposite him, David, his solicitor, is tapping away on a laptop. Apart from that, the only other objects in the room are a couple of disposable coffee cups and Miles's duffel bag – the most dreadful bag he's ever packed.

A few weeks earlier, when they entered this room for the first time, David explained that the lack of non-bolted furnishings and objects was a precaution. There could be nothing in here that could be used as a weapon. They were taking precautions, Miles instantly realised, against people like him: people who enter this place with their character in the grey purgatory between innocent and guilty.

David has been distracted by something on his phone. He frowns, then waves to get Miles's attention.

Miles's heart kick-starts. He hurriedly pulls his earphones out. 'What is it?'

'There's been a knock,' David says.

'A knock?'

'From the jury. They want to communicate something to the judge. It's probably just that they have a question for her. Eleanor has gone to find out.'

Miles sits up straight, pulling the fingers of his left hand. 'Could it be a verdict?'

'It would be very quick. They've not long been deliberating. They've probably just got a question about the evidence. It happens all the time.'

'But it could be a verdict?'

'Well, yes. It could be.' David adjusts his spectacles, straightens his navy tie. He's almost as fidgety as Miles. 'And if they've reached a verdict this quickly then it's probably a good thing for us.'

Miles stares at the bare white wall. 'Probably.'

'You know there are no guarantees, but I think we're in a strong position. Try to stay positive. Eleanor will be here in a minute.'

David gives him a reassuring smile, and Miles breaks eye contact. He looks down at his bag, which contains the essentials he was advised to bring – clothes, books, toiletries, a list of phone numbers – in case he's remanded in custody. Miles almost refused to pack it. Doing so added a real, tangible weight to the possibility that he might be found guilty, and he's been doing his best not to believe it could genuinely happen. Because it couldn't possibly happen, could it? He's read about people being unfairly accused, about miscarriages of justice. But it doesn't seem possible, in this day and age. In a developed country. It doesn't seem possible that someone like *him* could get sentenced to life in prison. But it's now undeniably possible, because he's packed a bag for it. His lawyers have done well to keep him on bail until this point, but a guilty verdict would mean immediate custody.

Miles stares at the door, waiting for his barrister to appear. He's restless, fidgeting, knitting his fingers together, jiggling his knees. Then he hears it: faint at first, the clacking of heels in the corridor. The sound grows steadily louder, then stops. After a short pause, there's a tap on the door, which then opens. Eleanor strides in, dressed in her wig and gown, and closes the door behind her.

'Hi, Miles.' She gives him a half-smile – he gets a lot of those, at the moment. They're smiles of goodwill and sympathy, because there is sod all to genuinely smile about. 'How are you doing?'

'I'm good.'

Again, she gives him that half-smile. But this time Miles sees something on her face he didn't notice earlier. Her make-up is always perfect, as if this is all showbusiness, which, he supposes, in a way, it is. But today it's been applied more heavily, especially around the eyes, and her skin has a matt glow. It knocks his heart up another gear; he knows there's only one reason anyone puts make-up on that thick – they're about to go on camera. Or they think they might be about to. 'Is it all right if I sit down?'

Miles gestures to an empty seat next to him.

Eleanor lifts the lower fabric of her black gown and sits. The smile has gone, her lips now pressed into a straight line. 'It appears things have progressed a little faster than we'd expected. Remember what I told you: if it's good news, try to take it with good grace, no whooping or punching the air. There's a family in there who have lost their daughter, their sister . . . and you can't be seen to be celebrating. No matter how relieved you might—'

'Wait, are you telling me they've made a decision?'

Miles is sure he knows the answer, but he needs her to say it anyway.

'That's right. We'll be going back into court soon. The jury has reached a unanimous verdict.'

CHAPTER 2

MILES

Miles no longer sits; he paces around the small space. He's asked to be alone, and he won't see another soul until it's time to go back into court.

It all comes down to this. What's about to follow is both the beginning and the end. But exactly what is about to begin and what will end is yet to be decided. If it goes his way, the curtain will fall on the grim drama his life has become this last year. If it goes against him, it will be . . . well, Miles has been advised not to dwell on that. Because it's unthinkable. Or at least it would've been, a year ago.

The thing awaiting him on the flipside of this binary split of fate – the unthinkable – carries so much weight it could drag him down to depths he'd have never thought possible. It's a life sentence. Literally. In prison. Not a metaphorical one, like the way people describe their office job or marriage. An actual prison, with iron bars and paedophiles and plastic plates. The institution that most people don't give any serious thought to because it's so far off, so foreign and abstract. That's the thing with the unthinkable. It takes a seismic change to your mindset and a lot of time to break through the impossibility of it. But eleven months is a long time when there's a murder charge hanging over you. And there's something about the words *you are hereby charged* that gives the brain the jolt it needs to start grappling with a new reality. Once you've started thinking about the unthinkable, it becomes very thinkable indeed, to the point where you'll barely think about anything else. And Miles has been given a heck of a long time to think.

Once again, his mind travels back to the week last year when everything changed. It was last December – nearly a year ago. Life was normal, then. Better than normal, even. It was an exciting time: he'd just been booked for the biggest job of his career so far, and he was planning a trip to New Zealand – somewhere he'd always dreamed of visiting. And, more fateful than that, he had a date lined up.

One night, that's all it was – one night that changed everything. Before that date, he'd never met Caira Kennedy, hardly knew anything about her. And now his name and hers will be inextricably linked in the most awful way, not only in people's minds but also as a matter of public record and the subject of internet speculation.

It was one of those sliding doors moments; there were so many tiny twists of fate that combined to set off a chain reaction and blew his entire existence to pieces. It left him to ponder all the what-ifs. What if he'd made different plans that night? What if he'd set the age range on Hinge a bit younger? What if he'd swiped left when Caira's image appeared on his phone screen? What if he'd cancelled on her at the last minute? What if he hadn't offered to walk her home?

He's gone over it plenty of times in his mind and concluded that his date with Caira was always likely to happen, whatever he did. Almost like it was preordained. Miles was free and single, and once she swiped right on him, he was always going to reciprocate. She was gorgeous and looked like a lot of fun. Her profile picture – the same image that was later used with many articles about her murder – was candid: she was at a restaurant table, in half-profile, smiling broadly, probably laughing with someone out of shot to her left. She looked almost exactly as she did on the night they met: her face framed by a mass of blonde curls, the smoky eyes, large hoop earrings.

She gave him her address, which was unusual, and told him to pick her up. This left him wondering if he should arrive with a bouquet like they were in some American rom-com. In the end, he opted for a single rose. And it was just before seven on a cold winter's evening when he arrived at her street under a dark and cloudless sky. He'd driven there, and found a parking spot on Caira's road, about a hundred yards from her address. He didn't need the car after that – the restaurant Caira had chosen was only a few minutes' walk away.

His memory of what happened is a little hazy. The date went well; that might seem an odd way of summarising it, given the aftermath, but it was true. All of Miles's dates went well. If you're fresh-faced and well spoken, and follow a few simple rules – mirror their body language, ask lots of questions, make no mention of politics – then there is no reason for any date to go badly. Caira liked him – there was no doubt about it. They were seated at a small table in a busy bistro, conversation rumbling all around. Her eyes shimmered and she spoke with animated energy when he asked about her life. She had a keen thirst for wine, and they put away two bottles: a Crémant and a Côtes du Rhône, as would later be coldly reported in court.

As a result of the wine, Miles can't remember their conversation verbatim, but Caira spoke about her job with an intensity that was unforgettable. Social work was no cakewalk, she said. Some days were hard; *many* days were hard. The domestic worlds lived in by some were so private, so messed up, and people really had no idea what was going on behind locked doors and perma-drawn curtains, or what it was like to be a child for whom that situation was the norm. Some days Caira came home from work and spent the evening in tears. But it was all worth it, she said. To make a *real* difference in someone's life. And safeguarding vulnerable children from harm: what could be more important and satisfying than that? The longer she went on about the vital and impactful nature of her work, the more aware he became of the triviality of his own. He felt faintly winded by the shame of it by the time she paused for breath and flipped the conversation with the inevitable follow-up question: *and what do you do?* They discussed his work, and then, somehow, the conversation switched to where they had gone to school. Caira's eyes widened when he said Holvine College. She had questions about Holvine, and about the investigation published in *The Times* a few months earlier. Was it true, what the whistleblowers had said? That there was systemic abuse? Had he heard anything? Miles told her as much as he knew; there were rumours about certain teachers, but they might be unfounded. Miles had never been a boarder — that side of school life, what went on after lessons ended, wasn't really known to him.

After the meal, they went to a pub across the road for more drinks — double gin and tonics that cost eight quid a piece, according to the receipts that were taken in evidence — and stayed until it closed at midnight. And then he walked her home. The temperature outside had dropped further, and their breath smoked on the December air. When they reached her apartment, he jammed his hands hard into the pockets of his coat and tensed his body, attempting to disguise his shivering. She must have noticed anyway, because she asked him if he wanted to come in and warm up while he waited for his Uber. Naturally, he said yes. As for what happened next . . . well, there's only one living person who knows the truth about that. That's why it's been argued in court for the last month.

◆ ◆ ◆

It was the day after the date when everything started to move fast. Miles was still mildly hungover when the police turned up in the early evening. And then began the impossible – the unthinkable – series of events: a chain of sickening experiences that no person should ever have to go through. It started with what the police described as a chat, that progressed to interviews and legal advice and no-comment answers. There were swabs inserted, fingerprints taken, accusations levelled. *You are hereby charged.* There was a court appearance, the ceremonious removal of his anonymity, the media reports. There was a committal hearing, a plea hearing, a pre-trial hearing, and months of barely bearable waiting, and it all led here, all built up to a three-week trial that will decide the course of his future.

Any minute now, he will go back into the courtroom. Hopefully, for the last time. Once again, everyone will be focused on Miles. Once again, they will all stare at him, weighing it up, wondering whether he did it, whether he murdered her. Only, this time, the jury will give them an answer.

Throughout the trial, the seven men and five women on the jury have all appeared to have doubts about his innocence. Even his family have doubts, he is sure of it. It might be just the faintest hairline in an otherwise solid wall of belief and support, but the crack has still showed. There is only one person in that room who knows for *sure* – with one hundred per cent certainty – whether he did it, and that is Miles.

There's a light tap on the door, and Miles stops his pacing. He waits for a moment, tries to slow his breathing, then opens it.

In the doorway is David, wearing another of those patronising half-smiles. Miles never wants to see another of those as long as he lives. 'Okay, Miles, are you ready? It's time to go back into court.'

CHAPTER 3

ELIS

Something's happening. This might be it. The judge and jury aren't in yet, but there's a tension building in the room. It's unsettling. This place, with its oak-panelled walls and high, ornate ceiling, is supposed to unsettle people like Elis. It has a dusty smell, like an old book. It's full of whispers. And today it's full of something else – a collective unease. On the front bench, Miles's barrister shuffles some papers, stony-faced.

Elis sits in the public gallery, which is mostly full, as it has been for much of the trial. The press bench is packed, too, of course. They wouldn't miss this. The reporters have been lapping up every minute of Miles's misery, and they'll no doubt be hoping for a guilty verdict. To them, Miles isn't even human, just the subject of a story – a more interesting specimen than is usually served up to them in the dock. If there was a bingo card containing all the clichés for the tabloids' dream defendant, Miles would have the lot: well-spoken, expensively educated, glamorous job. Most importantly, he's good-looking – objectively more so than ninety-nine per cent of the population. Good looks are interesting anyway; when our eyes are instinctively drawn to a face in a crowd. But, for whatever reason, that same attractiveness becomes overwhelmingly fascinating in the context of a fall from grace. A model at a fashion show might be lazily admired by a small audience, but when he or she tumbles face first on to the runway, the images are consumed by a hungry audience across the world. That's what they're getting here: a slow-motion car crash in which the vehicle involved is the sports car from their wildest dreams. It's the chance to see the man who has it all lose all that he has.

The whole thing has resulted in an orgy of coverage. The news sites, even the more sensible ones, have framed their headlines to highlight his advantages in terms of wealth and genetics. And, naturally, the more personal the dirt they can get the better. It was laughable the way the reporters started scribbling their shorthand at breakneck speed whenever the prosecution attempted to steer the narrative in a more salacious direction. At times during this trial, the Crown tried to paint Miles as some kind of deviant, which is ridiculous. Elis knows exactly why they did that – because they don't have a motive.

There's movement. A hush falls over the courtroom, and Elis's pulse quickens as Miles is led into the dock. He's accompanied by a stocky security guard in one of those short-sleeved polyester shirts that are only worn by security guards. Miles looks solemn and exhausted. He's in a black suit and tie, like a mourner at his own funeral. Most of the time, and in all his professional headshots, Miles has what you might call bed-hair – a charmingly tousled thatch that hangs close to his eyes. But today, and during the whole trial, it has been combed to within an inch of its life. His weight loss has pinched his face in unnaturally tight under his cheekbones, and his lips appear to be even fuller. The court artist's sketch looked almost like a caricature. *Maybe that's why,* Elis thinks, *people are able to write and talk and speculate about him as if he's not a real person.* What doesn't come across in any of the news stories is that he's pretty normal, really. A decent bloke. And Elis should know – they're mates. Maybe even *best* mates.

He felt a connection with Miles straight away. Elis never really fitted in with the lads from his school. They were all right, but something didn't quite click; he largely felt inclined to hide the fact he didn't like the same music or share their love of sports, and it bothered him that the people around him were so lacking in imagination. But Miles was different. They met because they were both hired to work on a police procedural drama being shot in Manchester. Miles had a supporting role, and Elis was a day player who ended up staying a whole week because the scenes he was in proved problematic. It was during the pandemic – everything was closed – and so they spent every evening killing time together at their hotel. By the last night it was like they'd known each other for years. Because they both lived in Bristol, they began to hang out, bonding over the craziness of the industry. Their personalities were so similar it was scary. That must be one of the reasons why it's so disturbing to see him there in the dock – it could so easily have been Elis up there instead of him.

The jury members file in, and everyone's ordered to stand as the judge makes her entrance. Elis looks around the public gallery. To his left is Miles's family – his mum, dad and sister. They hold hands and stare ahead, grim. It's surprising how few of Miles's mates have made the effort to come. George is here – as he has been most days, to be fair – but there are few others. Far more numerous is Caira's camp – her family members and their supporters. They sit to Elis's right, as far away from Miles's lot as they can get, and their anger is palpable. He makes sure not to make eye contact because their hatred extends to him, by association. He felt it from their stares as he gave evidence from the witness box last week. He gets it – why they are so angry. They're grieving and hungry for justice. But their passion has clouded their judgement; they can't see logic, can't see how obvious it is that Miles is not the person responsible for Caira's murder.

At the head of the courtroom, the judge and clerk finish a conversation, and the clerk approaches the jury. Elis takes deep, slow breaths. This is it, he can feel it. It's deathly quiet now, and he can hear even the faintest of coughs, the scratch of every pen.

The clerk asks the foreman to stand. 'Will you please confine yourself to answering my first question yes or no.'

He nods his assent.

'Have you the jury reached a verdict upon which you are all agreed?'

The foreman, a bald man in spectacles and a tweed blazer, waits a beat, then clear as a bell answers: 'Yes.'

Yes. Such a simple word, but it sends a shiver up Elis's spinal column. Behind him, a barely audible gasp escapes a throat. They all knew this was coming, but it still seems unreal. Like it can't really be happening. Elis's palms are clammy with sweat. God knows how Miles must be feeling.

The clerk continues: 'Members of the jury, do you find the defendant Miles Deverill guilty or not guilty?'

The beats are unbearable. *Say not guilty. It must be not guilty; it has to be.*

The foreman clears his throat. 'Not guilty.'

For a second, the bench and the ground below Miles seem to lose their density. The room slips out of focus. Elis's mouth falls open and he looks over at Miles, who has his eyes closed and appears to be going through something akin to an out-of-body experience. His family embraces. And to Elis's right, there are sobs: guttural ones, the kind that sound like they physically hurt. Those sounds are at odds with the warm wave of relief and jubilation coursing through his body, and the combination creates a curious, intoxicating blend of emotions. Of course, he feels great sympathy for Caira's family, but that can't dull his relief that the jury has reached the correct verdict. Elis chooses not to look over at Caira's supporters and instead fixes his gaze on the lead prosecutor. He looks well-and-truly pissed off. Good. After the way he went for Elis in the witness box and Miles in the dock, Elis is quite happy to see him taken down a peg or two.

Noise continues to rumble around the court. The judge tolerates the outbursts of emotion for a few more moments, then calls for order. She thanks the jury for their time and tells Miles he's free to go. After such a painful, drawn-out process, the end is abrupt. There is no apology, no acknowledgement of the hell Miles has been through. But it doesn't matter. Elis can't wipe the smile off his face. He has his friend back.

Outside court, a breeze cools the back of Elis's neck as he watches from the sidelines. A media swarm awaits Miles. They're all here; the TV crews have half a dozen satellite trucks parked along the street, their cameras already in position. A group of photographers is poised. A reporter gesticulates live to camera, occasionally looking over her shoulder towards the courtroom entrance. They're all waiting. And then he appears, flanked by his legal team. The photographers buzz into life, jostling for the best vantage. There are cheers and applause from the small group of Miles's supporters, but he keeps his cool, his lips pressed into a demure smile. Eleanor leads him towards the press pack. 'Good afternoon, everyone,' she says. 'Miles will be making a short statement. He won't be taking questions.'

Miles unfolds a sheet of paper from his blazer pocket, and it shakes a little in the breeze. He takes a deep breath. 'Today's verdict brings to an end what has been an extremely stressful and trying period. I'd like to thank the jury for reaching their decision, and my dedicated legal team. I'm beyond grateful to my friends and family for their love and support during this awful time of my life.' Miles pauses for a moment and appears to swallow a lump in his throat. 'I'd also like to take this opportunity to offer my sincere condolences to Caira's family. While I am not guilty of this crime, I remain as horrified as anyone by Caira's murder and it is my hope that the person responsible will be brought to justice. To that end, I hope the police will look deeper and carry out the detailed investigation that her tragic death deserves. Now that this episode is behind me, I have the chance to try and rebuild my life, and I fully intend to take it. Thank you.'

The end of his statement triggers a flurry of questions. All speaking over each other, the reporters' voices are raised and garbled. For a moment, it appears that Miles might respond, but Eleanor shuffles closer to his side and takes his arm, before leading him away.

The reporters continue to bark questions as Miles makes his way towards a waiting car. Photographers retreat down the street to hold their position in front of him. Elis isn't sure what to do – should he rush over and say something to his friend? What's the right thing to say? Before he has the chance to think, George, Miles's old school-mate, has hurried over and put an arm around Miles, giving him a playful shake.

A broad smile takes over Miles's face. He's done well to stay composed until now, but he obviously can't help it. The relief spills out. And, at that second, camera shutters explode into life, every lens, from every angle, hosing him down in the second it takes for his smile to fade.

CHAPTER 4

POLLY

The car pulls away from the kerb and heads towards their home. Polly sits in the middle seat feeling weightless and light-headed, a growing sense of euphoria tingling throughout her whole being. Her brother is free. After nearly a year of wretched uncertainty, Miles has been found not guilty. She has to keep reminding herself, because otherwise her fraught brain can't comprehend it. A lifetime's worth of good news has been served up unexpectedly quickly and in a single potent shot, and it's almost impossible to digest. But as more minutes and seconds pass, it *is* sinking in. She can feel it physically happening: the removal of the threat they were facing has allowed space for relief to rush in with such intensity that she's struggling to keep a lid on it. And yet, unexpectedly, somewhere deep in her belly, an odd queasiness remains. That's because, although her brother has been rightly acquitted, the awful context is unchanged. A woman has been killed – and no one knows why. Elation, as it turns out, can't be purely felt in circumstances as horrendous as these.

They round a corner, and Miles leans in towards her. He's talking, but not in any orderly way. Every sentence he utters has vaguely the same meaning as the one before it, as if he needs to keep summarising recent events in order for them to be true. *They found me not guilty. I'm a free man. I can't believe it's over. It's finally over.*

'You better get used to it,' says Carl, their dad, from the front passenger seat. 'It never should have got this far. This whole thing has been a giant waste of everyone's time.'

Polly senses her father is beginning to go off on another of his rants. Carl has been like this ever since Miles's arrest. While Miles defeatedly bemoaned his bad luck, their father was bullish and indignant, focusing on the injustice of it. He was furious at the police and the Crown Prosecution Service. The charges were laid, he said, not because the police really thought Miles did it but because there were no other suspects, and they were under pressure to act. The onus should never have been on Miles to prove his innocence but the police to find the person who did it. Carl is now making the point for the umpteenth time. 'At least the jury saw it for what it was,' he says. 'A complete bloody sham. Now, we all have to put this behind us.'

Polly wonders for a moment how straightforward that will be: to put it all behind them. But now isn't the time for such thoughts. Instead, she chooses to comfort her mum, Zara, who is sat to her right, with tears streaming down her face.

Throughout this whole thing, Zara has been so stoic. But now it's all coming out. Polly suspects her mother reacted to Miles's arrest in the same way as she did: silently fearing the worst. She knew how badly this could have ended. At times, Zara seemed to feel Miles's stress and turmoil as acutely as he did. Maybe even more so. In a strange way, Zara had almost as much to lose as Miles. Other than for her brief career as a dancer and fashion model in the eighties, she has dedicated her entire life to the well-being of her family. And this could have broken their family beyond repair.

Miles rests his head gently against Polly's. 'I'm not dreaming, am I? It really is over?'

Polly pinches the skin on her brother's hand. 'Feel that? You're not dreaming.'

He smiles. 'It's such a relief.'

'I know.'

'We really *are* going on the trip, aren't we?'

Polly says nothing to that, just smiles and nods with what she hopes looks like genuine enthusiasm. She assumed that once the verdict came in, he would move on from the whole idea of the trip. But apparently not.

His eyes are wide and wet. Childlike. 'You were right about everything, Pol. Soon we will be on a flight to New Zealand, and we'll forget about everything that's happened.'

Polly pats him on the thigh. She can't allow him to carry on like this – not right now. But if he does, she'll have no one to blame but herself. Over the last eleven months, Polly has mentioned New Zealand more often than anybody. But that doesn't mean she ever actually thought it would be a good idea to jet off the minute he got acquitted. Talking about New Zealand was simply the single easiest way of distracting him from the real issue he was facing.

It was largely symbolic. Before Miles was charged, he'd been planning his trip for a while. When he got arrested, those plans obviously got shelved. Even if Miles had somehow remained in the mood for a holiday, his bail conditions didn't allow it. Carl had to put down a lot of money as a bond to prevent Miles from being locked up on remand. If Miles had skipped the country, they'd have lost the lot. So, instead of going on holiday, Miles found himself giving notice on his flat and moving back home. Polly has spent a lot of time back here in Bristol, too. A family must stick together in a crisis, and she instinctively felt that Miles needed his big sister around. Before the trial Polly came back from London pretty much every weekend, to check on him. Sometimes she even came during the week, if her brother was due in court. Other than for those court appearances, Miles spent almost an entire year almost completely housebound as he waited for the trial to begin. The mood in the house was torturous, and Polly found herself using the trip to take his mind off it. 'Soon, this will all be over,' Polly would say, 'and, before you know it, you'll be on a flight to New Zealand.'

It was something vivid and exciting for him to focus on. Something positive. A sort of therapy. Miles had developed an ominous fixation on prison, so Polly would sit him down in front of travel programmes and encourage him to visualise himself among mountains and forests; floating through fjords; swimming in cool oceans – anything but picturing himself in a cell. You *will* get there, she told him. And *soon*. She did her best to sound more certain than she really was.

Now though, Miles has been found not guilty, and there's no reason to use the idea of the trip as a distraction. And he certainly doesn't need to be flying anywhere. What he needs is to focus on a return to normality.

She'll make all this clear to him, soon. But now isn't the time.

They're halfway home, and Miles has gone quiet, staring out of the window. Polly gives his arm a squeeze. She's so relieved for her brother. He's had an utterly miserable year. She's relieved too for their parents, who have been to hell and back. And, quite honestly, she's relieved for herself.

Polly's ordeal might not have been anywhere near as traumatic as her brother's, but the last few weeks have been particularly dreadful, especially given the amount of media interest the trial has generated. But that is all behind her. Tomorrow, she won't be forced to go to court. She won't have to decide which outfit she wants to be in when the press photographers shamelessly train their lenses on her. That's something they don't tell you when your brother's charged with murder: that you'll be photographed to the same extent he is, simply by virtue of the fact you are young and female. During the trial, images of Polly made the papers every day. Every. Single. Day. Once, she was even on the front page, as if it were her at the centre of this awful crime. One of the papers did a profile piece about her. The article, which contained a number of inaccuracies, now serves as the top search result about her on the internet, so that when anyone – a prospective client, for example – googles her name they'll immediately link her to a notorious murder. One doesn't have to work in PR, as she does, to know that's decidedly inconvenient.

Polly still doesn't know where the information came from, but the profile piece did manage to get a few things right, and some of her life's minutiae was recorded with an uncomfortable level of detail. It said she was based in London, but got the wrong area (her flat, which she hasn't seen the inside of for two weeks, is in Hammersmith, not Pimlico), and gave the address of her office, presumably in case any stalkers fancied tailing her on her way to work. They got her age right: thirty-three. And it was true that she habitually bought a £4 chai latte whenever she passed a Pret. It also said she was single, which wasn't true at the time of publication but is now. The piece was about five hundred words long, although the bulk of it was about her clothes. It pored over her wardrobe in great detail and included hyperlinks to stores where readers could buy some jacket or accessory she was wearing to court. *Get the style of a murderer's relative!* it seemed to be saying. It was surreal and dehumanising to read about herself that way, as if she were a public figure, a commodity, a celebrity even. As a naive teenager, Polly daydreamed about being a celebrity. But she never imagined this. What she's got can't even be described as fifteen minutes of fame; she's not famous – she's infamous. And there's a big difference.

The car turns on to their honey-stoned Georgian terrace and pulls up about three-quarters of the way down. Miles sits up straight, his body trembling with energy. Suddenly, after being so downcast and moping for the last year, it's like he's a different person. He turns to Polly and places a hand on her shoulder before opening the door. 'Come on,' he says. 'We can look up flights when we get in.'

CHAPTER 5

GEORGE

George sets a magnum of champagne on the step and rings the doorbell to the Deverills' place. He's glad to be back; it's nearly a year since he was last here, but he's always been made welcome by Miles's family. Their home is a five-storey townhouse facing the park, in one of those terraces built when developers still cared what housing looked like, and whoever built this one gave it the full beans: limestone front, multiple balconies, tall sash windows – the works. He expected a media scrum outside, but it's all quiet. Maybe now they're finally getting left alone. Down the street, to the west, the sun is setting, and the sky is peach and mauve above ragged rooftops and a cathedral spire.

Miles closes the door, and George stoops to pick up the champagne. 'A gift from Ma and Pa,' George says. 'From my family to yours.'

Miles accepts it with a small smile. His whole aura seems diminished by his ordeal; it's robbed the colour from his cheeks and the zest from his movements. 'Cheers,' he says. 'Although, I don't think it's going to be that kind of night.'

George raises one eyebrow. 'You're a free man again. You've got your life back. If that's not worth a glass of Bolly, I don't what is.' He slaps his friend on the back and follows him into the hallway. It's immediately warm and familiar: the oak parquet floor solid under his feet, the elaborate cornice work, the sweeping balustrade staircase. Home from home. They go to the rear ground floor, where a slow chatter echoes out of the kitchen. There are eight people in there: Miles's parents and sister, a few people from his legal team, and Miles's actor friend, Elis. There's a pleasant smell of baking, but the vibe is more solemn than he expected. It's not gloomy, just a little restrained, the wine and finger food being consumed almost apologetically, like at the beginning of a wake. It's strange, how some people can take an occasion as happy as this and still manage to suck the spirit out of it. Miles is lucky to have a friend like him, who can cheer the mood up a bit. But, even so, he's got his work cut out trying to spark joy in the miserable lot gathered in front of him right now.

As if the embodiment of a tough crowd, Miles's sister is staring at George, her arms folded. 'Congratulations, George, you're famous,' she says, and adds something under her breath. George didn't hear it but has no doubt it wasn't complimentary – Polly never has minced her words.

'What are you talking about?'

'You haven't checked the news, then?'

George takes his phone out of his pocket and opens the *Tribune* app. He can feel the group watching for his reaction. His eyes widen. The top image shows George with his arm around his friend; Miles's face is creased by the breadth of his grin, and George's head is cocked back in an open smile. Under the picture is a headline with a gleeful tone to match. *Smiles for Miles: Young actor's relief after being found NOT GUILTY of murder.* George reads a couple of lines of the story then slips his phone back into his pocket. He shrugs. 'So what?'

Miles purses his lips. 'It looks a bit more celebratory than we'd have liked.'

George snakes his left arm around Miles, locking his head tight in the crook of his elbow exactly as in the photo. 'We *should* be celebrating. We *are* celebrating. Forget about it – this will be old news before you know it.'

'George is right,' Carl says, 'this will all be forgotten about in a few weeks. You can't let this ruin your life for a minute longer.'

George crams a puff pastry tart into his mouth and speaks as he chews, the tang of red onion on his tongue. 'Cheer up everyone, it's like a bloody morgue in here.'

His eye lands on Elis and catches his reaction: a slight eye-roll – barely detectable. He's caught him doing that before. But if Elis has got a problem with George, then he's going to have to get used to him, because Miles is his best friend, and George was here long before Elis started following him about.

'So, where are we going tonight?' George asks, looking expectantly at Miles.

David, Miles's solicitor, unperches himself from a stool and sets his wine glass down on the island of white marble. 'Miles isn't going *anywhere*. Not tonight.'

'What's the plan, then?'

'Just a couple of drinks here,' Miles says. 'Reubyn will be here soon – we can finish planning our trip.'

Elis takes his phone out of his pocket. 'Actually, I've been doing some research for the trip, I've got loads of—'

'Elis, I didn't know you were coming?'

Elis looks at George and raises his eyebrows. 'Didn't Miles mention it?'

'I thought I did,' Miles says.

'Anyway, I've been looking at accommodation options for Fiordland,' Elis says. 'It's supposed to be one of the most stunning places on Earth. Look, I found these.'

George sighs inwardly as Elis swipes through pictures of log cabins in the middle of nowhere. Fiordland. They could save a fortune by going to Norway if they want to look at fjords. George waves at Polly and ushers her over, sensing he needs an ally. The trip is meant to be a *break* for Miles, a bit of light relief. He needs to be spending a lot more time in a jacuzzi than a pair of hiking boots. 'Pol, come here. What do you think of this?'

Polly strolls over and eyes Elis's phone with the look of reluctance George was hoping for. 'Yeah, I don't think now is a great time to be planning a holiday, do you? Miles probably wants to chill out for a bit.'

They turn to Miles, who shrugs. 'It's fine. I want to. The sooner the better.'

Polly gives Miles a look that George finds difficult to read. She has changed clothes since they were in court, into a loose-fitting black shirt that accentuates her dark features, the messy fringe and long, wet-looking eyelashes.

'And where do you want to go?' George askes Miles.

'Polly and I talked about starting in Queenstown. It's got the scenery that he wants' – pointing a finger at Elis – 'and enough fancy wine bars and vineyards to drain even your bank account, George.'

George smiles and makes brief eye-contact with Elis. 'Sounds lovely.' He's not entirely convinced by the plan, but Miles needs him to be positive right now, and besides, what he's suggesting makes a lot more sense than whatever Elis has in mind; if he wants to do climbing or orienteering or any other Duke of Edinburgh Award nonsense, he's picked the wrong group of people. Polly, for one, wouldn't be seen dead in a set of crampons. As for Reubyn, he would get out of breath just lacing up a pair of boots.

George raises his free hand to excuse himself. 'I'll be back in a sec.' He sidles over to the long kitchen counter, Bluetooths his phone to the Deverills' speaker set-up, and begins queuing up songs on Spotify. What's needed here is uplifting music, stuff that marks the occasion for what it is – the night when Miles gets his freedom back. He picks '*Drop It Like It's Hot*' by Snoop Dogg, and '*Celebration*' by Kool & The Gang to kick things off, then goes in search of titles that fit the context of what's just happened. There's a playlist called 'Freedom' created at the time of the Brexit referendum, and the top song is called 'Free Bird' by someone named Lynyrd Skynyrd. George doesn't know what it is, but, thematically, it sounds ideal, so it gets added to the queue. He picks a dozen or so more, then presses play on his newly curated Spotify list and smiles at the slow beat clopping out of the speakers: the first song is perfect. For a club tune it's tastefully down-tempo, and will warm people up nicely. The volume can go up in a few minutes when everyone has settled into the groove.

George scans the room and can't see Miles. He leaves the kitchen, swaggering to Snoop Dogg, and finds his friend in the hallway, staring at his phone. George peers over his shoulder. On the screen is the *Tribune* article he was looking at earlier.

'Why are you still reading that story?'

'I don't know. Some of the comments on it are a bit rough.'

George puts an arm around Miles's shoulders, speaks loudly into his ear. 'You can't pay any attention to it, mate. The people who write the comments are complete morons. Don't even look at them.'

'Yeah, I know, but it's hard not to.'

George is opening his mouth to reply when the doorbell goes – a heavy trill, like an old telephone. He raises one eyebrow. 'Want me to get it?'

'Nah,' Miles says. 'It's just Reubyn.'

George shrugs. 'All right, you let that hamster in, and I'll go crack open that champagne.' He slaps him on the shoulder and strides off towards the kitchen, matching his steps to the beat, and leaving Miles to answer the door.

CHAPTER 6

MILES

Miles pauses by the front door for a moment and grins as he weighs up how to greet his old friend. Should he pretend to be angry, scold him for not being in court today, or just throw his arms around him in a big hug? It might be funny to try the former, but even as a trained actor Miles can't pull that off – he feels the corners of his mouth being pulled upwards like a string puppet's, beyond his control – there's no way he can feign anger right now. Not at Reubyn.

He jerks the front door open, and immediately his smile falls from his lips. He hides his drink behind his back. The man standing on the step is not Reubyn, but a lanky bloke in a cheap grey suit. He's got a thin face and a downy receding hairline, and Miles recognises him instantly – he was on the press bench for much of the trial. The man clutches a notepad in his left hand and rotates a biro between the long fingers of his right.

'Hi, Miles,' the man says, in an accent from somewhere in the Midlands. 'I'm sorry to disturb you. My name's Anthony and I'm a journalist, here on behalf of the *Tribune*. It must have been such a relief to hear the verdict today?' He brings the pad in front of him, ready to record anything Miles says.

'I gave a statement outside court; I don't have anything else to say.'

The reporter nods briskly. 'I totally get it. You've been through one hell of an ordeal – I can't imagine what it's been like.' It's not a question, but his rising inflection demands an answer. He waits a beat, eyebrows raised at Miles, then continues. 'Did you get my letter?'

'Maybe. There were a few.'

'I just wanted to offer you the chance to tell your side of the story, Miles.'

Miles's eye twitches. How is it that he's got to deal with this after the day he's had? After the *year* he's had. A voice in Miles's head says he should tell this guy to piss off, but he knows he can't do that. He must be polite. Besides, isn't this reporter just doing his job? He probably doesn't want to have this conversation any more than Miles does. Miles steps outside and closes the door most of the way to cancel out some of the noise from inside, where, regrettably, someone has just turned up the volume on '*Celebration*' by Kool & The Gang. 'I appreciate that,' Miles says. 'But I'm not sure that's a good idea.'

The reporter starts nodding again, like he's battery-powered and someone just switched him back on. 'Yeah, of course, Miles. I totally get it, I really do. But the thing is: it's really one-sided, what gets reported from a trial like that. And you're a victim, too – being falsely accused, that's terrible. I can give you a chance to set the record straight.'

Miles claws at his hair. Answering the door was a mistake. Inside the house, '*Celebration*' is fading out, and above it comes the unmistakable pop of a champagne cork and George's hyenic howl. Miles needs this conversation to end, quickly. 'No,' he says. 'Thanks very much, but I don't want to do an interview.'

'There would be a fee, too, although I know that's not what's important; the important thing is that people will understand your side of things and know the toll it's taken on you.'

'Thanks, but I *really* don't want to.'

The reporter nods, slower this time, and raises a hand of submission in response to the slight change of tone in Miles's voice. Mercifully, the music coming from inside has moved on to something much slower and more sombre; what sounds like a church organ drones in mournful sustain over the soft strum of an acoustic guitar. 'I'll be honest with you,' the reporter says, 'people in your situation often think talking to the press will be a bad move, but the truth is that *not* doing it can make things worse. Right now, everyone wants to know what you're thinking, and one interview can make all that interest go away. And if you don't do an interview then—'

'Sorry, but the answer's *no*.'

'Okay, I hear you loud and clear.' The reporter narrows his eyes and nods towards the door. 'Are you having a party, Miles?'

'What? No, of course not.'

The notepad is back front and centre, and the reporter's pen is poised. 'Hey, I can't blame you after the ordeal you've had – of course you'd want to let your hair down.'

'I'm just catching up with a few friends.'

The reporter scribbles. 'And it's a champagne kind of night? Why not, eh?'

Miles wrinkles his brow. 'I don't know. It's just a couple of drinks. I need to go now.'

The reporter hollers as Miles opens the door. 'Hey, Miles, are you a fan of Lynyrd Skynyrd?'

Miles looks over his shoulder. 'What?'

'This song,' he says. '"Free Bird".'

'I don't know. I've got to get back inside. Thanks for your time.' Miles shakes his head, confused, and closes the door. His heartrate has cranked up; he's got a feeling that conversation didn't go as well as it could have. He's a little light-headed as he trudges through the hallway and into the kitchen, where George comes at him with a bottle and tops up his glass.

'Here you go,' George says. 'Where's Reubyn?'

Miles shakes his head. 'That wasn't him.'

'Who was it?' George's head recoils. 'Are you okay?'

Everyone in the room is looking at Miles, who stands stunned, staring vacantly into his drink.

'Miles,' Eleanor says, the pointed, courtroom tone returning to her voice. 'Who was it?'

'A reporter.'

'Oh no.' Eleanor rubs her temple and looks around at the group. 'Who let him answer the door? What did you say, Miles?'

'I thought it was . . . He seemed to think we were having some kind of a party.'

Eleanor shakes her head. 'From now on, Miles doesn't answer the door, doesn't answer the phone, doesn't so much as stand next to an open window, at least not for a few days.'

Miles stands silent for a moment. The rock song playing on the stereo, the title of which he is now unlikely ever to forget, is increasing in energy. 'Who put this music—' Miles shakes his head and lets the rest of the question crawl back into his throat. It's irrelevant – whoever chose the song – there's no undoing that now. But he feels it returning: the swirling doom. It's not as heavy or all-encompassing as it was, but still it's coming back, pecking lightly at his skin and curdling in his stomach, and right now he should be free of all that. Until Caira's death, he'd never felt it before, or anything close to it; the darkest shade of black in the spectrum of human emotion had not been visible to him and then suddenly it was – he was standing on a precipice and staring into it from a great height. He takes deep breaths, fills his lungs, and focuses his mind. He can't let the darkness back in. *Not* guilty – that was the verdict. He repeats it over in his mind. *Not guilty*. He needs it to sink in, to register with every fibre of his body: it's all over, he's a free man. Maybe George is right – they *should* be celebrating, just not in full view of the tabloid press. Almost completely out of tune with that thought, someone turns the music down to a barely audible volume.

'What did you say, Miles?' Eleanor asks again.

'Nothing. I didn't tell him anything, not really. But he said if I did an interview, it would make it all go away.'

'He would say that, wouldn't he?' She sighs and shakes her head. 'The thing is, these journalists are vampires – they suck blood, but they're fickle. Fickle as the wind. If you ignore them for a few weeks, they will move elsewhere.' She looks wide-eyed at Miles and must pick up on his need for reassurance because she inhales deeply and carries on. 'Right now, this case is red hot. Caira's name is trending, and people are clicking on stories about her, but soon the stories will dry up, and if there's nothing to click on, they will stop clicking. And when they stop clicking, the reporters will crawl back under their rocks and leave you alone. I've seen it happen a hundred times before.'

'Journalists,' George says, patting Miles on the shoulder. 'Bloody snakes, you can't trust them.'

'Don't worry, I won't be—'

The bell trills again, followed by a heavy knock. They look at each other, all serious, as if what's on the other side of the front door might be some mob or plague that could threaten them all.

'Here we go again,' Carl says. 'I've had quite enough of this. Miles, stay where you are. I'll get it.'

CHAPTER 7

REUBYN

Reubyn waits to make sure the journalists have packed up and left before he gets out of his Mini. Miles, the poor bugger, apparently had no idea there was a photographer papping him from a car window the whole time he was talking to that reporter. Reubyn could've stepped in, warned him off, but he's managed to go so long without getting caught up in this that it would be foolish to now. He feels terrible that he hasn't been in court every day to support his friend during his trial, but he's worked so hard to get his channel off the ground, and now that it's finally taking off, the last thing he needs is to damage his reputation by getting drawn into that media black hole. Miles will understand that, of course. And now that he's been acquitted, Reubyn can and will support him in any way he needs, just as long as it doesn't result in his name being used under any unfavourable headlines. The whole thing has been a complete mess – a nightmare for everyone involved – and now, the best outcome would be to draw a line under it as quickly as possible and move on.

Darkness has fallen, giving the windows an amber glow, and lining the street are orbs of light atop the cast-iron lamp posts. It's been a while since he last came here. This is one of the grandest streets in Bristol, and his visits come with incrementally more powerful reminders that Reubyn inhabits a different social position to his peers from school. His background was unlike that of the others at Holvine College, in that his family didn't have an endless supply of money. Reubyn's place at Holvine was heavily subsidised because his mother was a teacher there. When she died from a brain tumour, the school made the gesture of waiving all future fees for his education – including an option to start boarding. His father, whose work was temperamental and involved long days, eagerly took them up on that offer, despite Reubyn's protestations. And so that was it: he spent almost his entire life at that school up until the age of eighteen.

Reubyn crosses over and presses the doorbell, followed by three heavy raps of the iron knocker to make sure he's heard in the rear of the house. Miles's dad opens the door a crack and peers out, then swings it open and welcomes him in. Reubyn receives a warm handshake and spots Miles waiting sheepishly in the hallway.

'Mate!' Reubyn jogs over and gives him a hug. Miles's shoulders feel stony and fleshless through his shirt. 'It's such a relief.'

'Thanks, man.' Miles outstretches an arm, ushering him down the hall. 'It really is.'

Reubyn follows him into the kitchen and finds it surprisingly full, given how quiet it is. He is no stranger to social awkwardness, and he senses it the second he walks into the room; the air of discomfort hits him like a wave, invisible and silent, yet powerful – almost enough to knock him off balance. It's something to do with the journalist who was interviewing Miles on the doorstep just then, he reckons. The media want more dirt on him. Even though the poor sod has had a light shone on even the most private aspects of his life.

Miles's mum smiles at the sight of Reubyn. It's a broad, unconvincing smile, the kind of beam you'd get from a used-car merchant who knows what he's selling is a dud. She rushes over and pecks him on the cheek, filling the air around him with perfume. 'How are you? Are you excited about the trip?'

'I sure am. I've been looking forward to it.'

That last part is a lie; Reubyn wasn't as confident as the others that a not guilty verdict was coming. It was about six months ago that Polly sent the email around to a handful of his friends, explaining about the trip. *When* he's acquitted, she wrote – not *if* – like the whole thing was a formality and Miles only needed to show up to court and the charges would melt away. It's important to be optimistic in circumstances like these, Reubyn supposes, but he was never able to share in that optimism. Not completely, anyway. But now that it's all over, is he excited about the trip? Damn right he is. Not only does he get to catch up with his old friends, but it's also a free holiday courtesy of Miles's parents and a brilliant opportunity to create content. What's not to love?

'So, you're good to go?' Miles says. 'How soon can you leave?'

'Yeah, whenever really.'

'Good stuff,' George says, appearing by Reubyn's side and giving his back a firm slap. 'Do we need a visa or anything?'

'Sort of,' Elis says. 'But it only takes a few days to be approved. I'll set up a WhatsApp group and put all the details there, so everyone is across it.'

'No dramas, then,' George says.

Miles's dad stands between Miles and Reubyn and wings his arms around their shoulders. 'No dramas – exactly. This is what life's all about, you know; you stick together and look after each other. I'm proud of you lot. Just tell me what flights you want, and we'll get them booked.'

A conversation begins about flights and the various travel options available to them. New Zealand is bang on the opposite side of the world, so it doesn't matter if they fly east or west, with stopovers in Asia or North America, it'll take roughly the same amount of time – twenty-four hours, minimum – to get there. No one seems concerned about the distance. If anything, it's pleasingly symbolic: their friend is moving on, leaving his past far behind. Reubyn senses the mood in the room lifting at all mentions of it; voices are getting louder and gestures more animated, and hope soars all around – Miles is back, a new chapter is beginning, and soon they'll be off on an adventure where untold freedom and wilderness await.

The conversation meanders on, covering everything and anything concerning New Zealand – *is it true sheep outnumber people ten to one?* – until all their knowledge of the country, whether verified or supposed, has run dry. After about an hour, various threads of conversation fragment, and Reubyn finds himself in a corner talking to Elis. There was a short while when he saw Elis at least once a week, but this is the first time they've spoken since Miles was charged. They discuss the trial and Elis's stint in the witness box. It's all a bit heavy, and Reubyn is glad when he changes the subject. 'How's the channel going?' Elis asks.

'Good, thanks,' Reubyn says. 'It's really been taking off in the last six months or so.'

'I saw that one about the abandoned theme park. Didn't it get like half a million views?'

'Yeah, that one did well. You never know what people are going to like, I guess.'

Reubyn's being modest, of course. He's been a content creator for years now and has developed a pretty good feel for the kind of videos that are going to fly. When he first saw images of the derelict Wonder Park, with its broken rides, crumbling towers and rotting kiosks strangled by climbing weeds, like some post-apocalyptic hellscape, he knew he had to go in there and film. It was a tad risky, but it was worth it: the visuals were incredible, and it all fitted in perfectly with the emerging themes of a rebellious spirit and oddball sense of adventure found on his channel. But really, it was all in the selling. He didn't title the video 'Abandoned theme park', as summarised just now by Elis. Reubyn has learned to be more creative than that. When he made the thumbnail, he manipulated the colours in the image, making the gaudier shades of the broken roller coaster brighter and the sky a steelier grey, and overlaid a cut-out of his own face contorted into a Munchian scream, along with the words: *Is this the creepiest theme park on Earth?* Who wouldn't click on that?

'Are you going to be filming while we're away?' Elis asks.

'I hope so.'

'Like a travel vlog kind of thing?'

'No, not exactly,' Reubyn says. 'That's such a crowded space.'

'So, what then?'

'I'm thinking I might do a little wildlife thing.'

'*Wildlife?* That's a bit twee for you, isn't it?'

'This won't be.'

Elis raises his eyebrows – an appeal for further details.

Reubyn waves a dismissive hand. 'I don't like to discuss stuff like this when it's still in the planning stages – I feel like I might jinx it, you know? I do have an awesome surprise for Miles, though. For all of us, actually.' He scans the room for Miles but can't see him.

Elis tilts his head. 'What is it?'

For a second, Reubyn considers telling him. But, no, it can wait a little longer. Especially as the agreement isn't completely finalised yet. 'You'll find out soon enough.'

'This is like trying to get blood out of a stone.'

Reubyn laughs and checks the room again for Miles. He's distracted by the buffet on the sideboard, which is lined with trays containing remnant quantities of crostini and tartlets and other glistening gluten-y lumps that he can't touch because of his allergies.

Elis starts up again, talking about rock climbing and a trip he took to the Dolomites last summer. Reubyn is still scanning the room, half listening to something about limestone and the sunny side of the Alps. He nods along for a couple of minutes and then cuts Elis off, raising his voice in no particular direction: 'Has anyone seen Miles? He's been gone ages.'

CHAPTER 8

MILES

Miles lies on his bed, his eyes closed, while the last of the guests are being herded out downstairs. He's exhausted, his fuzzy brain ready to shut down, and it feels like a weight is being applied to his body from above, pushing him deep into the mattress. He didn't realise he was running on pure adrenaline, and once that wore off, his body turned lifeless and empty. After a few hours of well-meaning-but-awkward platitudes and congratulations, he was hit by a wave of tiredness so strong it wiped him out, and he had no choice but to remove himself from the situation and go upstairs. The massive sense of relief at being a free man still remains, but somehow even that has taken a toll. It seems that when all the tension and anguish left his body it took all his energy with it. He's happy, of course, but it feels hollower than expected, and there's something else – this growing sense that things still aren't quite right. That conversation he had with the reporter has been playing on his mind, and he suspects there could be more bad headlines coming his way. Maybe they've already been written. He knows he shouldn't check, but he can't resist. He opens the *Tribune* app on his phone, and, sure enough, there it is. A new story. A sickness forms in his stomach at the sight of the first picture: it shows him, standing at the front door of the house, wine glass in hand, stupid grin on his face. It must have been taken the second he opened the door, when he thought he was about to greet his old friend. The picture has been cropped so tightly around Miles that the reporter can't be seen. The headline says: *Free Bird! Miles Deverill hosts party with champagne and Lynyrd Skynyrd to celebrate not guilty verdict.* And there are other pictures, including one which is simply a close-up of the magnum George brought with him. They must have had a camera pointed at his house for hours – maybe they still do. He reads the story.

Exclusive by Anthony O'Neill

Aspiring actor Miles Deverill has toasted his freedom with a champagne-fuelled house party just hours after being found not guilty of murder.

Mr Deverill, 30, was acquitted earlier today after a jury took just four hours to conclude he was not responsible for the death of social worker Caira Kennedy, 40, who was strangled with her own scarf last year.

By 7 p.m. this evening, just hours after the verdict, friends had arrived at his family's £3 million home, including one who turned up with a £120 magnum of Bollinger.

And guests enjoyed the champagne while listening to party hits including 'Celebration' by Kool & The Gang, and Lynyrd Skynyrd's 1974 anthem 'Free Bird'.

Dressed in a casual shirt and jeans, Mr Deverill, a former public schoolboy who was educated at £40,000-a-year

Miles takes deep breaths to try to dispel the swirling in his gut as he scrolls through the rest of the text; from there it just repeats the story from earlier, which he's already read. It's a long article and it takes ten seconds or so to thumb all the way to the end, where the comments section begins. He knows he shouldn't look, but it's compulsive – he can't help it. There are 173 comments on this story alone, and he starts scrolling through them.

LilianM: *I'm not sure this is wise. There's a time and a place for a party like this.*

Drfc1963: *What's he supposed to do? Mope for the rest of his life? What he's been thru is every man's worst nightmare and if he wants to have a couple of drinks then good luck to him. I will buy him a pint if he comes to my local.*

Hunny Bun Bun: *This makes my blood boil!! Miles Deverill is an arrogant, overprivileged little rich kid who thinks he can do whatever he wants! Gross! Poor Caira!*

AlexB: *He'll get his comeuppance. Mark my words.*

After reading a dozen or so comments he closes the app. He knows they will continue in a similar fashion – a mixture of bile and support, with the occasional moderate, sober voice thrown in. He knows the views here aren't representative of the population (for a start, most people simply do not hold such passionate opinions about those they've never met), and he's been warned against reading below-the-line comments on news articles. But this isn't the only place the keyboard warriors raise their ugly heads.

When he got home this afternoon, one of the first things Miles did was change the privacy settings on his Instagram account. It was time he got back into the world – he needs to have a visible public profile, on his own terms, if he wants to get his career back on track – and it was good that he had a ton of new follow requests. But he's starting to wonder if making his account public again was a good idea. In the six hours since, several of his older posts have attracted some unwelcome comments. They range from backhanded compliments (*you're pretty cute, for a murderer*) to more cryptic suggestions of guilt (*where's the scarf, Miles, where is it?*) and outright abuse (*rot in hell, toff*). Miles blocked a few accounts and felt confident the abuse would cease in time, once the trolls were bored of his case and became obsessed with someone else. Now he has to block a few more. He considers making the account private again, although he won't do that – he can't let the trolls win. Miles has to trust that all this noise will die down eventually. Even his strongest critics will come to accept that, in the eyes of the law, he's an innocent man, whether they like it or not. There are no charges against him, now. Not so much as a speeding ticket. His slate has been wiped clean.

The problem is: he's been cleared in a criminal court, but in the court of public opinion the case seemingly still has a way to run. Even after being acquitted, this is going to define him. Forever.

After briefly discarding it, Miles picks up his phone again – he needs distracting from his thoughts. He opens his email app. Earlier, he received a dozen or so emails from friends, acquaintances and colleagues, all expressing their support. It left him with a warm feeling, verging on pride – something he hasn't felt for the best part of a year. His email account seemed to be a safe space, probably because it's a private forum – that's not of interest to the trolls, who prefer their words to be out in the open, so the whole world can breathe in their toxicity. In the hour since he last checked, only one new email has landed in his inbox – from his agent. He sighs. Kate tried to reach him earlier, but he ignored her call.

Miles thought he deserved better treatment from Starlight. He joined the agency as a kid, when he would do the occasional job in return for a boost to his pocket money (he appeared in advertising for breakfast cereal and funeral plans and everything in between), and he went full-time after finishing his A levels, positioned as high-end talent with even more agreeable – and rising – rates of pay. It was all going swimmingly. But when he was charged, the agency dropped him immediately – something he learned through a statement it had released to the media. It hurt more than it should've. The decision wasn't personal, he knew that – they were just trying to protect their business from bad publicity. But it could've been handled differently. Miles had been loyal (he could have easily signed with another agency), he never once cancelled on a job, and he made them a decent amount of money. He deserved an explanation, at least. Whatever Kate wants now, it can wait for another time. But once again, out of curiosity, he finds himself unable to resist. He clicks open the email.

Hello Miles!

I was sooo relieved when I saw today's verdict! You must be desperate to put all this behind you and get back to work, and we can't wait to see you! It's great that you're taking a holiday, but you must give me the dates ASAP so we can book your work around it. We've already had a number of inquiries since the news came out today and the offers are very varied and exciting! Please call me at your earliest convenience so we can discuss.

All my best,

Kate

Miles begins to type out a reply and then abandons it to the drafts folder. It's exhausting, this instinct to constantly try to please and be polite, even to people who don't give a toss about him. Yesterday, Kate wouldn't have touched him with a bargepole, and she makes no apology for, or even acknowledgement of, the fact that she so ruthlessly deserted him as a client at the first sign of trouble. Does she deserve a prompt reply? No. Yet, it will still irk him that he's keeping her waiting, and it will nag him more and more the longer he leaves it.

Out of habit, he opens the junk folder before closing the app. Miles glances down the list of spam emails. A sudden wave of prickly heat tingles through his exhausted body. In among the scam messages offering discounted Viagra and guaranteed cash prizes is an email with a subject line that stands out among the rest. *Hello again.* But what shocks him is the name of the sender:

Caira Kennedy. It only spooks him for a second – then he can see it for what it is: apparently, some trolls are so dedicated to their sport that they'll even go as far as setting up a fake email account in the name of a murder victim. Nothing is too low for these people. He stares at it for a moment, and then again curiosity gets the better of him. He clicks it open. The email is blank, except for an attachment: an audio file. He probably shouldn't play it – God knows what kind of abuse is on there, could it even contain a virus of some kind? – and there's no doubting the malicious intent of the sender. He's weighing it up, his thumb hovering tantalisingly close to the play button, when there's a knock on his door.

'Come in.'

His mother enters, peering around the door first, then drifting in, her arms arranged into a strange cross over her chest, like she's trying to warm up. 'I just wanted to check on you – do you need anything?'

'I'm fine, thanks.'

She sits on an upholstered chair in the corner. 'It's so good to have you here, but it doesn't feel real. You know, like I might wake up tomorrow and find it's all a dream.'

Miles sits up and tosses his phone on to the duvet. 'Mum, don't worry. It's all over.'

She opens her mouth to speak, then decides against it. After a few seconds of thought, she says: 'Are you sure about New Zealand?'

'Yeah, I'm sure.'

'I wish you weren't going so far away.'

'Mum, that's the point.' It hasn't always been the point, but it is now. When Miles and Elis originally discussed the idea of going to New Zealand, the distance wasn't a factor. But, right now, he needs to escape, and New Zealand is about as far away from here as he can possibly get without boarding a rocket and blasting out of Earth's atmosphere. It's *exactly* where he needs to be. 'Anyway, it's not for long. And, with any luck, by the time I get back, this whole thing will have blown over.'

Zara gets slowly to her feet. She appears to have a similar level of energy. 'Are you sure I can't get you anything?'

'I'm fine, honestly. I'm just tired – I'm going to sleep soon.'

She leaves, and Miles hauls himself up, starts getting ready for bed. He brushes his teeth, splashes water on to his face, dries his face on a clean towel. A routine like this at home feels suddenly surreal and it catches him unawares – his hands tremble and he tenses his facial muscles to hold back tears. If things had panned out differently, he would be spending tonight in prison. The fatigue is also having an effect, making him emotional. He needs to rest. Tomorrow, he'll feel better – when he has a clear head.

Miles gets into bed and turns out the light. Tiredness has made him slightly dizzy, like that giddiness you get towards the end of a match when you've been running for eighty minutes and your blood sugar levels are low. Sleep should come easy now. He's wrapped in comforts: the sound of silence, the smell of home-laundered sheets, the softness of memory foam. Yet still he can't settle. His mind, whichever direction it wanders, keeps circling back to the email lurking in his junk folder, with the audio file attached. He knows he shouldn't play it – of course he bloody shouldn't – but he wants to. He has to know. He *has* to. If curiosity killed the cat, then Miles's recently gained spirit of inquiry could take down a pride of lions.

He takes his phone off the bedside table, and his eyes, now adjusted to the darkness, sting as the screen lights up. He opens the email app, and his junk folder, and clicks on the email. He stares at it again, then turns up the volume on his phone and taps his thumb on the tiny black triangle. It starts playing. The audio clip is eight seconds long, and it only takes two of those seconds to jolt Miles's heart out of rhythm. His whole body turns cold. He plays it again. And then for a third time. What he's just heard isn't possible. It can't be.

CHAPTER 9

POLLY

Polly wakes late; she slips off her eye mask, plucks out her foam earplugs and finds her bedroom bathed in sunlight and alive with the sound of chattering birds. She rolls on to her side, stretches her legs, and a smile creeps over her face. For the first time in weeks, she feels calm. Today, she doesn't have to be anywhere. Today, if she's so inclined, she won't even have to leave the house. With any luck, she'll be able to spend the whole day catching up with work. Polly set up her PR company five years ago, and the last few weeks – while the trial has been happening – she's taken her first significant absence. It's not a massive business; she has three employees, or four if you include a shared receptionist. But she takes great pride in it and doesn't like to be away for too long. It makes her happy that she's inherited some entrepreneurial talent from her father. Carl is a self-made man from a working-class background – a shopfitter done well – and always insisted that Polly and Miles would have to make their own way in the world. It's a point of honour for Polly that she's built her own company from scratch, using nothing but a bank loan and hard work.

After a few minutes of consciousness, a slight unease begins to gnaw its way into her zen bubble. For a moment, Polly isn't sure what it is. But then she remembers: the trip. The way Miles and his friends were talking about it last night, they're hell-bent on making it happen. Unless she can talk him out of it very soon, they'll be going to New Zealand in the near future. Obviously, she can't afford to take endless time off work, but, at present, she can't see an obvious way out of it. She's effectively spent almost a year promising her brother she'll be coming with him. And, more importantly, after everything that's happened, someone needs to look out for Miles. Polly isn't convinced she can rely on his friends to do that.

Once again, her life will be written off as collateral damage of this whole fiasco.

Perhaps that thought is a tad melodramatic. It could be worse. It might be a fun holiday. She won't have to pay for anything because Carl is bankrolling the entire trip. But it still delays her chance of getting her life back on a normal track. And she's not keen on the idea of spending a fortnight with Miles's friends. Hanging out with her brother is one thing, but the other three? Jesus Christ, she can hardly bear to think about it. First up, there's George: an old-money twat with control issues and a non-ironic penchant for brightly coloured chinos. Then there's Reubyn: a deluded little numpty who thinks he's going to be the next Mr Beast. And lastly, there's Elis, who she's only met a handful of times. Polly doesn't know much about Elis, but he might be the most tolerable of all of them. He's also quite handsome, in a weird way. He definitely isn't her normal type – she doesn't generally do beards, as a rule – but there's an intensity to him that's hypnotic, especially when he holds her gaze with his pale green eyes. Still, there's no way in hell she'll be going near him; she knows better than to get romantically involved with her brother's friends.

Polly slips into a robe and ties her hair into a loose ponytail before padding down the stairs. She sighs at the sound of a non-family voice – muffled and deep, like the far groan of a cow – coming from the kitchen. All she wants is a cup of coffee, and she should be able to go and get one at 10 a.m. in her family home without the fear of having to socialise make-up free. She walks in to find their parents sitting at the dining table, opposite Miles and his solicitor, David, who stares at a laptop. They greet her briefly, preoccupied. Polly flips on the kettle and leans a forearm on the cold countertop as she listens in to the conversation.

'Frankly, I'm as confused as you are,' David says, peering over his wire-framed spectacles at Carl. 'But whatever way you look at it, it's harassment, so we'll just have to see what the police make of it.'

'I just don't *understand*,' Zara says. 'Do you think she's . . .' She shrugs, unable to finish the question.

'I really don't know. But none of this is a problem for Miles, other than the unpleasant nature of it, obviously.'

Miles points wearily at the laptop. 'I've blocked the sender.'

'That's good,' David says. 'But frankly, email accounts are easy to set up, and whoever sent it can do it again. That's why this needs to be a matter for the police. I suggest you record any and all malicious communications so they can investigate those too; it's entirely possible that one of those keyboard warriors' – he raises his fingers to indicate inverted commas – 'as you call them, is linked to the person who sent that email, or could even be the sender themselves, and let's not dis-count the possibility that . . .'

David is still talking, but the words are foggy as the kettle growls and hisses to a crescendo. Finally, it rumbles to a climax, and Polly turns her back, pretending not to listen as she pours hot water into a cafetière, and the bitter scent of Colombian coffee rushes up into her nostrils.

'What about the press?' Carl asks.

'They're bang to rights. Miles has been exonerated, and there's simply no excuse for them to continue their pursuit of him – it's not in the public interest.'

Zara frowns. 'The public do seem to still be quite interested.'

'Oh, they're plenty interested,' David says. 'But that's a different thing. It doesn't serve the interests of the public as a whole for their curiosity about Miles to be satisfied now that he's been proven innocent. I'll be sending a strongly worded letter to the *Tribune*, and I'll have the regulator make all sections of the media aware that Miles has no desire to talk to them, and that any further approaches would be in breach of the Editors' Code of Practice. That should put an end to it.' David drains his mug and stands. 'In the meantime, let me know if any other reporters turn up. You should send them away, but it's imperative that you make a note of the publications they represent.' He picks up his briefcase. 'I'm sorry I couldn't shed any light on the other matter. It's not something I've come across before.'

Carl shows David to the door, and Polly takes the seat he's vacated next to Miles. She's silent for a few beats, waiting for someone to answer the obvious question that's hanging in the air, and when they don't, she asks: 'Come on, then, what the hell's going on?'

Miles looks at Polly, bleary-eyed, and turns the laptop to face her. 'I got an email last night.' He points at the screen. 'Look at the sender's name.'

Polly squints at the laptop; she's a little hungover and it's hard to focus without her contacts in. 'Caira Kennedy? That's a bit weird.'

'It gets weirder.' Miles opens the email and presses play on an audio attachment.

A female voice comes out of the speaker: *Hi Miles—*

'Oh, you're not listening to that again, are you?' Carl says, stomping back into the room.

'Shut up, Dad! For God's sake!' Polly huffs at her father, then looks at Miles. 'Play that again, and everybody be quiet.' She leans in closer, and Miles presses play for a second time.

Again, the voice, a soft but purposeful purr: *Hi Miles. You might think this is over, but this is not over.*

Polly lasers her eyes at Miles. 'Is that *Caira's* voice?' She doesn't need her brother to answer to know that it *is* Caira Kennedy's voice – they all know what it sounds like. About five years ago, Caira took part in a documentary called *Guardian Angels*, which followed her and five other social workers in their day-to-day efforts to keep children safe against a backdrop of abuse and neglect. After her murder, the series was cynically rerun on TV and clips from it were regularly spliced into news reports. Polly and her family have all seen the series, and they all know Caira's voice. There's no doubting the owner of the voice that just played on the laptop – it's Caira Kennedy.

Miles stares out of the window towards the garden, where a blackbird twitches about on the grass. 'Well, it sounds a lot like her. A *lot* like her.'

'What does it mean?' Polly says. 'Did she send it?'

'Don't be ridiculous, Pol,' Carl says.

It *is* a ridiculous suggestion, of course. She just blurted out the question without thinking. Polly was in court when pictures of the murder scene, including Caira's body, were shown to the jury. An expert witness explained that the line around her neck had been caused by a ligature, rather than the human hand, and the scratch marks above and below it were caused by Caira's fingernails as she'd tried to slacken it. Is Caira still alive? Of course she isn't. But Polly can't immediately think of another explanation. 'What's going on, then?' she asks.

'It's an impersonation of some kind.'

'It's a damn good one.'

'It doesn't matter,' Carl says. 'The police will sort it. One thing we know for sure is that we're dealing with a very sick individual.'

For a while they just sit, the grimness of it soaking into them. There have been a great many gloomy conversations held around their dining table this year, all of them concerning Miles, and now, even with the trial behind them, here they are in the shadow of another.

'I don't like it,' Miles says. His hands form a V around his face and hold his head, as if his neck can't bear the weight of it. 'I've got a bad feeling about this.' He's quiet again for a moment, and Polly can sense the thought as it gestates in his mind. She knows him so well that she can guess the words – or the rough meaning of them – that are about to spill from his mouth. He looks at her. 'Let's get out of here, now. I don't want to wait – the next available flight. I want to be as far away from here as possible.'

PART TWO

CHAPTER 10

MILES

Getting everything organised for the trip took longer than Miles had hoped. The soonest flights were fully booked, and both Polly and Elis had work commitments that needed to be fulfilled before they could leave. In fact, Polly seemed to have a long list of reasons to delay their departure. But, thanks to Miles's persistence, they sorted it all out in the end. Their travel is booked, as is their first hotel – four nights in Queenstown. After that, they'll figure it out as they go along. Miles likes the idea of that: the freedom. This trip will be exactly what he needs. It'll be great to spend some quality time with the people who have been there for him during his ordeal, especially his sister and Elis, who has been unbelievably supportive. And it'll be a chance for Elis to properly get to know some of Miles's other friends.

It's now a whole week since Miles's acquittal, and he's busy packing the last of his things into his suitcase. They'll be going early in the morning, and Miles can't *wait* for take-off. Leaving the country will be the final step towards normality after the nightmare of the trial. He'd expected things to get back to something close to normal as soon as a not guilty verdict was delivered, but it hasn't quite worked out like that.

For a start, he's been feeling strangely down, like he's being confronted with Caira's death for the first time. Nothing makes a man more self-absorbed and inward-looking than being charged with murder. The strain of it is so intense that it leaves no room for empathy. And it's only now that he's experiencing what might be described as delayed grief – a lingering sadness at what happened to her. Miles was with Caira the night she died, and now he can't help but spend hours thinking about it: the terror she would have felt in her final moments, the tragic loss of her life, the pain it must have caused her family.

Also, Miles still hasn't left the house since he got back after the verdict. For the whole week, he's been holed up, never once venturing outside. It just doesn't seem like a wise idea. And it's not simply due to paranoia on his part. The reporters may have largely stopped knocking, but Miles can't shake his conviction that photographers might still be lurking out there somewhere, waiting for him to emerge. The media certainly hasn't lost interest in the case. On Sunday, a whole bunch of new stories dropped online, and Caira's face once again peered out from the front pages of the newspapers. Some focused on her job: *TV Angel's career hell*, a headline read. One had a lengthy interview with Caira's ex-boyfriend, Ben Knight, who spoke of his grief at losing who he described as his soulmate. The way Ben told it, their relationship – and the *domestic bliss* that they shared – had merely been put on hold and they'd been destined to get back together.

But the worst article dropped a couple of days later – only twenty-four hours after they booked their flights to New Zealand. One of the papers had been tipped off that he was going on what they described as a luxury getaway. The way it was reported made it sound as if he was revelling in his newfound freedom, when the truth was the opposite – he was desperate to escape this feeling of the world closing in on him again. There was also an element of betrayal to wrangle with; someone with a close knowledge of his life had tipped off a reporter. He should have made it clear to everyone he knows that they need to be tight-lipped about their plans. Too many people found out about the trip, and eventually one of them sold him out.

But even more unsettling is the content of his inbox. Even though most of the abuse and trolling died off after a day or two, he continued to receive the Caira voice notes. Three more arrived, making four in total. Each one essentially a repetition of the first message, a vague threat, signed off with the same four words: *this is not over.* Everyone Miles talked to seemed to be in agreement about how they were created; the recordings were made using some kind of AI voice simulator. Each was sent from an email account set up in Caira's name. Miles found it particularly menacing how much thought had been put into these communications. And the most recent was chilling for the way it referenced his upcoming trip: *Have fun on your holiday, Miles. This is not over.*

He has forwarded the messages to the police, but so far, he hasn't received a meaningful response other than an email explaining they are looking into it. He wishes they would hurry up. The sooner they identify the person sending them, the better, because, at the moment, the question is starting to eat away at him. Who is harassing him, and why?

When he arrives in New Zealand, he will allow his mind to clear. When he gets to the most distant land possible, where no one knows who he is, he will be at peace. He'll check his emails less frequently. He will engage in healthy, mindful pursuits and activities. He will reconnect with all the things he took for granted about a normal, carefree existence.

In the meantime, though, the emails have got him thinking back over the trial again, reliving it day by day. What if his harasser was in court, watching him? When the trial was happening, Miles was preoccupied by a completely different question. All he could think of, when he looked around at the jury, at the public gallery, was: did they believe him? Would they find him not guilty? Now, when he relives the experience, a different question is on his mind. Who in that courtroom was so convinced by his guilt that they would never be able to accept his innocence, whatever the outcome? Who there had already convicted him in their own mind? Who had established a loathing of him that couldn't be undone by any verdict?

CHAPTER 11

THE TRIAL

The first day of the trial is likely to remain the most vivid in Miles's memory. The build-up to it was so intense, and when it finally came, it seemed utterly surreal. He had been partly prepared for the experience; his plea hearing ten months earlier was in the same courtroom, with a similar level of media interest. But that day was more about navigating his way to the court – the photographers and camera crews. Now, it was all about what happened inside the court. How this played out would determine how he was going to live the rest of his life.

It began at 10 a.m., with the jury being selected and sworn in. It was a slow process that gave Miles a chance to examine his surroundings and get a feel for what they were up against. Miles found it unnerving that the Crown had three barristers for the prosecution, compared to his two for his defence. Sitting behind the Crown's KC on the front bench were two junior barristers. One of them, a pale woman named Victoria Penning, would later get involved to a certain extent, getting up now and again to read out some transcript or set of agreed facts. But the other, a nervous-looking man of about thirty named John Paul Bridges, didn't seem to have a role at all beyond watching the trial. When Miles asked what he did, Eleanor explained that Bridges was what's known as a disclosure junior, who wasn't really required to be in court and probably wasn't being paid to attend the trial. The way Miles caught Bridges staring at him from time to time made him think that maybe there was something personal for him about this case, although Eleanor assured him there wasn't. Looking back now, Miles isn't so sure.

When the jury was sworn in, it was time for the prosecution to open its case. It was clear that, for the media, this was the key moment. They scribbled their notes more vigorously for the next hour than at any other point of the trial. They, and the public, had waited for the best part of a year to hear the juicy details they so hungrily desired, and now, the Crown's senior barrister was about to lay it all out – exactly what the prosecution thought had happened to Caira and why they were so certain Miles was a murderer.

The lead prosecutor, William Cox KC, was exactly how Miles had imagined a senior barrister to be: broad, bellied and booming, with eyebrows so grey and unkempt that they matched his fraying old wig. When he stood to open the prosecution's case, he did so while holding a picture of Caira, which he raised aloft to show the jury. 'This woman,' he began, 'was a beloved daughter, cherished sibling and doting auntie. She was forty years old when she met the defendant, Miles Deverill. And she was, to coin a phrase popular with her millennial generation, living her best life. Caira Kennedy had a job that she found purposeful and rewarding, and, due to her warm personality and infectious sense of humour, she had a wide group of friends. She was single, and she enjoyed being single. As a gregarious character who loved meeting new people, she enjoyed going on dates. But the arrangement of one of these dates began a chain of events that would ultimately prove fateful for Ms Kennedy, and her happy life was to be prematurely brought to an end.

'That chain of events began in November of last year, when Ms Kennedy met the defendant, Miles Deverill, on an online dating app. The two of them hit it off, regularly chatting via WhatsApp, and eventually made a date. That date took place on the third of December. It was a typical first date, the sort of which most of you will have experience. Thanks to CCTV footage, receipts and phone data, we have a very clear picture of what they did. They went out for dinner – steak frites for him, and pan-fried sea bream for her. Afterwards they went for drinks, and then Miles Deverill walked Ms Kennedy home to her flat on Victoria Crescent. Ms Kennedy went inside, and so too did Miles Deverill. We know he entered her flat because Miles Deverill's fingerprints and DNA were found in the hallway and living room.

'Miles Deverill became the last person known to have seen Ms Kennedy alive. It was at that point that the trail of Miles Deverill's movements – as recorded by CCTV, phone data and receipts – went cold until the next morning.

'What happened inside that flat is to be disputed during this trial. There were no witnesses to the crime that took place. Instead, what we have is a collection of facts and evidence that creates a clear picture of how and why Ms Kennedy was murdered.

'As you will discover during this trial, Miles Deverill is a man who is accustomed to getting what he wants. He's a man who is used to having his whims and desires satisfied. It is the Crown's case that when Miles Deverill entered Ms Kennedy's flat that night, he was presented with a rare scenario in which he discovered his whims and desires were not going to be willingly satisfied. In short, Ms Kennedy rejected him. And he responded with violence. Miles Deverill strangled her, and the ligature he used was the very scarf she had worn on their first date. And then, in a display of calculated callousness, he took that scarf from the property and disposed of it in order to cover his tracks.'

As Cox went on with his opening, Miles's eye travelled around the room. He watched faces twitch and expressions morph as they listened to the prosecution's hideous explanation of what had happened to Caira. He glanced at each member of the jury – a mixture in terms of age, sex and race – and wondered who among them would be prepared to give him a fair hearing. Which of them had already decided he was guilty? He looked into the public gallery, where his friends and family were sitting. A couple of them met his eye and responded with the customary half-smile. He scanned across the benches, his eye moving more quickly as it passed over the section where Caira's family – her parents, sister and brother – were seated.

His gaze was drawn to a man on the front bench of the public gallery. He had a wide, bald head, and hooded eyes that were focused directly on Miles. Something about the man's unflinching stare, and its openly toxic energy, seized his attention. It might have only been for a second or two, but eye contact with that level of intensity seemed to tip time off its axis, making it feel much longer, and when Miles flicked his eyes back to Cox, he found an image of that hateful face seared permanently on his mind.

At the time, Miles had no clue who he was. And it remained that way for weeks, because the man only stayed for the first day of the trial. But he knows now. He was Caira's ex-boyfriend, Ben Knight. The same man who gave a full interview to *The Chronicle*, the same man who donned a baby-blue knit sweater and sat on his sofa, arms folded, as he posed for their photographer with a sad frown on his face. Ben told *The Chronicle*'s reporter that he once lived with Caira in a state of domestic bliss. But from the loathful look of him that day in court, the unguarded menace in his eyes, Miles found it hard to believe that anyone had ever, or could ever, live with that man in anything approaching bliss. More likely, he suspects, it was the complete opposite.

CHAPTER 12

ELIS

This is it, then: they're going to New Zealand. Seat belts are fastened, the cabin has been secured and there's no going back now. Elis has lucked out with a window seat, with Miles to his right and Reubyn next to the aisle. George sits in the row in front, next to an older couple, and Polly is out of sight – for reasons unknown to the rest of them she's sitting in a different part of the plane. Elis is all ready for long-haul travel, having changed into a pair of shorts and a loose-fitting T-shirt. The plane has taxied into position, and he feels his shoulders being pulled back into the seat as it accelerates towards take-off. The streets and buildings and fields around Heathrow drop away, becoming smaller until the ground below is a toy landscape of matchbox houses and trees of painted sponge, and for a second the view becomes misty and then it's all gone: Britain is lost below the clouds, and it'll be more than two weeks before he sees it again. He slaps Miles on the thigh. 'We're out of here. How does it feel?'

Miles glances nervously around the cabin. 'It feels . . . I'll be happier when we get on to the next flight, I think.'

'Just try to relax.'

He doesn't look relaxed, and Elis knows why; he noticed it too, when they were boarding – the way some of the other passengers recognised Miles, their double-takes and lingering looks, the surreptitious nudges and finger pointing. It's enough to make anyone uneasy. But it'll be over soon. Once they transfer on to the next flight, and the one after that, those gawpers will have been weeded out and removed, replaced with people who hail from lands thousands of miles from theirs and who have no interest in the tawdry tabloid tales of the UK. In a couple of days, no one will recognise Miles. He'll be anonymous. And free. Elis can't help but feel a smidge of pride for the part he played in that redemption. Who knows what would have happened if he hadn't been there in court to testify in Miles's defence? If it weren't for Elis, if it weren't for *Chinatown*, Miles might be starting a life sentence right now. But instead, here they are cruising at 30,000 feet with the world and all its endless opportunities spread out underneath them.

Elis claps his hands together and looks along the row. 'Right, then. We should get some drinks in. What are we having first?'

George peers through the gap between two headrests. 'Cognac is pretty good with morning coffee, I find.'

'Gross,' Elis says, wrinkling his nose.

Miles studies the in-flight menu. 'They do a Singapore Sling.'

'What's that?' Elis asks.

'It's a gin cocktail,' George says, through the gap. His head is tilted forward so he's literally looking down his nose at Elis. 'It's fruity, you'd probably like it. Although I doubt they make it fresh in economy class.'

'Sounds a bit pricey,' Reubyn says.

'All the drinks are included.'

'Oh, bloody hell. No one told me that. Sling me one of those, then.'

The drinks arrive, pink-hued in small plastic cups, and they disappear in a few swallows. Next, they have some lukewarm beers.

George has given up craning his head to stay in the conversation and is quiet in the seat in front, leafing through an in-flight magazine. Elis was slightly relieved to find George was seated in a different row. Of everyone in the group, it's George who's been the frostiest towards him. On the other hand, maybe being sat next to each other would be exactly what they need – a bit of forced proximity to allow them to get to know each other. He's happy to be next to Miles, of course. They've never been closer. Their shared experience of giving evidence in court, and the time they've spent together in the aftermath, has done nothing but strengthen the bond between them. But he still has a bit of work to do if he's going to fully integrate into this group as a whole.

It should be doable, though. If he'd met this lot twenty years ago, he would have stuck out as being different. Now, he should fit in fine. It helps that his accent has melted away. Being able to slip into an authentic Welsh Valleys voice remains a string to his bow, in an acting sense, but even as a teenager he instinctively realised that speaking with a strong accent wouldn't do him any favours at auditions and parties. Not if he wanted to be taken seriously. When he became friends with Miles, he noticed his voice changing even further, and his mannerisms and intonation syncing with those of his new friend. It was just a natural thing. Elis is more suited to the world Miles is from than the one from which he himself emerged. It's not that he's embarrassed about where he grew up. Far from it. But he needs to be around people who have a great passion for the arts, who can converse with him about the things he finds exciting, without fear of shame or ridicule. When Elis tried to explain this to Miles, he seemed a little confused. But if Miles went to a small-town rugby club in South Wales and tried to strike up a conversation about Shakespeare or arthouse cinema, that would quickly put paid to his scepticism.

Elis is halfway through his beer and already eyeing up the menu for their next tipple. He isn't a big drinker, normally. Too much alcohol makes it hard to maintain a good physique, which is important for his work. In any case, binge drinking is overrated and most of the things that come with it – the hangovers, the inflamed organs, the poor decision-making – simply don't appeal to him. He prefers adventure, the outdoors: seeing a view that isn't the generic interior of a bar. Alcohol is a complete waste of time. But right now, crammed as they are into an aircraft cabin and unable to move, all they have is time to waste. Eight in the morning might not be the accepted hour for a drinking session, but they've entered a brain-melting thirty-six-hour period of international travel, layovers and jet lag, so the time of day is irrelevant. If Elis wants an adventure, the only place he's going to find it currently is at the bottom of one of those miniature spirit bottles. He drains the dregs of his beer, then orders a vodka and soda. There'll be a few minutes before the drinks arrive, and he asks Miles and Reubyn to let him out so he can nip to the toilet while they wait.

Elis is smiling, and a little woozy, as he sways up the aisle, and his bladder is uncomfortably full – he's left it to the last minute before getting up. Who knew it was possible to have so much fun on a flight? He stumbles into the cubicle and finds it dimly lit, the air heavy with the smell of industrial soap and the whooshing sound of speeding air. He uses the toilet and washes and dries his hands as quickly as he can, his long arms awkward in the tiny sink, and after a quick grin at his reflection, he hurries back out into the main cabin.

Elis is only a few rows down the aisle when he realises something's changed. He slows up for a moment. George's laughter is loud and grating, even from this distance. And he's switched places. George has moved back a row and is now in Elis's seat.

Elis quickens his step down the aisle, his pulse rising with it. He stops by their row, and all three – Reubyn first, then Miles and George – turn their heads to look at him. Elis forces a smile. 'Everything okay?'

George raises a drink which Elis suspects is the one he just ordered. 'Yeah, mate. I hope you don't mind, but I've swapped seats with you for a minute.'

'Yes, I can see that.'

George grimaces. 'You look annoyed. I'm sorry. It's just that I saw you'd brought some reading material with you, and I haven't, so, to pass the time, we're playing this game, The Minister's Cat?' He raises an eyebrow, then shakes his head. 'It's a bit obscure, not many people know it. I'll give the seat back when we're done, yeah?'

Elis's jaw locks tight, and blood fizzes in his veins. 'Well, actually, I'd rather have it back now.'

'Why?'

Elis takes a deep breath. *Remain calm.* 'Because it's my seat. All my stuff is there.'

'Oh, that's no problem at all. Allow me to move it for you.' George reaches into the seat pocket and grabs Elis's stuff – sunglasses, book and pillow – and dumps it on the seat in front. 'Okay?'

'No, not okay,' Elis says. 'That's my seat – it says so on my ticket.' He points. '*That* is yours.'

George laughs. 'Gosh. Don't make a scene – you'll get us kicked off the flight.'

Elis leans over Reubyn's seat, lowers his voice. 'I'm not making a scene. I just want to take my seat.'

'Look,' George says, 'we're going to be on this plane a long time, and we can move about if we want. It's not a big deal.' He starts to say something in Latin, but Elis talks over him.

'Just *move*.'

Elis locks eyes with George and finds his baffled expression infuriating. A few seconds of silence seem excruciatingly long.

Miles presses his lips into a line. 'Look, George is a bugger, he shouldn't have done that. But actually, do you know what, it *has* been a while since we played this. You don't really mind, do you, Elis?'

Elis clamps his teeth. What's he supposed to say to that? With those words from Miles, his argument has been utterly defeated. He nods and folds his arms. 'Fine.' The two passengers in front, who have clearly been eavesdropping, make way, and Elis squeezes in, sweeps some wrappers off his new seat and sits down. He picks up his book, a paperback copy of *Touching the Void* his aunt gave him for Christmas, and flicks through to page 1. It's the first time he's opened this book. His heart is still beating fast, and his teeth grind on every syllable. He tries to focus, but it's not going in – the words on the page are no match for the ones uttered by the three men in the seats behind.

'Reubs, it's your go,' George says.

'I've run out of drink.'

'Don't worry – I've got you.'

Elis feels something jerk into the back of his chair and the sound of George rummaging in a bag at his feet, then the chair decompresses.

'Where did you get that?' Miles asks.

'Picked it up in duty-free.'

'Nice.'

'You've got to have some backup ammo if you're flying cattle-class; the cabin crew are far too slow with the drinks.' A screw cap cracks, followed by the sound of something glugging into a plastic cup. 'And why settle for a taste of the fruit, eh fellas?'

That last quip from George spurs a disproportionately enthusiastic reaction from all three of them: they laugh and grunt their approval like pigs watching scraps being slopped into a trough.

There's a tap on Elis's shoulder and he looks around to see Miles holding up a bottle of wine. 'Do you need a drink, mate?'

Elis makes eye contact for a split second. 'Nah, I'm good thanks.'

He turns back to his book. Still on the first page, he hasn't made it past the opening four-word sentence. He sighs. If only they were on a later flight, then he could bosh a zopiclone and wake up at their destination. This is going to be torture. And there are ten hours to go. Behind him, the game has started up again.

Reubyn: Hungry cat.

George: Imbecilic cat.

Miles: Jealous cat.

Reubyn: Knotty cat.

George: What? That's N, you idiot.

Reubyn: No, knotty, not naughty. His fur's knotted.

George: Oh. Fine. Long cat.

Miles: Mindful cat.

Pause.

Reubyn: Narrow-minded ca—

George: Piss off, you can't have that – it's a compound. And it was too slow, anyway. Drink!

Elis slaps his book shut. He stashes it in the chair pocket, and swipes through the menu of in-flight movies. It's all crap. But he needs noise – anything to block them out.

George: Observant cat.

Miles: Punctual cat.

Reubyn: Qu . . . qu . . . quick cat!

George: Too slow! Drink!

Elis tears a set of headphones out of its plastic wrapping and puts them on. He selects a film almost at random – a Jason Statham action – and turns up the volume to the max. He puffs out his cheeks. It's going to be a long, long flight.

CHAPTER 13

POLLY

Polly breathes a sigh of relief as the plane grinds to a stop on the runway. After three flights and two layovers, they've finally made it to New Zealand. She should be grateful; none of their flights were delayed, and they've faced no hold-ups or disruption of any kind, but right now she's too tired to be grateful. There will be plenty of time, later, to be grateful.

Eventually the plane doors open. Polly exits the aircraft and grips the chilly steel handrail that flanks a set of rickety stairs with a vertigo-inducing drop either side. The air is gusty, rocking the staircase, and carries a sting of cold that sends goosebumps flaring across her bare legs. This isn't what disembarking an aircraft is meant to feel like; she expected to get that hairdryer blast of hot, foreign air, the all-encompassing warmth that takes a few seconds to settle into your bones and says: *you're on holiday!* But there's none of that. If anything, it's slightly chillier than it was in Heathrow when their journey began thirty-six hours ago. November is springtime in New Zealand, and she thought it would be a little warmer. Already a voice has been telling her this is no holiday, and now it's been confirmed.

It's early morning, at least in the disorientating upside down of local time, and she wears prescription shades despite the faint light outside – she didn't sleep well on the flight and her eyes are swollen and dry. After a careful descent in which she never takes her gaze off the steel steps below, Polly reaches the tarmac and takes a moment to look around. It's like no airport she's ever seen. They're in a crater on the surface of what seems like another world, bordered on all sides by mountains that are cracked and barren at their peaks, with a great grey slope that casts a shadow over the runway and all but the furthest end of the terminal building. She thinks maybe there is even a trace of snow atop one of those mountains. Normally, you'd have to sit through a long and winding drive or hike for hours to get so close to such peaks. And yet, here they are. Immediately, it seems wrong, like the contravening of some universal law: who builds an airport slap in the middle of what appears to be a national park, pours concrete over the floor of a valley like this, litters it with industrial buildings, fills pristine air with the chemical stench of jet fuel?

She quickens her step in an attempt to keep pace with Miles, who marches towards the terminal building at a pace that's jarringly out of character with his normal, easy-going gait. By the time a queue forms, she's still half a dozen heads behind him. He wears a baseball cap – she's never seen him don one of those before – and appears full of nervous energy, shifting his weight from one foot to the other and turning his passport over in his fingers. As Polly stands in an unmoving queue, in a land a pole apart from home, this skittish, secretive version of her brother feels eerily alien to her, and she finds herself wondering how long it will be before he returns to his normal self, if he ever does. Maybe that old version of Miles has simply gone for good. Maybe the events of the last year landed on him with such force that they broke him beyond repair. She tries to remember the last time she saw the normal Miles. When was it, Christmas? She has a hazy image in her mind of Miles holding a tall orange drink (a Harvey Wallbanger?) and wearing a tissue-paper hat and that broad Deverill smile that is almost identical to, but annoyingly more flawless than her own. That thought makes her realise she hasn't smiled much in the last year, either.

It's odd to think that nearly twelve months have passed since the smiles disappeared from their faces. On the night of 4 December, when she received a push alert to her phone notifying her of a murder investigation in the city where she grew up, she opened the story immediately. The details were quite scant: the body of a forty-year-old woman had been found at a basement flat in suspicious circumstances. The discovery was made at four-thirty in the afternoon, and there was one of those bland statements from police: *We understand this incident will have caused some alarm in the community, and we would like to reassure residents that a team of detectives is working tirelessly to understand what has occurred*, et cetera et cetera. The most notable thing was the location, a quiet residential street in one of Bristol's nicer suburbs. Still, she didn't give it much thought, beyond the normal *that poor woman*, followed by the faint, doomy resignation that it was most likely another domestic, that some meathead husband had come home from the pub and been triggered by something, had his fragile ego dented and decided the right response was to pummel a woman literally out of existence. And then she slipped her phone back into her pocket and moved on. Quickly, she forgot all about it. It wasn't until the next day that the first tremors of something seismic began to make themselves felt among her family. And then, suddenly, everything moved impossibly fast, like one of those controlled demolitions where explosives are used to undermine a proudly standing tower, and everything starts to come crashing down.

'You look like a cold-eyed killer in that one,' George says, peering over Polly's shoulder at her passport which she holds open, ready for inspection.

She eyes the picture – he's not wrong, but passport photos always look like this: her lips, painted a boring, neutral shade, are pursed miserably. She glares at George; he's wearing that inane grin of his. Did he consider the obvious context before delivering that remark? Polly decides it didn't occur to him because he's so lacking in common sense. She gives him a half-smile. 'Stay away from me, George, otherwise a cold-eyed killer is exactly what you're going to get.'

A heavy-set border officer beckons her forward, checks her passport and waves her through. After the otherworldliness of outside, the brightly lit concourse she's just entered is so bland it could be a depot in Croydon. It's grimly quiet, full of travellers too weary for chat, and there's a faint smell of vacuum cleaners and upholstery. Inexplicably, Miles has stopped in the middle of the room, where he stands staring at his phone. He's oblivious to the indignant glances from other travellers as they wrestle their rolling luggage around him.

Polly pulls up right in front of him. 'For God's sake,' she snaps. He looks up at her, eyes wide and worried like a startled animal's, and instantly she regrets her tone. 'Miles, are you all right?'

For a moment he looks confused, and then he shakes his head, and the life returns to his eyes. 'Yeah . . . yeah, I'm fine.'

'Earth to Miles' – she clicks her fingers – 'what's going on?'

'It's the police. They're trying to get hold of me again.'

Miles continues to stare off into space, and it's another second or two before Polly realises it's not confusion or brain fog that he's suffering from. It's fear.

CHAPTER 14

MILES

Miles finds a quiet corner of the concourse and goes back to his phone. He's received a voicemail message and email from police in the time it's taken them to fly from Sydney to Queenstown. They're both from a detective by the name of Chris Lewin. He remembers that name from the trial. His fingers tremble slightly as he enters the number to call him back, and again he has to remind himself: *not guilty*. He hasn't done anything wrong.

Lewin picks up on the second ring. 'Hello?'

'It's Miles Deverill here, returning your call.'

'Thanks for calling, Mr Deverill.' His voice is deep and dour. 'I appreciate it.'

'Your name's familiar. Didn't you investigate the murder? Caira Kennedy's, I mean.'

'I was, I *am*, part of the investigation team, but we've not met before. It was my colleagues who interviewed you and such.'

Miles sticks a finger in his left ear to block out a tannoy announcement. 'So, let me get this right. You investigated me, helped to prepare a case against me, and now you're investigating these audio files on my behalf. Isn't that sort of a conflict of interest?'

A short silence, then in a weary voice: 'No, not at all. You've been eliminated as a suspect, and no one on the team holds any kind of animosity or resentment towards you for being acquitted.' The detective goes into a long-winded explanation of the situation: the investigation is still active, they had a duty to keep all lines of inquiry open, even during the trial, and the emails Miles received were passed to the investigation team as a potential strand of inquiry. Miles is only half listening; he wants the detective to skip to the voice notes. They've been bugging him, and the more he's listened to them the surer he's become that it's her. It's an amazing thing, the human voice: everyone is born with a speaking tone so distinctive it can be distinguished from eight billion others. You could go ten years without speaking to someone, and that person could call you up out of the blue and you'd know it was them the second they came on the line. So, after more than a week of playing it over and over, he's certain: the voice is Caira's.

Finally, the detective gets to the point. 'So, these emails you received. We've analysed the recording.'

'Okay.'

'It was created using a voice-cloning tool. Sadly, in these days of artificial intelligence, these kinds of' – he pauses, looking for the right word – '*services* are readily available, and scammers are using them more and more. All you need to be able to recreate someone's voice is a minute of audio of that person speaking, and there are recordings of Caira's voice publicly available.'

'So, you think it's a scam? Like, they're going to try and get money out of me?' Miles experiences a warm rush of relief as he says it; he doesn't care about money, never has.

'We should keep an open mind about that. At this stage it's not clear what the motive is, but they've gone to some effort and planning to do it, so I would suggest you be extra vigilant—'

'Do you know who sent it?'

'I was getting to that.' The detective's words are rifled off quickly, with a barely detectable trace of annoyance. 'We traced the IP address—'

'Excuse me, sir.' Miles snaps his head in the direction of the female voice interrupting his call. A uniformed woman, flanked by a restless beagle, glares at him stiff-faced. 'Did you pack this bag yourself?'

'Sorry, hold on one second.' Miles mutes his phone and faces her. 'Yeah, I packed it.'

'Have you got any food with you?'

He looks at her blankly, his phone pressed to his side. 'New Zealand takes its biosecurity very seriously, sir. Any food, animal products, nuts, seeds, any organic matter of any kind?'

'No.'

The dog has a good sniff of his legs and bag, and the woman gives Miles a weary nod. Miles unmutes his phone. 'Are you still there?'

'Yes,' Lewin says.

'So, you traced the sender? Do you know who it is?'

'As I was saying, we traced the IP address and found the first email was sent from a computer at the Central Library in Bristol. Whoever sent the email, it would appear that they've gone out of their way to hide their identity.'

'But don't they keep records of who's using the computers? They must have to sign in. Surely you know who was using it.'

Another short silence. 'Ordinarily, we would, yes. This person signed into the library as a guest. Let me ask you, does the name Alex Burnfield mean anything to you?'

Miles shuts his eyes, trying to fully engage the weary machinery in his brain. *Burnfield.* Something about that name rings familiar. Could it be someone he's worked with? Has he read that name somewhere? It's a distinctive surname – he would remember it, surely. 'No . . . I . . . I'm not sure. I don't think I know anyone by that name.'

'Okay. To be honest, that's not a complete surprise. It seems to be some kind of alias, a false identity. The library requires guests to provide ID and proof of address, and, in this case, they appear to have been fraudulently provided – they forged a utility bill, and the address given was for an empty building. And there doesn't appear to be anyone by the name of Alex Burnfield living in this region. There is someone of that name living in Scotland, but we're satisfied they have nothing to do with it. We do have one other lead we are looking into.'

A shiver of dread courses through him. All that effort, and for what? Just to freak him out. Whoever did it must be completely insane or dangerous, or both. An image pops into his head of a menacing, shadowy figure sat at a computer like in one of those anti-piracy adverts. 'Do you at least know what they looked like?'

'No. The librarian who signed them in was a volunteer, we've spoken to her, but she can't remember anything specific. And the CCTV was no help either.'

'Right.'

The line goes quiet. Now, it would seem, is his opportunity to ask questions, but his mind has gone blank. George, Elis, Reubyn and Polly stand gathered around their bags, staring at him. A generic voice comes over the tannoy, a warning about unattended luggage. It triggers a thought. 'The voice-cloning software, who provides that? You could contact the company and ask them which of their customers uploaded Caira's voice.'

'It's not as straightforward as that,' the detective says, sounding impatient. 'There isn't just one company that provides that service. Getting data out of them isn't as easy as you might think.'

'I see.' Miles thinks back to the forensic examination of his bedroom, his devices, his *everything*, after Caira's murder; if it was *him* under investigation, they would find a way to access that data, he's sure of it. They would have found some useable CCTV footage. They would have someone in custody by now. Now the tables have been turned, they just can't be bothered.

'Be assured that we are taking this seriously,' the detective says. 'And, again, I should make it clear how important it is that you be vigilant. Don't engage with this individual, don't hand over any personal or bank details. The person behind this has been reasonably sophisticated in the way they've gone about it, and the fact that the first email was sent so close to the conclusion of the trial suggests it was premeditated – that recording had been prepared in advance. The criminal intent is quite clear, and I'd be surprised if you've heard the last from them.'

'Right.' Miles's voice is so small he's not sure if it's being heard. 'I see.'

'Do let us know if they contact you again, and I'll be sure to let you know if we get any further developments our end.'

His tone suggests the conversation is over. He's clearly irritable. Miles isn't sure what time it is at home in Britain, but it's definitely evening and probably late.

'Wait.' Miles walks back and forth along the back wall of the concourse like a zoo cat stalking the perimeter of its enclosure. 'What can you tell me about the murder investigation? Are there any other suspects yet? Have you investigated Ben Knight, Caira's ex-boyfriend?'

The detective clears his throat. 'Mr Knight was eliminated as a suspect early in our inquiry. Cases like this can be very complex and take a lot of time, and' – a deep breath, or a yawn – 'after the acquittal we launched a formal review of the case to try and identify any missing lines of inquiry . . .'

Miles listens as the detective talks in circles without saying anything meaningful, like he's reading from a script full of technical language and police jargon. As he goes on, Miles can only think of one thing: the DNA. The police played down its relevance during the trial, but now they must be revisiting it. Surely, that's where they're looking. Police found Miles's DNA on Caira's body, which made sense – they spent the whole evening together before she died. But they also found the DNA of another, unknown person. A forensics expert told the court that it could have come from anyone; modern techniques for recording DNA are so sensitive that the transfer of material could've happened by her bumping randomly into someone on the street. It was easy for everyone to dismiss that mystery DNA when they were pointing the finger squarely at Miles, but not anymore. The detective finally concludes his meaningless spiel, and Miles jumps straight to the point: 'What about the DNA? There was unidentified DNA on her body, are you looking into that?'

'That is a strand of our inquiry, but there isn't a lot we can actively do at the moment in regard to that.'

'Why not?'

'As you know, that DNA didn't match any individual on our criminal database, but that won't necessarily be the case forever. What often happens in this scenario is, at some point, we'll pick someone up for a different offence – say, shoplifting or drink-driving, for the sake of argument – and then, bingo: there's a match.'

'So that's it? You just wait and see?'

'*No*, Mr Deverill, that's *not* what I'm saying. It's *one* strand of inquiry. In terms of DNA, we are still actively trying to find the scarf Caira was wearing, as we believe the killer's DNA will most certainly be on that.'

'And how are you trying to find—'

'Mr Deverill, I appreciate your interest, of course I do, but I don't have the time at the moment to give you a full debrief on our investigation. If there are any significant developments, we'll let you know, and if you have any further questions feel free to put them in an email and I'll do my best to answer them.'

The call ends abruptly, and Miles shakes his head as he tries to digest all this new information. He walks wearily towards the rest of the group, his brain crackling with noise but not focused on any one clear thought. All of their bags have been offloaded from the carousel, and everyone looks expectantly at Miles for an update but instead he just says, 'Let's go,' and they pick up their stuff and head for the exit. He's mute, lost in thought, as they weave through the other travellers.

It's a small airport and it doesn't take long before they're outside and loading their stuff into a white people-carrier at the taxi rank. Elis takes the seat next to the driver and the rest of them pile into the back and they head off. Fatigue and jet lag have knocked the life out of them and they're out of the airport and on to a main road by the time anyone speaks, and when they do it's Polly, speaking hushed into Miles's ear: 'What did the cops want?'

'Oh, nothing. They were just giving me an update.'

'About the emails?'

'Mostly, yeah.'

'And? What do they know?'

Miles knuckles his eyes. 'What do they know? I'll tell you what they know: the square root of sod all. We were right about the AI, though.'

She pats him on the knee. 'Try not to think about it. Whoever they are, they're on the other side of the world now.'

The taxi rounds a corner and everyone except the driver turns their head to the left, where a curtain of trees and buildings has been pulled back to reveal a spectacular view: a long body of water – a lake or inlet – stretches out for miles, and behind it and all along its edge rises a ridge of mountains. Miles allows his tired eyes to unfocus, and the landscape takes on a blurry symmetry, the ridge floating suspended between the greys of the water and sky like the stripes of a triband. He cracks open the window and cold air rushes against his face as they follow the road that tracks the edge of the lake. *Alex Burnfield.* That name continues to turn over in his head; he tries to reach high into the rafters of his mind for some memory of it, but the journey is short and there's barely time to think, or even admire the view, before they reach the town.

Queenstown is low-lying and reminds him vaguely of Aspen, the way the squat apartment complexes and chalets shrink against the looming landscape. The town is so small that within minutes they have driven through it and are pulling up at their hotel: a disproportionately huge, gleaming white lakeside building. They're dropped off outside and haul their bags into a bright and airy lobby to check in. Miles and Polly each have their own double, while George, Elis and Reubyn will be sharing a family room. Key cards and directions are issued, and the group leaves the check-in desk and – with the exception of Polly, who heads straight upstairs – pauses to confer by the lifts. Should they go out and explore, get their bearings? Grab some lunch somewhere, maybe? Elis seems keen, but even he has been drained of his normal get-up-and-go. They're all jet-lagged, unclean and exhausted. Miles calls the lift and knows exactly what he's in the mood for, and all of it can be done from the confines of his room: shower, white robe, room service. He'll try to stay up as late as he can – he's set himself a target of remaining conscious until 5 p.m. – but there is no guarantee he can hold off sleep for that long. Miles's friends leave the lift and he continues up to the fifth floor, then takes a left in search of room 508.

He swipes his way in, and the door swings closed, snapping the room into silence.

Miles drops his bag, slides open a glass door and steps out on to the balcony. He blinks, then stares wide-eyed, briefly paralysed by the panorama that's unfolded in front of him. It's incredible. The lake is vast and flanked by firs on one side and walled at its furthest reaches by sheer mountains that weave and cross into a gorge with such depth it could go on forever. He rests his weight on the balcony rail and tilts his head downwards to where the water laps at a thin and empty beach below. A small eruption on the surface grabs his gaze; a cormorant lumbering into the air with great effort, flapping its heavy wings and gliding on to a branch of some unidentifiable foreign tree. The sense of isolation is overwhelming. This is it, he knows: they've reached the back of beyond, a thousands-of-miles-away hinterland that has no knowledge or memory, and Miles feels the madness start to drift away, like steam from a cup, all of it: the murder charge, the incarceration, the trial, the press intrusion, the abuse, the trolls, the emails. Alex Burnfield. None of it matters anymore. Not out here. His mind is starting to clear, a sense of order returning. The sun emerges through a gap in the clouds, sets light dancing all across the surface of the lake, and paints the firs a vibrant green. The drained muscles in Miles's face ache from being pulled tight. How long has he been smiling? He has no idea – he didn't even realise he was. All he knows is: it's done. The nightmare is over. And it's time to start living again.

CHAPTER 15

THE TRIAL

After the opening statements, there was a week allocated for the prosecution to call witnesses and present its evidence against Miles. The whole evening in question was pieced together through WhatsApp messages, CCTV and phone data. It was creepy to see his movements recorded in grainy, covertly captured images: him driving, sitting in a restaurant, walking through the entrance of a pub. And it was disturbing the way the prosecution made a concerted effort to portray Miles as entitled and selfish, which seemed incredibly unfair.

Also disturbing was the evidence from Caira's friend, who had gone to call for her and spotted her body through the living-room window. Next called as a witness was a police officer who described the crime scene as they had found it. Some of Caira's clothing had been removed and neatly folded. Her hands had been washed in bleach. Even the first officers on the scene had a pretty clear idea of how she died: there was a visible ligature mark around her neck, as well as other inglorious physical signs she'd been strangled. A pathology witness explained that it would have taken multiple minutes of sustained pressure around her neck for the life to be squeezed out of her.

As unpleasant as this all was, it was also crucial to Miles's defence. In cross-examination of these witnesses, Eleanor had established that whoever killed Caira must have spent at least twenty minutes inside her flat. And that detail would be vital when it came to the testimony of the defence's most important witness: Elis.

It was the second Thursday of the trial when Elis appeared to give evidence. He looked nervous, rubbing the back of his neck as he approached the witness box.

As Elis was appearing as a witness for the defence, Eleanor went first, gently questioning him. She began by asking Elis about his friendship with Miles, how they'd got to know each other, then moved on to what he was doing on the day of Miles's date with Caira. Elis explained that he'd spent most of the day on a location shoot at a country house in Gloucestershire. The job – a two-line part as a footman in a period drama – finished late, and it was gone nine by the time he'd driven back to Bristol. Even so, he'd still managed to summon the energy to get himself down to the gym after work.

'Mr Pritchard-Jones, do you remember what sort of exercise you did in the gym that evening?'

Elis considered this for a moment. 'It was leg day, so I did squats, Romanian deadlifts, walking lunges, and calf raises.'

Eleanor nodded. 'You seem very certain about that. Would you describe yourself as someone who has a good memory?'

'I would, yes. Very much so.'

'And do you remember what you had for dinner that night?'

'I do. I had chicken thighs with broccoli and sweet potato.'

'Thank you, Mr Pritchard-Jones. And what did you do after you had your dinner that night?'

'It was late, so I just put my feet up and watched some TV.'

'And do you remember what you watched?'

Elis scratched his head. 'I remember I was flicking through the apps and not really feeling inspired by any of it, so I switched to the terrestrial channels. My favourite film was coming on, so I thought I'd watch a bit of that before I went to bed.'

'And what's the title of that film?'

'*Chinatown.*'

Eleanor retrieved a print copy of the *Radio Times* from a file and opened it to a page marked with a blue tab. 'Mr Pritchard-Jones, I'm going to ask you to look at an exhibit, now. Do you have a bundle in front of you?'

Elis confirmed that he did.

'If you could turn to page twenty-three, you should see a photocopy of a page from the *Radio Times*, which published a timetable of television programmes scheduled for broadcast on the third of December last year. Members of the jury, you'll find the exhibit at the same place in your bundle.'

There was a pause while everyone flicked through the documents to locate the right page. Eleanor bit her lip as one man appeared flustered and took a little longer than the others.

She turned back to Elis. 'As you can see, according to the TV listings, *Chinatown* came on at precisely twelve-thirty a.m. Does that sound correct to you?'

'It does.'

'Thank you, Mr Pritchard-Jones. So, at twelve-thirty a.m., you began to watch *Chinatown* by yourself, is that right?'

'Actually, no. Just as it was about to start, there was a tap at my window.'

'And were you expecting a visitor?'

'No, I wasn't. But there's only one person who taps on my window like that' – Elis pointed at Miles – 'and that's him.'

For a moment, every member of the jury turned to look at Miles, before switching their attention back to Elis and Eleanor.

'Thank you, Mr Pritchard-Jones. And when Miles turned up at your flat, did you let him in?'

'I did.'

'And how would you describe Miles's appearance at this point? Did he seem in any way agitated, stressed, on edge, out of breath, anything like that?'

Elis shook his head. 'No, not at all. He was calm, totally normal. It was clear he'd had a bit to drink, but otherwise he was just his regular, happy self.'

'Thank you. And what happened next?'

'We sat down to watch the movie. The opening sequence to *Chinatown* is quite long, so Miles told me a little bit about his date, and then I told him to shut up once we got to the first scene. Miles passed out on the sofa after about half an hour. Eventually I did, too. I woke again a few hours later. Miles was still asleep, and I dragged myself off to bed, at about five in the morning, I think.'

'Thank you, Mr Pritchard-Jones, you've been very helpful. Before I finish, I'd like to circle back to a very important point, if I may. You say Miles turned up at your flat just before twelve-thirty a.m. Are you quite certain about that?'

'I am, yes.'

'The reason I want to check is because the timing of this is quite a crucial detail. We know from Caira's phone data that she and Miles arrived back at her flat at twelve minutes past midnight. That would mean Miles had a maximum of eighteen minutes to go into Caira's home and then walk the eight hundred yards to your flat. Can you be absolutely sure that Miles arrived at your flat by twelve-thirty a.m.?'

Elis nodded firmly. 'Yes. I clearly remember telling Miles how lucky he was to have turned up just in time to watch the greatest movie ever made. It was just before twelve-thirty.'

'And you are one hundred per cent sure of that?'

'Yes. I've never been more certain of anything in my life.'

'Thank you, Mr Pritchard-Jones. No further questions, your ladyship.'

CHAPTER 16

ELIS

It's their first day proper in New Zealand and Elis is on a high – literally. He stands atop Bob's Peak, on the shoulder of Ben Lomond, one of the area's tallest mountains, and a cool wind feathers his face with alpine air, the clarity of which you only get at such an elevation. The sky is a thick blue, with furry claws of cirrus, and the sun has a burning intensity. It's an improvement on yesterday; *four seasons in one day*, the hotel receptionist chirped when Elis returned from a walk soaked through from a sudden shower. After that he skulked back to his room to sleep off his jet lag and was out by six o'clock. They all were. And so, as expected, today got off to a very early start.

Elis woke at two in the morning to the sound of Reubyn snoring, and it was another hour or so before his roommates grunted into consciousness, and another three hours after that before the sun started to break slowly through the stubborn darkness. Elis felt like a small child at Christmas, waiting patiently for the day to begin, excited by what lay ahead. They met Miles downstairs for breakfast, and Elis pitched a plan to ride the gondola up the mountain, 1,500 feet above the lake, to the track for luge racing – downhill go-karting, basically – and for views across the region. George protested the idea, and for a heart-soaring moment it seemed possible that he might not come, but alas, no such luck. The only person who stayed behind was Polly, who had already expressed a desire to get some work done that morning.

The luging wasn't as exhilarating as he'd hoped. He thought there might've been an opportunity to have a proper race, a chance to leave George in a cloud of dust. But it was kids' stuff, really. Every time he got up a head of speed in one of the rattly little karts, he had to brake to a stop because a member of some uncoordinated family had failed to take a bend. No one could knock the scenery, though. The vista from the viewing platform was epic; from there you could see the whole lake and deep into the wondrous landscape he'd read all about: to the east, the Remarkables, an enormous and nobbled alligator of mountains that dominated the horizon, and to the west, the magnificent Cecil Peak, rising ominously steep out of the water. This colossally ruptured, gloriously discordant corner of the Earth's crust was bellowing a reminder, if they needed one, of just how much there was out there to explore. He stared at it, lost in all the possibilities, until George ushered them into the cafe where English canteen-style food was being kept warm under lights.

They had a high-carb lunch that hit none of Elis's macros, and now, while they wait in a queue for a cable car to take them back down the mountain, he can feel his body tire as his digestive system works overtime to break down a gutful of refined fats and starch. They move forward on to the platform and wait as the group ahead of them boards a cable car and the next one trundles into position. It's a delicate, glass-sided pod with benches at each end. They file in, sit down and off they go. Elis's stomach drops as the ground slips away and they're suspended, thinly encased and dangling, and the mountainside – a chaotic mix of rocky cliffs and dull grassy terrain – falls further below, almost impossibly steep. Reubyn has gone silent, staring at his feet, as he did on the way up.

Elis leans forward and puts a hand on Reubyn's shoulder. 'Are you all right?'

Reubyn remains silent, head bowed, refusing to look out of the windows. His vertigo came on gradually on the way up, but this time he's started suffering immediately.

'You don't look too well, mate,' George says. 'How's that fish and chips settling in your stomach?' There's no response, and George grins – a sure sign that he's going to keep prodding. 'Maybe you should do a food review for your channel,' he says, and then, when Reubyn doesn't reply, adds: 'How would you rate the batter, out of ten? Was it greasy enough for you? It looked a bit oily to me.'

Reubyn still doesn't respond. His skin gleams an unhealthy shade somewhere between grey and yellow, like a raw chicken breast on the turn; globules of sweat have formed between the sparse hairs on his crown.

'You should've brought your selfie stick for this,' George continues. '*Sweaty Brit suffers vertigo-induced heart attack on cable car* – that would get some views.'

'Bugger off.'

Laughter echoes around the cabin.

'I'm no engineer,' George says, 'but that cable doesn't look very robust to me. And it sure is a long way down.'

They're about halfway back now, but it *is* still a long way down – both to the rocks directly below and to the base of the mountain.

After a brief silence, George smirks as if he's thought of something clever. 'You know, Reubs,' he says, 'New Zealand is one of the most earthquake-prone countries in the world.' He winks at Miles. 'We're right on a fault line here, and they have some *real* big ones. I wouldn't want to be in one of these cable cars when the next big shake happens.' He grabs hold of the bench and starts jerking forward and back, generating a slight rocking motion. 'Do you feel that? I think the earth's moving down there.'

Reubyn lifts his head a couple of inches and rolls his eyes to look at George. 'Stop it!'

Cackles reverberate around the small space.

'All right, all right,' Miles says. 'That's enough.'

On his word, the cabin falls silent. Miles and George turn their attention to their phones as the cable car approaches the bottom of the mountain. Eventually they're low enough that Reubyn raises his head and puffs out his cheeks.

Miles looks up, twists the corner of his mouth. 'Hey, I've been meaning to ask, have any of you ever heard the name Alex Burnfield?'

'I don't think so,' Elis says.

Reubyn shakes his head with the listless energy of someone who's dismissed the question without giving it any thought.

George stares through the glass, running his knuckles over his jawline. 'Burnfield? I don't think so, either. Why do you ask?'

'Oh, it's one of my trolls. No big deal.'

Miles goes back to his phone. After a minute of thumbing the screen, he cocks his head. 'Pol's gone to the pub.' He turns his screen so they can see. On it is a picture from Polly's Instagram; she's leaning back in the half-shade of a parasol, a wine glass resting in her hand.

'Marvellous,' George says, rubbing his hands together. 'Where is she? Let's join her.'

Miles taps at his phone. 'I'll find out.'

Elis clears his throat. 'Oh, come on, it's too early for the pub, isn't it, fellas? There's other stuff we can do.'

'Like what?' George asks, seriously.

'Well, there's this steamboat that takes you out on the lake for—'

'Oh, for heaven's sake!' George shakes his head. 'Can you stop trying to be Captain Cook for five minutes and just chill out a bit?'

Miles laughs, and Elis clenches his jaw. He feels a sting of real irritation – not so much towards George but at Miles. George's moronic comments are to be expected, but Miles should have his back.

'It's two o'clock in the afternoon,' Elis protests, a vein burning in his forehead. 'The day is young.'

'Yeah, and we've all scaled a mountain this morning,' George says. 'I think that means we've earned ourselves a nice drink.'

Miles shrugs. 'He's got a point.'

Elis mutters under his breath. But there's no time for any acrimony to fester in the cabin – they've arrived. They file out, and George slings an arm around Miles, glancing over his shoulder at Elis as he guides Miles out on to the street and towards the town. Elis hangs back with Reubyn, who staggers out, visibly disorientated. Elis grinds his teeth. What has he signed up for here? A two-week piss-up? They're in New Zealand, for God's sake, and all these guys can think of to do is go to the pub. It's such a *waste*. They make it out on to the street, and Reubyn slumps his backside on a low wall and hangs his head. The colour is returning to his cheeks, but he still looks pathetic, drawing the long deliberate breaths of the infirm.

Elis places a light hand on his shoulder. 'How are you feeling, man?'

'I'm fine. Just give me a minute.'

'I'm sorry – I didn't know about your thing with heights; you were fine on the plane, weren't you? Anyway, I didn't realise it would be that steep.'

'It's fine. I'm just glad to be off the bloody thing.'

Reubyn takes a bottle of sunscreen out of his bag and wearily smears factor 50 on to his forearms and head. It's already his second application of the day. When he's done, Elis offers his hand and hauls Reubyn to his feet.

'George can be a bit of a prick, can't he?' Elis says.

Reubyn raises an eyebrow. 'Oh, I know he can be a bit much, at times. But he's all right, really.'

'I get the feeling he'd rather I wasn't here.'

Reubyn shakes his head. 'That's not true. He can be a bit full-on, but he doesn't mean anything by it. You get used to him.' Reubyn registers the doubt lines on Elis's forehead and adds: 'Honestly, he's just having a laugh.'

'I'll take your word for it.'

Reubyn appears suddenly brighter, but Elis still sets a slow pace; it's only a ten-minute walk to where the town's bars are clustered on the lakefront, and he's in no hurry to get there. As he strolls, Elis's eye tracks along the ragged outline of the mountainous horizon. On a day like this, there must be plenty of climbers on those peaks, all in ascension towards life's most momentous moments; up there – where freedom is a real, touchable thing – ambitions are being met, bucket lists ticked, summits reached in eruptions of endorphins. His sight rests upon the highest visible point, a knuckle of rock raised triumphantly against the blue sky, and he imagines what it'd be like to be there standing on it, staring back down.

'Hey,' Reubyn says, wiping the image from Elis's mind, 'you know I told you I had a surprise for us?'

'Yeah.'

'Well, it's all confirmed. I think Miles is going to really love it. Do you want to see?'

'Of course.'

Reubyn fiddles with his phone, then turns it to the side and pincers his thumb and index finger to zoom in on an image. 'Check it out.'

Elis's head recoils with surprise. 'Bloody hell.'

'I know, right?'

He takes the phone from Reubyn to examine the picture more closely, and a tingle of excitement fizzes through him. 'Is that . . . is that for *us*?'

CHAPTER 17

REUBYN

Reubyn gets a rush of satisfaction from seeing the look of astonishment on Elis's face. He was hoping for this kind of enthusiasm, and seeing his expression go from surprise to elation – like a toddler being given a new toy – he can almost forgive him for that bloody cable car. Elis is right to be impressed, though. What he's looking at is something a bit special. And it's also the result of months of research and negotiations.

When he first got wind of the New Zealand trip, Reubyn put feelers out with all sorts of tourism businesses and travel PR firms to see what he could blag in return for a brand partnership. As normal, there was a range of responses: some polite nos, a few ghostings, a couple of rude rebuttals – mostly bemoaning *bloody influencers* – and a handful of offers, either of such low value that they weren't worth his time, or so boring he couldn't make any decent content from them. But a couple of months ago, he got an email from a public-relations firm owned by the parents of an acquaintance from school. He called in a favour and, unexpectedly, it paid off. In return for a video review, to be shared across all his social channels, they were offering a vehicle for a week. And not just any vehicle. The company who own it, a global enterprise called Waverley Travel, specialise in satisfying the whims of elite, wealthy tourists. Their clients demand the best, even when it comes to hiring a camper van. And, in this case, that appetite for luxury resulted in the most blinged-out motorhome imaginable and the biggest and most expensive vehicle of its kind in New Zealand. He accepted the offer immediately. It was a no-brainer. Not only would Miles love it, but it would make brilliant content for his own channel. Ideas for video titles immediately came to mind: *Inside the million-dollar motorhome*; *Touring Middle Earth in a mansion*; *How to go camping like a billionaire*. Now they can go anywhere they want, do anything. It opens the door to a whole new spectrum of possibilities – including one that could be brilliant if it goes to plan.

'When will you get it?' Elis asks, handing him back the phone.

'I should have the keys on Sunday.'

They start walking again, and Elis has more zip to his movements. 'This is amazing,' he says. 'A proper road trip.'

'Don't say anything to the others just yet. I want to be the one to tell Miles.'

'Sure,' Elis says. It's maybe thirty seconds before he speaks again. 'Can I ask you something?'

'Okay.'

'Why do you let George talk to you like that?'

'You mean in the cable car?' Reubyn waves a dismissive hand. 'He's just mucking around. It's totally fine, I'm used to it.'

'Fair enough.'

But there's a look of bewilderment on Elis's face, and Reubyn can understand why. It's easy to see how the exchange between him and George in the cable car could've been construed as mean behaviour. Bullying, even. But it wasn't. Reubyn is certain about that; you don't spend a decade at a boys' school as someone like him – small and physically uncoordinated, with an allergy list and

Ventolin inhaler – without finding out what real bullying is. And he would have dwelled a lot longer in that circle of hell if it hadn't been for George sticking up for him. George has a sense of justice. He's fiercely loyal to his friends. Yes, he will tease and provoke, and he's wary of outsiders. But he's not a bully.

They turn the corner to find Miles on his phone and George slumped impatiently against a post. George straightens up as he sees them. 'What's taken you so long?'

Reubyn shares a knowing glance with Elis and neither answers.

Miles hangs up. 'She's at The Globe' – he points – 'it's that way.'

They carry on, into town. Reubyn's stomach has settled now, and, with the sun beating down, a cool drink is suddenly urgent. They walk in silence, and Reubyn considers whether to tell Miles about the motorhome. Until he told Elis, the only person who knew about it was Miles's dad. But better to wait until it arrives – for maximum impact – and then Reubyn can film his reaction and send the video to Miles's parents. There's an outside chance that he won't like the idea, which would be a disaster, but that seems extremely unlikely. You'd have to be mad to turn down a trip in that thing.

After a few minutes' walk, The Globe comes into view. It's vaguely in the style of a Western saloon, with a wooden facade and veranda. There are a dozen or so tables outside in the full glare of the sun, and they're all packed out, rumbling with the sound of intoxication. Reubyn spots Polly immediately, his eye drawn to her bright slash of lipstick. She's unaware of them, her chin propped up on her knuckles as she talks to two other women at her table. Even from fifty yards away, Reubyn can tell instantly that these strangers, with their bare shoulders and shiny hair, are the gorgeous, fun-loving type. Who are they? What are they doing with Polly? Reubyn's only just recovered from the stress of the cable car and now he has to deal with this – it's a *nightmare*.

'Oh, hello,' George says, pulling up as he spots them. 'What do we have here?'

Miles adjusts his Wayfarers and squints in their direction. 'I have no idea who those girls are.'

'Well, you're about to find out. Who'd have thought – your sister is a better wingman than you'll ever be.'

George waves them across the street towards the bar. Reubyn looks at Elis, who shrugs and follows the other two. A thin knot of dread ties in Reubyn's stomach. Although he's been gaining confidence when it comes to talking to women, he'll never be in the same league as the others. This is going to pan out the way it always does: his handsome, dashing friends will charm the pants off them, and he'll be left sat there like a lemon. *You're going to look like an idiot.* He tries to slow his breathing. *No. Not this time. Just remember everything you've learned. You've got this. You can do it.*

They follow George, who sashays through the tables to greet the women. Reubyn slowly brings up the rear, and Polly has already started the introductions by the time he reaches the table. She points left, to a woman with her hair in long, neat braids. 'Faith is from Australia.' She then gestures to the opposite side of the table, where sits an intimidatingly beautiful blonde in a wide-brimmed hat and oversized sunglasses. 'And Jessie is from West Virginia. She's a cosmologist and—'

'A *cosmologist?*' George juts his lower lip as he shakes her hand. 'Blimey, I'd never have guessed.'

'Why is that such a surprise?'

Polly gives him a tight smile. 'Yes, I'm interested to know that, too, George. Why so shocked?'

Jessie has her eyebrows raised with a smirk.

'Well, she obviously forgot to bring her telescope.'

Jessie laughs. 'Good save.'

'You know, Jessie, we should talk' – George raises one eyebrow – 'I know a thing or two about the Big Bang Theory, myself.'

Everyone laughs – Jessie surprisingly loud – and Reubyn feels himself slipping to the fringe of this conversation already, ready to drift away into invisibility. Why are they laughing? *I know a thing or two about the Big Bang Theory* – what does that even mean? Reubyn once watched a podcast interview with the psychologist and relationship expert Dr Jane Sheridan, and one of the things she said was: *if you know someone who's good at talking to the opposite sex, watch them and see what they do.* But what the hell can he learn from this? What can be gained from observing George? This time, he has been called out for his unconscious bias and still managed to come up smelling of roses thanks to a couple of lame jokes. *I know a thing or two about the Big Bang Theory* – imagine if Reubyn had said that. They would have been disgusted. The difference is: George is tall and carries himself with a straight-spined authority that suggests what's coming out of his mouth must have some merit. Reubyn doesn't have that natural charm. It's not that he's devoid of confidence; he'd back himself to succeed in most situations. But the one thing they don't teach you at school is how to behave around girls. So how did his friends gain this effortless ability? How are you supposed to learn, when you've spent your whole young life at a boys' school, where girls are exotic, far-off creatures? He's trying to remember everything he's picked up from Dr Sheridan: her ten rules for success with women. *Shoulders back*; *If you're not confident, fake it*; *Shout your value.* What is the fourth rule? He can't remember.

George is still going on – no one else is getting a word in right now – and he's hamming up his accent, even posher than normal, if that's possible: the full James Bond act to impress the American. He has one hand planted on the table and he's leaning in, talking directly to Jessie. 'There's really nothing more awe-inspiring than looking into the universe, is there?' he says. 'What was it Oscar Wilde said? *We are all in the gutter, but some of us are looking at the stars.* How very true.' Jessie opens her mouth to reply but George has started again before she has a chance. 'The school we went to,' he says, 'is one of the only schools in the world to have its own observatory and planetarium. Those who studied physics in the sixth form, like I did, got to have lessons in there. It was an incredible way to visualise our place in the universe, to see the celestial movement, to—'

'To fall asleep,' Reubyn says.

George's mouth falls open at the interruption. 'What?'

Reubyn's fingers spider furiously in his pockets. 'He was so fascinated by astronomy, he used to fall asleep every time we went in the planetarium.'

The girls burst out laughing, and Reubyn feels a hot rush of adrenaline course through him. George looks stunned for a moment, then grins. 'To be fair, it was really dark in there. And it had these lovely, comfy leather seats. It was quite romantic, actually.'

'Not romantic enough for him to stay awake,' Reubyn says. George's mouth is agape again. Reubyn feels his tongue turning dry, but carries on: 'You could tell when he'd slept through the whole thing because when the lights came up, he'd have a little bit of drool' – tapping his chin – 'just there.'

More laughter. Reubyn's hand visibly trembles, and he whips it back into his pocket. He's forced himself into the conversation, but it's come at a cost – he's gone so faint he might pass out.

George's head is tilted at him in disbelief. 'On the subject of education' – George speaks slowly, coiling an arm roughly around Reubyn, squeezing his shoulder so that his fingernails dig into his flesh – 'this noted scholar here dropped out to spend more time on his YouTube channel.'

The girls look at Reubyn, and blood flares in his cheeks. He knows he shouldn't go into battle against George – he'll always find a way to humiliate him.

'What kind of channel is it?' Faith asks.

Everyone stares at Reubyn now. He hates this bit, having to summarise what he does in one line. *Shout your value.* 'It's entertainment. Adventure-type stuff. I'm still kind of figuring it out.'

'He's got thirty thousand subscribers,' Polly says.

'Wow.'

Be confident. 'Thirty-four thousand, to be precise.'

'You're famous.'

'Not quite,' Reubyn says.

George loosens his grip on Reubyn's shoulders. This isn't playing out how either of them expected. 'He's what's known as a micro influencer,' George says. 'It's a bit of a stretch to say he's famous.' George digs into the ice bucket for the bottle in the centre of the table and examines the label. 'Another of these? My round.'

Now Reubyn remembers. *Demonstrate generosity.* That's the fourth rule. How could he forget?

George beckons them inside. 'Come on, boys, I've got a treat for you at the bar.'

Reubyn turns to follow them, then feels a hand on his forearm. It's Faith, the Australian.

'Hey, Reubyn.' His name – *she remembered it.* 'The channel sounds awesome.'

His stomach tenses. He's winded by the compliment, by the dazzling glare of her smile as she stares up at him. They've all been so drawn in by the solar gravity of the blonde that they've barely noticed her – but she's just as beautiful; more so, even. 'Thanks,' he says.

'I'd love to know how you got it off the ground.' She speaks in a low voice, and it has a slight coarseness – as fine as gravel gets before it melts into sand. 'Can you tell me how you did it? I wish I could do something like that.'

Reubyn opens his mouth but for a moment he's speechless. Her gaze is intense, and it strips everything else away – all sight and sound; the house lights have gone down, and they're silhouetted in a spotlight, all alone. Did she . . . did she just flutter her eyelashes? Women don't actually do that in real life, do they? Just in period dramas and rom-coms. 'Of course,' he says, eventually. 'I'll' – he points to the bar – 'I'll be right back.'

He walks away, weightless, towards the bar entrance, where George is waiting for him at the door. Reubyn looks back over his shoulder to check she's still there, to check she's *real*. His heart is trying to beat its way out of his chest. That was surreal, dreamlike. Maybe he really *can* do this. Maybe he's *not* a complete loser. Dr Sheridan is right: it is possible; he just needs to project the right image, say the right things. This is *life-changing*.

George stops him at the door. His face has gone stiff, the way it does when he's pissed off, or about to do some damage to something. 'What are you grinning about?'

'Nothing.'

'What the hell are you playing at?'

'Sorry?'

'Drooling in the planetarium? What the hell was that about?'

Reubyn shrugs.

George leans in, so Reubyn can feel his breath. 'I don't know what you're trying to achieve, *mate*,' George says, 'but if you try something like that again, you'll be the one drooling – on a ventilator.'

CHAPTER 18

GEORGE

It might be busy outside the bar, but inside it's dead. There's no one else here in this dark wooden interior, apart from one woman – dressed in an odd summer/winter mix of vest and woollen hat – already at the counter. When a young, tattooed barmaid appears, George nods towards the other customer.

'You go,' the woman says, looking along a row of taps with gaudy labels. 'I'm still deciding.'

George gives her a thumbs up. 'What's your finest whisky?' he asks the barmaid. She stretches on her tiptoes for a bottle on the top shelf and places it on the bar. 'I'll have four doubles please, no ice. Plus, a bottle of that' – pointing towards the empty wine bottle he holds – 'and four pints of that' – nodding at a tap that reads Pacific IPA.

'Pay day, is it?' the woman queuing next to him says.

'Something like that.' George turns away from her and hands out the square whisky glasses to his friends.

Elis sniffs with caution, like the glass might contain something poisonous. 'What is it?'

George rolls whisky around the sides of his glass. 'It's Macallan. Single malt scotch. Aged thirty years' – he moves in between Miles and Reubyn – 'just how I like my friends. It's not the very best, but it's as good as you'll get this far from Scotland.'

'I'm not really a fan of whisky,' Elis says.

'Wait until you try this one.'

'Are these doubles?'

George rolls his eyes. 'Something you need to know about us lot: we don't do single measures.' He raises his glass. 'Why settle for a taste of the fruit, am I right?'

This is met with a roar from Miles and Reubyn, and the three of them tip the whisky down their throats in a single movement. George blinks rapidly, his body electrified by the liquor, and looks, watery-eyed, at Elis, who appears confused, still cradling a full glass. Elis smiles awkwardly and takes a sip, grimacing at the taste.

Why settle for a taste of the fruit – it's fast becoming the motto of this trip. Elis doesn't understand the reference, of course – one would only know it if one went to Holvine. It was an unofficial mantra at school. O'Mara, their head of sixth, was obsessed with high-style oratory and would invent these little rhetorical phrases and idioms. This particular line he had delivered in a speech at the Letters to Our Future Selves ceremony. As the name suggested, the event involved pupils from the lower sixth opening the missives they had written to themselves six years prior and then comparing their ambitions then and now. George laughed at the trivial goals set by his younger self: make a cricket century, see the Pyramids, some nonsense about designing video games. In the time that had passed, his aspirations had become more rational and bound to well-trodden routes into financial services and politics – the big-boy stuff that came with the big rewards.

If Holvine was good for anything, it was that it sharpened one's focus on what was important before it became too late.

People who went to lesser schools spent their lives squandering opportunities through fear and applying for crappy jobs with CVs that promised they *work well as part of a team*. A Holviner would never spout that tosh; they didn't work well in teams, they ran the teams. They're *leaders*. They didn't become local councillors, they became parliamentary ministers. They're bankers, not accountants. They didn't do am-dram – they went to Hollywood.

When O'Mara gathered them all together at the ceremony, he signed off with the line that, for various reasons, they'd never forget: *why settle for a taste of the fruit, when you can have the whole vine?* Whole vine . . . Holvine, get it? It received a few groans, as was often the case with O'Mara's wordplay, but without that it wouldn't have been so memorable. And O'Mara knew that a message of this importance needed to stick in the memory. It was about grabbing the most out of life, not settling for any half measures or putting limitations on oneself or being second-best – prosperity comes when one takes full advantage of life's bounty.

Of course, such a lesson doesn't get through to all. So much of the wisdom emanating from Holvine was lost on Miles – or, even worse, ungratefully rejected. Miles is lucky he has his good looks to fall back on, because he is completely lacking in natural ambition. After the Letters to Our Future Selves ceremony, Miles immediately took to parroting the phrase, initially as a way of mocking O'Mara, and then, after a while, it began to take on a life of its own. It got adopted ironically by the boys as a way of offering encouragement, especially during drinking games or any activity that required a modicum of bravery. Instead of *down that glass of wine, it was why settle for a taste of the fruit?* And instead of *you need to hit two more reps on the bench press*, it was *have the whole vine.* When you're at school together for long hours, you develop many of these privately shared sayings and in-jokes. If one is an outsider, one can't just gain access to all of that, no matter how much one might want to – that stuff is as exclusive as the gates to Holvine itself. And that's why George can't be bothered to try to explain the meaning of the phrase to Elis – because even if he did, he wouldn't understand.

Finally, Elis finishes his whisky and his chest lurches forward in a dry heave.

Miles takes his pint off the bar and takes a sip. He points to the exit. 'Shall we?'

'Wait.' George thuds his glass on to the bar like a gavel. 'You all saw how well I was getting on with Jessie, just then. Don't do anything to ruin my chances with her, all right? You might want to keep your distance.'

'Seriously?' Elis's face is still creased in disgust from the whisky. He gapes at Miles. 'Is he for real?'

Miles grimaces. 'I think he might be, yes.'

'Look,' George says. 'I don't want to sound uncouth, but I can assure you that Jessie has already begun to imagine her future with a tall dark Englishman – me. And I'm not going to stand idly by if you come in and attempt to deprive her of the chance to realise that dream.'

George looks at Elis, waiting for him to protest. But he doesn't; instead, he slides his hands slowly down his face, pulling at his cheeks to expose the deep tangle of veins along the base of his eye sockets.

'Okay, then,' George says.

Miles tuts and shakes his head. 'Another thing,' he says. 'Can we please not mention the whole, *you know what*.' Miles grimaces, and they all know what he's referring to. 'It's not about misleading anyone. I'd just like to get through at least one night without explaining it all, and to be treated like a normal person. You know?'

The other three nod in agreement.

'Yeah, of course,' Elis says.

'Absolutely fair enough,' George adds. 'In all honesty, I don't think it would help anyone to be bringing that up. Anything else?'

They look at each other. Elis mutters something inaudible.

'Good,' George says. He grins broadly and extends an arm towards the door. 'Once more unto the breach, dear friends. And stay away from Jessie. Jessie is mine.'

George hears a theatrical sigh and turns to find Polly has snuck up behind him. She has her arms folded in that semi-serious contemptuous manner of hers.

She gives him a withering smile. 'Have you ever thought about taking a break from being a complete prick, for literally *one* minute?'

George grins. 'Oh, look, the fun police is here. What's the charge? Are you worried I might steal her heart?'

Polly groans and rolls her eyes. The others head for the exit, and she turns to follow.

Before she has a chance to leave, George reaches out and grabs Polly loosely by the arm. 'Hey, wait. I've been meaning to ask you something.'

She stops and looks at him blankly.

George steps close to Polly and lowers his voice. 'What's your take on Elis?'

'What do you mean?'

'Well, I hardly know the man. And I just wondered what you thought of him.'

'I think he seems really nice, actually. He's been super-supportive of Miles.'

'So I gather. And what's his motive behind that?'

Polly raises her upper lip, exposing her teeth. 'Not everyone requires a *motive* to do something nice, George.'

'Don't they?'

Polly shakes her head and walks off, and George stands and watches her for a moment, considering just how wrong she is about that. All actions require a motive. Even well-intentioned ones. And people choose not to reveal their motives for a variety of reasons, good and bad. It might be through kindness or tact, deception or shame. George is normally pretty good at instinctively realising what those reasons are. He's accustomed to concealing his own. But there's one motivating factor that he can't quite fathom in all of this: why, exactly, has Miles chosen to bring Elis along with him on this trip?

CHAPTER 19

MILES

Miles opens his eyes, and it takes a second or two for him to remember where he is. At the same time, there's an assault on his body: deep nausea, eyelids of sandpaper, a head full of rocks. A proper hangover. He hasn't had one of these for a long time. Miles lies still, unready to move, staring vacantly towards the window. The room is dark, but a white glow around the edges of the curtains says the sun has been up for some time. A glass of water stands on the bedside table, but it's too much effort to reach for it. He closes his eyes. Maybe he can slip back into sleep. He lies, his head pulsing, and memories of the previous day start to splice together, disjointed fragments slowly interweaving to form a narrative. They were at that bar all afternoon, weren't they, and then there was a restaurant – Thai, he thinks – and then another place, not quite a nightclub but there was neon and a dance floor, and—

Suddenly the picture cuts to black. His body tenses, rigid. Something crawling up his bare calf. Someone. Someone in the bed with him. He turns over, and there she is.

'Good morning, Miles.'

He blinks. 'Jessie.'

She's smiling, lying relaxed on her side, ice-blonde hair fanned across the white pillow. Her make-up has bled slightly, leaving inky flecks of black under her eyes. Jessie is unnervingly comfortable in the silence, her smile unfaltering as they lie staring at each other. It's a closed smile that thins her lips and pulls a dimple deep into her cheek.

Miles rubs his eyes. 'What time is it?'

'Ten-thirty.'

'Oh.' Ten-thirty. He's slept for a long time. Or has he? He can't remember what time they came back here.

'I've been awake so long,' she says. 'You were dead to the world; I didn't want to wake you. You talk in your sleep – did you know that?'

He has been known to do that. Complete gibberish, normally. 'I hope I didn't say anything too offensive.'

She laughs. 'I couldn't make it out. And, believe me, I tried. Something about China, maybe?'

He rolls his eyes around, in thought. 'We had a layover in Hong Kong – that's probably it.'

'Right,' Jessie says. 'You seem to have gotten over your jet lag, anyway. It's a gorgeous day out there. We're going down to the beach. Do you want to join us?'

The way she talks is strangely relaxed, like they've known each other for years. Miles hesitates. 'Maybe, yeah.'

Jessie slides out of bed and stoops to pick up her clothes that are scattered on the floor. 'Polly's coming. Faith, too.'

'Okay. I'll let the boys know and we'll come down and meet you.'

'Cool. We need to enjoy the sun while we can,' Jessie says. She turns her back to him and fastens her bra. 'I've seen the weather report for the next few days, and it *sucks*.'

We need to enjoy the sun while we can. WE. Is she talking like they're a couple already? That's a bit keen. Jessie slips on her dress, still facing away, and Miles quickly averts his eyes as she turns to face him. She picks her phone up off the bed. 'I'll take your number.'

Miles lists the digits, and she taps them in.

She continues to thumb her phone, then pauses and looks at him. 'What's your surname, Miles?'

'D—' He stops. He's not ready for this. His real name would serve up some truly horrifying internet search results. 'It's Davis.'

She lowers her eyebrows. 'Miles *Davis*? Like the trumpet guy?'

Oh no. You idiot. 'Yep. My parents are big fans of, er . . . jazz.'

'Cool. But they didn't have to take it out on you.' She slips her phone into her bag, kneels on the bed, leans over and jabs him in the shoulder, stinging the muscle with her knuckles. 'Just kidding!' She leans closer and kisses him on the mouth, as easily as if they were married. 'See you soon,' Jessie says, cheerfully, waving as she leaves.

Miles waits until the door closes behind her, then turns on to his side and closes his eyes. He's done well there – Jessie is some girl; there's no denying it. And she seems *very* into him. On the other hand, she was eager to leave just then – what was that about?

Miles lies there, allowing more images of last night to form in his mind. Now it's coming back. He has a hazy recollection of leaving the dance floor to get a round of drinks, and Jessie turning up next to him at the bar. She asked him if he wanted to go outside for a cigarette, and then, when it transpired that neither of them had any – or even smoked – whether he'd like to walk down to the beach. An image of her forms clearly. She was even more stunning down there, by the lake, her large round eyes shimmering like the still surface of the water in the silver moonlight. He can't remember exactly how they decided on going back to his hotel room, but he has no doubt it was her idea – she was making all the moves, that's for sure. He smiles as more of the memory crystallises in his mind:

she was so loud, in a good way – fun, laughing easily at everything he said. All that aside, things didn't progress very far physically; he's still wearing his underwear as proof of that. After everything that's happened, he's been instinctively wary of putting himself in a potentially compromising position, and they wouldn't have ended up here together if she hadn't taken the lead.

Miles dozes for a while. Maybe thirty minutes later, he opens his eyes and grabs his phone off the bedside table. A long list of notifications covers the screen: news alerts, messages, emails. Three missed calls from George. Miles thumbs through the alerts and is relieved to see no mention of his name in any of them. That's the third day in a row he's been out of the news; maybe it really is starting to blow over. Finally.

He looks through his messages. They're not important; there's one from his bank and two from George, asking where he disappeared to last night. There's little point in replying to that now – George is most likely still furious. Besides, Miles's memories of what happened are vague. Instead, he taps out a message to the WhatsApp group: *Heading down to the beach. See you there.*

Then he opens his emails, and his smile drops. He stares at the list. A tingle of anger, like a needle pressing at his skin. All the emails that have come in overnight are spam, including one from 'Caira Kennedy'. *Here we go again.* He opens the email and forwards it to Lewin; this is for the police to worry about, not him. Miles has been expecting another of these emails, but even so, it's infuriating that there are trolls who still won't leave him alone. Again, the email is blank except for an audio attachment. And, again, he can't resist. *Hi Miles,* begins the AI-generated Caira voice. *I hope you're enjoying New Zealand. This is not over.* Miles tosses the phone. He won't be giving it any more thought. That's what they're trying to achieve, to torment him. But he won't allow it.

Miles hauls himself out of bed and lumbers unsteadily into the bathroom. He cranks the shower on and steps in through the glass door into a heavy, scalding blast of water. *This is not over.* Why are those words repeating on him? It's the voice – that artificial ghost – that makes it hard to ignore. It's quite clever, really, he begrudgingly admits. *I hope you're enjoying New Zealand.* Yes, he is enjoying New Zealand, thanks very much, although he's sorely regretting the fact it's been reported in the media so that every freak with a vendetta against him knows where he is. At least whoever is sending these emails is a long way away; this latest one was sent at 4.06 a.m. – a clear sign it originated from a different time zone. They're in Britain, still – of course they are. No troll would be insane enough to travel to the other side of the world to hammer their point home. All he has to do to escape this person is ignore them.

Miles steps out of the shower, towels himself dry and dresses for the beach – shorts, sandals, T-shirt – and heads out to the lifts. He reaches the lobby, and the slap of sandals echoes as he crosses the white-tiled floor towards the exit. Outside, he pauses underneath the portico and pulls his shades down from his head before stepping out into the full glare of the sun. It's noon, and the midday rays toast his face and arms with a dry heat. The lake is a wavering mirror to the trees and mountains. Miles hears the trill of birds and faint hiss of traffic. And he hears . . . something else. A faint clicking sound, rapid – like the shuffling of cards. He looks around. The noise has stopped. What was that? The rattling of some foreign creature? A sprinkler system? A bird? Did he imagine it? He listens carefully, but there's nothing. Just the sound of a car as it pulls out from the neat line of parked vehicles along the far side of the street and drives slowly west, disappearing behind the trees.

CHAPTER 20

POLLY

The three women lie in a diagonal, their towels aligned towards the sun, at the far end of the beach. Lake Wakatipu is so vast that they might be by the sea, but there are giveaway signs that they are not; the sand is more like shingle – hard, like a bed of concrete might lie a few inches beneath it – and a dozen or so ducks bicker to their left. After a chilly morning, it's now surprisingly warm. The sky is blue, and there's barely a breath of wind. The water is deathly still.

Polly has been at the beach for about an hour, and her skin shines from sunscreen and perspiration. Faith was already here, and Jessie turned up a little later looking sheepish. She didn't say where she'd been, but Polly has a pretty good idea, given she disappeared at the same time as Miles. Faith called her out immediately, though. *G'day, stopout!* she yelled, loud enough that it turned a few heads. Faith didn't notice how Jessie was wounded by that remark, how she turned away to hide her shock. It's surprisingly conservative behaviour for someone who Polly suspects is quite promiscuous. But it's a strange group, this. That's what happens when you're travelling – Polly remembers that from her gap year. When you're in a strange country, far from home, the social barriers that normally keep people apart are removed, and you band together with people even if you have very little in common. Here they are: three women from three different continents, all behaving like they've been friends for years. Jessie and Faith met via a Facebook group called Solo Women Travellers NZ. When they spotted Polly sitting on her own at The Globe they approached her and introduced themselves. Polly is glad of it – hanging out exclusively with Miles and his friends for the next fortnight could easily have sent her mad.

Polly turns, shifting on to her back, and spots Miles, who kicks off his flip-flops and carries them in his hand. She waves, and he waves back. *Stopout.* If any logic were applied, someone who's endured what he has would be very cautious about embarking on a one-night stand. But there is seemingly no stopping the cretinous impulses of young men. Her brother included.

Miles stops and beckons Polly towards him. Polly doesn't move, just turns her palms upwards, and Miles repeats the gesture. His face is serious. Polly sighs and gets to her feet, then plods towards him.

'Hey, sis,' Miles says, leaning in.

Polly recoils slightly from his hug – she doesn't like being touched when she's all sweaty. 'Good afternoon, Miles.'

He straightens up. 'I need to brief you on a couple of things.'

Polly rolls her eyes behind the lenses of her shades. She looks over her shoulder at the girls, checking they're out of earshot. 'Oh, great. And what have you done now?'

'It's nothing serious.'

'Okay.'

'Firstly, I told Jessie that our surname is Davis.'

'Oh for—' Polly shakes her head. Questions pop into her head but they largely answer themselves. 'So, I'm Polly Davis? Brilliant.' She doesn't like lying for him – it doesn't come naturally. She didn't think lying came naturally to him, either.

'Sorry about that. But it's for the best.'

'Is it? You'll tie yourself in knots, deceiving people like this.'

Miles rakes his fingers through his hair. 'I panicked, okay? I'm sorry.'

She sighs. 'Right.'

'Also, I received another email. Another Caira voice note.'

'Oh.' Polly wrinkles her brow. 'What did it say?'

'"I hope you're enjoying New Zealand."'

She shrugs. 'It was pretty well documented that you were going to New Zealand.'

'I know; I'm not particularly worried about it.'

'Have you told the police?'

'Yeah.'

'Good. Then you should forget about it.' She places her hands on his shoulders. 'Are you all right?'

'Yeah.'

'Come on, then, Miles Davis' – the reassuring smile she's forced disappears – 'oh, bloody hell – *Miles Davis?* You really are a moron.'

They walk over to the girls. Faith is sitting up, watching them, and Jessie lies on her front, propped on her elbows and reading a book. Some small talk ensues: benign chatter that is at odds with the awkwardness created by whatever Jessie and Miles got up to last night.

After a few minutes, Faith stands. 'Who's coming for a swim?'

'Sure,' chirps Jessie, sitting up and arranging her hair into a high bun.

Polly looks at the water. It's a clear tea-green for the first few yards and then it's dark and pondlike – a far cry from the inviting cyan seas found in places like Greece and Thailand. 'I'm good here, thanks.'

Polly sits and watches as the pair of them tiptoe towards the water, studying their bikinied bodies: Jessie slender and pale, and Faith, not. She remembers how Faith's body bulged dangerously in her dress as she cosied up to Elis last night. He didn't seem to mind. A tingle of irritation rises in her at the memory of it. Is she . . . *jealous*? No, that's not it; Polly might be attracted to Elis, but she doesn't actually *want* him. And besides, Faith was probably just being friendly – she was cosying up to Reubyn as well.

Jessie reaches the water first and shrieks as it hits her ankles. The shock on her face is instantly replaced by a bright, carefree smile and she places her hands on her knees to steady herself as she folds over in laughter. Jessie has *no idea* – no clue at all that she just spent the night with someone who's been on trial for murder. It'll be interesting when the truth about that comes to light. Polly wonders if Jessie gave Miles the full rundown of her own baggage: a divorce at twenty-nine, the nervous breakdown that followed. Polly got the whole story last night from Faith.

'We need to make a decision,' Miles says.

'What?'

'We've only got a couple more nights left at the hotel – where are we going next?'

She digs her toes into the coarse sand. 'There's no hurry, is there? We could extend the booking, if we want?'

'You like it here, do you?' Miles pulls his phone from his pocket.

'I didn't say that. But I need to get *some* work done, and it's hard to do that if we're moving around the whole time.' Polly's immediately aware her argument is undermined by the fact she's lying on a beach. It is true, though. Her business is currently being looked after by Dee, her most senior employee. Dee's been a lifesaver, but she can't manage everything on her own. Her other two employees, Marco and Callie, are quite green and need a fair amount of handholding. And there's admin to keep across.

'Yeah, sure.' Miles's words come out airy and slow, and suggest he's stopped listening. He's been distracted by something on his phone, and his eyebrows are low as he stares at the screen. Out in the lake, there's a scream as Faith splashes water on to Jessie's dry upper body.

Polly turns to face her brother. 'What's the matter?' she says.

'I've got another one. Another one of those Caira emails.'

'Yeah, you already told me that. Are you sure you're okay?'

He turns to look at her and shows his screen, on which Outlook is open. 'No, I mean I've got *another* one. Like, just now. Look.' Miles points to the timestamp. 12.39 p.m. – the same as on the digital clock at the top of the screen.

Polly removes her shades and folds them in her hand, squinting at the blinding sunlight reflecting off the lake. 'I don't think we should listen to it. Just send it on to the police.'

Miles presses his lips. 'Maybe we should listen to it – at least then we know what we're dealing with. Are you sure we shouldn't just play a—'

'Oh, just play it, then.'

His eyes widen in surprise, and he holds his phone out between them, eyebrows raised. 'Are you sure?'

'Go on,' Polly says. She leans in closer and fans herself with her hand.

Miles presses play, and Caira's voice, or more accurately the computerised reproduction of it, begins: *Hi, Miles. I hope you've not got a sore head after drinking all that Macallan. This is not over.*

Polly knew it was coming, but the voice still causes her skin to prickle. There's something about the way the words are delivered so dispassionately, in a matter-of-fact tone that is completely detached from the context. Exactly as might a ghost. Miles's eyes have lost focus, and she can almost see the colour draining from his face. 'Macallan,' she says. 'That's weirdly specific.'

Miles rubs his hand across his forehead. 'I know.'

'But you weren't drinking that, were you? You were on beer and wine, as I remember.'

Miles doesn't reply, then he lurches to his feet. 'Bloody hell,' he says, half under his breath.

Polly stands. 'What's the matter?'

Miles pulls at his fingers. 'This is bad.'

'What is?'

'The thing is: we *did* have Macallan yesterday. At the bar, when we arrived at The Globe. So how do *they* know that?'

Polly thinks for a moment. She needs to say something reassuring. But he's right, this is bad. 'I'm sure there's an explanation. Who knew about the Macallan? I don't remember you mentioning it.'

'Just the boys, as far as I know.'

'Maybe one of them posted about it on socials? Their accounts aren't private, are they?'

Miles glares at her. 'Or maybe one of them is trying to wind me up.'

'You think one of them is sending the emails? That's impossible.'

'Is it? Everything seems impossible until it happens. And a lot of things that I thought were impossible have happened to me, lately.' He turns to walk back in the direction he came, then looks over his shoulder. 'Nothing surprises me anymore.'

Polly starts after him. 'Wait!' She points at their belongings on the sand. 'I can't just leave all their stuff here.'

'You stay,' he hollers back. 'This is between me and them.'

CHAPTER 21

MILES

Miles stomps along the waterfront, past the main pier with its bright signs advertising boat trips, and sees his three friends ambling in his direction. He quickens his step, and his heart rate, already high, ticks up with it. George has spotted him. He points and says something to the other two. As Miles gets closer, it becomes audible – something about him being a *snake* – and, when he gets closer still, George addresses him directly: 'I'm only letting you get away with this because of your annus horribilis, you little—'

'Shut up,' Miles snaps. He pounds right up to them, causing all three to come to an abrupt stop.

'What's up with you?'

Miles jabs a finger in their direction. 'I think you know. At least one of you knows.' George, Reubyn and Elis trade looks. They appear genuinely baffled. Either Miles has got this wrong, or someone here is a convincing liar. 'If you're playing some kind of joke,' he says, 'then I want to know now, because it's not funny.'

They stand, bewildered, for a few moments, and then Reubyn breaks the silence. 'Honestly, I don't think any of us has a clue what you're talking about.'

'Okay' – Miles takes his phone out and opens his emails – 'maybe this will jog your memory. I received it about ten minutes ago.'

The four of them huddle around Miles's phone and he presses play on the audio file. Miles studies their reactions. If anything, they appear even more confused than before. Shocked, even. When it's over, they all stare at him, eyes wide.

'Mate,' Reubyn says, 'seriously, why would any of us do this? We're your *friends*.'

Looking at them now, the realisation that he's right lands with a thumping clarity. There is no plausible reason for them to do it. 'So how do they know about the Macallan, then?'

George shrugs. 'God knows.'

'Did any of you mention the Macallan? To anyone at all?'

They shake their heads.

'What about on your socials? Did you post it anywhere? Or write it in an email?'

'It was just a drink,' George says. 'It's nothing to write home about.'

'So, you're sure? We're the only ones who know about it?'

'We must be,' Elis says. 'Just us four and the woman who poured it.'

There's a silence, then Miles turns around, looking in the direction of The Globe. The bar staff – he's right, they might know something. 'I'm going over there,' Miles says. 'I need to talk to her.'

The others follow, and George falls in by Miles's side. 'What are you hoping to get out of this?'

'I'm not sure. But I've got to do something.'

'You'd be better off going to the police.'

Miles stops by the side of the road, waiting for traffic to pass. 'I will. But right now, they'll be asleep. It's the middle of the night back at home.'

'I mean here. We could go to the local police station.'

They seize a small break in the traffic and jog across. 'That would be pointless,' Miles says, slightly out of breath. 'I'm not spending the next two hours explaining this whole saga to PC Plod from Queenstown police.'

They arrive at The Globe. It's much quieter than yesterday, but it's early – they probably just opened. Miles tells the other three to stay outside, but George ignores the instruction, following him through the door. Inside are two men: one behind the bar who unfolds his arms as they enter, and one in a pale pink shirt who doesn't look up from his laptop. Miles heads straight to the bar, and George skips ahead of him.

The barman smiles. '*Kia ora*. What can I get you?'

'There was a girl working here yesterday,' George says. 'Blonde hair, tattoos, nose ring. Is she around?'

The smile disappears. 'Are you a friend, or something?'

'Not exactly. We just need to talk to her for a minute.'

'She's got a boyfriend, bro, if that's why you're here.'

'It's not that,' Miles interjects. 'We were in here yesterday and—'

Miles stops at the sound of an old throat being cleared, like a shovel being driven into hard ground. They turn around to see Pink Shirt, a short, grey man with a face full of broken capillaries, who has departed his laptop and crept up behind them. 'Is there something I can help with? I'm the owner.'

'They want to talk to Heather,' the barman says.

'I gathered that much.' The owner straightens, summoning as much height as he can muster. 'But I'm afraid we don't give out the contact details of our staff to random blokes.'

Miles shows his palms. 'Look, I'm not some weirdo. It's just I think she might be able to help me.'

'And how's that?'

'I think' – Miles exhales slowly – 'I think I might be being followed.'

'Right.'

'So, is she on shift today?'

'She's not here.'

'When will she be in?'

The owner pinches at the loose, ruddy skin under his chin. 'Look, I know who you are.'

Miles tries not to react. But his heart has just been punched out of rhythm. 'You do?'

'You're Miles, right? One of my staff recognised you when you were in here yesterday. I'm not judging, or whatever, but I don't want any drama in my bar.'

The heat in the room rises, and Miles feels strangely naked, feels the judgement of the man standing in front of him.

'He hasn't done anything wrong,' George says. 'He was falsely accused.'

The owner's eyes flick to George. He opens his mouth, and his attention is drawn towards the door. They all turn to look. Walking in with a backpack hanging from her tattooed shoulders is the bartender from yesterday. Heather, apparently. She stops in the middle of the room, confused by the four sets of eyes locked on her. 'Hi,' she says, with a drawn-out rising inflection that makes it sound more like a question. 'Is everything okay?'

'Give us a minute,' the owner says. He shoots Miles a look as he leads Heather to a table in the corner. Miles feels the barman's stare burning into him, also. His cover has been blown – all the staff here know who he is, and they'll all have been gossiping about him. How on earth was he recognised on the other side of the world? Do the people of New Zealand really take such an interest in the court cases of the UK? It seems unlikely. Although places like this have a high turnover of staff and it's plausible some of them are British.

'All right,' hollers the owner, beckoning Miles over.

'You stay here,' Miles says to George. He crosses the wooden boards to the table in the far corner where the owner and Heather sit on one side. Miles takes a seat opposite.

'Okay,' the owner says. 'What's this about?'

Miles takes a deep breath. How to explain this without sounding completely insane. 'I think I might have a stalker.'

They wait for him to continue. Heather's eyes narrow in confusion.

'Last night, my friend over there' – pointing to George – 'ordered four glasses of whisky from you. It was a specific brand, Macallan.'

'I remember,' Heather says, her voice light. 'We don't sell much of that.'

'Right. But the trouble is: someone is threatening me, and somehow that person knows I had Macallan last night.'

Heather's eyes widen and she glances sideways at her boss. 'Wait, you're not suggesting *I've* been . . .' – she shakes her head, lost for words – 'I've never met you before in my life.'

'No,' Miles says. 'I'm not suggesting you've done anything wrong – nothing whatsoever. But did you mention it to anyone? Does anyone else know that we had Macallan last night?'

'Remember, you don't have to answer anything you don't want to,' the owner says, unhelpfully.

'That's right,' Miles says. 'I'm not trying to put pressure on you. But someone is making my life hell, and I'd like to be able to report them to the police.'

Heather is silent for a moment. Her eyes wander, tracing across the ceiling, then fix again on Miles. 'Actually, there was something.'

Miles shifts in his seat. 'Okay. What was it?'

'There was this guy, he came up to the bar and asked what the English blokes were drinking. I told him about the Macallan, and he asked to have the same. I told him the price, and then he changed his mind and ordered a cheaper whisky. I did think it was quite strange.'

Miles leans in, elbows on the table. 'What did he look like?'

'Just an average guy,' Heather says.

Miles's eye twitches. 'Can you be any more specific?'

She shrugs. 'He was average height, dark hair – cut short, like your friend's over there.' Heather thinks for a moment. 'And he had a beard. Well, not a beard, exactly, but, you know, some stubble.'

'Anything else? What was he wearing? Did he have an accent?'

'All right, that's enough,' the owner says, as Heather opens her mouth to speak. 'Heather here needs to start her shift.'

Miles's mouth falls open. 'Wait. What? This is important.'

The owner stands. 'And so is the privacy of my customers.'

'This is going to be a police matter,' Miles says, also rising to his feet.

'And are you a police officer?'

'No, obviously not, but they'll be investigating this, I guarantee it.'

'That's great – you send them my way. They can talk to whoever they want. I've got CCTV cameras, receipts, the works. I'm all above board. Whatever they want, I'll hand it over, but for now, we're done here, so order a drink or piss off.'

The owner folds his arms and nods at Heather, who scurries off and disappears into a backroom. He lifts his tangled white eyebrows at Miles.

'Thanks for your time,' Miles says. He leaves the table and walks out of the bar, closely followed by George.

Outside, Reubyn and Elis are sat at a table in the shade of a parasol. Their conversation ceases. 'Any joy?' Reubyn asks.

Miles slumps heavily on to the bench. 'I'm definitely being followed.' His eyes dart all around – checking for eavesdroppers, especially any that might match the description given by Heather – and then he gives his friends the full rundown of what he's just heard, his heart galloping along with the whole story.

'Bloody hell,' Elis says after a short silence, once Miles has inflated his cheeks to indicate he's finished. 'What are you going to do?'

'There's not a lot I can do. Obviously, I'll pass on everything I've found out to the police, but I doubt they'll get on to it very quickly. And in the meantime . . .'

Miles shakes his head; he doesn't need to articulate it because they all know: in the meantime, this holiday has been ruined. The longer he sits there in silence, the more it dawns on him just how disastrous this all is. It's as if the problem facing him has gained a physical mass, has him surrounded and is pressing at his flesh from all angles. Now, there is no doubt: the person who's harassing him *has* travelled to New Zealand, and that raises a whole new set of questions to which the possible answers create increasingly dark and nightmarish scenarios. Who is Alex Burnfield, the stubbled barfly with the AI Caira voice? What's his motive? What's he planning to do? If *this is not over*, then what the hell is going to happen next? Is Miles in danger? And to what extent? Before, it was easy enough to dismiss the emails as the work of a troll – a keyboard warrior who was out to unsettle him from behind the murky veil of the internet. But now, this has to be taken seriously. Travelling to New Zealand is a significant investment – both in time and in money – and that points to this man being hell-bent on carrying out whatever he's got planned. There is every chance he could be unhinged, or completely insane. And what should Miles do before the police track him down? Hide away in his hotel room? Abandon Queenstown and flee somewhere more remote?

George waves a hand across Miles's field of vision, which has turned misty as his thoughts run wild. 'What if we don't have to wait?'

A sparrow lands on their table and skitters about, pecking at a few stray crumbs. They behave differently, here, the birds. They're bolder, reckless in the face of danger. The scruffy little sparrow is inches away – if Miles were so inclined, he could whip out an arm and snatch it.

'Miles,' George says, raising his voice. 'What if we don't have to—'

'I heard you the first time.' Miles glares at him irritably. 'What are you on about?'

'I mean, we should take action.' His eyes are piercing, serious. 'We should strike while the iron's hot.'

Miles huffs. 'And how, exactly, are we going to do that?'

'I've got an idea,' George says. 'A way to identify him. Whoever this bastard is who's following you, I wonder if we can smoke him out.'

CHAPTER 22

REUBYN

They arrive back at the bar early, around six o'clock, this time with the girls. Reubyn stays close to Faith as they walk in, to make sure he can get a seat next to her. She was friendly the previous night, enough to make him think he might have a chance, and this is an opportunity to deepen the connection between them. Yes, they're here for other reasons as well, but there is absolutely no harm in Reubyn getting to know her a little better and seeing where that leads.

In accordance with George's plan – or identification strategy, as he's begun calling it – most of their group sits at a large table in the middle of the room, and George, arriving separately with a baseball cap pulled low at the front, heads straight upstairs to the mezzanine level and takes a seat overlooking the whole space. His plan, when he explained it earlier, seemed almost too simple to be of any use. But, in the absence of any better ideas, Miles decided it was worth a try. Probably because the alternative is doing nothing.

The idea, which Jessie and Faith have been told nothing about, is to have a normal night out and behave as if nothing is troubling them whatsoever. Meanwhile, George – who the girls believe is absent due to a migraine – will be scanning the room for anyone who might be surreptitiously keeping an eye on Miles. If he can identify the person watching Miles, and if they match the description given by Heather, then they can follow him when he leaves. They've made the decision not to confront anyone in the bar. They don't want to risk making a scene and security getting involved. Plus, if they follow Miles's stalker, they might be able to find out where he's staying, which would be crucial information to pass on to the police.

Reubyn waits until Faith takes her position at the far end of the table and sits next to her. She's dressed casually tonight, her peacock-blue blouse chiming with her eyeshadow, and, as he pulls his chair in, he's gently intoxicated by the sweet woody scent of her perfume. Miles, sat opposite, isn't doing the best job of appearing relaxed: he pulls at the collar of his shirt and shifts in his seat. At least his eyes aren't searching the room, which is the main thing. Polly hands out the first round of drinks, and a discussion begins about the recent solar eclipse and how the viewing experience compared between Europe and America. Reubyn turns to Faith, boxing them into their own private conversation. 'So, do you still want to be a YouTuber, after everything I told you last night?'

'Are you serious? Of course I do, totally.'

'I thought I might have put you off for life.'

She laughs. 'I'm a recruitment agent. Compared to mine, your work is literally thrilling.'

Reubyn gets the conversation flowing by asking polite questions about her job. *Ask questions and really listen* – that was another key takeaway from Dr Jane Sheridan. And the more he listens to Faith talk about her job, the more he silently agrees with her – working in recruitment *is* a waste of her time, a waste of her life. She spends eight hours a day in an office she dislikes, doing work that she hates, which involves organising people into jobs that they, in turn, hate. And all the while she earns little more than enough to cover her living expenses in western Sydney. Faith is bright; there is no limit to all the exciting things she could do if she only believed in herself, and Reubyn makes a point of telling her that several times.

Before long it's Reubyn's round, and on the way to the bar he steals a glance up at George, who leans against the balcony rail, purportedly reading a book. As Reubyn waits for cocktails to be shaken and poured, he ponders how much he should reveal to Faith about his work. She hasn't asked how much he earns from his channel but seems to be under the impression he makes a fortune. It would be stupid to shatter that illusion right away. Faith seems to be in complete awe of his job, of how he's able to make a living doing something he loves. But the truth is, he really should've had a second job these last couple of years to supplement the income he gets from YouTube. But he didn't do that. Instead, he took out loans. And lately he's been struggling to stay afloat.

The trouble is: none of his peers do menial work to boost their incomes. There is a stigma around it, the way it lowers social standing. He could just imagine how George would react: *time is one's most valuable commodity*, he would say, and it so follows that no one should waste time on work that doesn't advance their career, raise their status or, at the very least, earn them shedloads of cash.

Reubyn should've swallowed his pride and got a job in a pub or shop – anything to help balance the books while he was growing his channel. But people from Holvine don't have jobs like that; they either get cool jobs, or jobs that progress fast, earning them a ton of money or power. If they're lucky, they get one that comes with all of those things, and then they're included in the 'notable alumni' section of the school's Wikipedia page. Reubyn isn't there yet, but, if he sticks to the path he's on, pours all his effort into it, one day he might be. In the meantime, all he's got is debt. And, like an invasive knotweed, it seems to grow and multiply no matter how much he tries to beat it back. He's committed to his business now, invested heavily, and he needs to make a success of it, and fast, or soon that debt is going to swallow him whole.

Reubyn sets a tray of drinks on the table, his fingers sticky from the syrupy spillage that's collected in a moat around the edge. He hands out the cocktails, saving the last two for Faith and himself.

Faith thanks him and takes a sip. 'So, you never actually told me how you got started as a content creator. You know, like you promised you were going to.'

Reubyn takes a sip of his own cocktail, and a few flakes of salt from the rim cling to his lower lip. 'Well,' he says, clearing the salt with his thumb, 'it wasn't my first choice. When I was younger, I assumed I would get a job in the TV industry.'

Her right eyebrow shoots up, as if on a string. 'You *assumed*? Isn't that quite a competitive industry to get into?'

'Yeah, I know, but you assume you can do the same job as your parents, right? And my dad's a TV producer.'

'Wow. Cool. What kind of shows?'

'He used to run a show called *Dealbreaker*, it was this game show where—'

'I know it!' Faith's face springs open. 'Oh my God, I loved *Dealbreaker* as a kid. We used to get it in Australia.'

Reubyn feels a warm rush of pride. 'That doesn't surprise me. It was massive, back in the day. They used to make millions off the phone-ins alone.'

'Did you ever meet Tony Meadows?'

Reubyn laughs. 'That's all anyone ever asks about it – do I know Tony.'

'And do you? What's he like?'

'I got to know him quite well, actually. He used to come round to the house a lot, especially after Mum died.'

'Oh, I'm sorry.'

The atmosphere between them has shifted, and Reubyn immediately regrets mentioning his mother. 'It's okay. I was pretty young when it happened – I've had a long time to come to terms with it.'

Her face is crumpled in sympathy. Reubyn wants it to beam back to life, so he turns the conversation back to Meadows. 'Tony was exactly like he was on TV – a mile a minute, never stopped talking. He and Dad were really close, and he even babysat for me, sometimes, when he needed a break.'

'Tony Meadows was your *babysitter*? That's insane. You guys come from a different planet, I swear.'

Reubyn shifts his chair a little closer. The music seems to be getting incrementally louder as the bar fills up, and now they can barely hear each other over the booming bass and thrum of voices. 'It was a strange time, that's for sure,' Reubyn says. 'I did work experience on *Dealbreaker*, as a runner – stuff like that. But it became clear pretty quickly that there wasn't going to be a career path for me.'

'Why?' Faith asks, glancing at him briefly before turning her head so Reubyn can speak directly into her ear.

'That whole industry has changed. About ten years ago, Dad's work all started drying up. And if there was any work, he had to travel to Belfast or Scotland or something, for weeks at a time. It's got to the point now where he's in the middle of his career and he's barely working. It's stressful. He's got no income. I'm not signing up for that.'

'But, why? I mean, why is there suddenly no work? He was the producer on *Dealbreaker* – surely he's in demand?'

'It's because these TV shows just aren't getting made anymore.' Seeing her lips pressed in confusion, he explains: 'Some programmes are getting made, of course, the really high-budget shows, stuff for the big apps, but all those light-entertainment shows that used to be on TV all the time, like *Dealbreaker* – the demand for all that has fallen away. Think about it: everyone is on the streamers, listening to podcasts, watching social media shorts—'

'Watching YouTube.'

'Exactly. When I told Dad I wanted to start a YouTube channel, he encouraged me, because he could see what was happening. He helped me get started, sorted me out with the lighting and microphones and background set-up. I've got him to thank, really.'

'You're too modest. You're good at it. I watched another of your videos this morning. They're great. You're amazing.'

Faith stands, and as she leaves the table, she places her fingers on Reubyn's forearm and a bolt of electricity shoots through him. She smiles and then swishes off towards the bar.

Reubyn takes deep breaths. *You're amazing*. What did she mean by that? Is she amazed by his videos, or could it simply be that she finds him, Reubyn Carmichael, *amazing*?

Don't get carried away, he tells himself. She's being friendly because she wants to get started in the business and needs Reubyn's advice – that is still the most plausible explanation for what's going on here. But he's helpless as his heart and mind are carried off on a wave of hope. He watches as she disappears into a queue at the bar, then glances around. The volume of the music has split the table: Polly and Jessie are huddled in conversation, and Elis is barking something in Miles's ear.

Reubyn's phone vibrates in his pocket. He unlocks the screen and finds a new message in their WhatsApp group.

George: I think I've got him.

Miles must be reading it too because his eyes widen and then he slips his phone back into his pocket, all casual. A few seconds later, he takes the phone out and taps with his thumb. A new message appears.

Miles: OK. What now?

George is typing . . .

George: We wait. Act normally.

George is typing . . .

*George: When I say now, Miles you come and meet me by
the bar. Straight away, no delays. Understood?*

Miles: Got it.

Miles's lips twitch as he stares into his drink. It's clearly taking a lot of effort to prevent himself from becoming visibly alert and searching the room. If he's nervous, it's understandable. Reubyn didn't expect George's surveillance to actually lead anywhere, and he suspects Miles was doubtful, too. So, what's going to happen now? Whoever this stalker is, he could be dangerous. Armed, even. Will they follow him? Front him up? The only thing Reubyn knows for sure is: he's not getting involved. If it was up to him, they would lie low until the police have time to investigate. But he knows they won't wait. George is reckless and impatient, and Miles's desire to know who's following him has become all-consuming.

Faith is oblivious to the tension as she arrives with a tray of drinks. She hands them out and resumes her chat with Reubyn. As their talk continues, Reubyn keeps an eye on Miles. He's no longer talking to Elis; instead, he stares at the phone in his hand, no doubt waiting for George to say the word.

Reubyn and Faith chat about all manner of things that his friends would normally find too boring to discuss: posting schedules, lighting equipment, SEO, editing, analytics.

More drinks arrive at their table. And then more. For a short while, Reubyn is so wrapped up in his conversation that he forgets about George and his plan.

And then, just after midnight, it finally happens – Reubyn feels his phone vibrate. Miles is already up on his feet before Reubyn has time to open the app and see George's message. As promised, he's only written one word: *Now*.

CHAPTER 23

GEORGE

As soon as he's pressed send on the message, George hurries down the mezzanine stairs. He's been sat up there for hours, watching this man for two of them, and he's not about to let the bastard get away now. Miles must have seen his message because he is out of his chair and walking towards the bar. George rushes over, grabs Miles and steers him towards the door. 'We need to move,' he says.

They step outside, the pounding music still ringing in George's ears. Miles says nothing, just looks at him for a cue. George checks right and left. He points left and whispers in Miles's ear: 'You see that guy in the denim jacket?'

Miles nods and moves in his direction.

George holds him back. 'Wait. Not yet.'

They watch as the man ambles under the yellow glow of streetlights, past a row of shuttered shops. He glances briefly behind him and takes the corner.

'Okay, let's go,' George says.

'Are you sure that's him?' Miles whispers.

'I'm certain.'

Miles quickens his step. 'I didn't see any facial hair.'

'He's had a shave, obviously,' George says. 'Trust me, it's him – that freak has been watching you all night.'

It was about nine o'clock when George spotted him. Three hours he was sat up on the mezzanine, and the whole idea was beginning to seem like a waste of time. And then suddenly a shiver ran through him. There he was, sitting at a table with two women on the far side of the room. Short dark hair, black T-shirt. A hooked nose and thin lips. And he was staring straight at Miles. Straight at him. It was so obvious. The man turned his eyes to his two companions but before long they were back on Miles. And that's how it continued – his attention moving back and forth between them. Shortly before eleven, the two women left, and the man stayed put. And from that point on, he barely took his eyes off Miles. George tried to gauge the expression on the man's face. He looked thoughtful and sullen, but was there something else? Anger, maybe? It stirred something in George, too – an irritation that grew stronger the longer he looked at him, until it churned into fury. How dare this man come after his friend? After everything he's been through. With the memory of it clear in his mind, George quickens his step, and Miles shuffles his feet to keep up until they reach the end of the road.

They slow down as they round the corner on to a quiet street that leads towards the lake. The man walks the pavement under the shadow of storefront canopies. He pauses and looks back over his shoulder, but his face is unlit and featureless – barely more than a silhouette. He carries on, apparently untroubled by their presence. They're closer to him, now – around fifty yards away – close enough that they can hear his hard-soled shoes clop against the concrete. It's the only sound, save for their own footsteps and breathing. They daren't speak. The air carries not even a murmur, and the sky is cloudless, black and dusted with stars. A waning moon lights a faint path across the lake.

The man leaves the pavement, briefly looking back at them as he crosses the road. George and Miles share a glance. They keep their pace until he disappears around the corner, then George gives his friend a nod and they cross the street. His heart knocks against the wall of his chest. The temptation to run after the man is almost irresistible. All the questions he has for him turn over in his head. But they must keep their distance, for now. They need to see where he goes. They need to know where he calls home, for now at least. After that, all bets are off.

George and Miles reach the end of the street, where the waterfront opens up before them. They take the corner. George freezes. The street in front of them is empty. Completely empty. 'Bugger.' He stares at Miles. 'Where's he gone?' Between the street and the lake is a footpath, flanked by a column of trees. The path, intermittently illuminated by streetlights, is also deserted. But George's eye is drawn to thrashing, shadowy movement on the grass beyond. Someone sprinting. 'There!' he says, pointing as he charges forward. George and Miles run after the man, who now has about a hundred yards on them. He must've started his sprint the second he went around the corner. How could they have been so stupid? They charge along the path, past a playground and the last buildings before the waterfront gives way to a wooded park. The man runs into it and takes a right where the path forks in two. George and Miles continue their chase into the park. It's even darker, here. Fewer lamps light the path, and for a moment the man disappears into the shadows. George tries to find an extra gear. Miles is falling a few paces behind. The man reappears, then darts off into the trees. Within seconds, he's faded into the darkness.

George chases across the uneven grass. His eyes dart about as he sprints, searching for any movement. He gambles and turns right. But it's dark and he can't see the man anywhere. He slows to a tentative jog. A grid of shadows, cast where feeble lamplight has struck the trees, quickly fades, and within thirty seconds he's shrouded by the pitch-black. The man has disappeared. And now George realises his mistake – he's completely exposed. They just followed some psychopath into a dark and empty park in the middle of the night, and now they don't know where he is.

George glances back to the path, which lies empty. He stops dead, listens. A hushed whisper from the leaves above. Light footsteps on the grass. A hand grabs George's shoulder, and his guts turn to liquid.

George spins around to see Miles, his face cut in half by a grey trace of moonlight. 'Bloody hell, don't do that,' he says, through gritted teeth.

'I think we should leave,' Miles says.

'Hard agree.'

George spins slowly, taking a final look around for any sign of the man, then walks back towards the path, with Miles at his side. Once they're under the glow of lamplight, George turns and shouts: 'Stay away from my friend!' There's no echo to his words – they die instantly on the night air. And there's no response.

Miles tugs at George's arm. 'Come on.'

They move quickly, back to the waterfront. On the way, Miles stares ahead as if in a daze. George vocalises his thoughts as they go. '*How did we let him get away? He was fast, wasn't he, faster than I expected. Who the bloody hell is he? What does he want?*'

Miles is monosyllabic in response to everything he says, to the point that George starts to wonder if he's being punished with silence. Is he annoyed with George because the plan didn't work out exactly as it should? Surely not. It was a good idea, and George sacrificed his whole evening to make it happen – he relished the thought of being able to hold that bastard's feet to the fire and force him to explain what the hell he was doing.

No, Miles has just gone quiet because he needs to crunch the ramifications of it all. On one hand, Miles's stalker doesn't seem overly dangerous – he fled like a hare when they caught him off guard. But there's no denying he still has the upper hand, for now. Assuming the police take this seriously, it shouldn't take them long to find out who he is. But in the meantime, this man knows who they are; he knows *where* they are. And only he knows what the hell he's planning next.

They're approaching the hotel when Miles snaps out of his stupor. He grabs George by the shoulder. '*Please* tell me you got a picture of him.'

'Of course I did.'

George opens the camera roll on his phone and swipes through the pictures he took in the bar. Some are, admittedly, blurrier than others – he was some distance away when he took the shots, and he had to be sly about it. He selects the clearest one and zooms in. And there he is. He's smirking, the smug prick. At that point, he had no idea he'd been rumbled. But now they have a picture of him. Whoever he is, the net is about to close, and fast. George hands the phone over for Miles to examine. 'Here's your stalker,' he says. 'Do you recognise him?'

CHAPTER 24

MILES

Miles wakes alone. Jessie was keen to come over last night, but after what happened, Miles's head was too fraught to be dealing with company. Plus, he needed to give a full update to Lewin while everything was still fresh in his mind. It was nearly four in the morning when he finally pressed send on the email. He included everything: the Macallan, what Heather told him at The Globe, and the fiasco that led him and George to the park. Miles was in two minds about whether to include the whole story about the man they chased last night – he didn't want to appear to be taking the law into his own hands. But, after some thought, he decided to include the lot. He and George didn't do anything wrong. They only wanted to talk to the guy, and the fact he bolted was confirmation enough that they'd identified the right man. Miles signed off his email with a plea for the police to take the matter seriously and promptly track down his harasser. Lastly, he attached the photo George took on his phone while watching the man in the bar last night. It's slightly blurry, not totally sharp on the man's face, but clear enough for him to be identifiable. Unfortunately, though, it isn't possible for him to be identified by Miles. He must have stared at that picture for the best part of an hour, and concluded he's never seen him before. Or at least he has no memory of it. He certainly isn't Caira's ex, or any of her close relatives, or that weird junior barrister, or anyone in the public gallery during the trial. But, still, it is something of a breakthrough – George did well to get such a good image. They've done all they can. The police have everything they need to find this man – including a picture of him.

Miles swipes through his apps. As is always the case lately, his stomach curdles as he opens his emails – they so regularly bring bad news now. There's a new one from his mum, and a reply from Lewin. There is nothing from 'Caira Kennedy'. It's possible, he supposes, that the man behind those emails might have been sufficiently spooked that they might now cease altogether. Miles taps open the email from Lewin.

Good morning, Mr Deverill.

Thank you for your very detailed description of yesterday's events. I can assure you that we, in coordination with our colleagues at New Zealand Police, will be treating this as a priority and will update you as soon as we've been able to speak to the person you've identified. Our work to identify the author of the most recent communications you've received is underway and ongoing.

I must warn you, however, it is imperative you don't make any more attempts to confront any suspect yourself. Not only would you be putting yourself and others in danger, but the law would not look upon you with any leniency if you were to commit a crime during such an undertaking.

I strongly advise you to maintain a very low profile while we investigate, even if that means keeping to the confines

Miles closes the app and sits for a moment on the edge of the bed. There's something in the tone of Lewin's email that he doesn't appreciate. He sounds impatient. Patronising, maybe. Ungrateful, definitely. But maybe Miles is being oversensitive – the tone of an email can so easily be misinterpreted, can't it? With the human voice and expression removed from a communication, a man can cheerfully type out what he thinks is a polite message and it will be taken as pure poison by the recipient. Still, there was no word of thanks from the police for the way he and George effectively did their job for them last night. Surely their efforts deserve some kind of acknowledgement. George seemed to think they were worthy of a medal.

Miles goes to the window and opens the curtains. Once again, Queenstown is a different place; today, strong winds have chopped up the surface of the lake, and low-lying grey clouds have reduced the brightness to near zero. Down on the street, Miles's eye is drawn to a gleaming white motorhome that's newly parked up. It's too big for the space it's occupying and encroaches into the bus stop outside the hotel. Reubyn must be intrigued by it, because he's down there, pointing at the rear doors and talking to a woman in a black suit – the owner, presumably.

Miles dresses for what looks like chilly weather – jeans and a jacket – and heads out. It's eleven o'clock; he's missed breakfast, so he'll have to go foraging for something to eat. As he waits for the lift to take him down, Lewin's words repeat on him: *maintain a very low profile while we investigate, even if that means keeping to the confines of your hotel.* That's all well and good, but Lewin wouldn't want him to starve. And, after watching his stalker run for his life last night, he can all but rule out the possibility of him attacking Miles in the street as he walks to the corner shop – especially in broad daylight.

The lift pings as it reaches the ground floor, and Miles walks through the foyer to the sound of chaotic jazz. He's relieved to hear it fade out as he passes through the revolving doors.

Outside, Reubyn is still in conversation with the suit on the opposite side of the road. She's pointing to a panel on the side of the motorhome, which looks even more enormous from street level. It strikes Miles as odd that she's giving him such a thorough tour, but, on second thoughts, it isn't, really. If you show a genuine interest – and Reubyn can come across as quite overexcited at times – the proud owner of pretty much any luxury vehicle will likely bore you to tears by running through its specifications in granular detail. For a second, Miles considers crossing the street and joining the conversation, but he's not in the mood. Instead, he takes a left and walks towards the town.

A cold gust lifts the hair off his forehead and blows straight into his eyes. The weather here is so confused and chaotic, the way it changes its personality completely by the day – sometimes even by the hour. Yesterday it was warm enough for the beach, and now it feels like autumn has suddenly blown in.

Miles is about twenty yards down the pavement and squinting into the wind when he becomes aware of someone out of the corner of his eye. A woman in an orange dress has left the bus stop opposite and is crossing the road in his direction. Miles glances at her and keeps moving, quickening his step. His focus is straight ahead, but, in his periphery, she is nearing – a body of blurry orange, her dark hair thrashing in the wind. When she's a few yards away Miles is forced to stop. He tenses, stares right at her. And she looks right back, her face soft. 'Miles?' she says, and as she holds her phone out in front of her, he knows exactly what's going on.

Miles's heart thumps into a new gear. He says nothing, just glares at her. There's no room left for politeness – what's happening here is completely out of order.

Her smile is even smaller this time. 'My name's Felicity and I'm here on behalf of *The Chronicle*. I just wanted to ask you a couple of questions about your trip – is it going well?'

'From *The Chronicle*?' Miles snaps. 'They sent you all the way over here?'

Again, that smile. But this time it doesn't show in her eyes, just pinches at the corners of her mouth. 'No, not exactly. I'm a freelancer, here on their behalf. I'm based in Invercargill. So, are you having a good time here in New Zealand?'

Miles stares out at the lake. He remembers that shutter noise yesterday as he left the hotel. It occurred to him then that it could've been a paparazzo, but he'd ruled it out – it had seemed absurd. Suddenly it doesn't. He fixes his stare back on to the reporter. 'Did you have a photographer here yesterday? Taking pictures of me.'

She shakes her head. 'Sorry, I wouldn't know about that.'

Like hell she wouldn't. Miles's eyes dart all around, examining the cars and trees. 'Is there a photographer here now?'

'No, definitely not. Now, tell me about your trip – what do you think of Queenstown?'

'I'm not talking to you.' He turns on his heels and walks back towards the hotel.

'Miles, I didn't mean to startle you. I'd love to hear about the first few days of your—'

He spins back around. 'Leave me alone!' His shout turns the heads of Reubyn and the suited woman across the road, and then

Miles storms back into the hotel, his veins electrified with anger. He hurries through the lobby and takes the stairs up to his floor.

Back in his room, he draws the curtains and slumps on to the bed, his hands cupped over his face. Miles squeezes his eyes as tears threaten. What on earth is going on? He came to Queenstown to escape, but seemingly he has escaped nothing. His stalker has followed him to New Zealand. The hounding reporters have found him, too. He thought he'd find anonymity here, but even the bar staff know who he is. Miles could have remained in Britain and stayed with his family for a few weeks until everything had blown over. Instead, he's a prisoner in a hotel room on the other side of the world.

Miles runs his name through Google News. There are no new articles yet, although he suspects it's only a matter of time. He tries to guess what the headline will be. He can't put his finger on the right combination of words, but he can imagine the gist: a rich kid who should be firmly behind bars is instead sunning himself in luxury others can only dream of. Miles is still doomfully envisioning the story – and the pictures, and the comments, and the shares – when there's a knock at the door.

He stands, suddenly light-headed. It can't be the reporter, surely? She wouldn't follow him into the hotel? The staff on reception wouldn't just give out his room number, would they?

Miles tiptoes over to the door, careful not to make even the slightest sound to confirm his presence, and peers through the spyhole.

CHAPTER 25

REUBYN

Anxiety is written all over Miles's face as he opens the door.

'Is everything all right?' Reubyn delivers the words with a grimace that suggests he knows everything is very much *not* all right.

Miles ruffles his hair with the palm of his free hand as he holds the door open. 'I just got accosted by another reporter.' He looks up and down the corridor and closes the door behind them. 'It's happening again.'

Reubyn perches on the desk, his lips pressed into a line. 'I saw the reporter. Is there anything you want me to do?'

'I don't think there's anything we *can* do.' Miles falls silent for a moment, then sighs heavily. 'I'm waiting for the police to get back to me about last night, and in the meantime, I can't even go to the bloody shop without getting harassed.'

Reubyn frowns and shakes his head. Poor Miles is really being put through the wringer, and the timing of these most recent unfortunate events couldn't be worse. Reubyn took ownership of the bus this morning, and it's incredible – even better than the pictures suggested. It's been months in the planning, and he's been so looking forward to showing Miles. But he has a feeling that unveiling it now might be inappropriate. Like cracking a joke at a funeral, it might be just the thing to lift spirits, but there's also a significant risk it could make matters worse. Reubyn walks over to the window and peers through a gap in the curtains. He looks at Miles and opens his mouth to speak, then changes his mind. He scratches his head. 'I don't know whether to tell you this or not.'

Miles clenches his teeth. 'Oh God. What now?'

'It's not like that. It's nothing to worry about.'

'Yeah, well, whatever it is, it can't make things worse than they already are.'

Reubyn's heart flutters as he grips the curtain and begins to pull it back.

'Don't,' Miles says. 'I think there's a photographer out there.'

Reubyn lets go, having widened the gap in the curtains by about a foot, and a shaft of light pierces the centre of the room. 'But I need to show you. The thing is, it's parked outside.'

'What is?' As soon as the words leave his lips, Miles's expression changes – his eyes bulge at a realisation. *He knows*, Reubyn thinks. Miles will have noticed the bus parked outside the hotel – it's not like it blends in.

Reubyn waves him over. 'Come and have a look.'

Miles walks to the window and peers out through the curtains.

Reubyn pulls a set of keys out of his pocket and tosses them into his hand. 'That motorhome down there, it was meant to be a surprise, but in light of what's been going on, I guess you're probably not in the mood for surprises.'

They both stare down at the vehicle, taking in its sheer magnitude – it's the size of a coach. It's also new and immaculate. The motorhome is on six wheels, and the body is covered in panels and hatches – all hiding fancy features powered by hydraulics.

'What is this?' Miles says. 'Have you hired it or something?'

'No, I got it through a brand partnership. Normal deal – I just need to promote it with some video content. It's ours for a week. If you want it, that is.'

Miles is silent. His eyes dart and flicker. And then he smiles, a broad, easy grin – the first time Reubyn has seen him smile in days – and it spreads like a virus to Reubyn's own lips. 'Mate,' Miles says, 'this is perfect. I mean, it's *perfect*.' He slaps Reubyn on the back. 'I can't believe you did this. It's *genius*.'

Reubyn beams. 'I'm glad you like it.'

'I have questions, though.'

'Fire away.'

Miles points out of the window. 'Do you even know how to drive that thing?'

Reubyn laughs. 'Yep. I had a go just now.' He decides not to mention the fact that, strictly speaking, he's meant to have an HGV licence – something he assured the company he had. 'I've had some lessons. It'll be worth it, I reckon. I should get some good content out of it.'

'When can we leave?'

'Whenever we want.'

'Tonight?'

Reubyn shrugs. 'We *could*. But I would suggest we load up on supplies, get everything we need, and then move on in the morning.'

'Okay, okay.' Miles nods, his eyes scanning the room, where his belongings are spread out across the space. He opens his case, and then picks up a pair of jeans, rolls them up and puts them inside. 'What about the girls? Can they come?'

Reubyn grins. 'I'm glad you asked. I've already told Faith about it, and she wants to join.'

'She does?'

'She wants to be a YouTuber, and she's offered to help as a kind of intern.'

Miles grins back. It's incredible to see how much his mood has suddenly lifted. He takes another look down at the motorhome. 'But would there be enough space? If they both came, that would make seven of us.'

'There's loads of room.' Reubyn hooks a finger to beckon Miles, whose newly found energy has caused him to wander all over the room, tidying various items into his case. He points at the vehicle. 'You see those panels on the side of the bus?'

'Yeah.'

'When it's parked up, those side bits can extend, so the interior pretty much doubles in size. We could fit ten people in there, easy. It's epic inside, it really is. Do you want to come down and take a look?'

Miles shakes his head. 'Not right now.'

Reubyn's smile fades. 'Yeah, of course. I wasn't thinking.' He bites his lip and stares out of the window for a moment, then turns back to Miles. 'So, will you pitch the idea to Jessie?'

'Yeah. I'll invite her over here later. It's not like I can go out anywhere.'

'Yeah, right.' Reubyn sucks in his cheeks. He goes quiet for a moment, his brow furrowed, then takes a deep breath. 'Look' – then after a long pause – 'do you think it's time to be honest with the girls about what's going on?'

Miles stops still and narrows his eyes. 'Seriously? I doubt they'll be thrilled about coming with us if we suddenly mention a murder trial and a stalker.'

Reubyn lets go of a nervous laugh. 'Look, I want them to come, too. I'm just saying we probably ought to be open about it, so they know what they're getting involved in.'

Miles stares vacantly at the sunglasses case in his hands. He turns it over several times, then tosses it into the suitcase. 'I hear what you're saying, but it's not like we'd be putting them in any danger or anything. The whole point is we are moving *away* from trouble.'

Reubyn twists the corner of his mouth.

'I'll tell them,' Miles says. 'Let's just leave it a few days, until everything has settled down a bit. I just want things to be normal for a little while longer. Fair?'

'Okay,' Reubyn says. 'Fair. Let's be honest, it's a miracle they haven't found out already – why ruin it?' He claps his hands together. 'Right, I better get on. We need to stock up, fill the bus with supplies. Any requests?'

'Hang on a minute,' Miles says. 'You haven't even told me where we're going.'

'We can go anywhere – that's the whole point.'

'But where first? You must have some idea?'

'Well, there's not a lot of point in heading south because there's not much between here and Antarctica.'

'So, we go north?' Miles takes his phone out of his pocket, presumably to open a map.

'Basically, yeah. Ultimately, it's up to you where we go – it's your trip.'

'Is it all right if we go somewhere quiet? Somewhere a bit out of the way?'

Reubyn smiles. 'Absolutely. I think I know the perfect place.'

CHAPTER 26

MILES

Miles spots Jessie as soon as she arrives in the hotel bar, on the sixth floor. He waves to get her attention, and, after scanning the expansive space for a moment, she spots him and makes her way over. The bar is modern and minimalist, with low-seated soft furnishings and a wall of huge arched windows that look out on to the lake. Jessie has just missed sunset, and the vista to Miles's right is fading to black. He stands to greet her and leans in as she approaches, but she pulls away. He ushers her to sit by his side. 'How are you?'

Jessie drops a large black handbag on to the seat next to her. 'I just ran into Faith and Reubyn outside.' She stares at him wide-eyed.

'Oh, cool. Did you see the bus?'

'Yeah, uh-huh, I saw the bus.'

'Good. That's what I wanted to talk to you about.'

'I guessed that.' She folds her arms. 'Why didn't you tell me you were leaving tomorrow?'

Miles takes a deep breath. 'It's complicated. The thing is, I didn't really know myself.'

Jessie is silent, staring at him with a bewildered look in her eyes. It seems they might be about to have their first tiff, the kind of disagreement an established couple might have, which is ridiculous – they've only known each other for a couple of days. This level of relationship fast-tracking is only possible with a holiday romance.

Miles stands. 'Let me get you a drink. Then I'll explain.'

Jessie picks up the cocktail menu and glances at it for a few seconds at most. 'I'll have a margarita.'

Miles heads to the bar and orders Jessie's drink. As the waistcoated bartender begins adding tequila and lime juice to a shaker, Miles ponders how best to deal with this situation. It's unfortunate that Jessie bumped into Reubyn, because it would have been better if Miles had told her about the motorhome himself. But the truth is it came as a complete shock to him, too. Albeit a good shock. It means they can leave behind his stalker and the gossipers and the reporters. And if any of those catch up with them, then they can just travel on a bit further up the road. This is what they needed, all along. Miles was never going to get free by flying to a new location and staying put in that one place. But Jessie doesn't know about his predicament, so his haste to escape Queenstown will make no sense.

After a few minutes, Miles delivers the cocktail to Jessie, placing it on the table in front of her. She's wearing a white, fine-wool sweater, and she rolls up the sleeves before picking up her drink.

'So,' she says, after taking a sip. 'What was it you wanted to explain?'

Miles sits and takes a deep breath. 'Why don't you come with us?'

Jessie squints at him. 'Are you serious?'

'Yeah.'

'But this is the first I've heard of it. Why didn't you mention this yesterday? Or the day before?'

'Because I didn't know. Believe it or not, Reubyn only told me about the motorhome today.'

She rolls her eyes. 'Where are you even going?'

'We're going north, starting with the West Coast. It's supposed to be beautiful.'

'It's beautiful here, too. I like Queenstown. And I've got three more nights prepaid on my hotel.'

'So?'

'So, I can't throw away that kind of money. I must make a lot less than you think.'

'I'll cover it.'

Jessie tilts her head, confused. 'And why would you do that?'

'Because I like you. And I want you to come with us.'

Her face softens, and she smiles for the first time since she walked into the bar. 'You really want me to come?'

'Of course.'

Jessie is silent for a moment, her lips bunched up as she stares into her drink. Then she gives him a coy smile. 'I guess I *could* come. I mean, Faith's going, right?'

'Exactly, everyone's coming. It'll be great.'

'I'm kind of surprised Polly and George want to come. They don't seem like camping types.'

'Well, it's not camping, is it, really. Anyway, I managed to talk them around.'

'Of course you did, Miles.' She looks away, but not quickly enough to hide the knowing smirk that has pulled a dimple deep into her right cheek.

'What?'

'I feel like all your friends just do whatever you tell them to.'

'That's not true.'

'Yes, it is. It's like you have some kind of power over them. And I don't get it. Why would they keep the motorhome a secret from you? Is it, like, your birthday or something?'

Miles laughs. 'No. I guess Reubyn thought it would be a fun surprise, that's all.'

'There's no other reason?'

'No,' Miles says, and when the word departs his lips, it leaves a sour aftertaste. After he gave her a false surname, he promised himself that it would be the only time he told Jessie a direct lie. But what he's just said amounts to another one.

Jessie drains the remains of her drink. 'Okay, if I'm coming with you, I can't stay here any longer – I need to go pack.' She leans over and kisses him, then grabs her bag and leaves, pausing by the door to give Miles a cheery wave.

Miles stays in the bar for a few more minutes, to finish his beer. But that sour taste – the one that gets exponentially stronger every time you double down on a lie – can't be washed away. *It's only for a couple of days*, he reminds himself. When they've got to know each other a little better, he'll get it all out in the open. By that point, she'll know him and understand why he's had to hold it back. Just a couple more days, and he'll tell her everything.

CHAPTER 27

ALEX

Have you figured it out yet? Do you know who I am?

You know my face. In a strange way, you know me. At the very least, you've now realised that I'm close, haven't you, Miles? Very close. I like that.

I've come to enjoy it, you see, this little game of ours. It's like a drug. Every time I imagine your fear and confusion and torment, it gives me a little high. Yesterday, I glimpsed it on your face, and, oh my, that was something: a proper rush, like nothing I've ever felt. To know that *I* had caused your discomfort.

It's made me wonder if I should keep this going a little longer. Aside from everything else, it's nice to have a purpose. I've never really had that before. I'm not a religious person, but I'm starting to think this all might be the true meaning of my life – what I was put on Earth to do. Everything in the universe is held in such delicate balance: all these equal and opposite forces. Without such forces, the world would spin off into chaos, wouldn't it? What you did – an act of unthinkable evil – demands an equal and opposite force. A jury of your peers should've been able to see to that. But they got it all wrong, didn't they? And in a way, that's a good thing. Part of me longed for that not guilty verdict. Because what would you have got, had you been found guilty? Twenty-five years? Out on parole for good behaviour after twelve and a half? Would that amount to an equal and opposite force, for what you did? No. Of course it wouldn't. You took the life of an angel, and it shouldn't surprise you that what's coming for you in her place will be suitably dark.

You surprised me last night. Your behaviour was more impulsive and careless than I had predicted. I don't know *why* that surprised me, given what you did to Caira, but it did.

And speaking of things that shouldn't have surprised me but did, I saw your RV today. Very nice. Very nice indeed. I'd love to know what's going on inside your head, why you suddenly feel so compelled to leave Queenstown. Is it anything to do with me, Miles? Are you feeling unsettled, by any chance?

When I saw it, I had a sudden, nonsensical fear that you might leave immediately. That would've ruined everything. I almost abandoned my plans, and that would've been a disaster. You can't imagine my relief when I returned and saw the RV was still there, parked up outside your hotel.

You don't know where I was this afternoon, do you, Miles? Of course you don't. How could you? You don't even know who I am.

Well, here's what I did. I took a bus to a nearby town called Cromwell. I was expecting the place to be pretty rough, given what I was there to do. But it was quite nice. Not completely unlike Queenstown, in fact.

I was there for a meeting. That makes it sound like a formal affair, and it most certainly was not. It definitely wasn't the sort of meeting you can set up on LinkedIn – more the kind that is organised via a dubious contact and an encrypted messaging app.

Now, I don't get nervous often, Miles. But honestly, when I arrived at the agreed location – an empty car park behind a closed industrial unit on the town's southern fringe – my heart may have been going a teeny bit faster than normal. It didn't help that I had to wait around for about twenty minutes before he turned up to meet me. And I must confess, my nerves were in no way settled when I saw the size of him.

The man I met is a member of a biker gang. A *real* biker gang. How cool is that? He had a patched leather jacket and a facial tattoo and everything. And here's a weird thing: he was quite nice. Nicer than you, Miles. Isn't that strange? He's had a hard life – that's obvious just from looking at him – and he still turned out better than you, even with all the coddling and head starts you've been granted.

Koa is his name. Well, that's the name he gave me, anyway. I suspect I wasn't the only one to give a false name: 'Koa' and 'Alex'. We had a nice chat. Did you know, that until 2019 you could walk into a shop and buy pretty much any gun you wanted in New Zealand? You can't do that now. But Koa says the country is still full of assault weapons. When the government brought in their new laws, they held a firearms amnesty, but, funnily enough, the gangs weren't inclined to hand over all their guns. Why would they? Especially when their street value was about to go through the roof. It's not cheap to buy a gun on the black market here, I can now say that from experience. And I suspect Koa put the price up even higher when he heard my accent.

The one he sold me was small and heavy, with the serial number filed off. He told me it was used. Quite chilling, that, isn't it? Perhaps it's been used to kill before. Or, maybe, someone has just used it to scare people, or simply for target practice.

I suppose I will never know for sure. But I like to think that you will be the first. I like to think that when I pull the trigger on this thing, the first life it will ever take will be yours, Miles.

Now, let's both of us get some rest. Tomorrow promises to be a big day. I must say I'm rather excited by all the unknowns. One thing is for certain, though – I will be close behind you, every step of the way.

Safe travels, Miles. We will meet soon. And in the meantime, I've left a gift for you at reception.

PART THREE

CHAPTER 28

GEORGE

They set alarms for 6 a.m., but George is awake before any of them sound, having been shaken from his sleep by a bad dream. It's the second night in a row that's happened. Something about sharing a room with other males – and their night-time rustling and breathing and snores – has caused his unconscious mind to go wandering into the past, back to his old dorm room. And, in his dream, roles were reversed, to the point where a bad dream might threaten to warp into a full-blown nightmare.

Unlike Miles, George was a boarder at Holvine College. He spent so much of his childhood there; it's perfectly understandable that his dreams could easily lead him back up the driveway to its fort-like entrance and through its heavy gates. He can well recall the first time he made the trip to Holvine himself, even if time has applied a misty filter to the memory. He remembers the silent, sombre car journey. The monstrous way the main school building loomed above them as they drove in. His parents' chatter echoing through the stone corridors as he followed. And then, later, alone as the door clicked shut on a dusty dorm with a jigsaw of beds with colourful duvet covers and a window that looked out on to a bare wall; how he doubled over and sobbed, as quietly as he could but unable to stop until there was nothing left, like a sponge squeezed until it was rendered rugged and dry and rough to the touch. That was the laying of the foundations for character building, he would later learn. The kind of sadness he felt, heavy and desperate, didn't last for long – the body wouldn't allow it; the human instinct for survival forces one to move on and cope with one's surroundings. But it left its fingerprints. Oh, it got in all right, and like the woodworm that bore tiny holes in the beams and joists that held the school together, it left a mark. Some had it harder than others, that's for sure. In the dream he's just had, he was one of the unlucky ones.

George might not have wanted to be at boarding school, but he made a bloody good go of it. And, while he hated it at first, it didn't take long before he established his place at the top of the school's social hierarchy. Even a place that breeds alphas has its own pecking order, and the social structure at Holvine was well defined and rigorously self-policed. That was encouraged, to a point, George reckoned. There was a benefit for all involved. The beta males at Holvine would be so traumatised by their experience that, as soon as they got out into the real world, they would alpha the hell out of anyone who got in their way. Even the most feeble and impotent of Holviners would be able to seize some kind of power, somewhere, once they burst free of its walls.

George's drowsy eyes fall on Elis, who lies open-mouthed on the far side of the room, his chest slowly rising and falling in the languid rhythm of sleep. If that boy had turned up at Holvine, George would have shown him his place, explained where he fitted in. But here, for some reason, he simply will not stay in his lane. Elis cannot grasp the order of things. But he will, if he hangs around for long enough.

George's train of thought is derailed by the alarms. They begin within a second of each other, on Reubyn and Elis's phones.

Reubyn kills his and is up and out of bed with alarming enthusiasm. 'Come on, boys,' he says. He walks around the room, flicking various switches to turn on the lights. 'Let's go.'

George groans. 'Ten more minutes.'

'No, mate. We can't let Miles down.'

George lumbers out of bed and pulls on his clothes. To his right, Elis is doing the same, although he's yet to say a word.

Miles insisted they leave at dawn, which seemed a tad dramatic, George thought. He's a tourist going on a scenic drive, not a field marshal planning a surprise assault. But ultimately George has reluctantly accepted that Miles's reasoning is sound. Even the most dedicated of tabloid photographers wouldn't bother getting out of bed before seven. And the same could be said, he assumes, for stalkers.

All that aside, something about this plan seems fundamentally wrong. It's not just that George is opposed on a recreational level; there's a flaw to the logic of it that he can't quite identify. When he does, he'll be able to put a stop to this nonsense and see that they're rightfully reinstalled where they belong – booked in at a half-decent hotel. Until then, he's got little choice but to go along with it.

George heads into the bathroom to brush his teeth. He's nearly finished when Reubyn appears in the mirror, standing in the doorway with a backpack on his shoulders. 'We're heading downstairs.'

George glances at him in the mirror, then spits and turns on the tap.

Reubyn takes a couple of steps closer. 'Would you mind doing an idiot check before you leave? Also, can you go knock on Polly's door, make sure she's up and about?'

George turns his head and rolls his eyes to signal a reluctant acceptance of his demands. This isn't the normal way of things: Reubyn calling the shots and George bowing to his whims. Everything here is being turned on its head.

With Reubyn and Elis gone, George finishes up at the sink, packs his washbag into his case and performs a cursory check of the room. When he's done, he wheels his suitcase into the corridor. Polly's one floor below and, instead of waiting for the lift, he elects to take the stairs. When he reaches the lower stairwell, he hears the muffled sound of Polly's voice. There's a sharpness to it that causes him to pause instead of entering the corridor. Just as he strains to hear, she stops speaking. About ten seconds later, her voice returns.

'I can't believe it. It's so underhand and so . . . *devious*. How could you do that to Miles?'

George's body tenses with interest. He stands stock-still and waits for her to continue.

'That's completely irrelevant,' Polly says. 'You've betrayed me *and* my brother. What would you have done if I hadn't found out about that email? Would there have been more?'

George peers around the corner and sees Polly standing by the lift with her phone pressed to her ear, suitcase by her side. He pulls his head back to avoid being seen.

'I don't know yet,' Polly snaps, after a longer silence. 'Frankly, I don't think it's going to do him any good at all to hear about this right now. He's supposed to be on holiday.'

As she's speaking, the whir of the elevator increases in volume until it clunks into position and a chime announces its arrival. George extends the pullout handle on his suitcase and hurries into the corridor to see Polly already stepping inside. 'Hold the lift for me!'

Polly makes no attempt to halt the lift, and George arrives just in time to wedge his foot in between the closing doors. Phone still to her ear, she glowers at George as he hurries in. 'I've got to go,' she says bluntly into the phone. 'We'll talk about this later.'

She shoves her mobile into her handbag, then frowns at George as the lift descends. 'Good morning.'

'Good morning, Polly.'

'Did you happen to hear any of my conversation, just then?'

He pulls up a single eyebrow. 'I most certainly did.'

Polly groans. 'Why doesn't that surprise me. And what did you hear?'

'Enough. Are you going to tell me what's going on?'

CHAPTER 29

MILES

Miles watches from his window as Elis crosses the street towards the bus. Elis hesitates and appears to shake his head before boarding. Polly and George follow, a few minutes later. For Miles, it's his cue to leave – everyone is now on the bus but him. He drains his coffee and takes a final look out of the window. It's unsociably early and a litter picker is snatching wrappers off the pavement in the half-light. The sun has risen beyond the mountains to the left, but a mixture of cloud and fog has muted the dawn.

Not everyone was keen to leave this early, but Miles insisted on it – the sooner they hit the road, the better. The others haven't been told exactly where they're going – only that their first destination is the West Coast. Reubyn thought it would make sense to explain it on the way, or not at all, in case anyone challenged the idea. As for Miles, he only has two rules, which he's written in their WhatsApp group. Rule number one: no one is to mention the Caira Kennedy case to the girls until he does. And rule number two: there are to be no social media posts – especially about the bus, or anything that could identify where they're going. They must not be followed.

Miles leaves the room and takes the lift to the ground floor. He informs the receptionist that he's checking out and slides his keycard across the desk.

The receptionist, a mousy man in his thirties, smiles and taps at his keyboard. 'I hope you enjoyed your stay, Mr Deverill.'

'I did, very much. Thank you.'

Miles is presented with his bill for room service, which he pays for with a tap of his phone and then turns to leave.

'Oh, one more thing, sir.' Miles turns to see the receptionist waving a small, padded envelope in his hand. 'You have some correspondence.'

'Thanks.' Miles accepts it with hesitation and flips it over. Handwritten on the front is his name, followed by the hotel. There's no postmark. 'Do you know who left this?' he asks.

The receptionist gives him a thin-lipped smile – a mixture of politeness and confusion. He shakes his head. 'Sorry, I don't have a record of that.'

'Of course. Thanks very much.'

Miles folds the envelope into his pocket and rolls his luggage across the lobby. By the time he reaches the exit, the sting of alarm he felt at receiving hand-delivered mail here in New Zealand is already abating. There's a perfectly good explanation for it. At the conclusion of the trial, he received a whole collection of letters from journalists, all grovellingly polite as they tried to convince him to give an interview. What he has here must be another one – almost certainly from the reporter who accosted him yesterday.

Miles crosses the street towards the motorhome. A window is open on the vehicle and the patter of conversation leaks out. As he makes his way around to its far side, he double-glances at the bus's front, which has the hulking build and intimidating height of a truck cab. A door is open to a small staircase at the middle, and Miles grabs the steel handrail and ascends.

He's greeted by the scent of alpine air freshener and a strain of voices: the combined, multi-pitched groan of six people trying to muster their enthusiasm for the man who called them here at this ungodly hour.

'I saved you a space up front,' Reubyn hollers from the driver's seat.

There's a clunk and hiss as the staircase retracts and the door closes behind him.

Miles tenses his lips to contain his reaction at seeing the interior for the first time. It's strange: less like boarding a vehicle and more like walking into a hotel suite – albeit a claustrophobic one. To his left, the girls are spread across an arrangement of corner benches either side of a bolted-down coffee table. Everything is slate grey, save for a spatter of mustard-coloured cushions, lamps, and other benign furnishings of the kind you might find in a clinic's waiting room. Every inch of wall space is taken up with either windows or cabinets, and there is the sense that a much larger room has been compressed into this one, the air and space drawn out of it. Beyond the living area, there are four seats in two rows facing the windscreen and control panel. To Miles's right is a galley kitchen and, beyond that, a door to another room. Their luggage is piled up in the kitchen, along with food, pallets of bottled water and newly purchased sleeping bags – all the supplies Reubyn picked up from the shops yesterday. Miles adds his bag to the pile.

Jessie and Faith mirror his smile as he makes his way through the living area, although Polly barely glances up from her laptop. Miles takes the front passenger seat, with Elis and George behind.

Reubyn leans over and whispers: 'Any update from the cops, overnight?'

'Nope.'

Reubyn shakes his head as he fiddles with the controls. 'They're rubbish aren't they.' His tinkering triggers a wiper, and it screeches back and forth over the dry windscreen several times before he figures out how to switch it off. 'What about your stalker? Anything from them?'

'No, nothing, thankfully.' Miles strains his neck to see out of the window. 'Look, do you mind if we get moving?'

'Of course.' Reubyn does a final check in his mirrors, then presses the accelerator and releases the handbrake, and the bus crawls into the road.

Miles shifts in his seat for the first ten minutes of the journey, looking all around for any vehicles that might be following. He ignores the conversation behind him, which is about sleeping arrangements and is dominated by George's views on who should have the right to occupy the separate bedroom. As it's a Sunday morning, the roads are dead, and Miles is soon satisfied they're not being tailed. Roadside buildings quickly get fewer until there are none, and in what seems like no time at all the single carriageway cuts a path through a wild and lonely landscape.

Miles hooks his arm around the headrest and faces backwards. 'How cool is this?'

He nods enthusiastically at the others, and while his smile is genuine, it's tempered by guilt. If Miles was being upfront and honest with Jessie, there would be an open discussion going on about all the messed-up stuff that's happened. There would be speculation about the identity of the man who's been following him. He would be tearing open the letter that's in his pocket and showing his friends the latest example of what he's had to put up with. Instead, there is a strange atmosphere of false calm mixed with genuine excitement, and it's left Miles with a numb feeling in his stomach.

'It's so cool,' Jessie replies. 'Where are we camping tonight?'

'We're going to be driving up the West Coast,' Reubyn says, without taking his eyes off the road. 'It's quite remote out there.

I've found us a good camping spot where we can stay tonight. The weather's going to be crap for the next day or two, so we just need somewhere to hunker down, really.'

George rolls his eyes. 'Brilliant. Somewhere to hunker down. I'm glad we travelled halfway across the globe for that.'

'The more remote, the better, I reckon,' Elis says. 'That was always the point of coming somewhere like this – to get away from everyone.'

'Too bad we can't get away from you,' George says, his quip garnering a couple of awkward laughs.

Polly hasn't engaged in their conversation and instead mutters expletives as she attempts to do something on her laptop. She's hotspotting off her phone but the signal is getting increasingly temperamental the further they get from Queenstown. Elis is equally untalkative, and the chatter in the back fades away.

With no audible distractions, Miles focuses all his attention on the landscape in an attempt to clear his head. The whole point of this getaway is to allow his mind to switch off from the awful events of the trial and forget about his stalker. He's determined to do it. Miles is still convinced he's in the best place for a mental detox: views as dramatic as these must be able to distract from any thoughts. He attempts to frame each vista and examine every detail – anything to set his mind on a different track.

They pass a barren vineyard, with rows of twisted remains, and another where vines flourish under black nets. Then a field with a cluster of stumps where a chainsaw has been taken to a copse. For hours they drive on, the views changing rapidly. The highway remains flat but around it the terrain oscillates – up and down, wide and then suddenly narrow. Mountain ranges tumble into hills, and plains give way to rugged slopes that corner into great gorges. They pass lakes and pine forests. Fields of grasses that are foreign shades of green and sickly brown. The road skirts an enormous lake, and, briefly, the sun is out and cuts shards off every inch of the water. Behind it, mountains are half obscured by heavy cloud.

In the back, Polly has given up on trying to work and has fallen asleep. Miles's limbs are increasingly restless, and his fidgeting hand creeps into his pocket, where the envelope is folded. He pinches at it, squeezing the blistered packaging under the surface. As he makes his way down, he feels something solid. The temptation to open the envelope itches away at him, but he knows he must wait until he's alone if he wants to swerve any unwanted questions. A new prickle of worry runs through him. No journalist's letter he's ever received has come in a padded envelope. And if a reporter didn't hand-deliver this package to his hotel, then there's an obvious and alarming explanation for who did.

CHAPTER 30

THE TRIAL

One of the defence's key jobs was to pick apart the alleged motive for Caira's murder. It was flaky anyway, this suggestion that Miles – a man with an unblemished record and no history whatsoever of violence – had launched a deadly assault on her simply because their date hadn't ended a certain way. But the prosecution still tried to make it stick. And Eleanor had her work cut out to not only show Miles's good character but also discredit the prosecution's attempts to sully it.

It was also down to Miles's defence to put forward more plausible motives for Caira's murder that might exist elsewhere. To that end, Eleanor called Briony Edwards, a regional manager of social services. She was a recently retired wiry, grey woman with a downturned mouth and baggy eyes, and the decades she'd spent dealing with human misery seemed written into the lines on her face. Once the oath had been sworn, Eleanor began by asking about her career background. Briony confirmed she'd spent more than twenty years working in the same department that had featured in the docu-series *Guardian Angels*.

'In your experience,' Eleanor said, 'have you, or any of the staff you've managed, ever been on the receiving end of hostile or intimidating behaviour while at work?'

A wry smile formed on Briony's face, combined with a barely detectable eye-roll. 'Unfortunately, yes. That's very common.'

'And why is that, Mrs Edwards?'

'Parents sometimes don't react well when they're told they're not providing suitable care for their children.'

'I see. And how would you describe a typical reaction?'

Briony shrugged. 'Denial. Frustration. Anger.'

Eleanor then gestured towards a TV set in the corner of the courtroom. 'I'm going to show you a clip from the documentary series *Guardian Angels*, in which Ms Kennedy explains to the parents of a child that there will be a court hearing to decide whether their son is to enter foster care.'

The video played, showing Caira calmly explaining to a man and a woman what their upcoming court process would entail and why it was happening. The man, dressed in tracksuit bottoms and a grubby grey T-shirt, appeared twitchy and unsettled from the beginning. Both parents' faces were pixellated, but even so, the man's behaviour became visually more aggressive as the clip went on. Anger flared in his body, and the video ended with him being restrained by two security guards while he attempted to move towards Caira, his neck straining angrily as he lunged at her.

When the clip was done, Eleanor resumed her questioning. 'Mrs Edwards, would you describe what we just saw on that clip as an unusual reaction?'

Briony considered that for a moment. 'It's quite an extreme reaction, but not completely unusual.'

Eleanor nodded. 'Have you yourself ever witnessed a social worker being subjected to this kind of physically aggressive behaviour?'

'Yes, I have.'

'And are you aware of any cases in which any members of the families you serve have developed an obsessive dislike for a particular social worker?'

'Yes.'

'And in such situations, have you ever been aware of any social worker becoming fearful for their own personal safety?'

Briony nodded, sadly. 'Yes. I'm afraid so.'

'And my last question for you, Mrs Edwards, have you ever come across a situation where a social worker has feared for their life as a result of their work?'

'Yes, I have.'

Eleanor left a long silence before thanking Briony and turning to face the judge. 'No further questions, my lady.'

CHAPTER 31

REUBYN

Reubyn sees the turning coming up ahead and indicates to leave the highway. It's been a long drive and he needs to stretch his legs.

It's now only ten kilometres to Hendrick's Forest. Having spent so much time reading about it, looking at photographs and studying it on Google Maps, he can't wait to see it for real. He discovered the forest while researching compelling subjects for video content. When on the hunt for ideas, Reubyn's normal instinct is to search for something dramatic and strange. But here in New Zealand, he needs to be careful and considerate – Miles has been through so much and he mustn't add to the stress by taking him anywhere weird. So, he's chosen somewhere peaceful. The reserve they're about to enter will be stunning and unspoilt – exactly the sort of scenery this country is famous for. And it has something else going for it, too: the kākāpō. Reubyn has been upfront about it to Miles, and he's fine with it. There's no reason for him not to be, really. And it's only for one night. Or maybe two, depending on how it goes.

Reubyn isn't a big nature guy, but when he saw videos of the kākāpō, a unique and rare bird, he knew it had the potential to captivate a large audience. The kākāpō is unlike any other bird on Earth. It's a ground-dwelling parrot; bulky and green with forward-facing eyes, like an owl's. And it's completely flightless.

Reubyn has prepared and memorised a bit of background on the bird, which he plans to use as a short piece to camera. Its story is a sad one, although crucially not without hope of redemption. For thousands of years, the kākāpō was abundant in New Zealand, where there were no mammals, and birds had free rein. But when humans arrived, they brought with them rats, dogs and other animals that picked off the kākāpō with ease. The birds were defenceless. Because they'd evolved in the absence of mammals, they didn't recognise their predators when they appeared. It didn't take long before the kākāpō were almost completely wiped out. Today, there are only a handful left. And if you want to spot one in the wild in mainland New Zealand, pretty much your only hope is Hendrick's Forest, where a reintroduction programme is underway. If Reubyn can track one down, he'll end up with a lovely little video. And if it goes *really* well, he can imagine it being a massive hit.

Ahead, the road is narrowing. And the surface is about to change, too — the smooth tarmac's soon to run out. There's no apparent reason for the sudden change, and Reubyn slows the vehicle before they reach the unsealed road surface. Even so, the bus begins to shudder and rattle over the rough ground, which is gravelly and pocked with potholes. Via the wing mirrors, Reubyn sees dust clouding up around their wheels.

They pass three heavy-set local kids on bicycles, who all stop pedalling and gawp at the bus, as if it's a spaceship that's beamed down from another galaxy.

In the interior mirror, Reubyn sees Polly stirring from her nap; she's been roused by the bus's shaky movements as it passes over the uneven terrain. Polly sits up and looks around, bleary-eyed. 'Where are we?'

'We came off the highway a while back,' Reubyn says. 'It would appear they don't bother sealing the roads out here in the sticks. Not enough traffic to make it worthwhile, I guess.'

'Reubyn, you can't take a vehicle like this down a dirt track – the hire company will go ballistic. Turn around.'

'It's fine,' Reubyn says. 'We're nearly there.'

'Nearly where?'

Reubyn groans. He's spent large chunks of the last couple of hours explaining to everyone else where they're going, and he's not about to go through it again. 'A camping spot. You'll see it in a minute.'

Reubyn makes a slow turn around a corner. The road ahead is flanked by small, shabby, rickety-fenced fields, some containing sheep. The uplands beyond are covered in forest.

'Jesus Christ,' Polly mutters under her breath.

Reubyn ignores her moaning; she'll be fine when they get there. He concentrates on the road. It's still wide enough for two lanes but there are no markings. On their right is a single mailbox and a farmhouse behind it, set back from the road. Thanks to his research into the area, Reubyn knows this is the last dwelling before they reach the reserve. From his elevated position, he can see over the fence and into the yard, where there are a couple of off-road motorbikes, and bits of old farm equipment and tractor tyres scattered across the dirty concrete.

Nobody speaks as the bus rumbles on towards the gate at the bottom of the hill, which Reubyn knows is the entrance to the reserve. He pulls up in front of it and climbs out, leaving the engine running. As he steps down on to the ground and looks up, he has the sudden sense of being small and insignificant. The forest is towering and wide. It's uglier than he expected. It has a startling effect on him – turning his stomach. Reubyn is surprised and almost ashamed to react that way to a collection of trees, but it's inescapable: there's something unpleasant about it.

A wooden sign says, 'Welcome to Hendrick's Forest', but it's weathered and dull and not particularly welcoming. Written underneath is a longer indigenous name that Reubyn won't attempt to pronounce. A yellow notice is attached to the gate, from the Department of Conservation, but Reubyn pays no attention to it – he already knows about the kākāpō reintroduction project.

The road on the other side of the gate is cracked and old but in better condition than the one they're on – it was at least once sealed with tar. There is no telling how long it is; the road is a dark, shadowy hole through the forest, visible for a few hundred yards until it ascends and bends and is lost in the trees. Penned in behind the perimeter fence, the trees jitter, their brushing branches creating an undulating whisper. There's a change in the air. Reubyn was well aware that there is a storm on the way, and now he can sense it – that heaviness all around. He's always been particularly sensitive to changes in barometric pressure, ever since he was a little boy, and now he can really feel it: that odd sensation when the tissues inside his body begin to expand ever so slightly and press against his nerves.

Reubyn tries the gate, and it creaks open. He breathes a sigh of relief. He has largely hedged his bets on being able to camp here, and, at the moment, he doesn't really have a plan B. He leaves the gate ajar and returns to the bus. There's an unexpected tickle of trepidation in his chest as he squeezes on the accelerator, and the bus rattles over a cattle grid and crawls into the forest.

CHAPTER 32

ELIS

The track is longer than expected, snaking deep into the reserve, and it's only just wide enough for the bus to make the corners. Elis's view is of little more than the mossy forest floor and the passing trunks of trees, some thin and straight and others that twist with grasping arms. It's gloomy under the canopy, but the sun must've briefly broken through the clouds because light strobes through the trees for a few seconds before they're returned to near darkness. The forest's low ceiling feels unsettlingly dense; here they are, in November, yet the trees are alive and sprung with green leaves that form a bristling barrier to the sky.

Elis shouldn't be here. That's clear now. He had his chance to back out, but, like an idiot, he didn't take it, instead hoping for things to miraculously improve. He should've stayed in Queenstown and taken the next available flight. Now it might be several days until he next has the chance to head for home.

He was a fool to think he might fit within this group. To the untrained eye, he probably looks a bit like them. He may even sound a bit like them. But you can't fool these people by changing your accent. The differences can be found if you look for them: in their confidence, their tattoo-less skin, their perfect teeth. That's a lesson he's learned on this trip: if you're required to make a judgement on someone's background, it's very much like buying a horse. You need to look them in the mouth. Elis's teeth are slightly misaligned, and he has dark fillings – both hallmarks of someone who went to a comprehensive.

He glances over at Miles, who's joking with George about some night out in their past. It's as if Miles is a different person to the one he knows at home. This trip was supposed to bring them closer, but it's had the opposite effect – Miles appears to have forgotten all loyalty to Elis, even after everything that's happened.

On their right, a haunted-looking shack of weathered timber is coming into view, half hidden by the trees. They pass it, round a corner and enter a clearing. Reubyn announces that they've reached their destination and pulls up into a small but empty car park, coming to rest across five or six spaces. Next to the car park is a patch of green, where two old picnic tables are half consumed by the long grass. Reubyn opens the doors, and they all file out.

'Is this it?' George asks of no one in particular, his hands planted on the waistband of his mustard-coloured trousers as he looks around.

Elis was asking himself a similar question. There's an information board at the far end of the car park, but there's little else to mark this place as a destination of any kind, other than some wooden signposts that point to several hiking trails. The forest looms high and close and all around. There is no view of anything beyond the trees, and above them thick grey clouds are gathering.

'It's just a camping spot,' Reubyn says. 'Somewhere to break up the journey.'

'Somewhere for you to film your bloody video,' George says.

'Think of that as a bonus. We have to stop somewhere.'

George scoffs. 'A bonus? Forgive me, but none of this looks like a bonus, does it?'

'Oh, come on, it's not that bad. We've got everything we need in the bus, don't forget.'

As Reubyn speaks, there's a faint growl of thunder. George says a few words in Latin, then mutters something about wine and heads back into the bus. He's followed by Reubyn and Faith, who are busy making plans for their video project.

With George and Reubyn out of the way, for a minute at least, now would be a good time to corner Miles for a quick chat. But he's already wandering off with Jessie. Elis watches as they amble across the car park, and then he feels a presence coming up behind him. He spins around to see Polly. She wears a small smile that is sweeter than normal for her, and Elis wonders if what lies behind it might be pity. He's becoming something of a loner on this trip.

'What do you think of this place?' Polly says.

Elis looks around and shrugs. 'It's all right.'

'You sound about as enthusiastic as I am.'

Elis laughs. 'It could be worse. Really, a place like this will be as much fun as you're willing to make it. Do you want to go take a look around?'

She twists the corner of her mouth. 'Yeah, okay. I think a walk might do me good, actually.'

They walk side by side to the end of the clearing, where there's a signpost at the entrance to a trail.

Elis ushers Polly ahead of him on to the path, which is wide enough only for single-file. Her pace is sluggish, a weariness to her movements.

'Is everything okay?' Elis asks.

She glances back at him. 'Oh, it's just been a lot, you know? What's been going on with Miles.'

'Of course.'

'And I discovered something today that was quite upsetting.'

Elis is silent for a moment, unsure what to say. 'I'm sorry to hear that.'

A question has formed in Elis's mind, but he's unsure whether to ask it. Polly would volunteer more information, wouldn't she, if she wanted to discuss it with him? They step over the dead trunk of a fallen tree and continue down the path. All about them are masses of wild ferns, and the forest smells of damp vegetation and rotting wood. Birds make an odd collection of sounds overhead: bleep and cackle and click. The trees, too, are peculiar and unknown. Elis can identify most of the trees he comes across in the UK, but not here. Some tower straight up, and others are bony-thin and poke out at strange angles. Many of the tree stems harbour life of their own – flesh-eaten, clumped with moss or strangled by the tendrils of climbing plants. After a minute or so of silence between them, curiosity gets the better of Elis, and he decides to ask. 'This upsetting thing you found out – do you want to talk about it?'

Polly looks back over her shoulder. 'Not really.'

'Okay.'

'Let's just say someone I thought I could trust has decided to stab me in the back.'

'Oh no, that's awful.'

Polly responds by glancing at him, her lips pursed to confirm the awfulness without words.

Elis says nothing more, and they carry on down the path. After a couple more minutes, the outline of the wooden shack is becoming visible through the trees. It's bigger than it appeared from the road – maybe thirty feet wide. At one point in time, the wooden boards that make up its sides were stained with dark varnish, but only streaks remain. A set of wooden steps leads up to the entrance, but there's no door.

Without discussion, they head straight for the shack. Polly continues to lead the way, climbing the steps and raising her forearm to banish a cobweb laced across the door frame. Her footsteps beat a hollow sound out of the wooden boards as she enters. Elis follows and finds three windows of grubby glass that look out on to a pond, with tiers of banked earth behind and a sparse collection of trees. There are a series of feeders, and that they've been replenished with seeds is the only sign so far that anyone else has ventured into this part of the forest in months.

'What is this thing?' Polly asks.

'It's a bird hide.'

Polly sits on the bench and presses her nose to the glass. 'I can't see many birds out there.'

Elis sits next to her. 'We might need to be patient.'

'That's not my strong suit.'

He points at a hole in the ground, a little like a badger sett. 'You see where the earth is dug out, just there?'

'I think so.'

'That might be a burrow. Keep an eye on it.'

They wait in silence. There's the occasional twitch of movement in the trees, but the sources aren't up to much – a silvereye and a robin.

After five minutes or so, Polly gives up watching the burrow and turns her face to his. 'Do you know what, Elis, I was thinking earlier – I hardly know a thing about you.'

Elis shrugs. 'I hardly know a thing about you, either.'

She places a hand on his bare forearm. 'Go on, then. Ask me anything.'

Elis is quiet, his lips bunched up in thought.

She grins. 'Anything at all.'

He scratches his head.

'Oh, come on,' Polly says. 'There must be *something* you want to ask me.'

Elis racks his mind for the sorts of questions he *should* ask in this situation, but none form. Meanwhile, the questions that *are* on his mind burn with a fire so fierce that it engulfs anything else. He frowns. 'What do you think happened to Caira Kennedy?'

Polly's smile vanishes. She removes her hand from his arm and her face stiffens. 'I try not to think about it.'

'Same here.'

Polly stuffs her hands in her pockets and stares out at the birdless scene in front of them.

The atmosphere between them has gone cold. Elis needs to explain himself, or at least fill the silence. 'It's just that, now Miles has been found not guilty, do you not wonder what *actually* happened?'

Polly shifts on the bench. 'Like I said, I try not to think about it.'

'Well, I think about it a lot.'

She continues to stare dead ahead. 'Do you?'

'Yes. And the more I think about it, the less sense it makes.'

Polly shakes her head irritably and flashes a scowl at him. 'What are you talking about?'

Elis pauses to think. Continuing down this road would be a bad idea. But, on the other hand, being consumed by thoughts about this, and not being able to discuss them with anyone, is a torment the like of which he's never experienced until this year. If there's anyone who is safe to talk to about this, it would be Miles's own sister. 'Look, I know Miles didn't do it. Obviously. But I was there listening to the trial, and a lot of what he was saying, it didn't . . . add up.'

'This isn't much fun, is it, birdwatching?' Polly quickly replies. 'I think I'm going to head back.'

With that, she stands and leaves the bench. Elis is startled by the sudden speed and purpose of her movement, her long legs marching towards the exit.

He opens his mouth to call her back, but no sound escapes his throat.

And he's glad of it.

There's no doubt it's for the best. Because, just then, for a sickening second, it crossed his mind to tell her the truth.

CHAPTER 33

REUBYN

Reubyn gently moves Faith a half-step to the side so he can check the shot from the second camera. It looks brilliant, with their small campfire dominating one side of the frame and filling the night air around it with an orange glow. Without the firelight, it's pitch-dark, and the crackle and spark produced by the flames only add to the atmosphere. Even with the shelter of the surrounding forest, the wind is picking up, blowing smoke into the trees. Reubyn's already done a soundcheck, and the wireless microphone clipped to his shirt seems to be coping with the elements, especially when he sits with his back to the wind. *All should be well*, he thinks. But something is nagging at him. He can't put his finger on what it is. Reubyn dismisses it; he's just freaking out because of the importance of the scene. Earlier, he and Faith got some great footage of him exploring the trails in the twilight, but this bit is key – he plans to use it to open the second video of what he now hopes will be a two-parter.

'Faith, can you move those plates, please,' Reubyn says. Their barbecued dinner was tasty enough, but the remaining smears don't do anything for the shot. He takes one last look at the framing. 'Okay, I think we're good to go.'

Reubyn sits back down, sets his phone to video mode and takes a deep breath. Around the campfire, everyone has gone silent, watching him with interest. It's awful having an audience for a piece to camera, but he has no choice – the firelight is too good not to use. 'All right, here we go,' he says. 'Everybody be quiet.'

Reubyn raises his camera stick and clears his throat. His normal 'show voice' is brash and loud, but for this he's going for something different, subdued. 'Hi guys,' he says, almost in a whisper. 'I'm not going to lie, I'm excited right now. Night has fallen here in this primeval forest in deepest, darkest New Zealand—'

He stops and looks over at George, who has burst out laughing.

Reubyn glares at him. 'What the hell?'

'Sorry. Couldn't help it.' George presses his lips into a line, trying to appear serious, then his face creases up with laughter again. It's an abrasive cackle that rips through the ambience. He shakes his head. 'It's just . . . *primeval*? I wasn't prepared for that.'

'Actually, you were prepared for it. I told you what I was doing.'

George shows his palms. 'All right, all right. I'll zip it. *Silentium est aureum*.' Then to Elis: 'That means silence is golden.'

'Thanks for that.' Elis stares into the fire. 'Maybe you should consider employing that mantra yourself.'

'Touché,' George says. '*Adversus solem ne loquitor*. That means—'

'Will you shut up? I am sick to death of this,' Elis says.

Reubyn gives them a stern look. 'Can you two calm down, please?'

Elis folds his arms. His face snarls, looking monstrous in the firelight. 'I am calm. I just couldn't give a toss about the meaning of his pretentious Latin phrases.'

'Guys! If you can't be quiet, can you *please* go somewhere else for five minutes so I can film this?'

Right on cue, Elis gets up and walks off, as if he's been waiting for an opportunity to excuse himself. It doesn't come as a shock;

George has been giving him grief all evening and it would appear he's finally had enough. It's not pleasant to witness, but Reubyn can't help but feel a guilty twinge of relief – if it weren't for Elis being here, Reubyn would himself be bearing the brunt of George's relentless snarking.

'What about you, George? Do you need five minutes?'

'I'll be quiet, I promise,' he says, miming a zip across his lips.

Reubyn takes a moment to recompose himself. He raises his eyebrows at Faith, who responds with a thumbs up. After a few deep breaths, he starts again. 'Hi guys. I'm not going to lie, I'm excited right now.' This time, he goes for a dramatic pause, looking left and then right. 'Night has fallen here in this primeval forest in deepest, darkest New Zealand, and we're all set up with our campfire, here' – pointing with his free hand – 'and if we listen very carefully, we might just hear the call of one of the rarest and most bizarre creatures on Earth, the kākāpō.' He pauses again for a moment, cups a hand to his ear. 'Forests like these were once full of these mad, flightless, nocturnal parrots. Early explorers found they could catch them by shaking the trees, and they would fall out as easily as apples. Nowadays, there are only a handful left. So, what's going to happen? Will we find one? Will I come face to face with the world's weirdest bird? Stick around and find out.'

Reubyn looks into the camera with a half-smile that he hopes conveys nervous excitement. He holds it for a few seconds, then simultaneously lowers his smile and the camera stick, and laughter breaks out around the campfire.

Jessie claps her hands. 'Reubyn, that was *so* good.'

'Thanks.'

Reubyn unclips his phone and watches the video back. It's good – excellent, even, for a first take. Out of the corner of his eye, he sees Jessie whisper something in Miles's ear, and the two of them get up and walk off. Reubyn stands and goes over to check the video Faith has captured. 'This looks great,' he tells her, as the clip nears its end.

Faith smiles. 'Sweet. Are we done?'

'No, we need to do another one.'

'But you nailed it first time. That was amazing.'

Reubyn's heart pulses with new energy. *Amazing.* Her words are more warming than the fire. He can't help but stare at her. She beams, her full lips stretching wide with lithe elasticity. He could just go on viewing her, the way someone might study the canvas of a master painter, observing each and every small detail.

'Reubyn?' She gives a small shake of her head. 'Why do we need to do it again? What's wrong with it?'

He blinks. 'If you want a slick edit, you shouldn't ever rely on one take. It might seem good now, but when you get home and look at it on your laptop, there might be a mistake, or some flaw you didn't realise was there.'

'Of course, that makes sense. Okay – let's do it!'

That smile, again. Her eyes gleam with enthusiasm and flicker with firelight. She likes him. There's no doubt about it now. Maybe it's finally happening. As he moves back to his spot by the fire and sets up for the next take, Reubyn is sure – as sure as he's ever been about anything. At last, he's entering a love story that might actually have a happy ending. And one thing has become suddenly clear, like the universe is sending him a signal – it's time for him to make his move.

CHAPTER 34

MILES

Miles follows Jessie into the bird hide, a shaft of artificial light from her phone guiding the way through the dark. It was her idea to come here, for some privacy. She stops, just a few feet into the hide, and pans the light around, illuminating each wall in turn, then every inch of the floor, followed by the ceiling. The wooden boards moan under her feet as she creeps over to the window. She presses the light to the glass, peers out and then returns to Miles with a puckish grin. 'It's just us,' she says, taking his hand and pulling him close. 'Alone, at last.'

'Were you expecting a late rush of birdwatchers?'

Jessie laughs. 'You never know what you'll—' A sound emanating from the forest has caused her to stop. Her eyes go wide. 'Do you hear that?'

Miles hears it – a call from deep in the trees. It's anxious, almost desperate in tone.

She lowers her voice. 'I grew up in the country; there are a ton of owls where I'm from, but I've never heard that one before.'

'Why are you whispering?'

Jessie giggles. 'I don't know.' Her chilly hands slide up inside his T-shirt and come to rest on his lower back. She leans in and nuzzles at his neck. The timid first drops of new rain tap against the metal roof. Her hair smells faintly of lavender.

'You're cold,' Miles says.

'Maybe I just need warming up.'

She kisses him on the mouth, her tongue doing a slow dance with his, and her hands travel southward, into his jeans. Miles gasps at her touch and closes his eyes, leaning into the physicality of the moment. His hands have found a way inside her coat, have located her soft, bare skin, and his fingers trace gently up her back, blood pulsing urgently around his body.

Suddenly their mouths break apart.

An explosion of thunder shakes the air so fiercely it seems to rock the hide. They stare at each other, Jessie's mouth having fallen open. The thunder has a long tail, rumbling on for a good few seconds. Her mouth relaxes into a smile. They turn to look out of the windows. Waiting for it. And then lightning forks flashlight the forest so that for a moment they can see far into the trees, strobes of ultraviolet briefly summoning the woods to life. As suddenly as they were illuminated, they are plunged back into darkness.

'Where were we?' Miles whispers. He takes Jessie by the waist and steers her a few feet to his right, so her back presses gently against the rear wall. He kisses her neck, and feels her warm, ragged breath against his ear. More thunder rumbles, this time not so violently loud. Miles ignores it, his hands tracing the curve of her hips and lingering when they reach her chest. The lightning flares again, but Miles doesn't open his eyes, just witnesses it as a bright pulse behind his eyelids.

A shocking sound storms his ears.

Jessie screams. A bad scream. High and hacking and harsh, like it's coming deep out of the darkest ditch of her throat. Her body has gone tense in his arms, her shoulders are raised.

Miles recoils. 'What's the matter?'

'There's someone out there,' she says, the words tumbling out on top of each other.

'What do you mean?'

She leans into him, and her hand trembles in his. 'I mean, there's a man outside, out the window.'

'It's all right,' Miles says, although he doesn't quite believe it. His skin has turned cold. The mood in this flimsy, remote structure has undergone an abrupt change. What felt playful and exciting is suddenly dreadful. The sounds of the storm, which seemed romantically dramatic twenty seconds earlier, are now menacing and unwanted. He can barely see further than a couple of yards in front of him. They're penned in by the dark.

Jessie activates the torch app and directs it in front of her, creating a spot of light on the middle window. She points a shaky finger. 'Right there.'

Miles takes her phone out of her hand, presses the device against the glass. 'There's no one out there.'

'There was, I swear.'

'You're sure?'

'I want to go back,' Jessie says, a tremor in her voice.

'Okay.'

Miles's heart thumps as he leads her by the hand towards the exit, shining the torch in front of him. It's a strange fear that's gripped him. Like the intense, irrational terror of a child convinced something lurks under their bed. He stares into the forest. In the hazy ring of light cast by the torch are shaking leaves and swaying branches, but beyond, the only colour is black. Is someone out there? Who the hell are they? And what do they want? *This is not over.*

Miles pauses in the doorway and pans the beam across the trees. There's no one in sight. Maybe Jessie imagined it? That's the most likely explanation, but right now that thought brings no comfort. He leads Jessie through the doorway, down the steps and on to the damp path.

'Watch your step,' Miles says. 'It's slippery.'

They walk the path as briskly as they can without losing purchase on the ground.

More lightning electrifies the air, and Jessie squeezes his hand. 'What if he's following us?'

Miles stops, and shines the torch behind them, then all around. 'There's no one following us.' He walks on. 'Are you absolutely sure you saw someone?'

'Yes!' There's a contained urgency to her voice. 'You don't believe me?'

'I believe you.'

The clearing is close; Miles can see the dying bonfire's red glow through a slash in the trees. Miles does another three-sixty with the torchlight. Maybe it's the harsh LED lighting, but Jessie's face is ashen and full of fear.

'Did you see his face?' Miles asks.

'No. He had a hood up. His face was in shadow.'

They reach the clearing, and Miles puts an arm around Jessie's shoulders as they hurry across the car park towards the campfire.

Faith must've seen the worried look on Jessie's face because she gets up and runs over. 'What's wrong?'

As she comforts Jessie, Miles tries to process what's happened. Instinctively, this feels bad. They've only been here a few hours, and already another nightmare seems to be unfolding. He takes deep breaths. *Okay, calm down and stop jumping to conclusions.* There will be a rational explanation for this – and it won't be anywhere near as dire as his imagination is telling him.

Miles's mind is feverishly alert and processing thoughts much more rapidly than normal. Perhaps one of their group went for a walk in front of the hide. Maybe what Jessie saw was nothing more than a trick of the light. Or even more likely, a trick of the mind. It would be understandable; they've entered a strange, remote place, and, with the weather, the whole atmosphere is unsettling. Maybe any dark shadow could take on the appearance of a figure, for a second or two, at least.

On the other hand, she seems utterly convinced about what she saw. The fear in her eyes appeared genuine. With Jessie firmly in the arms of Faith, Miles surveys the scene. Out here in the forest, they're seemingly isolated; the only people for miles around are those with whom he's travelling. And if someone really did try to sneak up on them just then, it was almost certainly someone from their own group. Miles checks exactly who is still sat around the fire – and, more importantly, who is not: Reubyn and Elis.

Miles walks over to where George and Polly are side by side, confused looks on their faces. 'Did either of you go over to the bird hide, just then?'

They look at him blankly and shake their heads. He immediately feels guilty about making the observation – it's his oldest friend and his *sister*, for heaven's sake.

Miles walks off towards the bus, and Jessie gives him a small smile as he passes. She knows he'll get to the bottom of this.

Miles opens the door and finds Elis and Reubyn standing in the kitchen, each holding a beer.

'Hey, man,' Elis says.

Miles raises a hand in acknowledgement, then goes to the fridge and grabs a bottle. 'This might sound weird.' He picks up the bottle opener and his beer hisses as he levers off the cap. 'Did either of you go over to the bird hide tonight? After dinner.'

'Nope,' Reubyn says.

Elis shakes his head. 'Me neither.'

Miles takes a sip and looks at Elis. 'When you left the campfire earlier, where did you go?'

Elis narrows his eyes at him. 'I came in here.' He shakes his head. 'Is that all right? What's this about?'

'It doesn't matter.'

Miles slumps down in the living area. He stares out of the window, at the fire, and he can hear faint whispers from the kitchen. Miles takes a long slug, trying to figure it out.

Could an outsider have come here? Could Alex Burnfield have followed, without them noticing? It seems impossible – there's no way someone could've tracked them along those rural roads without being seen. Or could they?

Could someone be tracking one of their phones? That too seems impossible – they all lost reception ages ago and no one has even a bar of signal. But what if someone fitted some kind of device to the bus? You see it all the time on films and TV shows; they stick a gadget to the underside of a vehicle and monitor where it goes using GPS. Do people do that in real life? It's too dark now to check. He'll do it in the morning. In the meantime, he rules it out as a possibility on the basis that it's extremely far-fetched. The fact he's even considered it is probably a symptom of increasing paranoia.

Could it have been one of the locals? The kids they passed earlier? They stared in amazement at the bus; perhaps one of them was intrigued enough to try to get a closer look. Or a birdwatcher? The exotic birds Reubyn is interested in are nocturnal, so maybe a nature lover turned up at night hoping to spot one. Yes, that seems likely. The more Miles thinks about it, the more plausible it becomes.

He racks his brain for another theory. But he can't think of anything. Miles tries to consider it rationally, calling upon the problem-solving techniques he learned at school: logical inference, abductive reasoning, Occam's razor. The simplest conclusion is usually correct. So, who or what did Jessie see at the bird hide?

The longer he thinks about it, the more certain he becomes.

Either Jessie was mistaken, or they simply had an awkward encounter with a late-night birdwatcher. The alternative doesn't bear thinking about.

CHAPTER 35

GEORGE

George wipes sleep from his eyes and lumbers into the kitchen to make a coffee. It's nearly noon and he is the last to rise. He tips out the remaining coffee machine pods and groans; all the sensible ones have been used up, and only a handful of unappealing flavours are left. He picks what he hopes is the least offensive – roasted hazelnut – and fires up the machine. It grumbles away at a similar volume to the rain's steady patter against the roof. He moves to the window. Outside, there is movement; leaves shiver, and the thinner branches shake and sway. George hears a voice, and the serious tone seizes his attention. It's not coming from the living area, where Elis, Polly, Jessie and Faith chat in hushed voices. It's at the other end of the van – the bedroom. The coffee machine falls silent, and George removes his cup. He places it on the sideboard, which is dark and flecked with grey: a synthetic imitation of the kind of black granite used to make modern gravestones. Miles sounds annoyed, or in some way animated. George creeps out of the kitchen and loiters by the bedroom door, where the voices of Miles and Reubyn are more audible.

'. . . I can't do that to her, don't you see that?' Miles says, a tinge of exasperation to his question. 'It's not fair, after what's happened.'

'You're being *way* oversensitive,' Reubyn says.

'I am not.'

'You are. She probably imagined it anyway. You know what Americans are like, they're dramatic. It wouldn't surprise me if she made the whole thing up as part of some damsel in distress routine.'

'That is incredibly unfair!' Miles shouts, and George takes a reflexive step back. 'She's really freaked out,' he says, his volume returning to normal. 'And, frankly, so am I. To be honest, Reubyn, I thought you would understand that.'

There's a silence, and George clenches his teeth.

'What do you want me to do?' Reubyn says.

'You know what I want – I want you to drive us the hell out of here.'

'And you know I can't do that, not yet. I've got a bit left to do on this video.'

'But I'm not safe out here.'

'Of course you're safe – this is the safest place you can be. We're miles from anywhere. Trust me.'

'You're putting yourself before everyone else.'

'Well, if it's altruism you're worried about, how about this: you tell Jessie the whole story, and I'll drive us out of this forest. Right now.'

Another silence.

'I'm not ready to do that.'

'I know. And I'm not ready to leave.'

George hears footsteps, and darts into the bathroom. The bedroom door opens and out comes Reubyn, who glances his way. George turns on the tap and pretends to wash his hands as Miles passes him.

That was . . . *odd.* One wouldn't describe it as a furious argument, but he can't remember the last time Miles and Reubyn had cross words.

And Reubyn doesn't want to leave? He's not *ready* to depart this dump? What's going on here? How bloody long does he need?

George towels his hands and returns to the kitchen for his coffee. He takes a sip and grimaces. It's absolute garbage. Coffee should never be flavoured with hazelnut – or any nut, for that matter. Isn't coffee a flavour in itself? No amount of flavouring – be it caramel, gingerbread or bin juice, as this tastes like – will improve upon it. He slams his mug on the side and approaches Reubyn, who stands by the door locked in a fierce battle with the zip of his raincoat.

'Hey, Reubs,' George says. 'Are we busting a move soon or what?'

Reubyn rolls his eyes. 'Not you as well? Why is everyone in such a rush, all of a sudden?'

'Because we're supposed to be on holiday right now, not languishing in a ruddy gulag.'

Reubyn huffs as he tries to free the fabric snared in the teeth. 'I need to do some more filming before we go. Plus, I'd like to see if this weather calms down a bit – it might be dangerous driving a vehicle like this in high winds. It's not like I'm an expert.' Finally, he zips up his coat and turns to Faith. 'Are you ready?'

Faith gives the affirmative, and they venture out into the rain, some of which blusters into the bus before the door swings shut. George sees Miles is staring at him from the kitchen, and when they lock eyes, Miles jerks his head a fraction – a discreet order to join him.

'Everything all right?' George asks in a low voice.

'Not really,' Miles says. 'It's looking like we're going to be staying here another night.'

George raises an eyebrow. 'We'll see about that.'

Miles's eyes are drawn to the living area, where Jessie sits with Elis and Polly. He turns his attention back to George. 'I need your help,' he whispers.

'Shoot.'

'Do you think it's possible we could've been followed here?'

'By your stalker, you mean?'

Miles nods.

George thinks for a moment. 'I don't see how. We definitely weren't being tailed by a vehicle. I mean, we were both looking out for that, and there was nothing, the whole way.' He pauses, deep in thought. 'Although . . .'

'What? What is it?'

George points towards the bedroom. 'Let's talk in there.'

They go inside and George closes the door behind them. The room – where Jessie, Faith and Polly slept last night – is a mess of clothes, make-up and bags. A bed is still made up on the floor.

'We've got outsiders with us,' George says. 'Isn't it possible one of them could be in cahoots with your stalker? I mean, how much do we really know about Jessie and Faith? Come to think of it, how much do you really know about Elis?'

'*Elis?* He's a mate. As for the other two, I don't think we need worry about them.'

George opens the door, checking for eavesdroppers, and closes it again. 'Are you sure about that?'

'Okay, let's test your theory,' Miles says. 'Let's suppose that, for some bizarre reason, one of them is working with my stalker and wanted to tip them off with our whereabouts. How the hell would they even do that? We all lost signal ages ago. And Reubyn has been super tight-lipped about where we're going.'

'Fair point.'

'So, it's not possible, is it?'

George goes quiet and rakes his fingers through his hair. 'All right, look. I wasn't sure if I should ask this, but have you considered the possibility that Jessie might have been lying about seeing a man in the forest last night?'

'What? No. No chance.'

'How can you be so sure? We only met her a few days ago.'

'Trust me. You should have seen her – she was terrified, shaking like a leaf. I think it's possible she was mistaken, but I don't think she's lying.'

George frowns. 'She probably wonders about you.'

'I'm not lying! I just haven't told her the whole truth yet. But I will.' Miles shakes his head. 'This is getting us nowhere.'

'Look, mate, for what it's worth, I get why you're anxious. But I really don't think we've been followed, so try not to worry.'

Miles exhales slowly. 'Thanks, I'm sure you're right.'

George nods and reaches for the door handle.

'Wait,' Miles says. 'One more thing.'

'Go on.'

'This might sound paranoid but hear me out.'

'Okay.'

Miles takes a deep breath. 'A tracking device. Do you have any idea what one looks like? And how we'd find it if someone fitted one to the bus?'

George places a hand on his friend's shoulder. 'I'll help you check over the vehicle, if you like, just to be on the safe side. But I'm afraid you *are* being paranoid, mate.'

Miles shakes his head. 'I need to show you something,' he says, digging into the pocket of his shorts. Miles reveals an object lying on his palm.

George's eyes go wide. 'Crikey. Where did you get that?'

'It was in an envelope left for me at reception at the hotel.'

'It looks real,' George says, examining it.

'That's what I thought.'

George turns it over in his hand. It appears to be a piece of live ammunition. But it's not the type he's used to dealing with – game cartridges filled with shot pellets. This is more compact, with a pointed front end. A more sinister kind. He's never held one of these before, and it sends goosebumps flaring across his skin. A bullet.

CHAPTER 36

REUBYN

'Are you ready?'

Faith grins. 'As I'll ever be.'

She stands on the trail, sheltering underneath the golf umbrella Reubyn bought in Queenstown. She grips it with both hands, and it trembles in the wind. His Lumix is clamped to the shaft, to keep it dry from the rain. Faith stares out from under her hood, eyes shining with mischief and excitement. She's gorgeous – even with her body hidden beneath the borrowed cagoule.

'Stay close,' Reubyn says. 'Keep the same sort of distance as we are now. And don't worry if the camera's a little shaky – it all adds to the effect.'

'Roger that.'

'Here we go. Take one.' He walks slowly down the trail, looking back over his shoulder at the camera. 'Okay, guys, we've left the camp in the centre of the forest and are heading east. We reckon we heard the call of the kākāpō last night, coming from somewhere around here, so let's have a look.' They reach a straight bit of path, and Reubyn turns around to face the camera, walking backwards along the trail, his feet squelching in mud. 'One thing's for sure, though – there is a strange aura in this place. It feels ancient, somehow, like we've gone back in—'

Reubyn's standing foot slides and gives way, and before he knows it, both his feet have left the ground and he's going down. He lands heavily on his side, his hip and shoulder slapping into the mud, sending splatters flying in all directions.

Faith is silent for a second, then the sound of her laughing tears through the air. She hurries to him, but she's laughing so hard it's difficult to tell if she's bent in concern or simply doubled over from hysterics. After a few seconds she manages to gasp out the words: 'Are you okay?'

Reubyn waves away her outstretched hand and hauls himself up. He assesses the damage; his shorts, socks, raincoat – pretty much all items of his clothing – are smothered with mud down one side. He sighs. 'A small dent to my pride, maybe, but I'm otherwise okay.'

'One for the blooper reel,' she says, and then her face opens again in laughter – great, shuddering laughs that shake her whole body.

Reubyn chuckles too; lightly at first, but Faith's laughter is contagious and soon he's lost control of himself as well. And they're laughing *together*. She's not laughing *at* him – they're just two people enjoying the moment, reacting to the absurdity of their situation.

She ushers him towards her, holding the umbrella out. 'Do you want to watch it back?'

Reubyn moves in and they stand shoulder to shoulder. Their arms are pressed together, through their coats. As she sets up the clip, Reubyn realises this is the moment. Although, he hasn't *realised* it – he's been informed by his heart, the way it's thumping so fiercely it might burst free of his chest.

Faith's eyes are misty, and even as she concentrates on the viewfinder, her smile remains. 'All right, here it is,' she says, and presses play.

The clip starts. Reubyn only knows this because he can hear the audio. He's not watching the screen. Just her. Faith's smile broadens as the video goes on, getting closer to his fall. Then Faith tilts her head back and laughs.

She turns to look at him, and her smile relaxes a touch, the plumpness returning to her lips. They're ripe and red, like summer fruit. Reubyn's skin tingles all over, from his ankles all the way to his scalp. *This is it.*

He tilts his head to the side and leans in towards her. All noise seems to cease in that moment, the world put on mute. He puckers his lips and braces for contact with hers.

But there is no contact.

Faith jerks her head back. Her face freezes into something serious, the kind of face a doctor might make before delivering bad news. 'Oh, Reubyn, I . . .' She shakes her head.

'I understand,' Reubyn quickly replies. And he does. His body has gone numb – stunned and wet feeling, like he's been doused with cold water. A roiling sickness thickens in his gut.

'It's just that . . . Oh God, I really like you,' she says, her brow furrowed. 'But I'm not in the right place for something romantic right now. That sounds like such a cliché, but . . .'

'Of course. I totally understand.'

'Are you sure? I'm sorry if I gave you the wrong idea.'

Reubyn stares vacantly into the trees. 'It's fine.'

'Right, well then, shall we do another take?' Then, after five seconds or so: 'Reubyn?'

He's dizzied, unsteady on his feet. His vision is unfocused, and, in front of him, he sees nothing but a blurry barcode of tree stems. Reubyn blinks hard, then turns to look at her. 'Do you know what, I think it might look more authentic if I film this bit myself, on my phone.'

Faith nods slowly, the life gone from her eyes. 'Okay. Is there anything I can do to help?'

'No, I'm good.'

'Right.'

'Do you mind taking the camera back to the bus? It would be good to get it out of the rain.'

Faith nods. She looks at the ground, then turns and trudges back up the path. After about fifty yards, she stops and looks over her shoulder. Reubyn pretends not to see, and fiddles with his phone.

When she's disappeared from view, Reubyn slips the phone back into his pocket. He closes his eyes for a moment and stands stock-still on the muddy path, listening to the rain patter against his coat, feeling it run cold down his burning cheeks. He turns his face upwards to accept more of it. Water cascades off the canopy and the leaves glisten with a green that reminds him of poison. The sky, as much as he can see of it, is a ruined charcoal sketch – smudged with too much black. All around him the trees bend and groan.

Reubyn breathes deeply, then lumbers up the trail towards the bus, each step requiring an effort, as if he's gained a few stone.

Why did he think this time would be any different? This is how it always plays out, after all. It's not possible to become suddenly attractive by taking an online course and watching a bunch of how-to videos. How stupid can he get? He can't escape what he is: the guy who's destined to be put in the friendzone. The platonic side-dude who the girl will turn to for support when she's having trouble with her boyfriend. The boy who was last picked for sport is now the remaining sack of sub-primal cuts left languishing at the bar in the great meat raffle that is dating.

The air crackles as he walks the path, and he kicks loose branches as he goes. Then, in a direct insult, the heavens break, and rain hammers tenfold, thundering against the trees and surging through the canopy in broken chandeliers. Reubyn doesn't quicken his step, just lets it pour on to him. Allows it to wash the mud from his clothes. He'll be damned if he's going to let the elements get in the way of what he's here to do. And he won't allow himself to be distracted by Faith, either. Not anymore.

Reubyn reaches the path's end and enters the clearing, greeted by the rain's raw power; unbridled by treetops, it lashes against the car park and the bus's roof in an angry din. He crosses towards the bus and slows up when he sees her. Only the back of her head and shoulders are visible through the window. Even that is warped – distorted by the run-off that bleeds its way down the glass. She sits next to Elis. Not only next to him; they're so close there's nothing to separate them at all. Elis snakes an arm around her shoulders, says something in her ear, and, in a moment of certainty that knots Reubyn's stomach, normality is restored to the universe.

CHAPTER 37

POLLY

There's a restless tension in the bus as they wait for Reubyn to re-emerge. He came back from his shoot soaked to the skin and with a face like a slapped arse. He barely uttered a word – just got straight into the shower. Since then, he's been loitering in the bedroom for the entire afternoon, avoiding them. But he can't avoid them forever.

The other six are sprawled about the living area, and, with the rain hammering on the roof, Polly can't hear the quiet conversation going on between Elis and Faith over in the corner. Miles, Jessie and George have been chatting, but the conversation has been listless and slow-moving and has now dried up.

Everyone has been growing more ill-tempered, tired and unsettled. But at least there's now an overwhelming consensus that they need to leave – today. Apart from anything else, it would be good to move into an area with some signal. There might be an update from the police. Just as importantly, Polly needs to do some work. She *desperately* needs to do some work. Being unable to check in on her staff, to ensure her business is running smoothly, is filling her with anxiety.

Even though she's managing a small team, poor Dee will be stressing out, because she's used to Polly at least checking in with her every morning. And her junior staff, who have already gone rogue in Polly's absence, will have now turned completely feral. If Polly had known she would need to take so much time out this year, she would've taken on staff with more experience, rather than a couple of trainees. Now she's got a potential disaster on her hands.

Marco is keen but has a tendency to screw things up. It's like working with a puppy. His eagerness is endearing but he needs reining in, and it wouldn't come as a surprise if he's already launched some ill-conceived campaign in the two days Polly's been unable to monitor his work. And then there's Callie. If Polly doesn't designate specific tasks, her default setting is to do nothing.

Preoccupied by these thoughts, before checking out of the Queenstown hotel, Polly decided to do an impromptu performance appraisal – going through Callie's work emails. Her activity was underwhelming, to say the least. In fact, she had sent so few emails that it didn't take long before Polly had sifted through more than a week's worth. It was at that point that she noticed an alarming thread in Callie's inbox. Next to the name James Gardner was a subject line that gave Polly a sudden chill. *Story about Miles Deverill*, it said. Polly clicked it open immediately. Gardner, it transpired, was a reporter from *The Chronicle*, responding to an email Callie had sent to their tip-offs mailbox. There were a total of six emails in the exchange, outlining the whole sordid arrangement – the story she'd sold to them.

The Chronicle had agreed to pay her £200 – barely more than Polly pays her for a day's work – and in return, Callie gave them everything: their flight details, the name of their hotel (which mercifully didn't appear in the resulting article), and who was going on the trip. She also provided them with Miles's motivation for going, later attributed to *a source close to the family*. Polly could barely believe it. Callie had sold out their whole family for the price of a good haircut. The discovery left her so boiling with rage that she had to take a cold shower to try to calm herself down before calling to confront her.

Callie hadn't picked up at first. And by the time Polly finally got through, she was preparing to check out. That hadn't helped defuse the situation at all. As Polly held her phone to her ear in one hand, and tried to manoeuvre her bulky luggage through the door with the other, she'd completely lost her temper. Callie obviously hadn't realised her boss had the right to trawl her emails – the shock at being caught was evident in her voice. But, luckily for her, it turned out to be a short conversation because George appeared out of nowhere, forcing Polly to end the call. She hasn't been able to speak to Callie since, and the way the situation was left is far from ideal. Essentially, she gave Callie a short but ferocious bollocking, then hung up on her and immediately went offline for days on end. And that's not great management. You don't need to be Richard Branson to realise that what Polly's done isn't the way to deal with an HR issue of this magnitude. If you need to fire someone, it's even more important to do things by the book. Otherwise, you're simply asking for an employment tribunal. Polly's stress levels keep rising the longer the situation remains unresolved.

The door to the kitchen opens, and all eyes turn to Reubyn. He flips on the kettle and rummages through the cupboards, pretending not to notice their stares.

'Reubyn,' George hollers. 'Can we have a word?'

He approaches, wearing a deadpan expression. 'What's up?'

'We want to get out of here. We *all* do.'

Reubyn looks around at their nodding faces. 'Okay.' He shrugs. 'So do I.'

'Great,' George says. He pushes his lower lip out, and glances at the others. 'Let's get packed up and get going, then.'

Miles rises. Polly follows suit, eager to move on.

'Wait,' Reubyn says. 'We can't go right now.' He points to the window. 'Look at it out there.'

'Jesus, Reubyn,' George says. 'It's just a bit of rain. It'll be fine, come on, let's skedaddle.'

'It's not just a *bit* of rain, is it? It's biblical out there – there's probably flooding. And it's not just the rain anyway, it's the wind.'

'Now you're just making excuses.'

'No, George, I'm trying to stop you from dying.'

George scoffs.

'It's not like driving a car,' Reubyn says. 'This is a high-sided vehicle – it could tip over in a gale.'

'It doesn't look gale-force to me,' Miles says, peering out.

'That's because we're in the forest. We're sheltered by the trees. It'll be different out on the roads.'

Everyone is silent, and Polly senses a stalemate. They need a compromise if they're going to get out of here. 'We could drive a little way, and see how we go,' she says. 'If it's really that bad, we can just pull over and camp up?'

'Sounds fair,' George quickly adds.

Reubyn shakes his head. 'We need to identify a spot to camp. You can't just park up on the street – it needs planning.'

'No one could blame us for parking up in a storm.'

Reubyn folds his arms. 'The answer's no.'

Polly opens her mouth but George comes in loudly before she can say anything.

'Screw that,' he says. 'You don't get to call the shots – this isn't a dictatorship, last time I checked.'

'That may be. But I'm the only one who can drive this thing, and I'm not driving it anywhere tonight, so it looks like we're staying.'

George puffs his cheeks. 'For heaven's sake.'

'It's only one more night,' Elis says. 'It's not really a big deal, is it?'

George jerks his head at him like a raptor. 'It *is* a big deal when all of us except *him*' – George points at Reubyn – 'want to leave.'

'Not all of us,' Elis says. 'I don't particularly care, either way.'

'Who asked you, anyway?'

'Sorry, George, do I need permission to speak?'

'If you haven't got anything sensible to say, then yes.'

Elis sighs. 'I'm not going to let you speak for me. As far as I'm concerned, this is a perfectly nice spot to camp, and I wouldn't mind staying another night.'

George ignores Elis and turns to face Miles. 'Will you kindly have a word with your beg friend and tell him his opinion doesn't carry any weight in this group?'

Silence. The atmosphere shifts before George has even finished his sentence. His words are delivered casually, as if a throwaway remark of no consequence. But the impact is stark. The group exchange nervous glances.

Elis appears stunned for a moment, then glares at George. 'Beg friend?'

Polly shakes her head. This situation is close to getting out of control. 'George, stop it.'

George fixes Polly with a serious stare, and, just for a second, it looks as if he might back down. Maybe even apologise. But then the corner of his mouth pulls up into a smirk and his eyes take on a maniacal glint – the look of a man who simply wants to watch the world burn. Suddenly, the rain beating against the roof sounds like a percussionist brushing a snare. It's like a drum roll to highlight the growing tension, increasing in energy and volume right up until this show's big reveal. Polly can almost hear the climactic clash of a cymbal as George begins to speak.

'Yeah, that's right,' he says, his eyes back on Elis. 'Beg friend. As in, someone who doesn't have real friends and has to desperately cling on where he's not wanted. Beg. Friend.'

Faith and Jessie look at each other, grimacing.

Elis slowly stands. His hands are tense, fingers clawing by his sides, which then ball into fists. 'Why don't you come here and call me that?'

George springs to his feet with a grin and walks towards him. 'I'd be happy to, *beg friend*.'

In a sudden, spring-like movement, Elis's arm uncoils and he strikes out at George, his fist thudding against his cheek. George stumbles and steadies himself on the sideboard. Reubyn, Miles and Faith rush in to fill the space between them. They bark at Elis, ordering him back, and form a barrier to stop the two men from reaching each other. Jessie is frozen, her hands covering her mouth in shock. Polly groans and makes a dismissive remark, but she too is shocked. Witnessing this sudden act of violence gives her a pang of nausea.

George appears dazed for a moment as he presses three fingers to his reddening face. Then his eyes bulge. Still holding his face, he jabs a finger at Elis. 'You'll regret that.'

Elis smirks. 'I doubt it.'

George's tongue forms a moving lump under his skin as it explores for damage inside his mouth. He slowly nods. 'Oh, you will.'

'Cut it out, you two,' Polly snaps. 'This isn't helping our situation one bit.'

Elis has already turned away. He grabs his coat off its hook and opens the door, and the sound of the storm intensifies for a moment before he walks out. The door slams shut behind him.

George begins a tirade about Elis, and Polly turns her back, trying to tune out his angry outburst. She slumps on to the bench and puts her head in her hands. They need to leave. But with Reubyn digging his heels in, and Elis having just wandered off, that's not happening. They're going to have to stay here a little longer – in a place that is totally cut off, both digitally and geographically.

And there's something else that's started niggling away at her since she witnessed that ugly scene. What if George is right? They don't know Elis that well, and he can seem quite intense – as evidenced by the assault he just launched. What if Miles has made a mistake in trusting this guy? Maybe they shouldn't have invited him along. And now they're stuck with him.

CHAPTER 38

ALEX

Should I tell you my name? My real name. Right now? Gosh, it's tempting. Do you know, Miles, I came so close to revealing myself to you last night. You see, I can hardly wait a second longer before I get to see that look in your eyes when you realise you haven't got away with anything. I confess, it's becoming difficult to keep my emotions in check. But I must, just for a little longer.

In case it isn't obvious, I'm right here in this forest. I like this place. It couldn't be better, actually. The weather leaves a little to be desired, but I suppose you can't have everything.

I keep thinking about what exactly has brought you here, Miles. Is it a need for isolation? A love of the great outdoors? A random pin in a map?

No, it's something else. Fate has brought us here, I'm sure of it. Perhaps fate is the wrong word, but nevertheless I feel it happening: these powerful, balancing forces moving to create equilibrium; immortal, unseen hands moving us carefully around like pieces on a chess board. I'm one or two moves away. One or two moves. And then that's it, Miles. Checkmate.

You don't realise this, but under the cover of this forest, I've been able to take a good look at you. In light of everything that's happened, you're not behaving at all as I expected. I'm coming to the conclusion that you're playing a part. You're acting. How perfect. You've embodied a role. If that is indeed what's happening, you are a slightly better actor than I gave you credit for.

When I look at you, I'm trying to fathom what, if anything, is genuine in your facial expressions. The only thing I know for sure that isn't faked is the perturbed look you get when you're trying to figure out who I am. Who is following you? You'd love to know, wouldn't you?

What if I was to give you a clue? What if I was to tell you that I'm not the man you followed out of the bar the other night? Would that help?

That I, too, am an actor? No, I couldn't do that – it would be too much of a giveaway. You'd know instantly who I am.

I'm a good actor, you know. A far superior actor to you, Miles. I'm certain of that, even if I am destined never to get the sort of success you are capable of.

What I've learned about our industry, Miles, is that talent will only get you so far. Your personal background is far more important. Anyone in any doubt about that should look up their favourite British actor and find out what school they went to, how their family came into possession of their generational wealth.

No, I would never be able to hit the heights that you could reach. But that doesn't mean I don't know what I'm doing. I'm able and prepared. You'll discover that very soon. And when you do, you'll have witnessed the performance of a lifetime.

CHAPTER 39

MILES

It's nearly dark, and Miles scans torchlight in all directions as he hurries down the path towards the hide. The sound of the downpour raises in pitch as he approaches, becoming a harsher din as rain rattles the roof and gushes through gutters and downpipes. Water drips from his hair and face. He pauses halfway up the steps and aims light into the hide as he creeps towards the door and peers inside. The yellow orb illuminates a figure sitting on the bench, his torso bent over, face aimed at the floor. Elis.

'Hey,' Miles says, doing his best to keep his tone calm, to hide his annoyance at having been dragged out here. The last thing he wanted was to come back to the hide, but he can't just leave him out in the forest in a storm. 'I thought I'd find you here.'

Elis turns his head to the side, wearily, but otherwise remains in his hunched position. 'As opposed to all the other places to find shelter in this forest?'

Miles takes a seat next to him. 'Look, why don't you come back to the bus? George has calmed down a bit, now, and if you apologise—'

'*Apologise?*' Elis straightens his back and glares at him. 'Why would I do that?'

'You did punch him in the face. Quite hard.'

'And he deserved it.'

Miles prepares to reply, then he reconsiders. Elis doesn't appear to have calmed down at all – he is every bit as het up as when he stormed out of the van an hour ago. 'Listen, mate,' Miles says, eventually. 'What George was saying, all that beg friend stuff. He knows it's not true, he just likes to stir things up, get a reaction out of people. You shouldn't rise to it.'

Elis mutters something, but Miles doesn't hear. The noise of the rain pounding against thin metal has increased, to the point where it sounds like a train is speeding past them.

'Come on,' Miles says. 'Let's go back.'

'So, we'll all just return to being happy campers, shall we?'

'Why not?'

The question hangs unanswered, and Miles feels his pulse tick a little faster. Why is everyone getting so dramatic about tiny things? Falling out over nothing. As someone who has experienced real stress, Miles wants to grab them all by the ears and give them a shake, let them know how bloody lucky they are.

'Why not?' Miles repeats, eventually. 'We'll be moving on tomorrow, exploring somewhere new. There's no reason we can't all get along. Let's put this behind—'

'Well, it's not exactly been a fun trip, so far, has it?'

Miles shakes his head. 'Tell me about it.'

Elis cackles a little too loudly, and not in a way that suggests he's found anything amusing.

'What?' Miles says.

'Well, this trip hasn't been such a drag for you, has it, hanging out with your new girlfriend and your treasured schoolmates.'

Miles's brow creases. 'Are you serious? She's hardly my girl-friend – I've only known her a few days. And have you forgotten everything that's been happening? To *me*?'

'Oh, I remember everything. It seems to me like you're the one with the short memory.'

'What the hell are you talking about?'

Elis shoots him a withering look, and Miles breaks eye contact. They both know *exactly*. The agreement was they'd never speak of it again, but, apparently, that agreement hasn't lasted very long.

'It wouldn't kill you to show a scintilla of gratitude,' Elis says.

'I am grateful. What makes you think I'm not?'

Elis scowls. 'George. Out here, you've been acting like the sun shines out of his arse. It's like I don't exist. You take his side on everything.'

'George is one of my oldest friends.' Miles's voice is raised to match Elis's volume. 'I've known him since we were five.'

'And that's all that matters, is it? Time? Never mind shared interests, or common goals, or loyalty.'

'I think you're being a bit harsh.'

'Really?'

'Yeah. For a start, I have been loyal to you. You were invited on this trip, weren't you?'

'I might have been invited, but it's pretty obvious your loyalty is with George.'

Miles takes a deep breath, giving careful consideration to what he's about to say. He doesn't want to upset Elis, but, at the same time, he can't allow him to carry on. 'Elis, mate,' he says, in the sort of measured but purposeful tone a schoolteacher might use. 'I'm glad you came on this trip, I really value our friendship . . . but you need to remember that I've known George for pretty much my whole life. We're almost like brothers.'

Elis stares at the darkening mirror of glass in front of them, his jaw set tight. Then he slowly turns his head to look at Miles, his eyes wide and burning with emotion: surprise, loathing or fury, or some combination of all. 'You're unbelievable.'

'I'm not sure what you want from me. Am I expected to grovel at your feet every five minutes? For the rest of my life? Is that what you want?'

Elis stands. 'You really are an entitled, spoilt, ungrateful little prick,' he says slowly.

Miles recoils, stunned by the venom in Elis's words. 'Am I?'

'You are.'

Miles gets to his feet and steps back, putting a few yards between them. 'Well, if you don't like me, you're free to leave any time you like.'

'Yeah, I am,' Elis says, as Miles turns and crosses the room towards the exit. 'And I'm also free to change my statement, any time I like.'

Miles stops in the doorway and turns to face him. 'Sorry, what?'

'You heard me. I'm free to change my statement. And I might do just that. Maybe I'll go to the police and tell them the truth about the night of Caira's murder, that you *didn't* come to my flat, that we *didn't* watch *Chinatown* together, and that, quite frankly, I haven't got the foggiest idea what you were up to that night.'

Miles is dead-still, a statue in the doorway. 'Now you're being ridiculous.'

'No, I'm not.'

'You are. Why on earth would you do that?'

'Because it's the right thing to do.'

'The right thing to do? You'd be admitting perjury. You'd go to prison.'

'Maybe I would. But not for as long as you'll get when they do you for murder.'

'No.' Miles shakes his head. 'That's not how it works. I've been acquitted.'

'Are you sure about that?'

'I'm not having this conversation.'

'I think you'll find we just had it.'

Miles's veins are electrified, fizzing with anger. How *dare* Elis turn on him like this, after everything he's been through? After bringing him on this trip, all expenses paid. He steps towards Elis, shining the torch in his face so that he squints into the light. 'You're deluded,' Miles says. 'What you're saying, it pretty much amounts to blackmail. What are you thinking, here, that you can hold this over me forever, like some sword of Damocles?'

'What were *you* thinking? That you could just treat me like crap and get away with it?'

Miles opens his mouth and immediately closes it, deciding against the first thing that comes to mind. He takes two drawn-out breaths. 'I'm sorry if I've upset you. I genuinely am. But I think it might be best if you make your own way onward once we reach the next town. And perhaps we should avoid each other in future.'

Miles turns and leaves the hide, unwilling to continue the conversation. He has no intention of staying for Elis's response, but hears it anyway as he makes his way down the steps.

'You'll do well to avoid me.'

CHAPTER 40

REUBYN

Reubyn sits at the kitchen table, editing software open on his laptop. On the screen, he's walking a trail through the forest and turns his head to face the camera. Reubyn can't look, rolls his eyes upward. He simply can't look at that pudgy face. Right now, he'd do anything to have a different face – to be someone else.

He stares vacantly into the living area. On the TV is an American sitcom Reubyn can't remember the name of, and the canned laughter that rumbles out of the speakers a few times per minute is completely at odds with the current mood. There's been a grim tension in the bus for the last few hours, and it's only got worse since Elis skulked back about half an hour after Miles. Elis offered no apology; in fact, he hasn't uttered a word to George since he punched him earlier. Now, the group appears to have split into three parts. Or four, if you count Reubyn. Miles and Jessie are curled up in the corner, her head resting on his chest as they converse in hushed voices. On the other side of the bus, George and Polly are sat, drinking wine and locked in a grim-faced discussion as they stare at the TV. But Reubyn hasn't been paying attention to either of these couples. Instead, his gaze skims over the top of his computer screen, way down to the front of the bus, where Elis and Faith are in the passenger seats, with no discernible gap between them. It looks cosy. *Very* cosy. When Elis returned from his sulk, he took the furthest available seat away from everyone else. And Faith didn't waste any time; within seconds she had moved down there to join him.

Reubyn knows he's got no one to blame but himself. He gave Faith the cold shoulder, pushed her away, and now she's probably about to fall straight into the arms of Elis. But, still, it's hard not to feel emotional about it. Everything has gone wrong. And Elis isn't right for her. That's what Reubyn finds so frustrating; what his friends are looking for is so shallow – they're motivated by one thing – and yet they get whatever they want.

Reubyn isn't like them. Yes, sex would be nice, but all he really wants is a connection to someone. He'd like to feel wanted. And he doesn't even want much in return. Certainly not anything weird. He'd just like to be present with someone, to lie with them. Someone like Faith. Maybe she would whisper softly in his ear. Stroke his hair. Is that too much to ask? Apparently, yes. Nice guys finish last. It's an old cliché, but for Reubyn it rings true.

If Faith had chosen him, he would've done anything for her, moved heaven and earth to make her happy and keep her from harm. Elis won't give a toss about her; he'll probably use her and then move on to someone else. Reubyn watches Elis's every gesture, every expression, and they all look fake. George was right; Elis should never have been invited on this trip.

Reubyn still has eyes on him a few minutes later, until his view is interrupted by George, who is out of his seat. He's begun clearing the floor and rearranging the furniture, to convert the space from living room to bedroom. It's gone ten o'clock, and it seems no one is in the mood to stay up late and socialise.

George has finished converting a bench into a bed and is carrying a large cushion across the room when the overhead lights cut out. A split second later, the television cuts to black, and the fridge ceases its hum. The sudden death of all noise inside the bus gives the whirling sound of the storm outside a new intensity. And it's fully dark apart from the artificial glow from Reubyn's screen. Its blue light illuminates him and no one else.

'Reubyn,' George says, from somewhere in the gloom. 'What's going on?'

'Well, my friend, it appears we've run out of power.'

Groans and murmurs of dissatisfaction reverberate around the space, under the sound of drilling rain.

Polly appears by the table, faintly lit by the laptop. 'What the hell? What do you mean we've run out? You never said anything about this!'

'Okay, let me explain. Electricity is stored in batteries, and if you use the electricity within them, eventually the batteries run out.'

Polly places her hands over the table and leans across. 'Don't get smart with me, you know exactly what I mean. How can we have run out already?'

Reubyn shrugs. 'They said it would last a few days without a recharge, but I guess we've been using more power than expected. I mean, it's not really surprising, is it? We've had the air-con on pretty much non-stop, the telly, music, we've all been charging our devices . . .'

In the time it's taken him to utter these few sentences, Miles, Jessie and George have joined Polly, and the four of them stare at him.

'Please tell me we can still drive the bus?' Miles says.

'Of course we can. It's just the leisure battery that's run out.'

'Are you *sure*?'

'Yeah. The vehicle battery is separate, don't worry.'

Miles exhales slowly, his shoulders untensing. 'Thank God for that.'

'It's still not good, though, is it?' George says. 'My phone is on ten per cent.'

'Who cares? We don't have any signal or internet, anyway, why do you care about your phone?'

'Because nothing works! We haven't even got any lights!'

Reubyn tightens his lips to stop a smile from forming. They're completely overreacting. 'It's only for one night,' he says. 'And it's getting late anyway – we'll be going to sleep soon. I'm really sorry, George, you're going to have to brush your teeth in the dark, but guess what? Tomorrow, the sun will rise.'

'Yes,' George says. 'And when it does, we better be getting the hell out of here.'

To underline his point, George maintains eye contact, and, for once, Reubyn chooses to hold his gaze. Then he scans the other faces – all similarly serious. They look utterly miserable. Angry, even. In a strange way it feels like solidarity. At least Reubyn's not the only one. They're stuck here now, for at least one more night, and they can all be miserable and angry together.

PART FOUR

CHAPTER 41

THE TRIAL

The worst day of the trial coincided with Miles's thirtieth birthday. In any other circumstances he would've been celebrating, but once more fate conspired against him and served up a wretched experience. On the morning he was due to give evidence, Eleanor visited him in the side room he had sequestered due to the public's interest in the case, and gave him a birthday card in a jolly yellow envelope. 'I'm sorry this is how you're spending your birthday,' she said. But, in truth, he was so deep into his nightmare that birthdays and celebrations of any kind had become meaningless. There was barely time to open the card before they were heading upstairs to the courtroom for the day he'd been dreading.

As he was a witness in his own defence, Eleanor addressed him first, gently delivering the questions he knew she was going to, and he gave his preprepared answers. And then, the moment he had hoped would never arrive. William Cox KC rose to his feet, acknowledged the judge, and locked his eyes on Miles. The courtroom fell so silent that every cough cracked the air like artillery. And Miles experienced a triple dose of pre-exam nausea, his shirt damp and sticking to his back under his suit jacket.

'Mr Deverill,' Cox said. 'On the date of her murder, you say you were at Ms Kennedy's flat for a total of around five minutes, is that correct?'

'Yes.'

Cox looked up from his notes and shot Miles a withering look over the brim of his glasses, as if surprised by his answer. 'I put it to you that five minutes is a peculiar duration for such a visit. Why go in at all?'

'It was cold,' Miles said. 'She invited me to come in while I waited for an Uber.'

'But you didn't call an Uber, did you, Mr Deverill, because' – he studied his notes, as if he needed reminding – 'your phone was out of battery?'

'That's right.'

'Did you ask Ms Kennedy if you could charge your phone at her flat?'

'She didn't have the right charger. I think she had an Android phone.'

Cox's eyes stuck on him for a moment, then slid away. 'What kind of phone was yours, Mr Deverill? What make and model?'

'It was an iPhone 15.'

He checked his notes again. 'An iPhone 15 *Plus*?' – waiting for confirmation from Miles – 'and how new was this phone? Months, years?'

'A few months old.'

Cox nodded. 'And do you know what the battery life is for this particular model?'

'No.'

'According to the manufacturer's technical specifications, which are available in your bundle on page forty-three, the battery life for this model allows for video playback of up to twenty-six hours. Does that sound about right?'

'I suppose so.'

'How was it then, Mr Deverill, that on that date, you had managed to use up the entire life of that battery?'

Miles touched his collar, under which heat was spreading across his neck. 'I'm not sure. Maybe it hadn't been charged properly. I can't remember.'

Cox let his answer hang in silence as he pretended to find something among his notes. 'According to the statement you gave, you then walked to a flat rented by your friend, Mr Elis Pritchard-Jones, is that correct?'

'Yes.'

'Earlier in this trial, you'll recall the jury being shown a map which plotted the quickest route from Ms Kennedy's home to Mr Jones's flat. It showed the most direct route, yet you elected to go a different way – along some smaller residential roads and through the park. Is that correct?'

'That's correct.'

Cox raised an eyebrow. 'As you said yourself, it was a very cold night. Freezing, in fact. You must have been in a hurry to reach the warmth of your friend's flat, yet you took the longer route. Why?'

Miles's heart thudded urgently. 'I didn't intend to take the longer route. I was disorientated. I'd been drinking.'

'Let me see if I've got this right.' Cox talked slowly, as if deep in thought, considering it all for the first time. 'The data from your phone can't confirm where you went, because it was out of battery, and you weren't seen on CCTV because you took the long route to your friend's flat.' Another pause, and Cox set down his notes. 'I put it to you, Mr Deverill, that you're lying. I put it to you that you stayed at Ms Kennedy's flat for much longer than five minutes.'

'I'm not lying.'

'This wasn't your first date arranged on the Hinge app, was it?'

'No.'

'How many Hinge dates have you been on, Mr Deverill?' Cox had gone up several gears, firing questions more rapidly.

'Maybe ten.'

'And how many of those dates have resulted in sexual intercourse?'

'One or two.'

'Please be specific, Mr Deverill, was it one or was it two?'

Miles's cheeks burned, and he became acutely aware of his parents' presence in the public gallery. 'Two.'

Cox chose to pause in that moment, his lips pursed in consideration, as if he needed time to digest what Miles had just said. It created an excruciatingly long silence. 'Let's return to your departure from Ms Kennedy's flat. Given your history of romantic success, it must have come as quite a disappointment that she didn't invite you to stay longer?'

'I wouldn't say that.'

'Did you expect her to *put out*?' Cox put the emphasis on those last two words in a way that suggested he was talking Miles's language rather than his own.

'I didn't expect anything.'

'But you would've been happy if she'd made a move, asked you to stay over?'

'I don't know.'

'Did it make you frustrated that she didn't?'

Miles's temperature rose at that, and he tried to slow his breathing to suppress it. The last thing he needed, in response to that question, was to appear frustrated. He took a deep breath. 'I wasn't at all frustrated.'

'Mr Deverill,' Cox said, his speech simultaneously slowing and increasing in volume. 'I put it to you that you're a young man who is accustomed to getting what he wants, and when Ms Kennedy rejected your advances, you reacted with anger and violence, isn't that right?'

Cox thumped out those last three words like a slow drum. *Isn't. That. Right.* And despite his subsequent protestations and denials, Miles left the witness box with a vile feeling in his stomach. There were people in the room who were ready to believe Cox's version of events. He was sure of it.

CHAPTER 42

GEORGE

When George wakes from a disturbed sleep the next morning, he instantly recalls the nightmare that unsettled him hours earlier. Again, he was back at his school; again, it was their dormitory that was being subjected to the night visits; and, again, in this nightmare version of his childhood, it was him being taken from his bed in the middle of the night.

He understands, now, why he keeps going back there. This place, just like Holvine, is the kind that blurs the boundaries of consciousness, where it becomes harder to tell where nightmares end and real life begins. Fortunately, his mind has emerged fully from the depths of sleep and landed on the shores of a new day. And he should be glad of it. Soon they'll be moving on, driving out of this miserable reserve and on to somewhere better. But glad isn't quite the right word. Instead, he has what some people call 'mixed emotions'. It's a curious expression that suggests feelings can exist separately yet be all jumbled up, like marbles in a bag, when the truth is they seep and bleed into each other – anger, frustration, regret – and become a single entity, a complicated cocktail that can't be defined by a single word. As a child, George used to find feelings overwhelming, to the point where he visualised them as a living, breathing thing: a burning red dragon to be wrestled with. Nowadays, they are much more sedate, like a cat that winds round his ankles or curls up on his midriff when he is still.

George sits up and cranes his head to see through a gap in the curtains. Unbelievably, it's still tipping it down outside, and the wind seems even stronger than it was last night. The rain is not only hammering the roof but also lashing the whole left side of the bus.

'How the hell is it *still* raining?' George mumbles, not directing his question at anyone specific. 'What is this, a *rain*forest?'

There's no response; the others are still dozing or lack the enthusiasm to respond. He suspects the latter. So, George lies back and listens to the sound of the rain. It's discomforting. Just like the soreness around his cheekbone. A distant echo of the smouldering fury he felt last night. He's also woken with a good half a dozen new mosquito bites. Since they no longer have air-con, they needed to open the windows last night, and the bitey little bastards found their way inside.

It's maybe ten minutes before the door to the bedroom opens and Faith pads into the main area, stretching her arms above her head as she yawns. 'G'day.' She picks up the kettle and turns on the tap. 'Anyone for a cuppa?'

'Good luck with that.'

Faith sighs and replaces the kettle. 'Ah yeah, I forgot.' After a moment's thought, she says, 'Shall we have a cold one? That's a thing, right? Iced tea?'

'The freezer's not working, so it certainly won't be iced,' George says. 'But given that we're on a voyage of discovery, I'll embrace the spirit of adventure and join you for a tepid tea.'

Faith opens the cupboard containing the mugs. 'Anyone else?'

Miles and Reubyn decline the offer, in weary voices.

Faith peers into the bathroom, before planting her hands on her hips. 'Where's Elis?'

They all turn to look at the heap of sofa cushions, pillows and red sleeping bag that has served as Elis's bed for the past couple of nights.

'He's probably gone for a walk or something,' George says.

Faith pulls back a curtain and peers out of the window. 'Not great weather for a hike. It's pelting pick handles out there.'

George stands and steps into a pair of trousers. 'You know what he's like; thinks he's bloody Ray Mears. He's probably fashioned a shelter out of logs and bear hides.'

'There are no bears in New Zealand,' Faith says.

'Rat skins, then.'

'He's probably gone to the bird hide,' Reubyn says. 'I'd be there myself, if I hadn't given up hope of seeing one of those bloody kākāpō.'

For an hour or so they lounge around, get dressed and drink weak room-temperature tea. Eventually Polly and Jessie join them, and everyone begins the process of reorganising the space and packing up their stuff. They have a late breakfast of cereal and lukewarm milk, and Jessie makes sandwiches for the journey. Lastly, Reubyn brings in the slide-outs that extend the living area, returning the space to how it was before they arrived. All loose items have been secured, and the only stuff left on the floor is Elis's. It's all in a heap next to his half-empty backpack: his sleeping bag, toiletries, clothes. In the couple of hours it's taken them to pack everything up, most of the chat has been about where the hell he's gone. They've speculated about his mood, what he's doing, when he'll be back. George, Miles and Reubyn are of the opinion that it's nothing to worry about. But the others – Jessie in particular – are becoming increasingly dramatic about it, as if Elis is a vulnerable child or pet that's gone missing, instead of a grown man with a love of the outdoors.

Now, in a physical manifestation of that split, they sit, three to a bench; the girls on one side, boys on the other.

'I think we should just get going,' George says.

Faith, directly opposite, glares at him. 'We're obviously not going anywhere without him.'

'Well, what does he expect? He knows we're leaving today. If he wanted to come with us, he shouldn't have gone AWOL.'

Faith doesn't respond, but, even out of the corner of his eye, George can tell she's giving him daggers.

'We should go look for him,' Jessie says.

George scoffs. 'In this weather?'

'We should at least check the trails and the bird hide.'

'Oh, should we?' George says, wide-eyed at Jessie. 'And are *you* volunteering to do that?'

'No, but I don't think—'

'Thought not,' George says. 'And I'm not going either. The bastard took a swing at me yesterday, so forgive me if I'm not in a rush to go out and find him.'

Jessie looks at Miles, asking a question with a hopeful raise of her eyebrows.

He shakes his head. 'I'm not doing it. My clothes still haven't dried out since the last time I went out looking for him.'

'But he's your friend.'

'And he's a big boy. If Elis wants to go walkabout, then that's his choice. He doesn't need me.'

Faith stands. 'I'll go.'

Jessie takes hold of her wrist. 'Not on your own. It's not safe.'

The girls look at Reubyn, who initially avoids their eye contact. It appears he's not in a hurry to search for Elis, either.

'Look, there's no rush,' Reubyn says, eventually. 'The weather's still horrendous, and I wouldn't mind leaving it for a bit before we leave, anyway, to see if the wind backs off a—'

'Reubyn,' Polly snaps. 'Don't you dare start this again.'

'Start what?'

'All that crap about waiting for the weather to change. Let's get one thing very, *very* clear. We're *not* staying another night.'

Reubyn shows his palms. 'I know. I know.'

'I don't care if this forest gets hit by a category five hurricane, we're leaving today. Understood?'

'One hundred per cent,' Reubyn says.

The others stare at him, as if waiting for Reubyn to pledge a higher level of commitment. George feels a rare smidge of sympathy for him. What's he supposed to say? Even Reubyn wouldn't stoop to using the phrase 'one hundred and ten per cent' – only a football enthusiast would do that.

'Look,' Reubyn says eventually, gesticulating, as if handling an invisible object. 'His boots and coat are gone. He's obviously gone for a hike. We'll just have to wait until he returns. And if he's still not back in a few hours, then, at that point, obviously we'll have a decision to make.'

There are a few sighs. An eye-roll from Jessie. They are sure signs an agreement, albeit a reluctant one, has been reached. It seems they'll remain in the forest for a few hours yet.

George slumps back into the corner of the bench and closes his eyes. Bloody Elis. Eventually, everyone is going to head out and look for him – George can sense it. And, eventually, they'll find him. George would rather they didn't.

◆ ◆ ◆

The afternoon passes with card games – mostly rummy – being glumly contested on the living-room table. Not everyone is partaking; Polly has been engrossed in her novel, and Reubyn is using the remaining battery life on his laptop to edit. In the time they've killed, the weather

238

hasn't improved. But they really need to get going. The sandwiches Jessie made are long gone, and there's not much in the way of food. Most of it requires cooking or will soon perish without refrigeration. In short, Elis's time is nearly up.

After some negotiating, they decided the cut-off – the time at which they would cease waiting for Elis – was to be five o'clock. That way there would still be a few hours of daylight left, and they wouldn't have to drive out of the forest in the dark. Now, it's gone four-thirty, and the mood is getting antsy.

They're between games, and Faith has been riffling the cards with a metrical precision. The steady thrum under her thumbs is stark against the chaotic weather outside. Such skilful shuffling would be pleasing to watch if done by a croupier, but George finds it mildly irritating – that she can shuffle like that, and he can't. Surely those cards are good and shuffled by now. This has become performative.

As if reading his thoughts, Faith places the deck on the table. 'All right, this has gone on long enough. It's obvious he's not coming back.' She folds her arms, waiting for a response.

'Maybe—' Miles clears his throat, having croaked the word. This is the first time he's spoken for a while. 'Maybe he's gone. He was in an awful mood last night, and it didn't seem like he wanted to be here anymore. He can be a bit impulsive, and it wouldn't surprise me if he's just left.'

'But all his stuff.' Faith points. 'He wouldn't leave his bag behind.'

'Maybe he wants to travel light?'

Faith moves swiftly to the spot where Elis's belongings are piled up on the floor. She crouches, stands his backpack on end, and unzips the front pocket, feeling inside. 'Keys,' she says, placing them on the sideboard, before going in for another rummage. 'Phone,' she says, repeating the action. Faith digs in again, then waves a navy-blue document above her head. 'Passport. I've heard of travelling light, but who goes running off into the wilds of a foreign country without this?'

They stare at each other, even Polly, who rests her book open on her lap. Until now, no one has thought to look through his stuff, and it is, of course, pretty obvious that Elis wouldn't have fled without such crucial personal effects.

Polly sits up straight. 'So, what? We can't wait for him forever.'

'We have to go look for him,' Jessie says.

Faith nods. 'What if he's been in an accident? With this kind of rainfall there could be landslips or God knows what.'

'I don't get why he would even go out hiking,' Jessie says. 'In this weather. It makes no sense.'

'I'm worried about him.'

'Me too.'

A funereal silence takes hold. George gets up and paces slowly to the far end of the bus, deep in thought. Someone needs to take charge, and naturally, it needs to be him. He clears his throat to command their attention. 'All right, look. Here's what we should do. We send out a search party. For half an hour, tops. And if we don't find him, then we drive out of here and let the authorities know what's happened, report him missing.'

'Report him missing?' Reubyn asks the question with a crease in his brow. 'That's a bit extreme, isn't it?'

'We don't know where he is though, do we? Hence missing.' Reubyn opens his mouth to reply, and George shows him the hand – a command to shut up. 'This way, we'll have done our due diligence, taken reasonable steps to check on Elis's welfare, and we'll still be out of here by six. Sound fair?'

'So, who is going to be in your search party, George?' Polly says.

'Not *my* search party. I'm not going.'

Jessie rolls her eyes. 'I think we should stay together. We should all go.'

Within five minutes, and despite George's protestations, preparations are being made to go out into the storm. All of them. Those who own hiking boots – Miles, Jessie and Faith – are lacing them up. Coats and umbrellas are unpacked. George zips up his windbreaker jacket, which he suspects will provide feeble resistance to the rain, and reluctantly joins the others by the door.

Faith grabs the handle, then pauses, looking over her shoulder. 'I guess we should start at the bird hide?'

'I reckon we should check that trail first,' Reubyn says, pointing towards the front end of the bus, in a direction George reckons might be north. 'Then we circle back that way, check the other trails, and check the bird hide last.'

'Why the hell would we check the hide last?' Polly asks. 'Surely that's the most likely place he'll be.'

'Because, if we don't find him, we can't just drive off with all his stuff. We'll have to leave it in the hide. We can't just leave it out in the rain.'

'Well, bugger me, he's right.' George slaps Reubyn hard on the back. 'That's probably the most intelligent thing you've ever said. As a prize for being so bloody clever, you can carry his bag. Come on, then, let's get this over with.'

Faith opens the door, the sound of the storm rushing in to fill the bus, and they file out. As the last to exit, George closes the door behind him. It slams shut, assisted by a gust. As he descends the steps, he calls after the others, but they don't hear. Shouldn't they be locking the bus? *Forget it*, George thinks. In the scheme of things, it really doesn't matter.

◆ ◆ ◆

As he predicted, George is soaked through to the skin before they even reach the first trail. They got deluged as they crossed the car park, and now, out in the woods, he finds the canopy is at breaking point. The trees are bearing all the water they can, saturated completely, so the rain's full load is finding passage to the earth, only unevenly, in great sloshes and drips. George deliberately didn't bring any boots or waterproofs on this trip, so no one could persuade him to go hiking. And yet, here he is, out in the middle of nowhere, in the foulest of weather. His hoodless jacket is proving hopeless.

Their progress is slow. The path is slick with mud, and, with every step, George needs to plant his feet carefully on the ground to avoid slipping into the muck. Ahead of him, the girls are shouting Elis's name. Miles and Reubyn are too, somewhat half-heartedly. With the wind blustering around, their voices are small and have no echo.

At a fork in the trail, they stop. They call for Elis through tunnelled hands, channelling their shouts up the trail they have no intention of following further. Then they turn right, into an area of denser forest. This path is narrow and overgrown, invaded by branches and long leaves that arc and bend under their own weight. George uses his forearm to pull back the wet, reedy fronds of a tree fern that hangs across the trail, revealing a deeper tangle behind. All around is that damp, composty smell that's only found in the most shadowy of places. The dark corners that are permanently out of reach of the sun. *Primeval.* A couple of days earlier that word gave him cause to laugh. Now, though, it seems simply to be the correct adjective, not only to describe this ancient and wild place, but also the feelings and instincts that are seeded into those who enter it.

The path twists, and them with it. Reubyn, just ahead of Miles, holds his phone sideways to take a video. He's had it out for less than twenty seconds before he shakes off water and slips it back into his pocket.

After a few more minutes of walking, the forest is sparser again. In that time, George has fallen behind. They were supposed to stay close, but he's at least thirty yards behind the others. He trudges miserably. Weaving through the wet foliage has soaked George's trousers, and the wet cotton sticks uncomfortably to his thighs.

Still, the others call Elis's name.

But their search is nearly over now. Through the trees, George can just about make out the outline of the hide, maybe a hundred yards away.

A great gust swipes at the trees, making them groan and hiss. It shakes water from the canopy, and more gets in under George's coat, its cold fingers tracing down his back.

He shivers.

The others are approaching the hide. From somewhere near to it comes a high-pitched sort of yelp. A squeal of surprise or shock. Like a hare learning its fate on the running ground at the end of a coursing match.

George pauses. And then a sharp sound pierces the air, an urgent frequency cutting through the storm's low growl. A scream.

CHAPTER 43

POLLY

They all stare at each other. No one is staring at the body. Oh God. The body. That's what he is, now. What he's been reduced to. Elis's corpse lies haphazardly on the muddy ground next to the steps to the hide. His torso is on its side, and because his waterproof is unzipped, the cause of his death is gruesomely apparent. Polly ventures no closer. The sound of the rain against the nylon of her coat crackles like a lit fuse. Inside it, she realises suddenly, her limbs have begun to tremble.

She only takes one look, but it's enough to see that the light in him has been extinguished. The wound at his neck is horrible, but it's the look in his eyes – or, more precisely, the lack of any look – that's seared on her mind. She averts her gaze, looking anywhere but there. A deep sickness swirls in her stomach. She looks at the faces huddled around, and they all do the same: scanning each other, as if one of them will reveal the answer to this crisis. Instead, they're stunned into muteness. The only one making a sound is Jessie, and her whimpering is barely audible, drowned out by the sound of rain, and the wind-shaken branches and fidgety leaves. They cup hands over their mouths and wear expressions of pure horror.

Jessie begins muttering what sounds like a prayer.

Faith is the next to speak. 'What do we do?'

Polly expects George to begin barking instructions, but he doesn't. In fact, he's furthest from Elis's body. And silent. There's nothing they can do for Elis – he's so obviously *dead*. This is bad. Really bad. And yet no one is doing anything. They're all just standing here in the pouring rain.

'Okay,' Polly says, unsure of what she's about to say. 'Has anyone got their phone?'

Reubyn pulls his iPhone out of his pocket. 'I do,' he says, in a small voice.

'Call the emergency services.'

'There's no signal,' he says.

'Just try it,' she snaps.

Reubyn taps at his phone, then holds it to his ear. A few moments later, he looks at the screen and shakes his head.

Polly cups her face for a moment and swallows a lump in her throat. 'We need to go. We need to drive to an area with a signal so we can call the police.'

'What about Elis?' Jessie cries. 'We can't just leave him here!'

'That's exactly what we have to do.'

'But it seems wrong. Shouldn't we cover him up or something?'

'We can't tamper with him. This is a crime scene.' Polly's surprised to hear these words pass her lips. It doesn't sound like something she would say. But this isn't a situation she ever thought she would be faced with. Is this a crime scene, really? Maybe it could have been an accident. Although that doesn't seem remotely possible. Suicide? Elis seemed a bit down for the last few days, but she's never heard of anyone taking their own life by a cut to the throat. Polly scans the ground around his body. But there is no knife, or any sharp instrument anywhere to be seen. It's obvious that Elis has been—

'Reubyn? Are you filming?' Jessie's spluttered words break through Polly's thoughts.

Reubyn lowers his phone sheepishly, but Polly notices it is still pointing towards Elis. Towards the crime scene. 'I thought it might be important to document this,' he says. 'For the police. You know, evidence.'

Polly's about to scold him for being insensitive, but she bites her tongue. Reubyn's right. Elis has been murdered – that much is pretty bloody obvious. Despite how impossible that might seem. And they're the only ones out here in this forest. Which means . . . Polly swallows another lump of nothing, and it lands nauseously in her gut. She shudders. Is that even possible? Of course it is. People are capable of shocking, terrible things. Especially men. The only one she can immediately rule out as a suspect is Miles. Her brother isn't capable of doing something like this. But one of them is. And Polly feels that rising dread, the feeling that accompanies her in dark alleys and empty train carriages. She's not safe.

'We need to go,' she repeats. She grabs Miles by the arm, and sets off, leading them back towards the bus. She walks as briskly as she can on the slippery path. It's becoming difficult to see the ground clearly. It wasn't a bright day to begin with, and now, with heavy clouds and treetops forming a double barrier to the sun, daylight is fading fast. 'Come on,' she says, yanking at Miles's wrist. Her heartrate is increasing with every step. Doomy scenarios compete for her attention. What if it was George? What if whoever killed Elis is still armed with a knife? With each dire thought, her pace increases. She's hurrying now, almost jogging. What if the bus doesn't start? Polly starts running. What if they're stuck here? What if—

Polly's foot slips from under her, and her ankle twists as she falls. She yelps as she hits the path. A hot rush of pain shoots to her ankle, and she lets out an animal noise – somewhere between a growl and a scream. A sound of pain and fear.

◆　◆　◆

Miles and George help Polly up the stairs into the bus and sit her down on the bench.

'Here,' Jessie says, placing two white pills and a glass in front of her. 'These should help. I take them for period pain.'

Polly swallows them with a sip of water and thanks Jessie. Reubyn is the last to enter the bus, and he closes the door behind him in a manner that is oafishly slow, given their predicament. 'Come on,' Polly says, glaring at him. 'Hurry up.'

Reubyn lumbers through into the front seat and fastens his seat belt. Polly waits for the sound of the bus starting up. The warm chug of the engine. She's become so gloom-ridden that she's almost convinced herself the bus isn't going to start. But it will. And when it does, it will provide pure relief, like a first gulp of air after being held underwater. She watches Reubyn as he reaches for the ignition, and, somehow, deep down, she knows that she's right to be pessimistic. She knows it before the initial look of confusion takes over Reubyn's face when the engine doesn't roar to life. She knows it before he starts muttering, loud enough that they can all hear. Not every word is audible, but, in among the expletives, the key ones are. Somehow, she knew it already. Things *can* get worse. They *are* getting worse. They're in a *nightmare*.

Reubyn looks over his shoulder, a dumb expression on his face, like he's forgotten how to drive. He clicks off his seat belt. 'I don't understand. I tested it. I started the engine last night and it was fine. Now nothing works.'

For a moment they all just glare at him, stunned. Then everyone shouts over each other. How the hell is this possible?

Is he sure it won't start? *You bloody idiot, Reubyn.* The bus echoes with chaotic noise: shouting, cursing.

Reubyn gets out of his seat and approaches them with his hands raised submissively. They continue their outburst, a firing squad of questions, but after a minute or so, they stop, and once again the only sound is the rain drilling at the metal shell of the bus. If they were in a state of shock before, now the mood is ramping up into panic. And panic is no good in a situation like this; they need to *think*. Jessie is making a strange keening sound, and her body shakes as if hypothermic. Even Faith has lost her composure, raking her fingers through her braids and muttering to herself.

'Does anyone here know anything about mechanics?' Polly says, breaking their grim silence.

'Enough to know that you can't revive a battery without a source of electricity,' George replies. 'So, I'd say we're buggered, unless you know how to harness the power of rain.'

Polly narrows her eyes at him. If there's ever a good a time for his smartarse quips, this isn't it. Her stare lingers on George, and she feels her suspicion of him deepen. He was furious at Elis last night, calling him every name under the sun. Come to think of it, George has been awful to him for pretty much the whole trip. Maybe there was an underlying reason for this animosity that she didn't know about.

'Someone needs to go find some signal,' Jessie says, snapping Polly from her train of thought.

'Is that a good idea?' George replies. 'It's getting dark.'

'That's why it needs to be *now*.'

George stands and peers out of the window. 'There's probably about ten minutes of daylight left. It must be five miles at least to the nearest house.'

'*So?* We can't stay here.'

'Someone's just been murdered. And you want to nominate someone to walk five miles through a remote forest in the dark?'

'It might not be so far as that,' Jessie says. Her voice is unsure, desperate. 'Maybe on some higher ground, there might be some signal.'

'I'm sorry to be the one to point out the obvious,' George says, 'but Elis went out searching for a signal. And look what happened to *him*.'

'How do you know he was searching for a signal?' Faith asks. Her voice is measured, but there is a detectable coldness to her question. It's accusatory.

George shrugs. 'I don't.' He points at Jessie. 'That was *her* theory. I'm just saying it isn't safe to go wandering around out there right now. Jessie saw some random bloke out at the bird hide before, and now Elis is' – he pauses, trying to find the right words – 'in almost exactly the same spot.'

There's a silence, while they consider what he's said. And, as much as Polly hates to admit it, George is right. Again.

'Reubyn, lock all the doors and windows,' Polly says. 'So that this thing is completely secure.'

Reubyn does what he's told, and moves around the bus, checking every opening.

Jessie lets go of a quiet whine. Another thought occurs to Polly. The bus was unlocked when they got back.

'George, check the bedroom,' Polly says. 'Check all the wardrobes and under the bed.'

'Why do you want me to—' He nods, realising the answer. George ushers Reubyn to join him and walks slowly through the kitchen and towards the bedroom. Reubyn follows timidly behind George, who peers inside. Polly holds her breath as she waits for them to return. They all sit in silence, staring at the door. After about thirty seconds, they return, and George shrugs.

'It's clear,' Reubyn says.

Polly sits up straight. The pills have taken effect. 'Are you absolutely sure? Is there anywhere else someone could be hiding in here?'

Reubyn looks around the space, scanning high and low. He shakes his head. 'The storage areas are all really small and compact. There's no one in here but us.'

'And are you *certain* there's no way somebody could get in?'

Reubyn nods. 'I guarantee it.'

Polly stares out of the window. They have no electricity and soon they'll be stuck here in the pitch-dark. The discussion turns to light sources. They have no idea how much life remains in the batteries of their torch. Only Reubyn and Faith have any significant level of charge on their phones. Faith goes rummaging about in search of any other electrical devices that might emit even the slightest illumination and finds a clock radio with a digital display of the time: 19:58. But that's all there is. George hangs the torch from a clip in the ceiling, creating a yellow shaft of light and a spotlight on the floor. When that runs out, they'll swap the torch for a phone and flashlight app.

Jessie is muttering to herself again, keeps repeating little phrases that suggest she is struggling to accept the reality of their situation. *You've got to be kidding me. No way. This can't be happening.*

But it *is* happening. Denial is the first stage of grief – Polly was taught that when she was thirteen and her lurcher Coco had to be put down. The second stage of grief, if she remembers correctly, is anger. Although there has been plenty of that flying around already. The subject of their grief isn't totally clear cut. No one has paid any kind of tribute to Elis, and everyone is stressed and in shock. Devastated, even. But Polly suspects most of them are currently preoccupied by their own mortality rather than Elis's. Their grief, at least for the time being, is reserved for themselves.

◆　◆　◆

Darkness settles over the forest, and the conversation becomes less frantic. A grim discussion takes place. It seems they'll have to wait until dawn before making their next move. Given what's happened, it's not safe to go anywhere right now. But, at first light, one, some, or all of them – depending on the state of Polly's ankle – will be walking out of this forest to get help and raise the alarm. At that point, they'll also conduct another search of the bus, including the storage areas that can only be accessed from the exterior. It's possible that a vehicle as blinged out as this one will have an additional battery or generator that they can use for a jump start. Both Reubyn and George claim they have the ability to perform one, but Polly isn't convinced – this kind of man-flexing is so rarely backed up by meaningful action.

The display on the clock radio reads 21:35. No one is exactly sure what time dawn will come, but their best guess is sometime between five and six. That means they'll be stuck in here for eight hours at least. Polly is certain no one will be getting any sleep in that time. Even if one of them possessed the kind of zen ability to nod off under such stressful circumstances, it wouldn't be safe. They need to be vigilant.

Their conversation peters out, and the only sound is the thrum of the elements. The view out of the window is of nothing but empty blackness. There are no trees or branches, just the reflection of Polly's own miserable face staring back at her. She has bags under her eyes, and her hair is frizzed and wild. The hair of an animal.

They've been sat silently for a minute or so, when Reubyn clears his throat. 'Guys. There's something I should probably tell you.'

The grave tone of his speech seizes the attention of everyone. They all sit up.

Reubyn opens his mouth to speak, then closes it. Their stares have clearly unnerved him, and he rubs at his temple. 'It's not a big deal, in the scheme of things, really.'

Polly feels a tingle in her veins. She's mightily close to losing her temper with him. 'What are you talking about? Come on, out with it.'

'I probably should have told you before we came here.'

'Reubyn,' Polly snaps. 'Stop blathering and say it.'

He takes a deep breath, shakes his head. 'The thing is, when the police arrive, they're going to have questions about why we're here.'

Polly's eye twitches. 'And why's that, Reubyn?'

'Well, strictly speaking, we're not supposed to be here. The reserve is closed to the public due to a conservation project.'

Polly growls with disapproval, along with a few others. 'It's because of that bloody bird, isn't it? The kākāpō?'

'Yes.'

'And that's why there's no one else here?'

'I suppose it is, yes.'

'For God's sake, Reubyn.' Miles rocks forward, spitting his words. 'What are you playing at?'

'All right, let's not get carried away. It's not that big a deal.'

'Yes it *is*, Reubyn.'

Reubyn's brow furrows and he pulls his head back defensively, like a boxer dodging a blow. 'Calm down. I accept it isn't ideal. But let's not blow it out of all proportion. Compared to a murder, it's pretty insignificant.'

Miles stands and begins gesticulating with his arms. 'I think it would've been fair if I could've decided for myself if it was relevant. Honestly, Reubyn, you act like a bloody idiot sometimes.'

Reubyn looks wounded by that last comment. He stares at his own fidgeting hands for a moment, then glares at Miles. 'Well, you haven't been entirely honest yourself, have you? With Jessie for example.'

Polly winces. Reubyn's words have changed the atmosphere, and the temperature seems to have suddenly dropped by a couple of degrees. Miles stares into his lap, and for a moment no one speaks.

'Miles?' Jessie's voice is timid and confused.

Polly puts her face in her hands. 'For God's sake, Reubyn, why now?'

'Sorry, I shouldn't have said anything. It's the stress of . . . of everything. I'm sorry.' He turns to Jessie. 'Forget I said anything, okay?'

Jessie ignores him; her eyes are trained on Miles. 'What's he talking about?'

Polly squeezes her eyes closed. She wishes they didn't have to go through all this now. But they do. Polly is certain of that. Because if Miles doesn't tell Jessie the truth, Polly will. If only to put him out of his bloody misery.

CHAPTER 44

MILES

'Miles,' Jessie repeats. 'What is it you haven't been honest with me about?'

Miles runs his hands over his face. Not for the first time this year, he wishes he could slip off into another dimension. Things weren't supposed to turn out like this. Everything is going wrong. Jessie's eyes are burning into him, demanding answers. 'Let's go to the bedroom and talk,' he says.

'No, it's pitch-dark in there.'

'I just think it would be better if we discussed it in private.'

'And I think we should talk here.' She folds her arms. 'Whatever it is, these guys already seem to know about it. So, what's going on?'

Miles bunches up his lips. He's thought about this for days, how he's going to explain it to Jessie, but now that the time has come, his mind has gone blank. 'I was planning on telling you, but *this*' – he gestures in no particular direction – 'is literally the worst possible context in which to bring it up.'

'Bring what up?'

The silence is deafening. Even the rain has backed off, down to a light patter, as if the universe is straining to hear.

Miles exhales audibly. 'There was a court case. Okay? I was accused of something, I didn't do it, and I was acquitted. But it was recent, and I didn't want you to judge me on it at first impressions, so I held off having this . . . conversation. I just wanted to go a few weeks where life was normal and—'

'You were accused of something. What was the something?'

Silence. Jessie's face has taken on a dreadful gravity. She asks again. 'What was the *something* you were accused of?'

'Murder,' Polly says, matter-of-factly.

Jessie looks at Polly, and when her eyes turn back to Miles, they are wide with shock and then, in an instant, they gleam with something desperate – haunted, even – that seems to bore into the darkest part of Miles's soul. Her chin shudders. 'Oh my God.' She fans her face with her hands. 'Are you for real? Who are you?'

Miles places a hand on her leg. 'I'm the same person you—'

'Don't touch me.' She stands. 'Get away from me.'

Faith leaps to her feet, puts an arm around Jessie and shoots Miles an angry look before leading Jessie down to the front of the bus.

'Jessie, let me explain.'

Faith responds by lurching at him. 'Stay where you are.'

Miles retreats and sits back down. He doesn't look at Jessie, but he can hear her all right. She's wailing, now. Letting it all out. There's no attempt to conceal her distress. Faith is stroking Jessie's arm – a soothing motion. 'You better start from the beginning,' she says, her eyes lasered on Miles. 'Leave nothing out.'

Miles sits, head bowed. And, for the next half an hour, he explains it all, in a gloomy monotone: who Caira was, where and when she was killed, how he became the accused. The whole thing sounds unreal, even to him, and, under the shadow cast by Elis's death, he's aware that the story seems even more sinister. Faith stares at him impassively as he tells the story, but Jessie only takes occasional glances as she sobs. And each time she does, she quickly averts her eyes, as if he's too hideous to look at for more than a second. Faith questions him on Jessie's behalf, and he has that feeling once again of being on trial. To his left, Polly, George and Reubyn say nothing. Several times, Miles stands and attempts to approach, to get close to Jessie, to comfort her. Each time, Faith warns him off.

Eventually, when Faith runs out of questions, Miles ceases his explaining. For a while, no one speaks. The explosive secret Miles has been carrying so heavily for the last few days is no longer contained, and now all they can do is sit among the rubble and consider the fallout.

For maybe twenty minutes, the only sounds are the light tapping of rain and Jessie's occasional sobs. Although she's calmed slightly, Jessie still won't look at him. Whatever fondness was growing between the two of them, it's over. If he'd volunteered this information himself, maybe it would have been different. Miles remembers what Polly told him on the beach. *You'll tie yourself in knots, deceiving people like this.* Well, now the knots are tied. Good and tight.

In the context of Elis's death, their short-lived romance seems an absurdly trivial thing to get upset about. But, even if the seeds of their relationship have been crushed, he has an overwhelming desire to try to get her to see his point of view. It's so exhausting being hated, especially by someone he really likes. Whatever it takes, he needs her to forgive him.

Miles stands and takes tentative steps towards Jessie and Faith.

He's only managed a few yards before Faith blocks the way. 'Keep away from her. She needs space.'

'I just want to talk to her.'

'And I'm just telling you that she needs space.'

Miles grits his teeth. 'Surely it's up to her, if she needs space?' He cranes his head to the side to see past Faith. 'Jessie, please, I just want to talk.'

'Guys.' George is on his feet now. 'Can you both chill out a bit? This isn't helping.'

'And you,' Faith says, jabbing a finger at George. 'I don't trust you, either.'

'Me?' George scowls. 'What have I done?'

'If no one else is going to say it, then I will. He' – Faith is pointing at Miles – 'might be a lying arsehole, but he had no reason to kill Elis. There's only one person here with a motive. And that's George.'

CHAPTER 45

GEORGE

'How dare you?' George scowls at Faith, his pulse rapidly rising. She's really starting to grind his gears now. 'It was Elis who punched *me*, remember? Not the other way around.'

'Yeah, after you provoked him. And you were pretty bloody angry afterwards.'

'I'm sorry. Was I supposed to sing his praises? Oh, yeah, that Elis, he's a top fellow. Spiffing chap. Just gave me a haymaker to the eye. Absolute gentleman.' George hears his words land heavily in the silence. It's unbecoming. He ceases his sarcastic line of defence, sensing it's not doing him any favours. They're all looking at him with varying degrees of seriousness. 'Look, just because I was angry doesn't mean I wanted to kill him. That's one hell of a leap.'

'Actually, I think I remember last night you *saying* you wanted to kill him, or words to that effect.'

He wags a finger at Faith. '*That* is a post hoc fallacy of the worst kind.' George feels his temperature rising. He needs to keep a lid on his anger, but it's not easy when Faith is coming for him like this. 'We all use that kind of language figuratively, and you've twisted it to make a fatuous allegation. It's nothing short of outrageous.'

Faith laughs humourlessly, then shakes her head. 'Your fancy words might work on them, mate, but they aren't going to work on me. I don't know what a post hoc fallacy is, and, frankly, I don't give a damn. All I know is, I spoke with Elis last night.' Her eyes move around, addressing everyone but George. 'He was anxious. Like he knew something bad was about to happen.'

'Oh, this is ridiculous.' Again, George abandons his outburst.

'He told me he felt uncomfortable here, and that he was going to leave at the first opportunity and fly home. Elis was trying to get away' – she points at George – 'from *him*.'

George's hands tremble with anger. He balls them up into fists. He's not going to put up with this. Faith and Jessie aren't even meant to be on this trip. And now, because Miles hasn't been honest with them, Faith is throwing accusations at George. 'All right. This has gone on long enough.' He turns to Miles. 'I'm sorry, mate. I've got to tell them, okay? It's not fair that people keep accusing me.'

'Oh, my God.' Faith throws her arms in the air. 'You can't be serious. Are you telling me there's *more*?'

Miles says nothing, but closes his eyes, and his face assumes a look of weary resignation. George takes it as permission to spill the beans. 'There is *one* minor thing left that he hasn't told you.'

'Oh, right. Let me guess. He's a terrorist? A known paedophile? A goddamn serial killer?'

George rolls his eyes. 'Miles has a stalker.'

Faith slowly shakes her head. 'Because . . . of course he has.'

'I wish that was the end of it, but it's not. This psycho . . . well, we don't know for sure that he's a psycho . . . but a man has been following him and sending him threatening emails. And' – George takes a deep breath – 'then he turned up in Queenstown.'

'And now he's turned up here in this forest,' Faith says, flatly, staring at the window.

'We don't know that,' Miles says. 'The whole point of coming here was to get away. We were careful, and we made sure we weren't followed. There's no way he could have found us here.'

'Right,' George says. 'But the point I'm making is, there are other, much more rational, explanations for what's happened to Elis. It's not fair to point the finger at me just because Elis and I had a row. And it's not fair to point the finger at Miles, either. He's done nothing wrong.'

Faith returns to the front seats to comfort Jessie, whose sobbing has entered yet another phase. Her wailing and hyper-ventilating have ended, and the sounds she's producing now are more defeated and laborious. Her body sporadically twitches, as if her skin is being pinched. George understands why Jessie is upset – they're all upset – but this Dying Swan act is a little bit over the top. Faith places an arm around Jessie, but her eyes remain focused on George and Miles. 'It's a bit rich to say he's done nothing wrong. You guys have lied about pretty much everything. And now you expect us to believe this?'

'It's true,' Polly says, tilting her head back in a show of exhaustion. 'Someone has been harassing him.'

'Thanks for that, Polly. Some friend you've turned out to be.' Faith glares at Polly, who doesn't meet her eye. 'Anyway, this doesn't change anything. If some psycho has got it in for Miles, why would he kill *Elis*?' She pauses, looking around to see if anyone wants to volunteer an answer. No one does. 'Some stalker didn't kill Elis. One of you arseholes did. And my money' – pointing at George – 'is on *him*.'

CHAPTER 46

MILES

Their arguments have ceased. Out of the gloom, the red lines of the digital clock display show 04:53. Jessie and Faith remain down at the front of the bus, and Miles sits on the bench next to Polly. Opposite them, George and Reubyn stare glumly into space. It must be at least ten minutes since anyone last spoke. For the first time in days, it's close to being properly quiet, the wind and the rain having abruptly died off. There's still a delicate tapping against the roof, but it's so faint that Miles doubts whether it's really rain or merely the memory of it, an imprint. Maybe it's been hammering the roof for so long that it's left an echo — like when you walk out of a loud concert and your ears ring. Mixed in with the sound is the faint, high-pitched whine of mosquitos. And, intermittently, there is something else: a strange, low boom that Miles believes must be coming from a bird.

In the absence of human conversation, Miles's brain has been afforded a moment of clarity. Until now, he hasn't been able to hear himself think under the noise of their own infighting. Now, there is a state of calm, albeit a very uneasy one.

There seems to be a growing suspicion towards George in relation to Elis's murder. George is a lot of things, but not a killer. Everyone would be a great deal more suspicious of Miles if they knew about the conversation he had with Elis last night. If they knew about the false alibi. If they knew about Elis's threats to expose it.

Elis was the only one who knew that Miles's alibi was made up. Although Miles thinks his solicitor and barrister might know too, deep down. In fact, despite his solicitor not suggesting it explicitly, it was basically his idea. It's amazing how much can be conveyed with just the eyes and a slight adjustment of facial muscles. His solicitor had asked him where he'd gone after his date with Caira and then said pointedly: 'Having a solid alibi would *really* help your defence.' It seemed as clear an instruction as Miles had ever received. It was his job to sort it out. Essentially, he'd been forced into the lie. Not by his solicitor, but by circumstance. By the police, who charged him despite failing to find any compelling evidence.

The lie worked fine. At least it did until Elis threatened to expose it. That could have been a significant problem. And now, it's resolved. As terrible and gruesome and tragic as it is, Elis's death appears suspiciously convenient for Miles. Or it would, if anyone knew the context. There's no denying it: Miles has the strongest motive for killing Elis. But Miles didn't do it. And that begs the question: who did? And why?

For a start, the location of Elis's body is strange. What the hell was Elis doing at the bird hide in the middle of the night? He wasn't out looking for a signal – he'd left his phone in his bag. When they first realised Elis was missing, Miles had assumed he'd legged it. But Faith's right: Elis wouldn't leave without his stuff – especially his passport. Miles's best guess is that Elis went to the hide for some late-night birdwatching, although that still seems unlikely.

As for the motive, Miles can only think it was a case of mistaken identity. The killer hadn't come for Elis – they'd come for him.

Miles and Elis aren't that similar in appearance, but in the dark – and nowhere is darker than the forest at night – it's possible someone could have attacked Elis thinking he was Miles. It makes him shudder. That knife was meant for him. It was *his* throat they wanted cut. It seems probable that the killer had already come for Miles once, when he was at the hide with Jessie. What would they have done, if Jessie hadn't spotted them and caused them to flee? It doesn't bear thinking about.

Despite having had no sleep, Miles finds himself restless. He rocks in his seat, picks at his clothing, digs under his fingernails. He has this overwhelming feeling that the person who has come for him is near. With every passing minute, he becomes surer of it.

Miles needs to get out of here. It doesn't matter what anyone says: when dawn breaks, he's leaving this forest and getting to safety. The longer he stays here, the higher the chance that his stalker will be able to get to him. The police have probably identified him by now, but Miles suspects they're yet to track him down. He's close, Miles can sense it. Alex Burnfield. He's nearby. And he wants Miles dead. Outside, the sky is turning red. Dawn is breaking. But what, and who, will it bring? Burnfield. That name has been driving him mad. Burnfield. Burnfield.

'What did you just say?' Polly whispers.

Miles realises he's been muttering under his breath. 'Oh, nothing.'

'You said Burnfield.'

'Yeah.'

'Why?'

Miles narrows his eyes at her. 'Because that was the name my stalker used. When they checked in to the library to send the first email. You know this.'

'No. You never told me that.'

'I thought I did.' But he didn't. Miles remembers now: when he discussed it in the cable car, he was with George, Reubyn and Elis. Polly wasn't there.

'Well, don't you think that's odd?' she whispers.

Miles sits up straight. 'Why?'

'Burnfield.' She says the name with wide eyes, nodding as if he should know the answer.

'It's a weird name. I thought I'd heard it somewhere before, but I haven't.'

Polly is still nodding, now more vigorously. 'Yes, you *have* heard it before. We both have.'

CHAPTER 47

ALEX

I overestimated you. I genuinely thought you might be able to figure it all out. But here we are, nearing the end, and you still have no idea what is going on. Something in your brain won't quite click, will it Miles? All those little neurons are furiously firing away, but the pathways they're on aren't lining up right. And now your time has just about run out. Such a shame, because all it would take to achieve that eureka moment is the tiniest synaptic transmission – a barely detectable pulse of energy in the brain.

I've become fascinated by the chemistry of the brain. It must be because mine is so difficult to understand and predict. When I think of my own, I imagine some malevolent lab technician with a pipette, adding a few too many drops of this, too small an amount of that, and then finally, while wearing a look that says *oh sod it*, tipping in a volatile set of reactants just to see what happens – fuelled by the curious desire to witness a human head fizzing with restless malfunction.

There's so much noise in here, Miles. My head is a loud, loud place. Too many bad thoughts and memories. Too many competing desires and ideas. I'd like to put an end to it: to pour water on this miserable experiment and snuff it out once and for all. Have someone pack away the apparatus and clean down the bench as if nothing ever happened.

Still, not long to go now. Just a couple more hours and this will all be over, Miles. For both of us.

CHAPTER 48

POLLY

'Burnfield Court,' Polly whispers.

Miles's eyes go wide at the mention of it. 'From the documentary?'

'Yeah. Burnfield Court was the estate where that horrible drug house was. The one Caira had to keep visiting. Remember?'

Miles slowly nods.

'It was awful. And judging from the documentary, there were some horrible people there.'

Polly watches Miles's face twitch and tense as he thinks it through. Again, he says nothing, just turns his head to stare out of the window, where the forest is reappearing under the red glow of dawn. 'I wouldn't read too much into it,' Polly says. 'The people in that house were mostly addicts and drifters. There is no way they'd have the guile or the means to follow you all the way here. Whoever it is, they're just a troll.'

'Yeah, maybe.' Miles gets up and grabs his walking boots, then sits back down and starts lacing them.

'What are you doing?'

'I'm going to find a signal and call the police.'

'Really?' Polly raises her voice so everyone can hear. 'I think it would make more sense if somebody else went.'

'I'm going,' Miles repeats, firmer this time. 'Come with me if you want.'

Polly puts some weight on her injured ankle and winces. There's no way she can walk for miles. 'I can't. But you mustn't go on your own.' She raises her voice and looks around. 'Who's going with my brother?'

'I'll go with him,' George says.

The sight of George getting to his feet and reaching for his coat is a relief to Polly. He might be the most annoying man on Earth, but at least he's loyal to Miles. 'Thanks, George,' Polly says.

'Of course.'

'Wait,' Faith says, also rising. She jabs a finger at George. 'He's not going anywhere.'

'Why on earth not?'

Faith ignores George's question and addresses Polly. 'George is the only one with a motive for Elis's murder. The cops won't be happy if they find out we let him just wander off into the bush.'

George scowls and his eyes dart around, searching for support. 'For heaven's sake. Being punched in the face isn't a motive for murder. I didn't do anything to Elis. I'm not a criminal.'

'Maybe you didn't. But the point still stands. And besides, you and him' – pointing at Reubyn – 'are apparently the guys who know how to do a jump start. I reckon you should focus on that.'

'Well, he can't go on his own.'

Faith glares at George. 'Why not?'

'Apart from the *obvious* . . .' George pauses, and the image of the hideous wound to Elis's neck claws its way back into Polly's mind. 'You've obviously never done orienteering,' George continues to Faith, 'but the number one rule is you don't do it alone. What if he fell and injured himself like Polly? Even if you don't take into account what happened to Elis, it's a bloody long walk out of this forest.'

'Fine.' Faith folds her arms. 'I'll go with him. I've done plenty of bushwalking.'

Jessie shakes her head, and makes a pathetic, whimpering noise of discouragement.

'Don't worry,' Faith says to Jessie. 'I'm not scared of *him*.' Then to Miles: 'No offence.'

'None taken,' Miles says, miserably.

Miles walks over to the door and bites his nails as he waits for Faith, who dons her boots and jacket, and packs sunscreen and bottled water into a backpack. Polly has mixed feeling about Faith going with Miles. She would rather that the person accompanying her brother was a bloke over six feet, like George. But, begrudgingly, she concedes. When the police arrive, everyone will be interviewed, and they'll all have to tell the cops about the tension that's been growing between George and Elis. In light of that, it would seem pretty weird if they'd chosen George to go off and find help. Also, Faith is one of the only ones who has hiking boots and some remaining phone battery life. They could've sent Reubyn instead, but he would be no more useful than Faith in a crisis.

The light outside is a now a fiery yellow. There's enough visibility to see far into the forest. When Faith is ready, Miles unlocks the door and opens it with a haste that Polly finds alarming. 'Be careful,' she tells him.

Miles gives her a tight smile. 'Don't worry, we will.'

They leave, and Polly watches from the window as Miles and Faith walk side by side across the car park and on to the road. This is all happening too fast – the decision was made too quickly. She's slightly reassured to see them regularly turning their heads, being vigilant. They walk at a brisk, purposeful pace – also good. But a heaviness in her gut tells her there's something wrong with this plan. The doomy feeling rises in her with such force that, if she physically could, she would jump to her feet and run after them with a warning. Instead, she watches helplessly as they disappear into the trees.

CHAPTER 49

MILES

For the first ten minutes of their hike, Miles and Faith barely utter a word to each other. They've been on high alert, and the only sounds are the dawn chorus and the pounding of their boots. But now the sky is clear, bluish even, and the brightness and visibility have increased so they can see reassuringly deep into the trees. Miles is confident that, given the time of day, they're the only ones out here. Still, he orders himself not to get complacent. He continues to scan every inch of the forest, searching for even the slightest movement.

'You should've just told her, you know,' Faith says, breaking the silence.

'I know.'

'Jessie likes you. Well, she did. But you lied to her, and it came as a shock.'

Miles puffs his cheeks. 'I know.'

'I see your quandary, though. If you'd told her about your history, she wouldn't have gone near you.'

'I know I should've told her. It was a mistake.'

'You can say that again.'

Miles doesn't say it again, and they walk the next hundred yards or so without a word. Faith keeps a couple of paces between them as she walks. And as she scans the forest for threats, Miles can't help but notice she takes regular glances at him, too. Her vigilance includes keeping Miles under observation. In her mind, he must also pose a threat.

'Faith, can I ask you something?'

'Okay.'

'Do you believe me?'

She squints at him. 'About what?'

'About how . . .' Miles searches for the right words. It's an absurd statement to have to make, and he's tired of having to point it out. 'I didn't kill anyone.'

'You said that last night. About twenty times.'

'Because it's true.'

'Well, it doesn't make much difference to me. As soon as we're out of this forest, the chances of you and I running into each other again are pretty damned small, I reckon.'

'I guess that's true.' *No one will be in a rush to get together and reminisce about this trip*, Miles thinks. The fewer reminders, the better. 'Where are you going to go?'

Faith takes a swig from a bottle of water. 'Home. I'm not really in the mood for a holiday anymore.'

'Same.'

She raises her bottle. In doing so, she closes the gap between them. 'Here's to travelling on to home.'

'Cheers to that.'

They walk on in silence.

Miles hadn't given any thought to getting home. And now, the moment he entertains the idea, he realises that home will not bring the same comfort that it will for Faith. He needs to brace himself for another ordeal. When the media finds out about this latest development, a new storm will be set in motion. It'll be a gift for anyone peddling clickbait articles: another murder, connected to him. The public will eat it up. He imagines people rage-scrolling; thousands, if not millions, of hateful eyes poring over his image, and minds reaching for their between-the-lines conclusions about what's happened. They'll share their theories, discuss him with loathful tones and furious faces. At water coolers and bus stops and school gates.

He immediately feels guilty for these selfish thoughts, given what's happened to Elis. His friend is dead. Murdered in the most awful of ways. But that doesn't change the dismal fate that awaits Miles.

There needs to be compelling evidence against someone else for Elis's murder. The police have to find out who did it. If they can't, there remains the unignorable possibility that they will find a reason to accuse Miles. And then, his nightmare will begin all over again.

CHAPTER 50

GEORGE

It's been about twenty minutes since Miles and Faith began their trek out of the forest. Reubyn and George have been stood at the front of the motorhome for thirty seconds or so, picking and prodding at the hatch with their fingers, trying to figure out how to open the panel to reveal the engine.

George scratches his head. 'Reubyn, go have another look at the dashboard. This must open from the inside.'

Reubyn nods and heads back into the bus.

'I don't think that's where the engine is,' Jessie says. 'It will be in the back.'

George glances over his shoulder at her. She's stood a few yards behind him, her arms are folded, and her eyes are puffy and red. He turns his attention back to fiddling with the panel. George runs his fingers around its edge, trying to find a latch, and then, after about twenty seconds, it pings open by half an inch. Reubyn must have found some button or lever on the inside. George lifts the panel and reveals a space roughly the same size as a regular car boot. And it's empty.

'The engine must be somewhere else.' He looks at Jessie. 'Maybe we should try the back.'

She looks at him, deadpan. 'Yeah, maybe we should try the back.'

They walk around the rear of the bus and find a larger hatch with a prominent lever. George grabs it and opens up the panel, revealing the engine. It doesn't look massively different to what you'd find under the hood of a car, albeit on a larger scale. Along one side is a set of tools, different-sized wrenches neatly clipped into a line. Two of them are missing, he notices. Then his eye is drawn to the starter battery, and George immediately knows something is wrong. Very wrong.

'The battery's been tampered with,' George says. He's no mechanic, but even he can see that. The cable clamps have been disconnected from the battery terminals. And not only that; one of the cables has been cut clean through.

Reubyn and Jessie draw closer. From their faces, they've realised it, too. The motorhome hasn't malfunctioned or run out of power. It's been deliberately disabled. It's been sabotaged.

CHAPTER 51

MILES

They've been walking for a good half an hour, now. Miles reckons it'll only be another ten or fifteen minutes before they reach the gates to the reserve and get out on to the main road. Although that's probably not the best way to describe the gravelly track that led them here. It's not like any main road he's used to, but it's a highway of sorts and Miles will be glad to be on it. It's not visible from here, though. The road he and Faith are walking has entered an area of denser trees and foliage. They remain vigilant, constantly looking in all directions, but their range of vision is more limited now that the vegetation is thicker. Miles is still confident there's no one out there in the forest watching them, but the reduced visibility causes him to quicken his step. The thud of his boots echoes under the thick canopy overhead. He can also just about make out that odd noise he heard before dawn – that strange booming sound.

Miles stops for a moment. His increased pace means he's gained a few yards on Faith. When she's back in line with him, he hikes on and points to the phone in her hand. 'Any signal yet?' It's been five minutes since she last tried, so it has to be worth another go.

She taps at her phone a few times and stares at the screen. Then she shakes her head. 'Still nothing.'

They keep on, and Miles continues to pan all around. He tilts his head to look high and low, from the hanging branches to the gnarled undergrowth. The forest glistens, and shards of light flash overhead where the sun catches the wet leaves.

Miles stops. Movement in the bushes has grabbed his attention. He stands, frozen to the spot. A gasp would've just escaped his throat had he not clamped his larynx to suppress it. For a moment he thinks his eyes might be playing tricks on him – a consequence of sleep deprivation and stress.

'Faith.' He places a hand on her shoulder and whispers urgently as a wave of adrenaline rises through his body. 'Don't move a muscle.'

CHAPTER 52

POLLY

Polly sits alone in the bus, straining to hear the conversation taking place outside. George, Reubyn and Jessie went out to examine the engine and battery, to see if there's any way they can get the vehicle running. She's frustrated to be stuck in here, not knowing what's going on, but trying to hobble anywhere is painful. Her hopes are low, and although she can't hear what's being said outside, the tones of the voices have sounded anything but triumphant.

A few minutes ago, the door opened and Reubyn clambered in. He sat in the driver's seat, looking high and low for some switch or other, and then, after ferreting around for a bit, he made a noise that suggested some kind of achievement – the first positive noise she has heard in about twelve hours. He hopped back out before she had a chance to quiz him.

She should've told Reubyn to unlock a window. Their voices were just about audible, but too muffled for her to make out the words. She listened to them a little longer and then she heard footsteps. All three of them – George, Reubyn and Jessie – walked past her window, along the side of the bus and disappeared from sight. Now she can barely hear a thing. Where have they gone? Polly's thoughts begin to race, and hand a baton to her heart, which in turn picks up speed. They wouldn't leave her here on her own, would they? Not after everything that's happened.

Polly imagines what she would do if some assailant turned up and found her here alone. She'd be completely defenceless. In normal circumstances, pretty much her only option would be to scream and run from an attacker. But right now, she can barely even walk.

For maybe ten minutes she sits, craning her head to peer out of the windows. Straining to hear voices. She takes deep breaths. *You're overreacting. They'll be back soon.* But Polly's attempts to self-soothe aren't working. Not when the image of Elis's lifeless body keeps forming in her mind. Not when that artificial Caira voice increases in volume inside her head. The longer she's here alone, the more her panic ramps up. She pictures her brother, walking helplessly through the forest. *This is not over. This is not over. This is not over.*

A shrill sound stops her heart. She turns her head towards the kitchen. *Deet-deet-deet-deet-deet.* It's an alarm. She looks at the table, which is bare apart from a couple of half-drunk bottles of water. The digital alarm clock is no longer there. Someone has packed it away in the kitchen, she assumes, and now the bloody thing is going off. She waits for it to exhaust itself, to stop bleeping. But it's incessant. Worse, it's compounding her panic. It's as if someone has picked the world's most appropriate sound to accompany her anxiety: this relentless, high-pitched alarm. It's an infuriatingly perfect soundtrack to her current mental state. The sound warps in her mind, morphing into a famous piece of music from a famous horror movie. She can't remember its title – she's hasn't actually seen the film; it's ancient – but that shower scene is iconic. It's everywhere. The beeps of the alarm become synchronous with her memory of the music, the awful staccato violin screeches. The sound that was deemed the most apt sonic accompaniment to the sight of a young, defenceless woman being set upon by a knife-wielding . . . *Psycho*, that's it. *Deet-deet-deet-deet-deet.*

She can't bear it any longer. Polly hauls herself on to one foot and hops towards the kitchen. The bleeping is loud here. Polly slides open the top drawer and finds it crammed with cutlery. She tries the second one down and sees it's empty. She opens the third drawer, and the sound of the beeping intensifies. The digital alarm clock is in there. Lying on top of it is a small piece of paper, folded in half. Polly picks up the paper and it trembles in her hand gently, then more violently as she reads downward. Her stomach twists as the words on the page register. Then, she drops the paper and starts banging on the window with all her strength – not caring if she breaks the glass with her fist – and screams: a desperate wail for help.

CHAPTER 53

MILES

Miles stares at it in amazement: the kākāpō. For a moment, the sight of the bird is so miraculous and exotic that it strips away all thoughts of anything else. It's bigger and rounder than he imagined from Reubyn's description. The kākāpō is vibrantly feathered, with bright shades of lime and yellow, and flecked with black. It has a curious beak: wide and hooked into a downward point. Miles almost doesn't dare to breathe, for fear of frightening it away, but it seems completely unalarmed. It's a puzzling sight, the bird's calmness. But then Miles remembers what Reubyn told him about this species. *They don't recognise their predators.* The bird turns its head to look at him, and barely reacts, just continues on its haphazard path, lumbering heavily from foot to foot, doddery and oblivious to danger.

'Do you see it?' he whispers to Faith, without taking his eyes off the bird. She doesn't respond; presumably, she hasn't heard him or is as transfixed as he is – stunned into silence.

He'd like to take a photo or video, but his phone is dead. 'Faith,' he says, a little louder, his eyes still fixed on the kākāpō. 'Can you get a video?'

Still, she says nothing. The kākāpō pecks at something on the ground, then carries on, unperturbed, in its curious and clumsy motion.

There's a clicking noise behind him, metal on metal.

'Faith,' Miles says, turning to face her, 'can you take a—'

The sight of her shocks him into silence. His next instinct, a split second later, is to laugh. But his laugh only half emerges. Because he's realised: this isn't a joke. The blood freezes in his veins.

The look of anger and determination on Faith's face isn't for show. It's real. And so, he suspects, is the gun she's pointing at him.

CHAPTER 54

REUBYN

Reubyn looks nervously around, to make absolutely sure there's no one lurking nearby. For the second time, he stoops to check under the bus. George is fiddling with the starter battery, but there's no way he'll be able to fix it. Jessie looks as she has for hours: dazed and frightened. Reubyn can't blame her for that; she has every right to be scared. Reubyn is scared, too. He's also sick with remorse. This is all his fault. Why did he bring them out here? If anyone else gets hurt while they're stuck in this forest, it'll be on him. And he's powerless to help. He'll just have to hope that Miles and Faith are safely making their way out of here. With any luck, they'll soon raise the alarm. With any luck, the air will soon fill with the wailing of sirens as the emergency services arrive to deal with this mess.

His train of thought is broken by a noise coming from inside the van. The sound of muffled shouting. It's quickly combined by a fist banging against the window. Reubyn, George and Jessie glance at each other, then dart around to the door of the bus.

George gets to the door first. 'Polly!' he shouts. 'Are you all right?'

Reubyn finds Polly sitting on the bench, her face contorted in shock and a slip of paper trembling in her outstretched hand.

George grabs it, and as he stares at it, his face buckles. 'Oh no.'

'What is it?' Reubyn asks.

George hands him the sheet. 'Here, see for yourself.'

Reubyn takes the piece of paper and holds it so he and Jessie can see. It's a note, written neatly in blue biro. Reubyn's pulse quickens as he reads.

To Reubyn, Jessie, Polly and George.

None of you are in danger. I'm sorry you'll have to deal with the mess I'm about to create. It won't be pretty. I have my reasons, and I'm sure you'll find them out soon enough.

I'm sorry about Elis.

I'm NOT sorry about Miles.

Faith.

CHAPTER 55

MILES

Miles and Faith stare at each other for a few seconds. In that time, a hundred thoughts race through Miles's mind. These frantic notions raise more questions, and some half-conclusions. And a decision, of sorts. He elects to say nothing. He raises his hands, palms faced towards her, and takes a half-step forward.

'No further,' Faith barks. She jerks her arm as she speaks, and snarls. There's something about her voice that sends a shiver running down his back, an icy chill that begins at his shoulder blades and travels right down to the tail of his spine. It's not just the aggression in her voice. There's something else.

Miles's heart is hammering a warning. He stares at the gun in her hand. Miles doesn't know what kind of gun it is. What does he know about guns? Nothing. But it looks real. Solid steel. It must be Faith who's been threatening him, who taunted him with a bullet. But why? Whatever is going on here, he needs to take that gun away from her. She appears unhinged, and the longer she's stood there pointing that thing at him, the greater the chance that she'll do something stupid. Miles calculates the distance between them; it must be about six or seven yards – the whole width of the road. He needs to close that gap if he's to have any chance of disarming her. Miles take a smaller step, moving his left foot forward.

Faith lurches and pokes the gun at him. 'I mean it. Take one step closer and I'll shoot you in the kneecap. We can make this as painful as you want.'

Miles keeps still. He swallows. He realises what it is now about her voice. It's the accent. The Australian burr has gone, and her speech is eerily familiar. She doesn't speak exactly like he does, but it's close to home. There's a detectable trace of the regional accent of the west of England. This geographical reminder brings one place immediately to mind: Burnfield Court.

'Who are you?' Miles asks. There's a tremor to his voice.

'You tell me,' she says, coldly. 'Who am I?'

'Alex Burnfield.'

She laughs. A joyless, angry laugh. 'Did you rate my Aussie accent, Miles? I can do a whole load of accents. It makes my acting range a little more impressive than yours, wouldn't you say?'

Miles doesn't respond. He re-examines her, in light of that last remark. Is she someone he's worked with? There's a trace of enjoyment on her face, and Miles wonders for a second whether this should be his moment to try to ambush her. But he abandons that thought. Behaving in haste could be a fatal mistake. He waits for her to continue.

'Anyway, Faith *is* my real name. But you're right. I did send the emails.'

Miles shakes his head. 'No. No, it wasn't you. There was a man following me in Queenstown. One of those emails was sent while you were swimming in the lake.'

Again, she laughs. Although this time it sounds genuine. Amused. 'Seriously? Did you not know you can schedule an email to be sent at any time? Did they teach you nothing in that forty-grand-a-year school?'

Miles shuffles his feet in tiny, imperceptible increments. Nudging forward a few millimetres. He needs to keep her talking if he's to close the gap between them. 'But why?'

She stares at him for a moment. Shadows waver across her face, where sunlight is streaking in through gaps in the leaves. 'I wanted to watch you suffer. I had hoped the courts would see to that, lock you up. But what I've realised is, it's not possible to make you suffer. It all just washes off, doesn't it?' She spits the last two words. A lash of venom to her rhetorical question.

Miles says nothing.

'Murdered someone? Oh well, just hire the best lawyer. Getting some bad press? Never mind, just take a luxury holiday for a few weeks. Maybe get yourself a top-of-the-range motorhome.'

'That wasn't even my idea.'

'I know!' Her face springs open in mock delight. 'Sometimes it just falls into your lap, doesn't it? Everything just always seems to work out for Miles. You never even saw the inside of a cell. If you were from my estate they would've locked you up on remand, you know that, right? But not you. Just get Daddy to chuck a bit of cash at the judge and you're a free man until the trial.'

'Is that what this is about? Money? I can give you money. How much do you want?'

'Trust me, this is *not* about money. Although I must admit' – she shrugs – 'I have found it quite revolting, seeing this privileged existence of yours, up close. But this isn't about privilege. Or money. It's about justice. What I've learned about justice is you can't expect to get it through the courts. If you want justice, you've got to go out and take it for yourself.' There's a wild look in Faith's eyes. She's been working herself up; the longer she talks, the angrier she gets.

'Look,' Miles says, sensing the urgent need to derail her from her current train of thought. 'Let's have a proper discussion about this. Talk it through. But put the gun down. We both know you don't want to shoot me with that thing.'

'Oh, do we? Actually, I think that's one of the ways where we are different. One of the *many* ways.'

'We're not that different.'

Again, that mirthless, angry laugh. 'You have *no* idea how fortunate you are, no awareness whatsoever of your privilege, no idea how deep it runs.'

'I do. I know how—'

She jabs a finger in his direction. 'No, you don't. Because you have nothing to measure it against. You've never been on the other side of luck.'

'I have. You don't know what it's been like for me, being falsely—'

'For *you*?' Her eyes have changed. Everything has changed. It's as if Faith has gone and this is a whole different person. 'Oh, my heart bleeds. As it happens, I've been keeping an eye on you for a while, and I *do* know what it's been like for you. I'll tell you what, though, you haven't got the first idea of what it's been like for *me*. But I'll tell you, if you like.'

Miles swallows. 'Please, tell me.' He tries to make his voice sound sympathetic and encouraging, rather than eager. He really needs her to keep talking. He continues to shuffle his feet in tiny movements. So far, he's moved maybe a foot closer without her noticing.

'I didn't have the sort of cosy upbringing that you had.' She taps a finger against her temple. 'My mum wasn't right in the head. She didn't have the ability to look after herself, let alone a child. She was whacked out on heroin most of the time. And she brought bad men to the house. Men like you, who took whatever they wanted without a care about the damage they left behind.' Faith pauses and takes a deep breath. Her speech has been slowing, and now her words are airy and drawn-out. 'Only one person ever looked out for me, back then.'

She pauses again. Her eyes have a sheen that reflects the rays flittering across her face. Miles's dread deepens. When someone is pointing a gun at you, the last thing you want is for them to become emotional.

Faith appears to clear a lump in her throat. 'I remember when Caira started coming around to the house. I was one of her first cases. I was so fascinated by her. To a seven-year-old girl, she looked like a doll, or a princess, with her bright yellow hair and pretty dresses.'

Faith's voice has taken on a floaty, wistful quality. For the first time in minutes, her eyes leave his, looking off into the trees, as if distracted by the memory. Then she quickly turns her stare back on to Miles. 'I remember thinking she must have been really special to have two security guards following her. But I also got the feeling she was hiding something. Because in the picture on her lanyard she had a big beaming smile, and yet the face she used with us was always serious and sad. It made me suspicious. Especially as my mother hated her. And it was a long time before I realised that what she was doing was for my own good. She wasn't a doll, or a princess, at all. She was an angel. An angel sent for me.'

Faith's composure appears to be waning further, the gun now visibly trembling in her hand. 'You see, Miles. People have given up on me my entire life. But not her. She kept showing up. She wasn't obliged to stay in contact with me once I left the care system, but she did. She was the only constant thing in my life. Pretty much the only good thing. And you killed her.'

'I didn't kill—'

'Shut up! I'm talking.' Faith dries tears from her cheeks with two brisk sweeps of her left hand. Her speech is fast again, now. 'I know your defence. I read all the court reports, so there's no point in repeating it now. What I don't understand is, why. Why you did it. So, go on. Tell me. Why did you do it, Miles? Why did you kill her?'

'I *didn't* kill her.'

Faith growls and shakes the gun in her hand before steadying it again, so he can see directly into the barrel. Miles's breathing is rapid. For a heart-stopping moment, he thinks the gun is going to go off.

'Don't you *dare* deny it. If you deny it one more time, I'll kill you right now. I'm not interested in your denials. You can argue it until you're blue in the face, but I know the truth.' She wipes her face and breathes deeply, appearing to compose herself. 'You're a good liar, though,' she says, speaking slower and softer again. 'You almost had me believing it myself. This whole lie, it's like you're method acting. The way you behave and carry yourself. All innocent. I'll be honest, once I met you, I really didn't think you had it in you to kill someone.'

'I don't have it in me. That's what I'm trying to—'

'Shut up.' She tilts the gun slightly, so the barrel points towards his knees. An unspoken threat. 'Believe me, I've been struggling to figure you out. You seem so gentle on the face of it. How could a nice, well-brought-up pretty boy like you commit murder? You got me doubting everything. I had to check. I had to know for sure that you did it. And now I know.'

'What are you talking about?' Miles whispers the question.

'Elis. I suspected he was lying for you, to cover up what you'd done. So, the night before last, I gave him my own version of the lie detector test.' She raises her eyebrows, as if inviting a question.

Miles says nothing.

'After you lot fell asleep, I promised Elis I'd give him a good time if he came with me to the bird hide in the middle of the night. And his cock and balls couldn't say no to that.' She laughs. 'You men are all the same. When we got there, I asked him about your alibi. Whether that story he told the court was true.'

She glares at him. Again, Miles decides to stay silent. But his stomach is sludgy with dread.

Faith points at him with her free hand. 'He was loyal to you, I'll give him that. He told me it was *all* true, everything you and him told the court, that that's how it happened. But then he started to change his tune. It's funny, when you put a sharp knife to someone's throat, they start to tell the truth. They start telling the truth pretty damn quickly.'

'You killed him.' Miles feels tears prick at the back of his eyes. Elis is dead because of him. Deep down, he knew it already.

'I didn't mean to kill him. The trouble was, I had a very sharp knife pressed against his throat when he admitted he lied to save your skin. And it made me upset. I'm not very nice when I'm upset, Miles. In fact, I can be pretty horrible when I get upset.'

There's a silence between them, and Faith raises the angle of the gun, so it points directly at his face. Miles stands dead-still, but inside him, his blood fizzes, electrified with fear. Faith isn't mucking around. She killed Elis, and she's going to kill him. There's no doubt about it. Faith has said what she wants to say. Any second now, she's going to pull the trigger. 'Can I ask you one question?' Miles says. It's a gamble, but he hopes curiosity will get the better of her.

She pouts, in thought. 'All right. *One* question—'

But before she can finish her sentence, Miles is already on the move. He ducks as low as he can and, in one movement, charges towards her.

CHAPTER 56

GEORGE

George pulls on his trainers, which are still wet and muddy from the previous day. He ties the laces as fast as he can, with trembling hands. They keep slipping from his grip. Why is it that such simple tasks seem to become impossibly difficult when needed to be done with the most urgency? When his laces are tied, he leaps to his feet. 'Jessie, you stay here and keep an eye on Polly. Try not to—'

'For God's sake, George, just *go*.' Polly glares at him.

'Okay, okay.' George darts to the kitchen and opens a drawer, removing two kitchen knives. He hands the smaller one to Reubyn, who accepts it with a look of horror. 'Come on, let's move.'

George and Reubyn leave the bus, bouncing down the steps and sprinting across the car park. The cold steel of the knife feels absurd in George's hand. Not to mention dangerous. Running with an unsheathed blade probably isn't the most sensible idea. And what the hell would he do with it, if called into action? George hasn't got it in him to cut someone. Reubyn definitely doesn't. As they leave the car park and run down the road, George vaguely recalls reading some statistic about how carrying a knife significantly raises the likelihood of the carrier being stabbed. For a moment, he considers abandoning the knife, but decides against it. Faith is likely armed, and they have to help Miles.

They charge down the road. The asphalt is covered with trembling spots of light, and the trees link bony arms above them, encasing them under a tunnel of leaves and branches. George wonders if he's set the starting pace too high. There's a knack to distance running, and Reubyn was never very good at cross-country. They've only done a couple of hundred yards and Reubyn sounds out of breath already. His cheeks flush and his under-chin wobbles in a way that doesn't appear sustainable over a long distance. And what distance is that? Miles and Faith set off more than half an hour ago, albeit at a walking pace. George's ears are full with the sound of his laboured breathing and the pounding of feet as he performs a mental calculation. Half an hour at a typical walking pace, say three to four miles per hour, would be around one and a half to two miles. That's quite far. Assuming they maintain their current pace, which doesn't appear likely, it would take them—

A bang causes them to stutter their steps and scatters birds from the trees.

Reubyn slows to walking pace and turns to look at George. 'What was that?'

'I'm not sure.' George chooses not to vocalise the most likely answer, for fear of frightening Reubyn. He also isn't keen to admit the reality of it to himself. If they were out in an area of British woodland, George would assume what they just heard was a twelve-bore shotgun: the completely normal sound of country folk hunting pheasants and grouse. But here? In an area closed off for wildlife protection? That's not possible. More benign explanations – that it was some kind of firework or other small explosive – seem equally far-fetched. That leaves one possible answer: what they just heard was the sound of a gun being fired with nefarious intent. And the source of it is dead ahead.

They jog hesitantly onwards. Holding their silly kitchen knives. Bringing a knife to a gunfight. That's a phrase he's used countless times to describe being underprepared. Never in a million years has he thought he might literally find himself in that scenario.

Another shot rings out across the forest.

George and Reubyn have stopped running. They stand and look at each other, wearing expressions of bewildered horror. Whatever was happening between Faith and Miles is finished. It's over. They're too late to do anything about it.

CHAPTER 57

MILES

A hellish sequence of sensory firsts is unleashed on Miles as he charges towards Faith. It all happens in a rapid, confusing blur, within one or two paces, in a single second. A terrible onslaught of sound, agony and terror.

He's halfway towards Faith when he feels the impact of the bullet. It doesn't propel him backwards, like when someone is shot in an action movie. His forward momentum remains. The initial hit is simply a realisation – his skin and muscle registering the contact with a sudden signal to his brain.

Then comes the sound. The deafening crack of gunfire. The blast splits the air and sets a dull pulsing in his ears.

And then, as he's still running the no man's land between his starting position and his target, comes the most profound experience of all – the physical pain. It's a sudden agony, like nothing he's felt before – an explosion of white heat that pokers deep into his right shoulder. He's still running when that searing pain intensifies, blooming out from the point of impact.

Miles didn't see the bullet leave the barrel because his head is down as he charges forward. There's no time to dwell on the pain. He continues to rush on, bracing himself for being shot a second time.

His shoulder screams anew as it crashes into Faith. He roars as he hits her with a tackle from straight off the rugby field. His injured shoulder slams into her chest and her body gives way, hurled backwards under his momentum, and he lands in a heap on top of her on the road. Miles instinctively grabs her forearms. He needs to get her hands under his control. He can't let her point that gun at him again.

He slides his grip up her arms, to her wrists, and Faith is writhing beneath him, kicking, and jabbing with her knees. She screams, inches from his face. Miles gets a grip on Faith's wrists and quickly hoists her arms so they are outstretched above her head. The act of doing so causes a fiery sensation in his right shoulder. Her face is so close that her growls and groans are loud. Miles tilts his head to look up her arm and sees she has a tight grip on the handle of the gun. He, in turn, has a firm grip on Faith's right hand – the one holding the weapon. But his grip on her other arm is failing. He should be able to overpower her easily, but the injury to his shoulder means the muscles aren't working as they should. He strains to keep hold of her left wrist but he's losing his grip, one finger at a time. They both make low, guttural noises through gritted teeth as Faith tries to free herself from his grasp. Miles simply cannot keep his shoulder tense any longer. He loses his grip. Faith lashes her left arm free, and, in one quick motion, grabs the gun, switching it from her right to her left hand. Miles shifts his body, and attempts to restrain her arms under his weight, but it's too late.

Another shot. It's even louder at this close range, like the slamming of a steel door right next to his ear. Miles braces for the pain. But this time, the pain doesn't come. This bullet missed.

Miles makes a desperate lunge to try to gain control. Again, he grabs hold of her arms, and brings her hands together above her head. He braces against the burning pain in his shoulder and lifts her hands off the ground, then brings them down. Faith squeals as they thud against the tarmac. But she retains her grip on the gun. Miles repeats the action, this time summoning every ounce of strength to fight against the agonising pain in his shoulder. He lifts higher this time and slams her hands down on the road. Faith groans, and there's a rattle as the gun falls loose. Miles reaches out and sweeps the gun away. He scrambles to his feet and runs over to it. Faith is up in pursuit, but Miles gets there first. He grabs the gun and sprints up the road.

Faith chases after him, but Miles is quicker. He runs twenty yards further and turns, pointing the gun at him.

She stops dead, and a rush of relief sails through Miles's body. Her power over him has gone. It's over. He holds the gun in his left hand, keeping it aimed at the centre of Faith's chest. His right arm hangs loosely at his side. Any movement of it only increases the agonising pain in his shoulder.

Faith stands in the middle of the road, her shoulders sagging miserably. She glares at him and nurses her right hand. She's hurt. But it's impossible for Miles to find any sympathy regarding any injury she may have suffered – not when he's enduring such crippling pain in his shoulder. Pain she inflicted.

Faith takes a step forward, and Miles responds by taking a step back.

'What are you going to do, Miles? Shoot me? You get off on that, don't you? Killing women.'

Miles doesn't respond. The overwhelming relief he felt has already abated. What *is* he going to do? He has no idea. Miles might be lucky to be alive, but the situation he finds himself in – pointing a loaded gun at someone – is still one of mortal jeopardy.

The weapon feels unreal in his hand. Cold and heavy. His rests his finger delicately against the trigger, as lightly as he can. He can hear the beats of his heart – reassuring markers of life and time – but the passing of each heartbeat brings him no closer to the answer of what he should do.

Faith simply stares at him, pure venom in her eyes. After maybe twenty seconds of silence, she folds her arms. 'Just tell me why you did it.'

'I *didn't* do it.'

Faith shakes her head.

'I shouldn't have lied. I shouldn't have dragged Elis into it. But I *didn't* kill her.'

She says nothing.

'I'll tell you what happened. What *really* happened.' The power balance between them has shifted, and now Miles can do the talking. He takes a moment, trying to formulate the right way to explain it: the truth. He's recounted the alternative narrative – the lie – so many times that it almost feels like it really happened that way. 'I admit,' he says, nodding earnestly, 'I lied to the court about where I was. But I *didn't* hurt Caira. I didn't touch her. I know you don't want to believe me, but when I left Caira's flat that night, she was fine. She was happy.'

Faith turns her head to the side, dismissively. She stares vacantly into the forest.

Miles takes a deep breath, then continues. 'When I left her flat that night, I wasn't sure how I was going to get home. My car was parked on her street, but I'd drunk way too much to drive. On a normal night, I would've called an Uber, but my phone had died.' Miles winces at the pain in his shoulder, which is getting worse as the adrenaline wears off. 'So, I got in my car and had a lie-down on the back seat under my coat and fell asleep. I woke up shivering with cold about five hours later and drove home. And that's it. That's the whole story. That's what happened.'

Faith scoffs. 'And you expect me to believe that?'

'No!' Miles shouts. 'I don't expect you to believe that. I don't expect *anyone* to believe it. That's the whole point. It doesn't sound very bloody believable, does it? That's why I had to come up with something that *was* believable – someone to back me up – otherwise there was a chance I was going to get locked up for something I didn't do.'

'You've lied and lied and lied. You lied to the court. You lied to Jessie and me. How do I know you're not lying to me right now?'

'Because you haven't got the gun pointed at me anymore, have you?' He waves the pistol. 'I've got one pointed at you. If I was the murderer you think I am, wouldn't I just put a bullet in you right now?'

'Yeah, well, maybe you should.'

Miles points the gun high into the air and pulls the trigger. It fires, the gun kicking back in his hand. It's an unreal sight: the bullet leaving the barrel in a shudder and a wisp of smoke. Branches shake and wings flap as birds scarper from their perches.

Faith also flinches at the noise. She closes her eyes for a moment, then takes another step forward and throws her arms in the air, her brow and nose creased with fury. 'Just do it! Get it over with. I wasn't planning on walking out of this forest alive, anyway.'

Miles takes a step back, and fires another shot high into the trees. He can taste the sulphurous tang of gunpowder on the air. 'Maybe I should. But I can't. This is one of those times where being totally wrong about something has saved you.' He aims the gun upwards again and fires another shot. 'Because I'm not a killer.' Again, he fires into the air. 'I couldn't kill you even if I wanted to.'

Miles pulls the trigger again. But this time it responds only with a click. He pulls the trigger once more, and again it doesn't fire.

He's emptied the chamber. He lets go of the pistol, and it falls to the ground, landing with a heavy metallic clack as it strikes the road.

He watches Faith for a reaction. She doesn't move. He can't read her expression; is it surprise, or something else? Has he made a mistake? Faith's backpack is still on her shoulders; could she have another weapon in there? If she does, she isn't reaching for it. Her arms dangle limply by her sides.

Miles outstretches his good arm – an open gesture. 'Look at me.' He speaks at a slow, calm pace that is at odds with the urgent thumping of his heart. 'Look at me. I've never harmed anyone. I hate violence.' Miles touches his shoulder and grimaces. When he removes his hand from the wound, his fingers are crimson with blood. 'I've never been in a single fight, until just this minute. I've never raised my hand to a woman in my life. I don't even kill bugs.'

Faith stares silently at him. He's staring at her, too. It's a strange feeling, like they're meeting one another for the first time. And then, like a magic eye coming into focus, Miles sees her: the girl who suffered years of neglect and abandonment. He sees the woman who felt a loss so great that her feelings couldn't be controlled. A woman whose grief turned to anger and then hate. Hate that fuelled a need for revenge that brought her all the way here.

Something has changed in her eyes, and Miles knows exactly what it is. He's received so much scrutiny, so much judgement, that he can tell from the look in a person's eyes whether they believe him or not. And Miles can see it. She knows he's telling the truth. She believes him.

The expression on her face remains impassive. She's thinking. So is Miles. The way she looks at him reminds him of a cat, the way they stare you down with round eyes as they consider their options: fight or flight.

And then, without a word, she turns on a heel and runs. She's made her decision. The pace she sets off at tells him it's unequivocal.

Faith isn't coming back. Miles uses his good arm to gingerly lower himself to the ground, and he sits and watches as she sprints down the road, becoming smaller until she disappears around a bend. The person who has been following him, tormenting him, has gone.

Miles pulls up his shirt to examine his shoulder. It's nothing but a flesh wound, oozing blood. It hurts a hell of lot worse than it looks. It's not even bleeding that heavily. The longer he stares at it, the more it loses all importance. Eventually it will be nothing but a small patch of scar tissue. A blemish. A triviality. What he has is a wound that will easily heal. Unlike Faith. Unlike Caira. Unlike Elis.

Hunt for suspect after tourist slain at West Coast beauty spot

Greymouth Times, November 26

Police are appealing for sightings of a British woman after the suspected homicide of a tourist in a remote area of forest.

Faith Jackson has been missing for more than eight hours since police arrived at the scene, in Hendrick's Forest on the West Coast, around 10am this morning.

The victim, a 33-year-old British man, suffered a fatal stab wound. A second British man, 30, suffered a gunshot wound and has been admitted to hospital. A 33-year-old woman, also from Britain, received treatment for a minor ankle injury, police said.

The incident happened after a group of seven tourists chose to camp in the forest, which is currently closed due to efforts to reintroduce native wildlife.

Jackson is believed to have left the forest shortly after 8am, and a warrant has been issued for her arrest.

The authorities were alerted when another member of the group hiked out of the reserve and flagged down a motorist to raise the alarm.

Police are also investigating the theft of a motorcycle from a neighbouring farm, and it is believed Jackson may have used the vehicle to travel out of the area.

Checkpoints are in place on State Highway 6, and a police helicopter has been deployed as part of the search.

Jackson is 170cm tall, of medium build and has braided hair. Members of the public have been asked not to approach Jackson but to call 111 immediately if they see her.

Police are not looking for anyone else in connection with the incident.

Access to Hendrick's Forest is currently prohibited by the Department of Conservation. Any unauthorised person entering the area could face a penalty of up to $30,000.

CHAPTER 58

MILES

Miles is travelling backwards at speed, staring at the rapidly changing scenery outside: fields and hedgerows and cattle give way to warehouses and factories and car parks. Polly sits to his right, and George and Reubyn are opposite. They occupy a table on a train to South Wales, all dressed conspicuously in black suits – their funeral attire. Today will be a dreadfully sad occasion, but it promises to bring with it closure. And it's been a long time coming. It's taken nearly three months for Elis's body to be repatriated from New Zealand – time for healing of wounds both mental and physical.

For the physical wounds, the process was relatively straightforward. Miles had some minor surgery before leaving New Zealand and has now regained full mobility in his right shoulder. The medics assessing him informed him that he'd been lucky. The bullet had embedded itself in his pectoralis minor, the muscle where the chest meets the shoulder. Despite the intense pain he felt, there was no damage to arteries or bones.

Three months is also plenty of time, it turns out, for the media to lose interest in his life. After a brief frenzy when they returned home, the reporters stopped caring once it became obvious that he wasn't going to be giving interviews. His lawyers were right: a couple of weeks is a long time in the world of news. There are now plenty of other shiny new scandals to keep journalists occupied. The media has also been put on notice that reporters are not welcome at Elis's funeral, and their attendance would be an unreasonable intrusion into grief. With the clamour for stories having ebbed away, there's no reason to think any reporters will turn up and cause any trouble today.

As the media spotlight on him dimmed, Miles found the internet trolls began to leave him alone as well. After a couple of weeks, during which he barely left the house, things rapidly started to improve. Miles started going whole days without receiving abuse or pestering of any kind. He began to venture outside, starting with the odd walk to the shops or a drive across town to visit a friend, and then, before long, he was behaving in a similar way to how he did before his arrest. Life is approaching something close to normal.

It was on one of his small excursions about two weeks ago when he last heard from Lewin. Miles was sitting in a cafe, reading a job advert on his phone, when the screen showed an incoming call. Hearing from the cops didn't make him flinch like it used to; Lewin had kept in regular contact, continuing to provide updates on what became a complex investigation involving multiple police forces. He accepted the call. 'Hello.'

'Hi Miles, is now a good time to talk?'

He looked around to see if anyone was listening. Most of the customers scattered about the place were engrossed in their own conversations, but one or two were not. 'Can you give me five minutes?'

'Sure. I'll call you back in five.'

Miles grabbed his stuff and set off towards a nearby park. On the way, his mind skipped ahead, dreaming up possible reasons for Lewin's call. Most probably it would be about Faith, who was still missing, presumably somewhere in New Zealand. The police had kept him fairly well informed on that matter, always notifying him of developments before they released details to the public.

As it turned out, when the police had arrived in the forest on the day Miles was shot, they already had a warrant out for Faith's arrest. By that point they had noticed that her name, which they recognised as a minor beneficiary in Caira's will, had been on the passenger manifest for a flight to New Zealand just one day before Miles was due to travel. From there, police soon figured out that it was she who had authored the threatening emails.

The last major update Miles had received on Faith's movements was when the bike she'd stolen was found abandoned on the outskirts of a village about ten miles away from Hendrick's Forest. What Faith had done when she got there remained a mystery. New Zealand's West Coast is so remote, it's simultaneously one of the easiest and most difficult places to disappear into. There are no crowds to get lost in, but there are hundreds of miles of wild and empty landscapes where you might not encounter another human for weeks at a time. Could Faith still be there? Hiding in the wilderness? Or could she have escaped the region and blended in elsewhere? Maybe she'd escaped the country entirely. Or maybe, just maybe, Lewin was calling to let him know they'd finally found her.

Miles arrived at the park and sat on a bench to wait for Lewin's call. It was a mild, overcast day, and a father and son, with near-identical floppy blond hair, were playing football about fifty yards away. Jumpers for goalposts. A minute later, Miles's phone rang.

Miles answered immediately. 'Hi, again.'

'Hello. If you're ready, I've got an update for you.'

'You've found her?'

'No, it's not about Faith.'

'So, it's about Caira? You've had a breakthrough?'

'No, no. It's nothing major like that.'

'Right, okay.' Miles tried to hide the disappointment in his voice. A shriek caused him to turn his head, and he saw the little boy wheeling away in celebration at scoring a goal.

'Anyway, New Zealand Police have provided us with some answers to a couple of your questions. I'm sorry it's taken so long. As I'm sure you can appreciate, a lot of resources have been tied up by—'

'Yeah, I totally understand,' Miles says. 'Honestly, it's fine.'

A pause on the line. 'Good. Thank you. Now, let's start with the man you pursued in Queenstown, the chap you sent me the photograph of.'

'Oh.' Miles was surprised to hear him bring that up. It had lost all significance. Suddenly, he was curious again. 'So, who was he?'

'He was completely unconnected. He's a resident of Queenstown, and he'd never heard of you before. Officers have spoken to him and are satisfied he's telling the truth about that.'

Miles's mouth fell open in surprise. 'But, why? Why did he run like he did? He sprinted for his life. We chased him halfway across the town.'

Lewin took an audible breath. 'This man had witnessed homophobic violence in the past, so when he realised he was being followed by two men as he walked home from a gay-friendly bar, he decided, rightly or wrongly, the safest option was to run.'

'Oh, God.' Miles bowed his head and dragged a hand through his hair. 'We traumatised a completely innocent man.'

Lewin remained silent.

'But why had he been looking at me for the whole . . .' Miles's words trailed off. There was no point in finishing the question. 'This man, can I talk to him? I'd like to apologise.'

'He's requested that we protect his privacy. But if you want to write to him, I'll pass it on.'

'Thanks. I'd like to do that.'

'You also asked about the Macallan whisky, and how Faith knew you ordered it.'

'Yes.'

Lewin took another deep breath. 'Well, after officers looked at the CCTV from The Globe, they were able to identify a man who approached the bar and asked what brand of whisky you'd bought. When police talked to him, the man explained that a woman matching Faith's description had approached him on his way to the bar and offered him a hundred dollars to buy the same whisky as the four Englishmen before him. He decided to take her up on it, no questions asked.'

Miles wrinkled his brow as he tried to process what Lewin was telling him. 'Why didn't Faith just ask the bar staff herself?'

'I suspect she already knew what you were drinking. This was probably all about throwing you off the scent.'

'Right.'

'That's our best guess. We can't ask her, of course.'

'And you're still no closer to tracking her down?'

'I'm afraid not. Of course, if there are any significant updates, I'll let you know.'

Before he ended the call, Miles asked, as he always did, about the Caira Kennedy case. And Lewin patiently explained – no surprise to Miles – that the police were no closer to solving it.

Strangely, Miles has begun to feel a trace of sympathy towards the detectives working the case. When looked at objectively, it's not the easiest to solve. It doesn't help that there remains no known motive. Her killing wasn't sexually motivated – the autopsy confirmed that. And aside from a few minor grievances through her work, Caira didn't appear to have any enemies. Miles's best hope is that one day there will be a DNA breakthrough that will bring the perpetrator to justice. Whoever they are, they lit the touchpaper on this whole sorry affair.

Whoever they are, they're responsible for the deaths of two people: Caira, at their own hands, and Elis, as an indirect consequence.

It remains much more likely that the next time Miles hears from Lewin, it will be with an update about Faith. Although he doesn't expect that to be resolved any time soon either. Faith managed to deceive and bamboozle Miles at every turn. Her ability to do this has left him convinced that she will evade capture for some time yet. And she's shown considerable ingenuity. When police looked at her Google history, they found searches on how to disable a vehicle battery. But, even so, it was remarkable that she managed to do it while everyone in the bus was presumably asleep. Her talent for dissimulation means Faith has probably morphed into a completely different person by now. New accent. New appearance. New backstory.

He tries not to spend too much time thinking about the awful events that happened in New Zealand, but it's hard not to dwell on them. And there are other reminders. Last week, he received an email from Jessie. She got in touch to let him know she wouldn't be attending Elis's funeral. Her tone was cordial enough; Jessie made it clear there were no hard feelings, but she also left him in little doubt that she was in no hurry to see him again. He can hardly blame her.

Miles stares out of the window of the train. The view outside is now dominated by heavy industry: huge smoking towers that confirm life is churning on, the way it always has. For most people, anyway. Miles hasn't returned to work yet. He still has some decisions to make, in that regard, and had granted himself the period up until Elis's funeral to mull it all over. Now, that thinking time is nearly up. In a couple of hours, Elis will have been laid to rest. After three long months, it'll be time for Miles to start making some decisions about his future.

An announcement blares from the speakers in their carriage, one of those inhuman-sounding voices informing them that they will soon be arriving at their destination. As the train slows, the four of them clear the detritus from their table, then stand to collect their coats from the overhead rack. The platform appears, lined with passengers waiting to get on, and Miles stares into the crowd, scanning the faces. He does this now, every time he's presented with a gathering of people. And every time, Miles half expects to see her among them. But deep down, he knows he won't. Faith's not pursuing him anymore. She knows he's not her true target. If that weren't the case, the emails would've started up again. But they haven't. He's no longer receiving messages telling him *this is not over*. Maybe that's because it is. Maybe, once the funeral is done, Miles will finally start to believe it *is* over.

CHAPTER 59

POLLY

There was a good turnout for Elis's funeral, as would be expected for a man in his thirties. All pews in the small church were taken, and dozens more mourners filled the rear and wings. Afterwards, having been carried nearly twelve thousand miles – by car, plane and who knows what else – Elis's body made its final journey to a corner of the graveyard, where he was laid to rest under a clear blue sky.

Now, they sit in the back room of a flat-roofed pub, a few hundred yards down the road, for the wake. Along one side is a buffet of pale food. Polly hasn't touched any of it. She never has much of an appetite after a funeral and fails to understand how anyone can happily chow down on a piece of quiche having just watched someone get buried. Her funeral sickness is worse than ever, today. All thoughts of Elis inevitably conjure up that horrendous final image in her mind. The boys don't seem to be put off, though. Miles has managed to eat a couple of mini sausage rolls. Reubyn and George have put away a decent plateful and have now returned from a second pass at the buffet.

Elis's family are sat around a table in the opposite corner of the room. The Pritchard-Joneses have been remarkably civil to them, so far, all things considered. Although Elis's death is no fault of

Miles, Polly isn't convinced she would be as forgiving if the tables were turned.

'Oh, bollocks,' Reubyn exclaims. He's bitten into a doughnut and jam has oozed down his lapel. 'I've got to wear this suit again tomorrow.'

'Since when do you wear a suit two days in a row?' George says. 'Has someone else died?'

'I've got a meeting,' Reubyn replies, dabbing at his jacket with a napkin.

'What about?'

'A work thing.'

'Don't be so bloody coy, Reubyn, what's it about?'

'I'll tell you after. I don't want to jinx it by talking about it already.'

George rolls his eyes and drains the remainder of his beer. He raises his empty pint glass. 'Shall we have another? My round.'

'I think we should call it a day,' Polly says firmly.

George's lips twitch, as if he's about to say something, then he breathes a sigh. Whatever glib statement he was about to make will remain unsaid. It's a rare and welcome showing of self-restraint on his behalf. The others respond by finishing their drinks and grabbing their coats; they're all in agreement – an hour here is more than enough. They've paid their respects, and now it's time to get going before there's any trouble. Although the Pritchard-Joneses haven't vocalised any resentment yet, that doesn't mean for certain that no bad feeling exists. And with drinks being consumed at a liberal pace, the chances of any suppressed hostility revealing itself will only increase the longer they stay.

Polly has another reason for her haste: she could really do with getting on with some work. Although she only has a few clients at the moment, she still hasn't replaced Callie, and so they're a little thin on the ground.

They return their glasses to the bar and make a French exit. George and Reubyn lead the way, the former pestering his friend for more details about his upcoming meeting.

Polly walks slower, falling in step with Miles along the pavement. He walks at a weary pace but there's no point in hurrying him – the next train doesn't depart for half an hour. Miles is quiet, like he has been all day, and Polly walks silently next to him, allowing him space for contemplation.

A few minutes go by before Miles chooses to speak. 'I think I might abandon the whole acting thing.'

'What?'

'I'm not very good at it, Pol, let's be honest.'

'Yes, you are.' Polly gives him a look of robust encouragement. He might not be Daniel Day-Lewis, but he isn't talentless.

When Miles doesn't respond, she wonders if he might be serious. 'What would you do instead?'

'Something more worthwhile. I'm thinking maybe I could do social work.'

Polly raises an eyebrow but says nothing. Miles has been extremely emotional today, and he can be prone to fanciful thoughts like these. He'll come to his senses soon enough.

They walk back under the motorway and turn a corner towards the railway station. It's close to sunset and most of the street is in shadow; only a single pavement and the terraced houses on one side are bathed in the wintery yellow light. Polly grabs the cuff of Miles's coat and guides him across the road to the sunny side. It's still cold, but the delicate rays have just enough strength to provide a mellow warmth on their skin.

'We're lucky, aren't we?' Miles says.

'*You're* not.'

'Are you sure about that?'

Polly gives him a look. Now isn't the time for a deep philosophical discussion on fate and privilege awareness.

'When are you going back to London?' Miles asks.

'I'm not sure yet. There's no massive rush.'

Miles frowns at her. 'But what about the business, your flat, your tenant? There's a lot to look after, isn't there?'

'Ah, Miles.' She slings an arm around his shoulders, nudging him forward, and they continue moving slowly down the pavement. 'We've known each other for more than three decades, and you still don't see what's going on here.'

He squints at her, gives the slightest shake of the head. 'I don't?'

'All those things you just mentioned, they largely look after themselves. There's only one thing I've ever really had to look after, and that's my little brother.'

EPILOGUE

REUBYN

Reubyn sits alone at a black conference table in a medium-sized studio. Every inch of the walls is covered in black open-celled soundproofing foam, and behind him is a screen showing the logo for Danny Mascall's podcast. Reubyn has seen this room before so many times, on video. But to be here in person, to be the *subject* of an episode, is something akin to a religious experience.

Danny has a three-camera set-up, including a Sony FX9 – a serious piece of kit – for the master angle. Reubyn makes a mental note that he should aspire to own one of those. Pointing towards him is a Shure SM7. An identical mic is opposite, in front of an empty chair on the other side of the table. The key light is positioned high to his left, tilted at a 45-degree angle, and he can feel its heat against his cheek.

Danny was on the phone when he arrived. He put it on mute, greeted Reubyn with a bone-crushingly firm handshake, and directed him into the studio before wandering off to finish his call.

'Sorry to keep you waiting,' Danny says, strolling back into the room and closing the door behind him.

'No problem at all.'

'I really appreciate you coming in.' Danny visits each camera in turn, making final adjustments and getting everything rolling.

Reubyn watches him with interest, fascinated by how he works. It's the first time he's seen Danny in real life, and he's impeccably groomed. His black pompadour fades to a number one at the mid-section of his crown, and his beard also contains some kind of oil that makes it glint under the lights.

He sits. 'I'm all set. Are you good to go?'

Reubyn gives him the thumbs up. He had expected there might be a bit more small talk before the cameras started rolling, but apparently not.

Danny checks some notes set out in front of him, then begins. 'Hi everyone, and welcome to a very special episode of the Danny Mascall Podcast. I've got a really exciting guest today.' Danny's speech is smooth and assured – the kind of authority and confidence that Reubyn attempts to emulate when making his own content. 'Here with me in the studio is Reubyn Carmichael, the executive producer and star of *Escape to Hell*. If you haven't heard of this true-crime series about the murder of Elis Pritchard-Jones in New Zealand, then you must have been living under a rock because I can't seem to go a day at the moment without hearing somebody talking about it. Reubyn has kindly agreed to come on and tell us a little about the making of the series and his plans for the future. So, Reubyn. Thanks for coming on. How are you doing?'

'I'm doing good. It's great to be here.'

'To kick things off, and for the benefit of anyone who hasn't seen the series, why don't you give us a quick rundown of what the series is, and the story behind it.'

Reubyn takes a deep breath. 'Sure. I mean, I could fill the whole hour with this story so I'll try to keep it as concise as I can.' Reubyn starts with the whole saga with Miles and his court case, and then the trip to New Zealand, culminating with Elis's murder.

He concentrates on trying to get the pace of his speech just right –
it needs to be engaging and enthusiastic without him flustering over
his words. When he reaches the bit about Elis's demise, and Miles's
brush with death, he allows his tone to become graver.

'It must have been a super-traumatic experience for all of you,'
Danny says. 'And what's also crazy about this situation is that, while
this was all unfolding, you were there, the whole time, filming
everything on broadcast-quality equipment.'

It's not a question, but from Danny's rising inflection, it's
clearly Reubyn's turn to speak. 'That's right. Well, I wasn't filming everything. But yes. I have my own channel, and I was trying to shoot a couple of videos. When we got home, and the
dust settled on this whole thing, I was watching all this footage
back and realised that what I had was really quite a unique
documentation. It was all there. And out of this terrible tragedy,
we were able to create something quite powerful and moving,
something we could dedicate to Elis in his memory.'

Danny nods. 'I love the way you dedicated the series to Elis.'

They spend a few minutes talking about Elis, the way he and
Reubyn bonded in New Zealand, about how deeply his loss has
been felt.

'And what about Miles? He didn't take part in the series, did he?'

'That's right. He chose not to be involved.'

'There were some reports that you and Miles had fallen out
over it, and that he tried to stop the series from being aired. Is
that right?'

Reubyn has been expecting this question. He pauses, pretending
to give it a moment's thought, before delivering his preprepared answer.
'Miles is one of my best friends. It's true that we had a difference of
opinion when it came to this project, but he'll always be one of my
best friends.'

'Have you spoken to him recently?'

'No, but we've both been really busy. I'm sure I'll talk to him soon.'

'Right then.' Danny entwines his fingers and cracks his knuckles. 'Let's talk about Faith Jackson.'

Reubyn grimaces for the camera. 'Yes.'

'Because, when you made the series, she was on the lam, right? Has there been any update on that?'

Reubyn shrugs. 'Not that I know of. As far as I'm aware, they're still looking for her. The New Zealand police, the British police, Interpol – she's evaded them all, so far.'

'She's slippery,' Danny says.

Reubyn laughs. 'She's clever. Faith's good at disguising herself, and it wouldn't surprise me if the police never track her down.'

'Now,' Danny places a finger on his notes and begins reading his next question directly off a sheet of paper, 'the police are saying they're not looking for anyone else in relation to Elis's murder, so that makes Faith the only suspect. The internet is awash with rumours about why she might have done it, especially after the series aired. I'm not going to repeat any of this speculation, for legal reasons. But do *you* have a theory?'

Reubyn sucks air in through his teeth. 'The truth is, I think Elis was just unlucky. We were out there in the forest with Faith, who was unhinged and chaotic and had her sights set on Miles, and Elis somehow got caught in the crossfire. You have to remember, none of us knew what we were dealing with when it came to Faith. She seemed totally normal, but under the surface, Faith had a burning desire for revenge. She was extremely emotional, inwardly volatile and possessed by an urge to kill.'

Danny takes a sip of water. 'All right, why don't you finish up by telling us a little bit about your channel and your plans for the future. I gather you've brought something in to show us?'

'I have.' Reubyn reaches for his bag and pulls out a gold plaque, which he stands on the table in front of him. 'This arrived this week.'

'I remember getting one of those. Explain to our listeners what it is.'

'It's a Gold Creator Award. YouTube sends you one when you get to a million subscribers. A little marker of progress.'

'Congratulations, Reubyn. Welcome to the club.'

'Thanks. Since the series aired, I've had more and more people coming to the channel and discovering my content. I'm going to make that my focus again, for the foreseeable. In fact, I've got a bit of exclusive news for you, on that front.'

Danny tilts his head to the side, with a look of pleasant surprise. 'That's what I like to hear. Do tell.'

'I'm planning to go back to New Zealand for another project. I'm going to retrace our steps. And, who knows, maybe we will be able to succeed where the police have failed. Maybe we'll be able to track Faith down.'

They continue to discuss his project for a few minutes, and Reubyn offers a few more details. He explains that, as was the case for the first series, Jessie is the only other member of the original group who has agreed to take part. He hopes he might be able to persuade the others to change their minds. A lot of the people who were heavily featured in the first series – like Caira's ex-boyfriend Ben Knight – aren't really relevant for the second. But a greater financial incentive, available this time around, might tempt George to get involved.

Reubyn also reveals the working title for the project: *Finding Faith*. He chooses not to reveal the true extent of his aims, that Faith remains a source of fascination for Reubyn. Of course, he knows she was never really interested in him. Faith had simply identified him as weak and manipulable – someone she could latch on to in order to gain access to Miles. She was never attracted to Reubyn one bit. And disappearing into the wilds of New Zealand without a trace was simply another ghosting – albeit an elaborate one. But still, he finds himself thinking of her often, sometimes from the very moment he wakes of a morning.

Danny wraps up the interview with some enthusiastic praise and encouragement for Reubyn's work, then rises from his chair and turns off the cameras. 'Thanks for that, Reubyn. That'll be a great episode.'

'Oh, no, thank *you*. This is brilliant exposure for me. I really appreciate it.'

'I'm always happy to help a brother out. We've got to lift each other up, you know. The odds are stacked against people like us, these days. We've got to fight harder for every win.'

As Reubyn wraps his plaque in a towel and places it into his bag, Danny stops next to him and perches on the edge of the table. 'Tell me, what are your goals? What does Reubyn Carmichael want to achieve this year?'

Reubyn scratches his head. He doesn't want to embarrass himself by appearing unambitious. 'Five million subscribers.'

Danny nods. 'Achievable.'

Reubyn slides his backpack on to his shoulders. 'Do you really think so?'

'Absolutely. It's important to set yourself goals. They keep you honest. Once your goal is set, it's on you to make it happen.'

'I'll do my best.'

Danny holds the studio door open for Reubyn. They enter a bright corridor and walk towards the exit. 'Ask yourself, what would the world's most high-value men do in your situation? You've got to think like a CEO. Behave like a CEO. Get up early every morning and hustle. Successful people don't take a day off, and you won't achieve your goals by sleeping in on the weekends.'

Reubyn nods vigorously. He's heard this advice before, on video, but to hear it here, for an audience of one, is nothing short of thrilling.

They stop by the door. 'I've booked you a car,' Danny says. 'It'll take you wherever you want to go.' He offers his hand. 'Thanks so much for coming on the podcast.'

Reubyn accepts Danny's handshake and once again feels that crushing, vice-like grip. This time, Reubyn reciprocates, squeezing with similar force. An equal.

◆　◆　◆

Reubyn leaves the studio and climbs into a waiting Mercedes, his heart still giddy from the excitement of being featured on Danny's podcast. The driver is smartly dressed in a dark suit, and a compartment in the armrest contains a selection of snacks, bottled water and mints. It's a nice touch. Nice things like this seem to be happening more regularly for him these days. Reubyn gives the driver his address, and leans back on his leather seat, basking in the afterglow of his performance.

What just happened feels like a pivotal moment. It's funny how many pivotal moments in Reubyn's life can be linked to the Danny Mascall Podcast. The subjects of Danny's interviews are so varied; Reubyn has lost count of the number of vital life lessons he's learned from watching his show.

He's been given eye-opening insights about business, health and politics. But if he had to pick a single episode that had the most profound effect on him, it was the one with the psychologist, Dr Sheridan. Her tips for success with women. In fact, all the crazy events of the last few years can be traced back to her ten rules. More specifically, to rule number five: *If you know someone who's successful with women, watch them and see what they do.* It was such a simple piece of advice. And the more Reubyn thought about it, the more he realised he knew the perfect person to watch.

When it came to success with women, there was no one better to learn from than Miles. Whatever he was doing, it worked – women kept falling helplessly into his orbit. But what was it that made Miles so much more luminous than other males? What was he doing that meant girls were drawn to him as helplessly as moths? The answers to these questions would hold the key, Reubyn realised. If he could understand the secrets of Miles's success, he could use them for himself. It would be transformational.

To begin with, he started making notes, listing the latest clothing brands Miles bought, the hair products he used, the drinks he ordered. He observed his movements: the way he walked, talked, danced. But it wasn't enough. It didn't provide the answers he craved. The real magic was happening away from view: in Miles's one-on-one conversations, on his dates, in private. When it came to those situations, Reubyn had only his imagination to guide him, and that was useless. What he needed was empirical information. But that wasn't possible to gather. He couldn't just follow Miles around in his most deeply personal moments – the mere idea of it was absurd. He continued to think about it, though. Reubyn imagined being an invisible witness as one of Miles's dates went so spectacularly well that it progressed into something else. Something more intimate. And it would have happened, too, on the night Reubyn followed Miles and Jessie to the bird hide. That was the closest he ever got: himself like a moth behind a pane of glass, tantalisingly near. He would have seen one hell of a show if that bolt of lightning hadn't given him away.

The car pulls up outside Reubyn's London flat, which has been his home for nearly a year. He decided to move to the capital shortly after the contracts for *Escape to Hell* were signed. He needs to be here, really, if he's serious about trying to make it in the entertainment industry. Reubyn gives the driver a generous tip, grabs his bag and leaves the car. He swipes into his building and takes the lift to the fifth floor.

His one-bedroom flat is small and has a view of several mid-rise residential blocks of similar proportions to his own. Reubyn enters the bedroom and unzips his bag, removing the gold plaque and holding it at arm's length. He's been thinking about where best to display it. For now, it just needs safekeeping. He opens his wardrobe and places the plaque carefully in the top compartment, where he keeps his other precious things. His passport and birth certificate are up there, along with some *Dealbreaker* memorabilia and, most importantly, a leopard-print scarf. He pulls out the scarf and toys with it. As is always the case when he takes it out, it brings back a memory.

It's important to remember that what happened with Caira Kennedy was a one-off. A unique event. But the evening it happened had started off normally enough. That night, Reubyn went to the pub to edit. Sometimes he was more efficient and productive when he got off his sofa and worked somewhere else, be it at a cafe, library or, in this case, the local boozer. He was at a table in the corner, with his noise-cancelling headphones on, and a pint of Heineken 0.0 in front of him. And then fate walked in. Or more accurately, Miles did, along with a woman he'd never seen before. They were on a date, it appeared. Reubyn's skin tingled to life. He found himself in a sort of trance, brought on by sudden feelings of surprise, excitement and uncertainty. Miles hadn't noticed Reubyn; he was completely focused on his companion as they waited at the bar for their drinks. And when they sat, because Miles was facing slightly away he continued not to notice Reubyn.

At this point, Reubyn stopped caring about his edit. He was transfixed by the scene playing out in front of him. By chance, he'd found himself in one of the precise scenarios he had daydreamed about, and he wasn't going to waste it.

He watched studiously and noted how Miles appeared completely engaged – as if what she was saying was fascinating. He was generous, paying for both rounds. And he became increasingly tactile as the evening went on: a playful touch of the arm to begin with, and later nudging his chair closer to hers.

When the bell sounded for last orders, Reubyn knew he couldn't push his luck by staying any longer. He packed away his things, scooped up his change, and made his exit through the rear door, where he emerged into the gloom of a side street. Removed from the warmth of the pub, it was freezing, and Reubyn should've hurried home. But he didn't. Instead, he paused in the shadowy space by the bins and entertained himself on his phone. He couldn't identify the force that was keeping him there, but something was stopping him from moving on. A draught of cold slid through the opening of his coat and licked against his skin, raising the follicles on his neck. And then he saw them: Miles and Caira, walking briskly on the other side of the street, so enthralled by each other that they didn't so much as glance in his direction.

Reubyn watched as they walked on, the sounds of their footsteps and voices fading to an inaudible volume. Their silhouettes diminished, following the curve of the road until they were almost out of sight, and then stopped. They'd reached her home, he assumed. Miles and Caira remained there, chatting on the pavement. After a minute or so, she gestured towards the building, and Reubyn's heart began to thud. She was inviting him in. Reubyn had conceived of a scenario similar to this, but only as a fantasy. This was happening for real. It was a sign, he thought. Life comes with many signs and signals, and the trick is to figure out which ones to ignore and the ones to take heed of. But sometimes, it's completely obvious. Sometimes, life takes you by the hand and shows you the way.

When they'd descended from view, Reubyn waited for a minute and then followed, his laptop bag slung over his shoulder. He crept down the stone stairs to a narrow courtyard outside a basement flat. He found himself in a dark cavity, sandwiched between two tall stone walls, with a view into the living room. No one could see him there, as if it were a hiding place designed specifically for him. The perfect place to watch. And he could hear them, too. Just about.

Miles and Caira talked for a few minutes, Reubyn straining to hear their muffled voices. But then, unexpectedly, they left the living room and walked back into the hallway. He heard the front door latch. Reubyn straightened his posture and kept deadly still, pressing his back to the wall as the door opened. He held his breath, praying he wouldn't be seen. Miles kissed Caira on the cheek and told her goodnight, then made his way back up the steps and on to the pavement. The front door closed. But as the sound of Miles's footsteps faded, so too did any feelings of relief. Reubyn's stomach twisted with frustration. Why was Miles leaving? His date was so obviously up for it. It was such a waste.

Reubyn remained where he was, his hands deep in his pockets, the cold in the air stinging his face. The longer he stayed there, the less inclined he was to leave. The warm light emanating from Caira's flat was inviting. After a minute or so, Reubyn was hit by a thought of such clarity that it cancelled any argument going on inside his head: he'd waited long enough. His watching brief had run its course. Now, it was his turn.

He may not have been invited. But, sometimes, that's a good thing. Like when you break into a derelict theme park – or a forbidden forest, for that matter – sometimes, if you've gained entry with no given right to be there, it adds a delicious dash of jeopardy to whatever you're doing.

As he moved towards the entrance to her flat, he wasn't sure what he was going to do or say. But he knocked on the door anyway, and she answered almost instantly. She was smiling. The way she had been smiling for Miles all night. But the smile fell from her face when she saw Reubyn. Her eyes swam with a look he didn't recognise. And then everything moved in a blur of speed and struggle.

What happened next was a one-off, Reubyn reminds himself again. It's important to remember that. The other important thing to remember is: he didn't do anything weird. He was just present with her, lay next to her. He whispered softly in her ear, stroked her hair. Nothing weird. Nothing weird, at all. He's not some pervert.

But he can't deny that it was a thrill to be there with her. Just the two of them. He wants to return there, to that night with Caira, to relive it, but the memory has become murky, like it happened in a deep fog. It's the same fog that descends on him when his mind attempts to trace back to those wretched nights at Holvine, when he was led from his dorm by a dank, ageing hand in the grim hours, and the same fog that filled the house when his dad shut the door on those dreaded evenings when he was left alone with Tony Meadows. He used to wonder, why him? But now he knows: he was a soft target. He might not have been the best-looking boy, but he never fought back, never spoke out, never caused a fuss. Except he's not a soft target now, not anymore.

He runs the scarf under his nose, breathing in the last remaining scent of her, those final remains that diminish more with the passing of each month. Soon that last lingering trace will disappear, and all memory of her will be gone. He wants to go back, to see through the fog. To remember the feeling. But it was a one-off. A *one-off*.

The more he tells himself that, the less believable it is.

Could it really have been a one-off? Why should he be denied that feeling of human connection, when everyone around him takes it for granted? Maybe it *wasn't* a one-off. Maybe it was just the beginning. If it was the end, it would go against everything he's been taught: why settle for a taste of the fruit, when you can have the whole vine?

ACKNOWLEDGEMENTS

The person I most want to acknowledge here is you, for reading. I'm grateful you found this book. Thank you.

Cheers to my brilliant agent Maddy Milburn and her lovely team at the MMLA, notably Meghan Capper, Georgia McVeigh and Rachel Yeoh. Maddy and Georgia made valuable editorial contributions to the development of this novel.

I'm hugely grateful to my editors Maisie Lawrence, Hannah Bond, Sadie Mayne and Gemma Wain, who were a joy to work with throughout.

I owe a great debt to Laura Shepherd and Graham Bartlett, who guided me on courtroom and police procedural matters, respectively. They didn't run the rule over everything, though, and any mistakes in these areas are entirely my doing.

I spent four happy years living in Aotearoa/New Zealand, and it was fun to travel back there for the writing of this novel, if only in my mind. Thanks to my Kiwi mate Anna Loren for encouraging me to use Aotearoa as a setting for this book and being an early reader. She and her well-travelled partner Matthew Butt provided useful advice and discussed possible locations with me. Hendrick's Forest is a made-up place, so don't go looking for it. The kākāpō, however, is very real, as are the efforts to protect it from extinction. At the time of writing, there are only 238 kākāpō left. Anyone wanting to help these amazing birds can do so by supporting the recovery programme here: www.doc.govt.nz/kakapo-donate.

My research for this book forced me to listen to some fairly toxic podcasts, which I'm not inclined to publicise here. Instead, I'd like to highlight the work of the Survivors Trust and Refuge – charities that support victims of sexual violence and domestic abuse.

I'm lucky to have received support from many brilliant authors. There are too many to list here, but I must acknowledge everyone in the LMAG writers' group for keeping my spirits up every day.

Biggest thanks to my wife Sharry, son Grayson and dad Dave, and my wider family. Hopefully it's evident from this story how valuable I think it is to have a supportive sister. I'm lucky enough to have two.

Did you love uncovering the dark secrets at the heart of Miles's life? If so, then you'll be absolutely gripped by *The Best Man* by T. H. Murdock. It is supposed to be the happiest day of your life, but he knows your deepest secret . . .

Keep reading for an exclusive extract!

PROLOGUE

LUCY

I must have walked this path at least a hundred times, but today it feels different. Lonelier. More exposed. The gorse seems sharper, the sea a more seething sound, the wind harsher against my face.

Or maybe it's just that I've become aware of something behind me. A dark blur that appears in my periphery when I look seaward.

I quicken my step.

My fingers touch the spot at the opening of my coat, where I should be able to find it – his parting gift. It was a strange choice for someone who never showed any belief in fate. The closest I heard him get to that was to quote Sod's Law: *If something can go wrong, it will. Usually at the worst possible moment.* But I suppose when someone is close to death, it's understandable to want to abandon that sentiment in favour of something more hopeful.

In any case, I'm glad he gave it to me. To begin with, it gave me a chill each morning, a trace of a shiver, the metal cold against my skin. Close to my heart. Nowadays, it's a comfort. Or it would be, if I could find the thing.

It's for protection: that's what he said when he pressed it into my hand.

So what fate is this? The one time I really, and I mean *really*, need protection, I don't have it.

I glance over my shoulder, and my stomach pulls tight.

He was right all along.

If something can go wrong, it will. Usually at the worst possible moment.

CHAPTER 1

I'm leaving court when my phone rings. An old friend. I almost don't answer; I mean who calls people up these days? There's nothing that can't be said by text, or in an app, and that way I can ignore it until I've worked up the required energy to engage in social contact. If it's important, there's always email. But dialling your mate's number on purpose, making an unsolicited call for a live conversation, in the middle of the working day: what kind of maniac does that?

'Ed,' I say, 'what's all this? Have you butt-dialled me again?'

He laughs. We haven't spoken for months but I'd recognise that laugh anywhere: a nasal squawk like an old gate opening on a rusty hinge; it was the soundtrack to half of my youth. 'No, I meant to call you this time.'

'What's the matter then? You feeling needy? Want a cuddle?'

'Shut up, it's important. Do you have a couple of minutes?'

I do, as it happens. I have about five minutes before I descend into the communications blackspot that is the London Underground. I've just finished work after spending the afternoon at Westminster Magistrates', no doubt looking like a typical London clone in my black suit, phone pressed to my ear as I weave through the masses on Marylebone Road.

Ed takes a deep breath, so exaggerated I can hear it through the phone, then blurts out: 'I'm getting married.'

'You what?' For a moment I'm sure I've misheard him under the growl and horn of the building rush-hour traffic.

'I'm getting married. Next spring.'

'Bloody hell.' I sit down on a bench, breathing in the acrid fumes from a nearby exhaust. 'But you're only twenty-five. You're not a footballer or a Mormon – aren't you a bit young to be getting married?'

'Nah, it's fine. Kim's been keen on the idea for a while, and I'm not going to find better, am I? You've seen her – I'm punching above my weight, and we both know it.'

'I can't argue with that.'

He laughs. 'Exactly. So why wait?'

I'm silent for a few seconds. It all seems a bit rushed to me. But he sounds happy, excited – at least one of us is. And who the hell am I to lecture anyone on their life choices?

'Congratulations,' I say. 'I'm happy for you. This is great news.'

'Thanks, JP.' Ed pauses for a moment. 'There's another thing.'

Something in his voice, a slight tremor, tells me he's a bit anxious about what's coming next. 'Go on.'

'I . . . I was wondering if you'd be best man. Well, there'd be two, you and Merl. What do you say?'

Oh no. Being a best man is a nightmare. 'Of course. I'm honoured.'

My heart rate cranks up a few notches as Ed carries on, thanking me, and telling the story of how he proposed in view of the Eiffel Tower. I'm only half listening; my mind has already raced off into the distance, way down the track and through some stomach-churning hairpins to the certain car crash that lies in wait. Me, best man? That's a misnomer if I ever heard one. I'm the *worst* man, if anything. I shudder at the thought of martialling guests, cosying up to Kimberley's family, doing the speech. Oh God, the bloody speech. I'm not the man for this; Merl is the funny, confident one, he could easily do it by himself – why does Ed need me? Ed is probably only asking me because he thinks he should, and there's no way I can turn him down. I'm being killed with kindness.

An even more unsettling thought hits me, prompts me to cut him off mid-sentence. 'Have you decided where you're holding the wedding?'

I swallow a lump in my throat as I wait for his response.

'Kim wants to get married in church, and I'm not going to argue, you know what she's like. If it had been up to me, I'd happily do it down at the registry—'

'Yeah, but where? Have you booked somewhere for the reception?' *Please don't say St Hellion. Anywhere but there.*

'The Dolphin. We're going to have a big marquee. A classy one, mind.'

I'm breathing quickly, but can't get enough of the heavy, polluted air into my lungs. 'In St Hellion?'

'Yeah, of course. Where else would we do it?'

Shit.

Ed runs through the arrangements that have already been made, and I'm monosyllabic in response, staring across the street in a daze, the world around me slipping out of focus until all I see is the red smudge of a London bus drifting from right to left. A knot of dread tightens in my stomach. It's immediately obvious there's no hope of changing his mind. Everything is settled. The wedding will be held on the 24th of May, and I will be best man, which leaves my brain about eleven months to focus on it relentlessly, no matter what I'm doing, whether it be work, trying to sleep, running on a treadmill, waiting to be served at the Oxford Arms, being crammed on a Bakerloo Line train, heating a preassembled dinner, or any other of the repeating parts that make up the persistent cycle of a city existence.

I guess I knew this would happen, eventually. Something was always bound to come up that would force me to go back. Yet, even now, I can't bear the idea of it, even after so much time has passed.

It's been more than nine years since she died. *Nine years.* For nearly a decade the episode has played over in my mind, like some awful soap opera stuck on repeat, plaguing my thoughts, fracturing my sleep. What happened to her? Every rational thought I've had about it tells me we had nothing to do with it — it wasn't our fault. There had to be another explanation. The problem is, even now, I have no idea what that other explanation is. I can't be one hundred per cent sure.

Of course, we didn't really kill her. We couldn't have. Could we?

CHAPTER 2

To understand what happened all those years ago, it's important to know a bit about where I grew up. Maybe you were sent a postcard from there at some point. Maybe it was one of those kitschy ones that are split into quadrants. If it was, it probably had a picture of the beach and the Pellar's Stone, and maybe a photograph of the old mine, or an aerial shot that looks down on the V-shaped bay and its two uneven headlands – the giant Tregarrick and its smaller brother Penleaze – that hold the village in a crooked vice. The sea on these postcards always seems to have been altered slightly to make it bluer than it really is. *Wish you were here!* they shout from every side of every spinning rack in every shop. But if there is a slogan that sums up the feeling among the locals it would be the exact opposite: wish you *weren't* here.

To say St Hellion is a bit backward would be an understatement. To say the locals are set in their ways would be a bigger one. The biggest point of pride for the people of St Hellion is how far back they can trace their family name in the local cemetery. It's as if the place is stuck in a kind of time warp, where medieval stubbornness has stopped minds from being corrupted by science and logic. If you went there on holiday for a week, you would probably dismiss the everywhere-you-look references to olde Cornish lore as a novelty to entertain the summer hordes. But if you stayed for a winter – when the second homes are empty and the whole place is frozen and quiet – and you really opened your eyes and ears, you'd realise the people there actually believe it. They live it. You'd discover it's a place where horseshoes are nailed above doorways and people salute magpies for good luck. After a while, if you met someone wearing the breastbone of a bird hanging around their neck, that wouldn't be conversation-startingly unusual. The people of St Hellion range from the mildly superstitious, to dedicated herbalists and pagans, all the way up to the full-blown occultists. Some believe in haunted stiles and cursed fields and sea spirits. They bathe their babies in salt water to protect them from something or other. There are people in the village who honestly believe the sight of a lamb in the graveyard means a child could be about to die. Renovations on some of the older buildings have found skeletons, some human, embedded in the walls and foundations. The gift shop on Fore Street dedicates about a third of its cluttered display space to healing crystals and the like.

The popular belief is that people from St Hellion are a bit mental. But the truth is we're not. We are no crazier than any of the billions who believe in a god. When you grow up immersed in a culture, you don't think anything of it – it's always there, in the background. And while you can dismiss something as nonsense all you like, eventually, when you've heard it so much – be it in a local phrase, an off-curriculum lesson from your schoolteacher, a playground rhyme – it seeps into every pore of your brain, becomes completely normal. You don't realise it's happening. Not that any of that concerns you one bit when you're sixteen years old. Back then I had much more important things to worry about.

On 9 September 2015 – the day before everything went to shit – I was on a mission. I trudged the streets around Bayview – Lucy Rowe's housing estate up on the shoulder of Tregarrick Head – for more than an hour, trying to muster the courage to knock on her door. I had been there the previous day and failed. Would I have the guts this time?

After an hour or so, on my fifth approach, my galloping heart told me I would – it was happening. I turned the corner on to her street. As unreal as it seemed, I was going to do it. I was going to ask her out.

Back then, Bayview was part-finished after the developer went bust halfway through its construction. Lucy's street was eerie and carless, with houses on both sides in various stages of completion. With no traffic, and the pavements unsealed, I walked up the middle of the road to its far end, where Lucy's was one of only a handful of occupied houses. It was late afternoon and the light was fading, a little dry heat clinging to the air. My mouth was parched, and a trickle of sweat in the crease of my back went cold as I crossed the driveway and rang the bell. Lucy's mum opened the door immediately, as if she'd been poised behind it waiting for me.

'Is Lucy home?' I was in a daze; I'd left my body; the words were being spoken by someone else. They must have been, because I'd gone over what I was going to say a hundred times and they still came out in the wrong order. 'I'm revision for her science retakes, here to help.'

Lucy's mum cupped a hand over her mouth, stifling a laugh. 'She's in her room, love. Turn left at the top of the stairs.'

My stomach swirling, I removed my trainers and crept up, thinking how awful it would be if I was sick on the pale, almost white, carpet. Then I got to the top and there she was. Her door was ajar, and Lucy was lying on her front, on the bed. She scrambled to her feet and turned her back to me, hiding whatever was in her hands. 'Do you always turn up unannounced?'

'I was passing.'

'Passing?' She crouched at the base of a tall bookcase. Her eyes were wide. 'There's nothing past here but a load of salt water. Were you on your way to Canada?'

I forced an awkward laugh and looked at the floor, fumbling the coins in my pocket. *This is not going well.* 'I did say I'd help you with your chemistry revision.'

'That's great, JP, but maybe give me some notice next time, yeah?' She rolled her eyes, then looked at me with a playful smirk that melted my anxiety. 'You better come in, although, honestly, I think I might be beyond help.'

We sat at her desk, in front of a small window that looked out on to a sliver of sea. She wore a white vest that burst bright against the deep bronze of her skin, and her sleek inky black hair framed her heart-shaped face in a perfect arch. Her elbow brushed against mine. I suggested we start with some chemical equations. Nothing that was coming out of my mouth was what I wanted to say, and yet every word exchanged between us, however cold and empirical, was thrilling because it was said in private; we were alone, cloistered against it all, every breath amplified, her musky scent warm around me. Time spun off into an incalculable vortex and I'd no idea how long I'd been there when Lucy got called downstairs for dinner.

She put her face in her hands. 'I'm never going to get my head around this.'

'You will. I can help you again tomorrow, if you want.'

Lucy groaned. 'I can't bear it.'

I took a deep breath. 'Actually,' I said, suddenly light-headed, a tingle spreading over my skin. 'I was wondering whether you might want to do something that isn't chemistry revision. You know, only if you want?'

She peered through her fingers. 'OK, strictly no chemistry.'

'Strictly no chemistry.'

Lucy smiled. It was a big, broad, luminous smile, her eyes wide with it, and for a moment the brightness of it seemed to light up the entire world.

'I'm working at the cafe tomorrow, but I should be free in the evening,' she said. 'One thing, though. Don't just turn up at my house this time. Text me, OK?'

I did text her, straight away. And all evening, and the next morning, every phone bleep launching dopamine fireworks through my whole body. I had the unshakeable feeling that my luck was about to change. And it was – just not in the way that I'd hoped.

ABOUT THE AUTHOR

Photo © 2024 Tom Murdock

T. H. Murdock was born in Redruth, Cornwall, and lives in Bristol with his wife and son. Before turning to fiction, he worked as a journalist for fifteen years, in the UK and New Zealand. *The Date* is his first novel.

Follow the Author on Amazon

If you enjoyed this book, follow T. H. Murdock on Amazon to be notified when the author releases a new book!

To do this, please follow these instructions:

Desktop:

1) Search for the author's name on Amazon or in the Amazon App.

2) Click on the author's name to arrive on their Amazon page.

3) Click the 'Follow' button.

Mobile and Tablet:

1) Search for the author's name on Amazon or in the Amazon App.

2) Click on one of the author's books.

3) Click on the author's name to arrive on their Amazon page.

4) Click the 'Follow' button.

Kindle eReader and Kindle App:

If you enjoyed this book on a Kindle eReader or in the Kindle App, you will find the author 'Follow' button after the last page.